While a horrified world waits, these men are vying for ultimate control. . . .

The Caretakers—When the job is too desperate or tricky for anyone else to handle, they're on the scene.

The Ferryman—He escorts the dead to their final resting place—and when he kills them, they stay dead.

The Freeway Killer, a.k.a. Vampire, a.k.a. Gemini—Under these and many other names, murder was his only pleasure.

THE EIGHTH TRUMPET
It may signal the end of the world. . . .

THE
EIGHTH
TRUMPET

Jon Land

FAWCETT GOLD MEDAL • NEW YORK

A Fawcett Gold Medal Book
Published by Ballantine Books
Copyright © 1989 by Jon Land

Library of Congress Catalog Card Number: 88-92202
ISBN 0-449-13398-2

Manufactured in the United States of America

First Edition: March 1989

For Walter Zacharius, who took a shot
and
Daniel Zitin, who took another

ACKNOWLEDGMENTS

The help and assistance of so many becomes more important and valued with each book. For several of those listed below, mere mention is hardly sufficient to express my thanks and appreciation.

I must start appropriately with the wondrous Toni Mendez, as great a human being as she is an agent. The creative support of Ann Maurer makes all of my books far better than they have a right to be. But, of course, they wouldn't be books at all, if not for the Fawcett family under Leona Nevler and Dan Zitin, who publish people as well as books.

Thanks to Dr. Mort Korn more than ever this time for being the only person to suffer through this book in its most infantile stage, and to the brilliant Emery Pineo for helping it grow up.

Thanks as always to Shihan John Saviano for help with the choreography of the many fight scenes, and to Colin Burgess, Alan Foster, Andy Stearns, Andy Lewis, and Dr. David Bindleglass for assistance with geography. I am also indebted to David Schecter and Tony Shepherd for their contributions along the way.

Last, I must acknowledge John White* and Richard W. Noone** for a pair of excellent books which figured prominently in my research. Their devotion and commitment to their field enriches and enlightens us all.

*Pole Shift, A.R.E. Press, Virginia, 1986

**5/5/2000 Ice: The Ultimate Disaster, Harmony Books, 1986

THE FIRST TRUMPET

PAYBACKS

Sunday, November 15; 11:30 P.M.

CHAPTER 1

"**G**ATE, THIS IS CENTRAL. CONVOY IS APPROACHING."

"Roger that, Central. I can see their headlights."

At the central monitoring station in the mansion's front foyer, Nelson leaned closer to one of the three screens that provided a complete view of Ridgepoint Circle, the only access road to the Lime estate. He could see the limousine clearly now, squeezed between a pair of trailing cars and single leading one. His earpiece filled with the heavy *wop-wop-wop* of a helicopter an instant before a new voice came over it.

"Central, this is Sky Chief. All clear to the rear."

"Roger that."

"That you, Nellie? What's up, pulling a double shift?"

"Other guy called in sick. Just call me lucky."

"I'll think of you when I'm home and warm."

Nelson sneered, and his eyes turned to the view from the front gate camera, which was just now picking up the limousine's approach. Under close observation from the chopper, the convoy's journey from midtown Manhattan into the wooded heart of northern Greenwich, Connecticut had proved uneventful. Nelson had planned to be home in bed himself by now until orders came down assigning him to spend the night with a bank of twenty closed-circuit monitoring screens.

One thing about high-tech security, Nelson reckoned, after watching a pair of armed guards usher Jordan Lime through the foyer and up the spiral staircase, was that it totally removed anything even remotely resembling privacy. Hell, three of the twenty screens before him broadcast views of the man's bedroom. The billionaire couldn't even take a shit without being eyeballed the whole way.

Of the remaining cameras, four provided pictures of other areas within the mansion while ten tirelessly watched the grounds beyond. In addition to the standard lens, each of the cameras was equipped with an infrared optic nerve that received signals from transmitters worn by the dozen guards who patrolled at all times. That way, if an intruder managed to somehow bypass the eight-foot-high electrified fence that enclosed the estate, the camera would trigger an alarm and proceed to follow his path, automatically passing him on to the next camera when the grid changed. There was no room for human error. Amazing what $25,000 a day could buy you.

Nelson sat before the monitoring board and watched Jordan Lime make his way to his third-floor bedroom. Two guards followed close behind. The stairway camera had given way to the one mounted on the corridor, and Nelson focused on another pair of Pro-Tech guards standing outside the electronically sealed chambers. Lime approached, greeted them, and inserted a flat, square pad into the slot tailored for it. There was a click, and the door parted from its seal. Once Lime was inside, the door could be opened again only by him or by the monitor on duty—in this case, Nelson—who possessed the sole other access card. This was to protect clients against the possibility their enemies would retain Pro-Tech's own personnel to do away with them. Human greed had been programmed out, along with human error.

On the screen that broadcast the picture from inside the bedroom, Nelson watched Lime toss his tuxedo jacket onto the back of a

Chippendale chair halfway to the bay windows. He crossed toward the bathroom, passing the fireplace on the way. On the chance that a killer might choose this as a route for entry, an electrified field had been set up along the outer entrance to the chimney. It would stun an intruder senseless while simultaneously setting off an alarm. And on the chance that this and other precautions were rendered void by a power failure, a generator capable of running all systems with no decline in service had been installed in the basement.

Nelson settled back in his chair for what promised to be a very boring night.

He tried to keep his eyes off Lime as the billionaire went about his nighttime rituals in the bathroom, feeling he was invading the man's privacy. But that was what Pro-Tech was being paid $25,000 a day for, so he made himself watch at least sporadically, his eyes otherwise occupied with the screens that covered the grounds. He paid particular attention to the gardens, which contained the likeliest possible hiding places.

Lime, now clothed in satin pajamas, turned off the bathroom lights and padded softly across the luxurious Oriental carpet. Before climbing into bed, he slid his bay windows open and hit a switch that sent a set of glass curtains, bulletproof as well as electrified, into place before them, so his penchant for fresh air could not lead to his overnight demise. From his bed seconds later, Lime flicked a switch above the headboard which plunged the room into a darkness impenetrable to all but infrared cameras. Nelson watched as Jordan Lime began the slide toward totally protected sleep.

The next hour passed innocently, as Nelson tried not to nod off. The earpiece that relayed sounds from Lime's bedroom broadcast only snoring. What Nelson really wanted was to be home in his own bed enjoying a similar repose—minus the cameras.

Suddenly Nelson's earpiece registered the sound of glass breaking. Shocked wide awake, he leaned toward the screens. The pair of cameras sweeping Lime's bedroom had stopped. In the next instant their screens on the monitoring board filled with garbled interference.

"What the hell . . ."

He was about to call up to the guards at Lime's door when screams filled his right ear. Two tours in Nam, and he had never heard anything like this high-pitched wailing that curdled the blood in his veins. Through the ragged interference, Nelson made out something splashing against one of the camera lenses.

Blood.

He was out of his chair by then, striking the panic button before him with a trembling hand. A piercing shrill split the quiet of the night, but Nelson's right ear was still locked on the screaming coming from Lime's bedroom, screaming that now gave way to rasps and gurgling, along with the harsh sound of something being torn. All this came through his transistorized earpiece while he hurdled up the stairs, joined by guards converging from all angles. Logic told him whatever was happening in the bedroom was impossible. Lime was safe and alive, and all this was a terrible mistake.

Outside the mansion the helicopter cut unceasing patterns through the night. Its huge halogen floodlights illuminated every crack and crevice to reveal nothing amiss on the grounds. The alarm continued to shriek.

In Nelson's ear there was only a dripping sound.

He sprinted down the third floor corridor to find guards working futilely at the electronically sealed door.

Drip . . . drip . . . drip . . .

"Out of the way!" Nelson jammed his access card into its slot without a fumble. The door parted from its seal, and he threw his shoulder against it, the professional in him still issuing the proper orders.

"Stay out!"

Drip . . . drip . . . drip . . .

And then he was inside: Jordan Lime's eyes glared up at him, open and bulging. From the rug. Where his head had been separated from his body.

The dripping sound now came in twisted stereo—electronically in his right ear and live in the left. The dripping was blood. And the blood was everywhere.

Nelson leaned over and retched. Vomit spilled up his throat and drenched the already sodden rug. He mopped the excess from his mouth as his eyes struggled to focus on the scene. The remnants of Jordan Lime's headless torso lay half on and half off the bed. A severed arm was near the pillow. A leg hung over a chair next to the bed.

Jordan Lime had been torn apart limb from limb.

The door and window seals had not been broken. No penetration alarm had sounded.

Then how? Nelson wondered, as the floor seemed to waver beneath him. *How?*

CHAPTER 2

"**I**T'S THAT RIGHT JUST UP AHEAD," DAVID KAMANSKI TOLD his driver.

"That's not a road," the man said.

"It's not paved, but it'll do just fine."

They had been driving for three hours from an airfield carved out of the Vermont forest. Kamanski had directions, but in Vermont it was difficult to tell where one town ended and another began. They'd been doing fine until they got off Route 3 and entered a maze of roads with few markings.

The Ford sedan thumped and stumbled down the narrow dirt road, branches scraping at both sides. An hour before, they had stumbled upon Lindenville quite by accident. They'd stopped at a diner to ask directions, and it turned out to be Miss Lindenville's, in the very town they sought.

The Ford took a hump badly.

"Easy," Kamanski instructed, as he tried to decipher the final scribble of instructions. "Okay, this is far enough."

"What?"

"Pull over. I'll walk the rest of the way."

"Any reason why?"

8

"Because he doesn't know you. If he sees you first, he may shoot, and he never misses." Kamanski tilted over to check himself in the rearview mirror. The part in his hair kept dipping lower and lower as more and more strands disappeared. God, he looked old. His eyes could pass for sixty, and he was barely two-thirds of that. "Hell," he told his driver, opening the door now, "he might even shoot *me*."

Kamanski leaned over the backseat to grab his overcoat and headed on down the road.

It ended another hundred yards away. Kamanski thought of his Italian loafers and turned reluctantly onto a foot trail through the woods. Ten minutes in he caught the scent of wood smoke, and not long after, the cabin came into view—a one-story, sturdily built structure whose slight imperfections added to its rustic appeal. Kamanski crossed a bridge over a bubbling stream to reach it. Christ, this was really the middle of nowhere. Not even a power line for the last five miles. A man could die out here and it would be ten years before anyone bothered to come look for him.

He reached the front of the cabin and noticed a jeep parked alongside. Four steps brought him onto the porch. He hesitated slightly, then knocked on the door.

"Hello?" he called when there was no response. He knocked again, then called out louder.

His hand slipped to the knob and turned it. The door squealed open. Cautiously, drinking in breath, Kamanski stepped inside.

And found himself face to face with John Wayne, as big as life, sitting on a horse with the reins in one hand and a shotgun in the other.

The whole trip to Vermont, Kamanski had replayed his first meeting with Jared Kimberlain. The stockade cell was grubby and stank of ancient urine. There was no window.

"Good morning, Private," he said to the man seated on the single cot.

"Since you're not in uniform, I don't know how to address you," the man replied in a voice as chilling as his steel-blue eyes.

Kamanski looked him over and knew his instincts had been correct. The man was big and strong enough to rip another apart with his bare hands—that much was certain. But there was more. Beneath the surface, Kamanski discerned a suppressed tension and an undercurrent of violence coupled with the will to use it. This man was almost too dangerous.

"I don't wear a uniform, but I can get you out of here just the same." Kamanski gazed about the cell's narrow confines. "Not much of a place to spend the next twenty years."

"You've got my attention."

"Then I'll come right to the point. You have skills that are perfectly suited for a special group I represent."

"What group?"

"You've never heard of us. Very few have. We're called The Caretakers. Capital T, capital C. No fancy initials for the boys on Capitol Hill."

"And what exactly do you do?"

"We take care," said Kamanski. "Of the country. And I mean that quite literally. . . ."

He went on to explain that the group had been formed to safeguard the U.S. at any cost. That task, once ably performed by more traditional groups such as the FBI and CIA, could no longer be entrusted to them because of restraints affected by recent scrutiny of the intelligence community. The government had suddenly found itself more concerned with the Qaddaffis and Khomeinis of the world than with the Soviets and Chinese. A single hydrogen bomb in the hands of a fanatic could start a chain reaction of untold damage. And beyond this there were resources to be protected. Oil had been most important for a while, more recently it had been food, and down the road almost certainly water and maybe even air would be in danger. In all cases national safety and prosperity depended on the continued maintenance of all precious resources and the elimination of potential threats to them. In this respect, the world was composed of an incredibly small number of individuals whose actions determined the fate of the rest. Thus, these actions needed to be monitored, kept in check, and altered or redirected when necessary. Through any and all means available.

The Caretakers, Kamanski had explained that day, was an idea whose time had come. All field operatives were limited to a single three-year term to avoid burnout. There was no rank, no pecking order to ascend. There were just field operatives and conduits, and the latter were merely the glorified delivery boys of whom Kamanski was in charge. If a man survived the three years, he would be financially set for life.

Kimberlain had gone for the proposal with little thought, not quite enthusiastically but not reluctantly either. He really had no choice, and Kamanski had walked out of the stockade prepared to report to the shadowy blind leader of The Caretakers that he had found the man destined to become the best of them all.

"I'm willing to die trying to keep 'em. Question is, are you willing to die trying to take 'em?" John Wayne challenged the townfolk who were gathered on the other side of the stream. With that, he vanished, and the living room of the cabin returned to normal.

"It's called multidimensional television," a familiar voice announced. "A friend of mine rigged it up for me. Nothing like it will be on the market for years."

"Jared?"

"Over here, Hermes."

Hermes . . . Kamanski hadn't been called by his Greek anonym in years. Jared Kimberlain, on the other hand, had never been able to shed his, the Ferryman, after Charon, the Greek boatman who delivered the dead to their final resting place across the River Styx. Kimberlain himself had done plenty of delivering—more than any man Kamanski had ever known.

Kamanski turned toward his voice: he could have sworn it came from the corner but he found the corner empty. He located Kimberlain finally on the opposite side of the room, and as he approached the dark, hulking shape he made sure the Ferryman could see his outstretched hand.

"Been a long time, Jared."

"Not long enough."

Kimberlain took the hand cursorily and squeezed just hard enough to let Kamanski sample his strength.

"Hell of a place you got here, Jared."

"You should have let your driver join you."

"I was afraid you'd kill him."

"I tied him up instead. Don't worry, he's comfortable."

Kamanski's mouth dropped open.

"That same friend of mine rigged up a high performance defense system. I was waiting in the bushes when you pulled over. You're getting old, Hermes."

"I was never a field man."

"But you used to keep better company. That kid in the car might have a college degree and a forty-dollar haircut, but I wouldn't want him watching my back."

"Times have changed."

"If that were true, David, you wouldn't be here."

Kimberlain stepped further out of the shadows toward the oddly shaped holographic video machine and pressed the eject button. Some stray light through the partially open cabin shutters caught his face. It was the same face as the last time they had met, Kamanski reckoned, no different even from the first time he had laid eyes on Kimberlain in the stockade. A pleasant face that was somehow too soft for the man who owned it, too tailored, too fine. Eyebrows perfectly groomed. Dark, heavy eyelashes reaching outward. Not a single furrow on the brow or sag beneath the eyes. The thick hair showed no signs of receding, which sent pangs of jealousy through Kamanski. And the eyes. Oh, those eyes. Crystal blue and piercing, sharper than any knife. They didn't fit the face at all, but they were the one feature that fit the man.

Kimberlain placed the Wayne tape back in his huge video library.

"I never knew you were such a movie buff," Kamanski said,

moving closer to inspect the titles. The library was surprisingly diverse; from Capra to Hitchcock, from Wayne to Ladd to Eastwood to the Mad Max series. James Bond, too.

"I need you, Jared," Kamanski said suddenly, standing so that the Ferryman couldn't help but notice him.

"I've heard that before," Kimberlain said emotionlessly. "About three years ago, wasn't it? Not much more than two years after I left The Caretakers."

"There was a murder Sunday night. An industrialist named Jordan Lime."

"And here it is Tuesday morning and you haven't found the killer yet. You must be slipping, Hermes."

"Lime was worth billions, Jared," Kamanski went on. "Hired the best security firm money could buy and wired his mansion with equipment that would amaze even that friend of yours." He paused. "He was ripped apart, mutilated behind sealed doors and windows. No evidence anybody was even in there. The first man was in the room less than a minute after the first scream and found . . . We've got videotapes. We've got recordings. We had over twenty guards on the property. No one could have gotten in or out. What happened was impossible."

Kimberlain's eyes flickered for the first time. "If my literary knowledge serves me right, you should be looking for a gorilla right out of the Rue Morgue."

"A gorilla would have been fried by 20,000 volts if he'd tried to get down this chimney, Jared. I've had men on this for thirty-six hours straight. The police, too. We're no further along than we were at the start."

"We?"

"Pro-Tech, the security firm I'm associated with now, was hired to keep Lime alive."

"Don't expect it's the best time to look for new clients, then. What happened to the Bureau?"

"I thought it was time to move on."

"Imposing three-year tours on yourself now? I'm impressed."

"I'm afraid the Bureau agreed with me."

"I'm not surprised."

"But the money's better too. Much. And I'm authorized to offer you any sum you name to help us."

Ignoring him, Kimberlain moved to another wall of the living room. It was filled with weapons dating back from a hundred to a thousand years. Muskets, flintlocks, six-guns, a collection of knives and swords fit for a museum. Kamanski followed Kimberlain across the room and found himself transfixed.

"I restore them," Kimberlain told him. "Helps pass the time."

He took a three-hundred-year-old samurai sword from the wall and sat down with the sword in his lap. A good portion of the blade looked shiny and new; the rest was old and scarred. Kimberlain grasped a set of ultrafine polishing stones from a table next to him and set to work on the weathered portion of the blade. His large, callused hands moved as agilely as a surgeon's back and forth against a section halfway down from the hilt. Such gentleness, Kamanski noted, and yet alongside it a capacity for such—

"I don't work for money anymore, David," the Ferryman said suddenly without looking up. "You should know that."

"But you remain available. Your file needs updating constantly. You're quite a busy man, from what I've been able to learn."

"Paybacks, Hermes. They're to make up for all those assignments you delivered to me from Zeus. I'm doing my best to take care of innocent people who've been fucked by bastards like you. Take care, no capital t or c."

"Taking vengeance is another way of putting it. It's against the law so far as I know, but I don't want to quibble."

Kimberlain looked up coldly from his work. The polishing stones squeaked against the blade. "Are you threatening me, David?"

"I'm not that brave."

"But you're still smart; I can see that. Probably smart enough to turn around right now and walk out of here so I can finish watching my movie."

"What I've got might be a challenge for you."

"That's what you said about Peet—when was it, a little over three years ago, right?"

Kamanski tried very hard not to react.

"Come now, David, you remember Winston Peet, don't you? Giant, about seven feet tall, a bald head. He killed seventeen people in as many states. Ripped their heads clean off their bodies after he strangled them. Papers called him the worst serial murderer in modern history. Back when you were with the Bureau. You boys were getting nowhere so you begged me to track down your killer for you, and I came up with Peet. Wanna see the scars? Only you bastards couldn't get him executed, couldn't even get him imprisoned."

"We put him where he'll never hurt anyone again."

"In that nuthouse? Bullshit. Someday he'll get out. Just watch. He writes me letters and tells me so."

"This time it's different," Kamanski said.

"No it isn't, not to me. See, after the Peet thing, while I was lying there in the hospital damn near dead, I realized I had three choices: I could die, I could become like you, or I could change the course you set my life on. That's when the paybacks started."

"But they've never stopped, have they?" Kamanski wondered whether the Ferryman would spring on him now. "They come from everywhere, I'm told. You have no phone, no listed address, but still they find you. It's out of control, can't you see that?"

"You're wrong, Hermes," Kimberlain said quite calmly. "The paybacks reduce the world to something manageably small: just somebody who got fucked, the person that fucked them, and me. The last resort. They're willing to do whatever it takes to find me, because they've got nowhere else to turn. And each one I help brings me a little closer to making up for my actions with The Caretakers."

"You would have rotted in that stockade, Jared. You owe me for that much. Call *this* a payback."

"You used that same argument three years ago when you came to me about Peet. My payback to you is finished."

Kimberlain went back to his sword. Kamanski figured it was time to toss him the bait.

"Jordan Lime wasn't the first. There were two other successful industrialists murdered before him. Three incredible, impossible murders. All the victims were among the best-protected men in the country."

Kimberlain tried to keep on with the polishing, but clearly his mind was starting to drift.

"Come on, Jared, do I have to spell it out for you? Somewhere out there is a serial killer operating on a supersophisticated level. Think about future targets for this nutcase. Maybe the President will be next. You think the country could handle that right now?"

"You're asking me to become a Caretaker again."

"I'm asking you to go after a madman who may soon be in a position to hold the entire country hostage. You're the only one who can do it, Jared. This is your game."

The Ferryman inspected the progress he had made on the ancient sword. It was slow work, but it was gratifying to see the past come back to life in his hands.

"I'll think about it," he said, without looking up. "I'll let you know."

"When?"

"Get out of here, David, and let me finish this side."

CHAPTER 3

"**Y**OU MENTIONED THERE WERE TWO OTHER MURDERS," KIM-berlain said to Kamanski an hour later in the backseat of the car. The driver kept one hand on the wheel; with the other he massaged a shoulder sore from the pressure of his arms being laced together.

"Two that we know of," Kamanski said. "There could be more. Law-enforcement agencies aren't admitting there's a pattern yet." They were still two hours from the airfield, and he wouldn't feel sure the Ferryman was with him until their plane took off for Connecticut.

"Tell me about those two."

"Not as puzzling as the murder of Jordan Lime but just as effective," Kamanski said. "The first was Benjamin Turan."

"Experimental metals. Steel with the weight and texture of plastic and all the resiliency of iron."

"I thought you were out of touch."

"Not entirely."

"Turan did plenty of traveling abroad. Brought the importance of security home with him. He employed round-the-clock guards and even had a dummy car."

"So what happened?"

"Grabbed the latch to open the rear door of one of his limos one morning and got fried by fifteen thousand volts."

"Interesting. Chauffeur around?"

"In the front seat. Got fried too. That kind of voltage doesn't discriminate."

"Okay, how was it done?"

"A separate battery was installed in the trunk to supply the power source, and the car was wired with superconductive fusing. The killer didn't waste an inch, either. The only terminal we found was the one plugged into the latch Turan grabbed for. Thing was, the car was locked in the garage all the time. And the dummy limo wasn't wired, just the one Turan planned to use that morning."

"He would have used it eventually."

"You miss my point. Turan's use of a dummy car included using a double for himself. The odds were fifty-fifty that it would've been the double that got fried instead of him. I can't accept that. The killer wired the right limo because he knew it was right even before Turan made his choice."

"Psychic maybe?"

"I wouldn't dismiss anything."

A few moments of silence passed before the Ferryman spoke again.

"What about the other?"

"Adam Rand."

"Rand Industries?"

"You do surprise me, Jared."

"News reaches even the backwoods of Vermont. Rand Industries revolutionized the auto industry with their hypersensitive transmission. A whole new way of driving. The fuel injection of the nineties. Rand had to be worth a billion on his bad days in the market."

"Which puts him in the same league as Turan. And Lime. You can see what I was getting at back at the cabin. We're facing the ultimate serial killer here."

Kimberlain looked at him across the seat. "That's a pretty strong statement considering the last time we worked together."

"With good reason. Jordan Lime ordered twenty-five thousand-dollar-a-day security from Pro-Tech *after* the Rand murder two weeks ago. And in spite of that, this killer still found a way through, impossible as it seems."

"How'd Rand buy it?"

"In his sleep."

"Really?"

"His bed was blown up." Kamanski hesitated to let his point sink in. "Our killer likes a challenge and takes on a greater one each time. He's proving that nobody's safe. He's rendered all levels of security impotent."

"How can you be so sure it's one man?"

"Simple. A group would have an aim, a purpose. Someone would have heard from them by now with a list of demands. But there's been nothing. This is sport for our man. I can feel it."

Kimberlain was nodding. "So what we've got so far are a new kind of steel and a revolutionary transmission. What's Lime's claim to fame?"

"Most recently, a transistor coupling that resists burnout. Since these couplings had such a high breakdown rate, that discovery would have placed him above Turan and Rand before too much longer." Kamanski realized what the Ferryman was getting at. "You think our killer is keying on the product, not the people, in choosing his victims?"

"Probably a combination of the two. Anything's possible with the kind of mind we're facing here, if you're right about it being only one mind," Kimberlain told him, unaware that his hands had clenched involuntarily into fists. "Serial killers key on something that attracts them and keeps attracting them. While they're active no other factor is as important as that one single thing, because it allows them to attain their own version of superiority. It dominates their consciousness. Killing allows them to maintain the illusion that they're still in control, and even to increase that control. And killing the object of their obsession maintains their feeling of superiority."

"You're talking about Peet."

"A worthy suspect."

"Forget it. He remains under twenty-four-hour guard. He never even leaves his cell without a four-man escort."

"That's not much for him to overcome."

"A three-mile swim through frigid waters would follow even if he did."

"He could manage it. Believe me."

"Not behind bars he couldn't."

Kimberlain smiled. "I'm glad I didn't kill you back at the cabin, David, but I should have three years ago."

The plane brought them to a small airfield in southern Connecticut, where a helicopter was waiting to carry them the short distance to the Lime estate.

"I had the room sealed," Kamanski explained above the chopper's roar as they buckled themselves in. "Body parts removed, of course, but nothing else altered."

"You're a true professional, David," Kimberlain said. And when they were in the air, through the headset, "I'll want to hear and see your tapes first. I want to experience it from the perspective of all your helpless security guards."

"I'll arrange it."

The vastness of the Lime estate was the first thing that struck Kimberlain. It was much too large for anything but an entire army to patrol. Kamanski said Pro-Tech had made it impregnable and boasted that the surveillance equipment could pick out a fly if it wasn't wired properly. The Ferryman nodded and let him drone on, not bothering to point out that all that hadn't been able to stop Jordan Lime from being mutilated in his bedroom.

The front gate was still manned, but the perimeter guards had been dismissed. The sprawling mansion was shrouded by the misty, damp day, and the drizzle felt like ice against Kimberlain's cheeks as Kamanski led him up the steps to the mansion's entrance. The marble foyer that had contained the surveillance station was empty, so they made their way to the library, which had a big-screen television with a built-in VCR.

The tape in question was already loaded.

"There's nothing to see," Kamanski claimed. "I've been over it myself a hundred times."

"Push PLAY, David."

Kamanski punched the button and the screen filled with the last image of Jordan Lime's bedroom, its occupant resting beneath the covers, unaware of the awful violence that was to come. There was the crash of glass, and in the next instant the picture became a snowy, almost total blur.

"What was the crash?"

"Picture fell off the wall."

"How?"

"We don't know."

Now the blur was in motion, darkened seconds later by the splash of blood against the lens. Kimberlain rewound the tape and watched it a second time. "Any idea what caused the video breakup?"

"The feed line running from the wall was partially severed."

"And the line ran close to the picture that conveniently slipped from the wall?"

"Close enough."

Kimberlain watched the tape again, this time with the volume turned up higher. He didn't know precisely what he had been expecting, but this was worse. Total silence, then the sudden, awful screams—sounds of a struggle, maybe—followed by the dripping of blood.

"What if the killer was already inside the room when Lime hit the sack?"

Kamanski shook his head. "No way. The room was checked before Lime entered and was under guard all day. Even supposing the killer could have hidden himself for a number of hours, the security system is equipped with motion detectors sensitive enough

to pick up breathing. No readings all day. I'll show you the print-
outs if you like.''

"I'll take your word, Hermes. I also assume you've had the audio
on the tape slowed and filtered.''

Kamanski nodded. "We brought every single sound up to a hundred times its normal resonance and separated each one into individual segments.''

"Footsteps?''

"Not that we could find. If there were any, they got lost in the
screaming.''

"Let me see the bedroom,'' said the Ferryman.

Kamanski hadn't been exaggerating in the helicopter. Other than
the removal of severed body parts and other remnants of the corpse,
nothing in Jordan Lime's bedroom had been touched. Huge pools
of dried blood were everywhere—on the floor, the sheets, the rug.
Fingers of near black reached out from the walls in frozen anima-
tion, seeming almost to slither as Kimberlain gazed at them.

He moved about the room and in his own mind could see it all
happening, Jordan Lime being torn limb from limb. But he couldn't
visualize the actual murder. All he saw were the pieces being scattered to the sounds of the horrible screaming he had heard on the
tape downstairs. He tried once again for a fix on Lime, tried to
envision what had done this to him, but drew a blank. Very often
when the Ferryman walked onto a crime scene he could feel the
residue of the perpetrator as clearly as he could see the crawling
fingers of blood in Lime's bedroom. But now he was coming up
empty. *Stick with the technical, then,* he urged himself. "The
floors?'' he asked.

Kamanski was just behind him. "Dusted and electronically
scanned. No footprints other than Lime's.''

"Inconclusive. The killer could have worn shoes with Teflon-
coated soles. No marks or residue that way.''

"Granted, except Teflon squeaks on wood. We'd have heard
something on the tape.''

The Ferryman continued to gaze about the room. He focused on the window. "Was that open Sunday night?"

"Yes, but the glass curtains covering it are reinforced with steel linings. Bulletproof and electrified. Our man didn't come through that way. Nothing living did, anyway."

The Ferryman was still looking that way. "A ray," he said. "A ray fired from a good distance beyond the window. Your steel lining might not stop that."

"But a ray would certainly have left heat fringes on the severed body parts. Lime's limbs were sliced off. A sword like the one you were polishing back in Vermont. That's what we've been thinking about."

"Wielded by a killer who couldn't possibly have been in the room."

"The theory's not perfect."

"I want to bring that inventor friend of mine in on this," the Ferryman said.

"The best minds in the country have already run the circle."

"Conducting a search based on what they can legitimately accept to be real. My friend can accept anything. Nothing gets ruled out."

"Call him in. Whatever it takes."

The sun was down by the time Kimberlain pulled into a parking lot adjacent to Sunnyside Railroad Yard, a resting place for mothballed railroad cars in New Jersey, just outside the tunnel under the Hudson River to Penn Station. He danced across dead tracks as if current might still have been pumping through them.

The gray and brown steel corpses of Amtrak and New Jersey Transit cars were lined up for a good eighth of a mile, rows squeezed so close together that there was barely enough room for Kimberlain to shoulder his way between them. The pair of rusted brown cars he was heading for had carried cargo, not passengers. They were off to one side, apart from the neighboring lines of Amtrak cars, and were in relatively good condition; they seemed to be begging to be hitched onto engines once more.

"Ferryman here," he said softly into a small slit, cut at eye level on the side of one of the rusty cars. The car's rear door opened with a familiar *whooosh*.

"Welcome aboard," said Captain Seven.

The captain's hair had hung past his shoulders, wild and unkempt, for as long as Kimberlain had known him. The only difference lately was the graying edges along his temples. He wore cut-off jean shorts which exposed his thin, knobby legs, and a leather vest over a black Grateful Dead T-shirt. A medallion with a sixties peace sign embossed on it dangled from his neck, even though he'd spent much of that era fighting in Vietnam instead of protesting about it. Kimberlain didn't know the captain's real name and never had. He knew him only as a spaced-out tech whiz who'd made his mark in Vietnam as a brilliant flake from the seventh planet in another galaxy. "Captain" wasn't his real rank, but it sounded nice when you ran the "Seven" after it. He seemed content never to return to his own identity, and Kimberlain never pressed him about it.

"Hope you haven't come to complain about the video system," the captain said.

"Not a chance. Works like a charm."

"Course it does," Seven said proudly.

Kimberlain followed him through the doorway into his decidedly unhumble abode. The furniture was stunning. Each shiny black leather piece was built precisely to fit in its location. The carefully arranged interior was filled with flashing lights, diodes, CRT screens, monitors, switches, and assorted machines and data banks from floor to ceiling. Kimberlain caught the pungent scent of marijuana and flared his nostrils. "Ventilation system needs to be flushed." He smiled.

From a nearby table, Captain Seven lifted a plastic contraption bristling with tubes and dominated by water-filled chambers. "This shit's too good to flush out," he said, wrapping his mouth around a small hole in the device and sucking air from it deeply.

Kimberlain could hear bubbles churning. Almost immediately smoke poured through the various serpentine chambers, funneling ultimately into Captain Seven's lungs. He inhaled until the smoke was gone. The bubbles stopped.

Seven held his breath briefly, then let it out, stray smoke following with it. His eyes fell fondly on the marijuana-filled thing. ''Best bong ever,'' he reported, voice thinner with each word. ''Don't need to be lit. Breathing in supplies all necessary combustion. Don't remember how I came up with it. If I'd had it over in Nam, though, I'd be in the millions now.''

''Retire right,'' said the Ferryman.

''Yeah. Just imagine. All those boys in their foxholes at night lighting up a joint and sending a signal to the Cong for hundreds of yards. They had these, they could smoke themselves silly and the Cong would never know. We might even have won the war. Who knows?''

''Maybe you should take out a patent.''

''Too fuckin' late.'' Captain Seven sighed. ''World's turned to that powder shit. Freezes their minds. This stuff, well I been smokin' it for damn near thirty years now, and look at me.''

''Right.''

''Sure you don't want any?''

''Yup.''

Captain Seven plopped down in a black leather chair under a terminal board with a dozen flashing red lights. He turned to Kimberlain. ''So what do you want?''

''Got a challenge for you.''

''Oh?''

''Ultimate locked-room murder. Got the best tech boys in the country baffled.''

''Not the best, old buddy, but please go on.''

Kimberlain told him about Jordan Lime's murder, told him everything in the clearest, most deliberate terms so that Seven's brilliant but often frazzled mind could absorb it. When he was finished, the captain just sat there expressionless, not even blinking, the slight motions of his chest in and out the only reminder he was alive.

Without warning or word, his eyes flashed alert again and he drew the bong back to his lips. Once more bubbles churned like water boiling in an open pot on a stove. Smoke filled the chambers, and then it was gone.

"I need to know how it was done," Kimberlain added after the captain had exhaled.

"You asked all the right questions already."

"And got all the right answers. What am I left with?"

"The impossible."

"Your specialty."

Captain Seven started to lift the bong back to his lips, then thought better of it. "They didn't like my style in Nam. Know why? 'Cause it was too damn effective. I come up with perimeter mines that really knocked the shit out of the Charlie bastards. Lucky ones died quick. Not so lucky ones had their balls blown off. Thing was, I designed the mines thin and dark so we didn't have to busy ourselves burying them. Coated them with a special epoxy that made dirt stick to the frames. Ultimate camouflage. In-fucking-credible. Anyway, the brass hears about them and instead of giving me congrats and a medal, they tell me I'm in violation of the Geneva conventions. We're losing boys who barely got hair on their balls and they tell me *I'm* in violation. I realized then that they had sent us over there but they never wanted us to win. You read me?"

"It was before my time."

"Right. You and The Caretakers came later, when they wanted to avoid another Vietnam. Suddenly all the skills that violated Geneva were very much in demand. Nobody gave a shit anymore, and the object was to win, so I figured when they asked me to sign on, sure, what the hell. Only I couldn't tell the difference. Yanked myself out 'cause the winning and losing all felt the same."

"This time the winning or losing is up to you."

"Ain't that nice."

"There's more. Need you to work a little computer magic for

me, Captain. Like I said, we know of three murders but there have probably been more. Either way, there's got to be something the victims have in common besides the obvious."

"Expecting more impossible murders?"

"I'd bet on it. Be a bonus if you could come up with a few potential next victims for me based on whatever it is you turn up."

"No sweat. And where will you be while I'm sneaking into data banks and solving impossible crimes?"

"Seeking out an expert on the homicidal personality," Kimberlain said. He paused. "Winston Peet."

Kimberlain had been in his hotel room for twenty minutes and was nearly ready for bed. He was thinking how much he missed the quiet of the forest when the phone rang.

"Yes," he answered, expecting to hear Kamanski's voice.

"Ferryman, how good to hear your voice again."

Kimberlain froze. He squeezed the receiver tight. "Hello, Zeus."

"After so long some measure of enthusiasm might have been exhibited."

"Excuse my manners."

"They're excused. Now switch on your television. Channel three."

Kimberlain placed the receiver on the bed and moved to the television. A moment later channel three sharpened before him.

"Very good, Ferryman," said the voice, now coming through the television speaker as well while a shape gained focus. "I wish I could say it's good to *see* you, but of course . . ."

Zeus sat centered in the screen at the head of a conference table, sunglasses in place over his sightless eyes. His hair was jet black—dyed, probably—his features milky white and unchanged since last they'd met. The camera pulled back just enough to include in the frame the hulking brutes flanking him on either side.

"Neat trick," Kimberlain said.

"It seemed a practical expedient. I wished to avoid unpleasantries."

"Then you shouldn't have called."

"The knob's there, Ferryman. Turn it off." The sightless man's eyes seemed quite impossibly to regard him from the other side of the screen. "You can't, can you?"

"What do you want, Zeus?"

The picture blurred a bit, then sharpened to crystal clarity. Kimberlain realized his initial impressions of the former leader of The Caretakers had been mistaken, as if Zeus had fooled him, controlled him, even here. The old man's cheeks were creased and worn, his chin and jowls tired and drooping. There was an instant of pity for the blind man before the memories came flooding back. The screen filled with Zeus from the shoulders up as Kimberlain felt his heart beat faster.

"I need you," said Zeus.

"You've got to be kidding."

"I created you. Gave you your name, your—"

"It stops there, Zeus. You gave me my name; you gave all of us our names. And you were the god in ultimate control. We were part of a game you were playing. Don't expect me to play again."

"I was right, though, wasn't I?" I called you 'Ferryman' after Charon, who took the dead across the river Styx, because I knew that would be your specialty. You see, I knew you better than you knew yourself."

"Forgetting that last mission, aren't you, Zeus? You abandoned me, left me to die. I knew too much about the way The Caretakers really functioned, about the truth behind our operations. My term was almost up. You couldn't have me coming out alive."

"And wasn't I proven right? You talked after you came in, didn't you? It was the beginning of the end, it lead to our dissolution. We're talking about my life here, Ferryman."

"What about *my* life, Zeus?"

"It's all behind us. I never meant for you to die. Believe that or not as you wish, but my own heart is secure. I would have helped you if I could have. Don't you think I knew you would survive anyway and what the consequences would be to me? Think, man!"

"That was never one of my options during the term."

"Leave the past," Zeus pleaded, "for both our sakes."

Kimberlain started to reach for the knob.

"Millions of people may be about to die," Zeus said before he could turn it.

Kimberlain stopped his hand in midair and held it there.

"You are familiar, of course, with C-12 plastic explosives?"

"Roughly twenty times more potent than C-4. The most deadly incindiary short of an atomic bomb."

"Five hundred pounds of it is unaccounted for."

"Stolen?"

"In a very subtle fashion. Inventory sheets were altered, security circumvented at all levels. Very deep. Very professional."

"If you've gotten far enough to realize all that, you don't need me."

Zeus's features became less sure. "At this particular installation, security was my responsibility."

"Ah," Kimberlain said. "So you have yet to report your discovery to interested parties within the government and military. Worried about your reputation, Zeus, your career?"

The blind man sneered. "Nonsense! Acting as if the theft has gone undiscovered gives us the best chance of recovering the C-12."

" 'Us' as in you and whatever army you're running these days. I'm out."

"There's more." Zeus started to reach into his jacket pocket. "We interrogated a man believed to be one of the perpetrators. Killed himself with a cyanide capsule before we could confirm our suspicions, but something else about him told us plenty." He pulled a photograph from his pocket and signaled the camera to draw closer. "This tattoo was found on his right shoulder, Ferryman. Might be of interest to you."

The camera zoomed in. A death's-head with a spear running through it from temple to temple filled the screen. The death's-head was smiling.

"The Hashi," muttered Kimberlain.

"It's good to see your memory has not deserted you. The Hashi indeed. An international society of assassins for hire dating back a thousand years."

"You didn't believe me when I told you they still existed."

"But if the Hashi are anywhere near as dangerous as you claimed years ago, imagine the potential calamity we're facing if the C-12 has fallen into their hands. We have a concrete trail to follow this time, Ferryman. Find the explosives and you find the Hashi."

"And save your ass in the process."

"A minor subtext. Consider this as my providing sanction for your pursuit a bit after the fact, though not too late, hopefully, to save millions of lives."

"I don't need your sanction anymore, Zeus," Kimberlain said quite calmly. "And I'm done chasing ghosts."

The blind man yanked off his sunglasses to reveal the crystalline lenses that had never functioned as eyes. "Now you're chasing other people's ghosts, hiding behind a veil of morality to justify the kind of actions I used to justify for you. You're still the Ferryman. Only your passengers are different."

"Because they're chosen by me, not by some omnipotent organization that alone knows what's best for America."

"This conversation concerns the present."

"No, it concerns the past, and mine doesn't exist anymore."

"Damn it, Jared, I need you!" Zeus screamed like a spoiled child.

"Yes, Zeus, how does it feel?"

THE SECOND TRUMPET

WINSTON PEET

Tuesday, November 17; 8:00 P.M.

CHAPTER 4

"COME ON! GET A MOVE ON, LADIES. OFF WE GO!"

The women were herded off the van like so many cattle being led to the slaughterhouse. Of the six, four were reasonably attractive, one pleasantly plain, and the last a blonde of stocky build with a head too small for her body. The streets of Nice, France, were not exactly teeming with prostitutes at this hour of the night. Those available brought with them the risk they might take something from the villa besides compensation for their services.

"Right this way, ladies. Follow me," continued the huge, bearded guard in poor French. He led them toward the double-door entrance of the old converted hotel. Its isolated location and fortified exterior stone wall suited its present occupants well. Before becoming a hotel it had been the summer residence of a French nobleman. It had been built centuries ago by a famous Frenchman who'd made a successful living as a sea pirate.

The whores' faces glowed as they passed through the entrance into the surfaced granite foyer. The huge guard poked a finger like iron into the breast of the chunky blonde.

"Look but don't touch, bitch."

She swore at him in French and feigned a spitting motion.

The guard laughed heartily. "Upstairs, ladies. Touch any of the paintings and I'll slice off your fingers."

He led them to the fourth floor, where a right turn at the head of the staircase brought them to a series of six doors, three on each side spread equally apart.

"One hour with each man," came the guard's next instructions. "We're on a tight schedule here. The next shift will knock on the door when their turn comes." Then, with a crude wink, "Make sure all the coming is done by that time, eh?"

The whores giggled.

The guard started directing them through the doors, and the blonde drew the second one down on the left. Once inside with the door closed behind her, her eyes fell on a thin boyish figure lying naked to the waist on the bed.

"Well, hello, there," he said, licking his lips. "You're a big one, aren't you?"

Bravado talking, the blonde figured. The boy couldn't have been more than sixteen, seventeen maybe.

"Like to find out, wouldn't you?" she teased, but her eyes wandered to the tattoo on his right shoulder: a smiling death's-head with a spear running through it from temple to temple.

The boy started fumbling with his zipper, but the blonde was over him quickly, pinning him with her weight as her mouth lowered to his.

The boy moaned and hugged her tight.

The blonde returned his hug briefly, then let her hands glide to his chin, one on each side. The boy didn't see her eyes. If he had, perhaps he would have moved, or at least tried to.

The blonde jammed both her hands forward under his chin, jolting his head straight back at an impossible angle as she threw her frame forward to provide the final thrust she needed.

The boy's head snapped back and went slack. The body spasmed and stilled instantly, toes twitching and nothing more.

The whore lunged out of the bed as quick as a cat and yanked her dress off over her head. Under the discarded garment her body was wrapped with packs of explosives expertly positioned so that a body frisk would have revealed nothing but normal contours.

Twenty-two minutes later all the plastic explosives had been divided into individual blocks and the detonators readied. The grenades she pulled from a hidden pouch were the Soviet-made square variety which clung comfortably to the belt. The gas canisters were bulky but necessary. All she lacked was a hand-held weapon, and a search of the boy's closet yielded her a choice of many. She draped a pair of Ingram machine pistols over her shoulders and wedged an oversized Beretta into her belt. Then she completed her transformation by rolling down the sleeves of a top that was the companion piece of the tights worn beneath her dress.

This done, the woman settled the mounds of C-4 *plastique* into a pack she'd also found in the closet and lifted the strap over her neck. She wedged the set of detonators into her belt for easy retrieval. Stilling her breath, she pressed her ear against the door. Once confident the corridor was empty, she glided stealthily out. The only sounds came from the Ingram butts clicking against each other.

She started down the corridor, one with the darkness, stopping at regular intervals to wedge packs of the *plastique* home. This first set was purposely misplaced. There would be lots of noise but minor structural damage on this level, the idea being to draw attention and bring the majority of the building's inhabitants up here.

The second batch of explosives, which she now began to set, would bring the entire floor down. When this set followed the first by a generous sixty seconds, the rest of the villa's occupants would have had ample time to charge to the source of the initial blasts and be gathered conveniently when the next series erupted. A five-minute timer for the first, a six for the second.

The blonde finished packing the fourth floor and moved to the stairway. Her plan called for the packing of the third floor with C-4 as well. When both crumbled she would have the freedom she needed to move about on the floors below. Packing the third floor with *plastique* took precisely three minutes, which left her comfortably ahead of schedule.

She checked her watch: under two minutes to go now before the explosions began. She had to be in position by that time to complete the second stage of her plan. The guards patrolling the walled courtyard enclosing the villa had to believe the attack was coming from outside the compound as well as inside; confusion had to be created, with illusion as the framework. Her reports indicated that the headquarters for this stronghold was in the basement. She would rely on the confusion to allow her to gain access. The woman started for the stairway, intending to descend to the second floor.

A door on the corridor opened. She pressed herself into a doorway and froze. A man was approaching, whistling to himself. An instant before he reached her she sprang out and used the butt of one of her Ingrams against his face. Dazed, he reeled back and went for his pistol as the blonde's knife came up. Her free hand had looped around his throat before he could aim. She spun him around with a hand clamped over his mouth. In the next second her blade plunged into his back and found his heart. The man stiffened and slumped. The woman tried the door closest to her and found it open. Effortlessly, she dragged the body inside and closed it again.

Just a minute left. Damn!

"Henri, what the hell . . ."

Her eyes met those of the huge, bearded guard as she crossed back toward the staircase. He seemed to recognize her.

"*You!*"

But then he made his mistake. He lunged for her, confident he could cover the ground between them before she could steady her rifle, never expecting she would choose to encounter him hand to hand, meeting his attack with her own. The guard was huge and quick for his size, twice her weight at least, but the blonde slid by him in a blur, a hand whipping up and catching him in the throat with a *whap*! The man sidestepped, gagging, and felt a knee buckle as she sliced a kick into it from the side.

He tried to swing, but by then she had come up in front of him, and his groin exploded in pain. He lashed out wildly with his tree trunk of a right arm and felt the blow captured and redirected. Then a hand snaked around his chin and twisted as the one grasping his wrist pulled.

This time the snap was muted. His head flopped utterly loose. The woman let him fall and was in motion again.

Thirty seconds. No . . . Twenty-eight.

The plan had to be altered slightly, but with so much at stake nothing was slight. She bounded down to the second floor with no time for care and rushed to the first door on the left side of the corridor. This room would overlook the front of the compound. A clear view. A clear shot. When the explosions started, doors would open immediately, and the hall would fill almost as fast. Timing. The blonde had to use it to her advantage.

Fifteen, fourteen, thirteen . . .

At the count of eight, she lifted a foot to the door and put all her thrust behind it. Wood shattered at knob level, and the door flew inward. The three men inside responded instantly by grabbing for their weapons.

The blonde fired just as the first series of explosions sounded. The men danced backward with her bullets tearing into them. Her spray was too wide, too much ammo wasted, but she had to be sure. The last of the first wave of explosions rumbled as she shoved the broken door back into position. As she rushed to the window she heard the corridor behind her pulsing with screams, shouts, and the heavy pounding of feet.

Her view of the courtyard and stone fence was clear. The chaos on the outside was as widespread as inside. Men ripped rifles from their shoulders and rushed toward the house. The blonde stripped the first two square grenades from her belt and tore the pins from each.

Ten more seconds until the next wave of explosions sounded. Everything was going perfectly. She could hear dozens of footsteps pounding up and down the steps in confusion, but it was the screams of the women she had accompanied here that rose above all else.

She hurled the first of her grenades not for the center of the guards in the courtyard but well beyond them, toward the outside of the wall. This would induce them to think that the attack was two-pronged, that they were about to be penetrated from outside the wall in addition to whatever was occurring inside the house. The explosions coughed fragments of stone skyward. Inside the courtyard the guards dropped to their stomachs. A few scaled the top of the wall and began to return nonexistent fire.

The blonde hurled her second grenade and followed up quickly with two more. Her fourth lob was aimed for the inside of the courtyard now that she was confident the enemy's forces had been splintered.

She had lost track of time when the main explosions from the floors above shook her to the bloodstained carpet. Plaster cracked, and only a nimble roll to the left saved her from being crushed under a section of the ceiling as it tumbled down. Ignoring the chaos around her, she eased back to the window and hurled another series of grenades. Then she was moving toward the door, weapons shouldered as she mentally catalogued what remained of her arsenal.

Emerging into the corridor she caught the hot smell of fire and smoke, intermixed with the scents of exposed wood and the musty innards of the ruined walls. The stairway leading up was jammed with debris. She could hear the screams of those who'd survived the blast only to be buried by the rubble.

Debris also covered the flight down to the ground floor, and the blonde had to choose her footing carefully. Reaching the first level, she turned her attention to the basement entrance, but just then the double doors in the foyer rocked inward. The blonde brought both her machine pistols from shoulders to hands and was firing almost instantly. She wheeled to bring herself closer to the basement door and dropped more of the figures pouring through the entrance. She remained exposed, oblivious to the bullets ricocheting wildly around her. One dug a chunk from the wall just over her shoulder, and she twisted in time to find a pair of gunmen racing down the stairs from the second floor, firing as they came. She felled them both with a burst from one pistol while the other she continued to blast blindly toward the door.

Click.

One clip had exhausted itself, and the second quickly followed. The blonde abandoned one of the Ingrams and used her free hand to snap a fresh magazine into the one she still held. She pulled a grenade pin with her teeth and laid down suppressing fire long enough to allow her to hurl it at the heavy cellar door. The explosion rocked her, and the door shattered at the frame. The blonde yanked both of the gas canisters from her belt and tossed them down the now exposed stairs. As the noxious smoke began to spread, she wedged her last two packs of C-4 against the nearest wall and activated the ten-second detonators. That done, she lunged through the remains of the shattered door.

Thick gray gas filled the entire stairwell leading down into the basement. The blonde stuck a small portable breathing apparatus not much larger than the mouthpiece of a scuba tank into her mouth and disappeared into the smoke. She fired her rifle wherever motion or coughing alerted her to the possibility of a weapon. She reached the bottom of the stairs and followed her instincts toward a door behind which she could hear desperate screams and people moving about.

Boom! Boom! Boom!

Upstairs the *plastique* charges she had set on the first floor had just brought much of the ceiling down, entombing the entrance to the basement. The blonde tossed a final grenade against the door where she heard the sounds and pinned herself against the wall to shield her from the blast. She lunged back into motion before the echo had fully subsided, charging through the splintered door with rifle ready.

A few of those inside tried to fire at her, but her eyes had already locked onto them. Four were felled before she switched to the

Beretta, using her shots more sparingly but with deadly effectiveness. Even as she was firing, her mind registered the smoky fire at the back of the room. She shot a man hurling himself at what she realized was a flaming barrel. Though dying, he still managed to drop a sheath of white paper into the fire.

Pistol clutched tight before her, the blonde whirled across the room. Without hesitating, she dropped her free arm deep into the fiery barrel. The flames tore at her flesh and had her nearly gagging on the pain when her fingers closed on the last pages dropped in, which had not yet burned totally. Lifting them out, she fought to ignore the burns that ran from her elbow down. She forced herself not to feel the pain.

She could hear activity above her now, the remnants of the courtyard guards regrouping, probably realizing they had been played for fools. She had time only to rush to a closet that, as expected, opened onto a secret escape tunnel that would take her safely from the fortress she had destroyed.

The man in monk's robes moved closer to the fire in a futile effort to ward off the room's damp chill. The crackling flames provided the only light as they played against his cheeks.

"We could make nothing of the documents, Danielle," he said to the blond-haired woman who had just taken a seat in the dimness behind him. "They were too badly scorched for our equipment to yield anything more than a single raised seal." He hesitated, the gesture dramatic without trying to be. "The seal of the United States government."

"America," Danielle muttered. Her left forearm was wrapped in gauze, and the pain of healing had begun to set in. She swallowed it down like a bitter pill.

The man in monk's robes spun slowly around, still rubbing his hands together to force warmth into them. "The lead must be followed up," he told her. "We know their base in Nice was a key stronghold, and its destruction may have yielded even more than we had a right to expect."

"The men in the basement could have defended themselves, but they didn't," Danielle said. "Defending the pages, then destroying them, was more important to them."

"They had their priorities, as we have ours. You will go to America immediately. Bring all our resources there to bear. At last we may be able to stop one of their vicious actions instead of following in its wake."

Danielle was already rising.

"I can't tell you why," the man in monk's robes continued, "but I have the feeling we're facing something more here, as if, as if . . ."

"Don't bother," she said. "I have the same feeling."

CHAPTER 5

"**Y**OU GOT BUSINESS IN THAT NUTHOUSE, MISTER?" THE DRIVER of the launch asked Kimberlain.

"Just visiting a friend."

"Ain't been safe in these parts since they built it. People try to sell their houses and nobody wants 'em, not with that view from their backyard."

The launch driver pointed disgustedly at the island's rocky shoreline and the parapets rising there like the horns of some ancient beast with daggers for teeth.

Watertown was closer to Montreal than New York City, and Kimberlain had spent the drive steeped in apprehension. To meet Winston Peet again after three years . . . He had to admit he was looking forward to it, as if something remained unfinished in what had passed between them.

Kimberlain had been on the road at seven A.M. sharp Wednesday to make his drive north through New York State. Just outside Syracuse, the slight morning mist over Route 81 changed to a wet sticking snow which made the remainder of the drive unnerving and uncomfortable. Three inches had piled up by the time he passed through Watertown en route to the small town of Cape Stone, which overlooked Lake Ontario near the U.S.–Canadian border. Bowman Island was visible from anywhere you stood, and from the water so was Graylock's Sanitarium for the Criminally Insane. No one called it that, though. To those who knew of its existence, it was simply "The Locks."

The launch driver slowed his boat as the dock came clearly into view. A single attendant stood on it. The accumulated snow was virtually untouched in the shadow of the huge gray-stone structure of The Locks. Few of the occupants within would ever see the world beyond Bowman Island again; in point of fact only a small number would even see Bowman Island. The Locks had been constructed for survival but not for what could be construed as life. In seven years of operation, though, there had never been an escape.

"Excuse me for not waiting," the boatman apologized, not bothering to tie down before Kimberlain climbed off.

"You Kimberlain?" the attendant asked, helping him steady himself on the snow-crusted dock.

"That's right."

"Got a car right over here for you. Dr. Vogelhut's expecting you."

"Hope I won't be disturbing him."

"Tell you, friend, the one thing the docs up at The Locks got is plenty of time to talk to normal folks."

Three minutes into the drive down the single two-lane road, the towers of The Locks rose on all sides, seeming to grow out of the island itself. The United States judicial system stored its worst criminally insane here, those given virtually no chance at all for recovery. The capacity for violence lurking within those walls was something Kimberlain could feel even from this distance as clearly as the cold and the snow.

The car's worn wipers fought a losing battle with the accumulation on the windshield. The driver spoke again without taking his eyes from the slick road as the front gate appeared. "I understand you're here to see Peet."

"Know him?"

"Not when I can help it. Got a wing all to himself, that guy. His guards don't even eat with the rest of the personnel." A pause. "Dr. Vogelhut asked me to brief you on the security."

"Go ahead."

"Two twenty-four-hour armed guards outside the cell. His cell's been reinforced, the bars double thick. No window. Video surveillance, too. And on the chance that Peet manages to escape, there's a foot-thick door at the head of the corridor for him to contend with, manned by another pair of guards, and none of the guards in the wing with him have keys."

"You mean you lock them up in there?"

"Essentially, yes. We know what Peet's capable of. The men have been specially trained and are specially paid."

"Salaries sent on to their survivors in the event something goes wrong?"

"It's doubtful that it could." They were waved immediately through the front gate. "None of the guards ever get within reach of Peet. Don't even have to open the cell door to give the animal his food. Got ourselves a whole different system for him."

"Glad to hear it."

"Please, Mr. Kimberlain, sit down."

Dr. Alan Vogelhut was an old-looking forty-five with a paunch. Nervous sweat coated his palm as he shook hands. Vogelhut reseated himself at his desk as Kimberlain settled into a leather Queen Anne chair angled in front of him.

"You understand that technically Winston Peet is permitted no visitors. I agreed to make an exception in your case in view of Mr. Kamanski's phone call and because of your rather unique interest in this patient and his history."

"I wouldn't call him a patient."

"Be glad that I do, Mr. Kimberlain, for there is no power on earth that could have induced me to permit this visit unless I felt it would have some bearing on Peet's therapy."

"Therapy? Don't tell me you're trying to help him?"

"I do have an obligation."

"Do you have an obligation to the seventeen people he killed?"

"Mr. Kimberlain, it was precisely because of his capacity for violent behavior that I chose Peet for experimentation with a new behavior-modification drug."

"For a minute there I thought you were going to tell me he found God."

"You didn't let me finish. Maybe it was the drugs and maybe it wasn't, but Peet's changed. I won't say reformed or cured, just changed—and for the better."

Kimberlain shook his head in dismay. "You tell him I was coming?"

Vogelhut nodded. "He believes it to be a reward in the positive-reinforcement end of his therapy, an extension of the letters I have permitted him to write you." A pause. "Are they what brought you here?"

"Have you read them?"

"I respect my patients' privacy."

"Then I suppose I should, too."

Vogelhut leaned forward, slightly agitated. "It is my feeling that your visit here today will help me evaluate his progress. I'm the only one he converses with, and under the circumstances that doesn't tell me much. I'm using you as a barometer and thought it best to prepare you for what you'll be facing."

"Don't bother. I know Peet."

"Not this Peet."

"Seven feet tall, bald, wide as a house, and just as solid?"

"A quirk of evolution is the way he describes himself. Does a minimum of a thousand push-ups and two hours of isometrics a day."

"And the rest of the time?"

"He reads."

"Reads?"

"Philosophy. Nietzsche mostly, everything he ever wrote. Peet has taken to quoting him extensively. I've obtained dozens of books for him."

"Not in hardcover, I hope. A man like Peet could turn those edges into weapons like you wouldn't believe."

"I had the covers removed. From the paperbacks as well."

"What else does he read besides philosophy?"

Dr. Vogelhut, keeper of The Locks, settled back in his chair. "Martial arts, specifically a form called aikido."

"A bit too nonviolent for him."

"I told you he'd changed. He practices the moves day and night."

"You can't practice aikido alone."

"Peet does."

Vogelhut led Kimberlain to the isolated wing where Peet had been kept these last three years. He opened the door with his own key but stopped short of following him in.

"Don't you want to observe the momentous occasion firsthand, Doctor?"

Vogelhut shook his head. "It would be best for his therapy for the two of you to converse alone. Besides, I'll examine the tapes later."

"I'll send him your regards," Kimberlain said, and the door closed, sending an echo through the hallway beyond.

The first pair of guards, armed with automatic rifles, stood just ahead of him. One led Kimberlain down the hallway toward the single lit cell where another pair of guards stood six feet away on either side. Kimberlain felt his heart thumping as he drew closer, the memory of pain rising in the tissues of the scars left from their one previous encounter. When he reached the cell, he found the huge, bald figure sitting cross-legged on the floor, looking strangely calm and placid.

"Hello, Ferryman," said Winston Peet.

Kimberlain loathed dwelling on the specifics of their one and only meeting, either in his own mind or aloud to others. For three years he had done his best to forget it, but the frequent nights when the pain woke him from sleep made this impossible.

Eight murders had been committed before any pattern was discerned, and another seven before Kamanski, then of the FBI, called in the Ferryman. There could have been more—dozens more—but Kamanski and others involved doubted it because the killer seemed to enjoy having others critique his handiwork. All the bodies had been found with their heads missing, ripped from the torsos *by hand*, following death by strangulation. Impossible strength was clearly involved. Don't look for a man, the advice went, look for a monster.

The Ferryman went looking for a monster. The methodology indicated that whoever it was wanted to be caught, or at least challenged. He was leaving an easy-to-follow trail, fifteen murders in fifteen different states, no pattern in the victims other than the condition their corpses were found in. But Kimberlain knew there had to be more clues because the killer would have wanted to leave more. He could almost feel him out there laughing, thinking, *I'm giving you everything you need to catch me, and this is the best you can come up with?*

Murder number sixteen took place while the Ferryman was on the case. He and Kamanski spent long hours before a map of the U.S. on which sixteen numbered flag pins indicated the spots where bodies had been found. The apparent randomness was striking, though Kimberlain knew this had to be because they were looking in the wrong direction. Poring through the piles of information in the victims' files accomplished nothing. Computers came up empty because the data didn't suggest any logical conclusions.

The frustration of digging so deep suggested to Kimberlain that perhaps they had neglected the clues that were on the surface. He went back to the files, made copious notes, and after a solid day found the answer: each killing had taken place in the previous victim's birthplace. The first had been killed in Boston—the Ferryman guessed that was where the killer was from. That victim's birthplace was Gilford, New Hampshire; the victim there was born in White Plains, New York. And so it went, with no state ever repeated. The killer was plainly in need of a pattern, a purpose, anything to string his acts together. And the most terrifying ramification of this was that, obviously, significant research went into his selections. After all, no victim could be chosen until it was ascertained that a birth state would not be repeated as a result.

The sixteenth victim was born in the town of Medicine Lodge, Kansas, and, not surprisingly, the killer had not paid that state a visit yet. The Ferryman knew a full mobilization, at least a publicized one, might force his man deeper into the shadows. On the other hand, he felt that a challenge to the killer would provide his best chance for confronting and stopping him. He had his own picture leaked to the news services, a clear shot of the specialist who had been brought in to take up the hunt. The killer would see the picture and not be able to resist going for number seventeen, if for no other reason than to prove himself superior.

Medicine Lodge was a small town, with one thousand people for each of its two square miles. Kimberlain convinced Kamanski to limit their work to surveillance until a positive identification was obtained. By him. It was similarly agreed that the latest discovery would be held back from the people of Medicine Lodge, in effect making the entire town the bait, a decision that would ultimately force Kamanski from his job.

The Ferryman showed just enough of himself in town to be sure the killer would see him. The madman was present all right; there was no mistaking that feeling. He knew the man had arrived just as surely as he knew none of Kamanski's surveillance would pick him up. Kimberlain sat in the town's single bar from five o'clock on, listening to Kamanski's team issuing their reports from various sectors and wondering how it would be when the inevitable confrontation occurred. Halfway into the night, the waitress became his only company. She was a pert and pretty brunette, maybe twenty years old, with a knockout figure. Kimberlain nursed club sodas as if they were thirty-dollar shots of the finest cognac, and every ten minutes or so the waitress would appear to ask if he wanted another. Sometimes he said yes just to have reason to tip her. All the time he listened to Kamanski in the walkie-talkie set on the bar.

Kimberlain never really had a concrete reason to suspect something was wrong. In the end it was his watch that told him. Eighteen minutes had passed since the waitress's last appearance from the kitchen, and she hadn't once gone that long between tips.

Oh, Christ.

In that moment the Ferryman knew the killer had taken his challenge to heart. He also knew he should have anticipated that the man would do it just this way. He was so agitated he punched the wrong button on his walkie-talkie and jammed it in the receive mode.

With no time to lose fretting over that, Kimberlain leaped over the bar and crashed through the kitchen doors. He saw him standing there in the bright light; huge, without question the biggest man he had ever seen. Kimberlain had met plenty of giants in his time, either abnormally tall or abnormally well muscled, but he had never laid eyes on a creature who was so much of both.

The bald monster grinned and slid the pretty waitress's head across the floor toward the Ferryman's feet. The rest made history of a sort, lasting exactly the fifty-seven seconds it took for Kamanski and his men to be attracted to the sounds of a struggle.

The Ferryman's first thought was to go for his gun, but the monster was upon him in one swift lunge, and he abandoned the notion in favor of striking a blow hard and fast. He tried for the throat, but the monster snatched his hand out of midair and twisted it violently away. Kimberlain went with the move, into it in fact, but the giant was ahead of him again, pulling with a savage motion that dislocated Kimberlain's right shoulder with a sickening *pop*.

The Ferryman tried for his gun then, but just as he pulled it free, a huge blur whipped against his wrist and the weapon was gone. The giant smiled and tightened his grasp. Kimberlain understood what the monster was fighting for. If he killed the Ferryman, he would surely be the greatest killer alive.

Kimberlain felt the monster's hands going for his neck. They clamped on. This was the way the monster dismembered his victims; he tore their heads off when he had killed them.

But this time the victim was still alive.

The monster started to twist, and the Ferryman saved himself by turning his whole body with the move. The giant had great strength and relied on it totally. But great strength is at its best when it meets resistance, and Kimberlain's motion offered none. He ducked when he felt the grip slacken slightly, and then he was free, backing off.

The monster gazed at him, puzzled yet almost happy; the level of this challenge pleased him. Kimberlain sidestepped and nearly slipped in a pool of the waitress's blood. A few feet in front of him was her headless corpse. The top of his head clanged against hanging pots and pans, and the monster's face was temporarily swallowed by them as he stalked forward.

Kimberlain's ruined shoulder was really throbbing now. He thought of going for his pistol, but where was it? There was no time to look. He felt behind him and realized he had backed himself against the kitchen stove. Next to it was a coffee station where a pair of pots simmered.

The monster chose that moment to lunge, the same moment Ferryman reached behind him and grasped the handle of one of the pots. He felt a hand like a knife pierce his kidney, and the pain blinded him as he started the pot forward. At first he had planned to hurl the boiling contents into the monster's face, but he was too close for that now and opted instead to crash the glass pot against the huge bald dome.

The monster howled in pain, flapping at his ravaged skin and scorched eyes. His next wild motion stripped a dozen pots and pans from their hooks. Kimberlain saw the opening and seized it, kicking out once, twice.

In the midst of the second kick, his eyes locked on the pistol near the dishwasher, and without thinking he stooped to reach for it. The monster whirled in the same direction and lashed a blow to his wrist that shattered bone. He managed to evade the next blow by backpedaling agilely, but with one wrist ruined and the opposite shoulder dangling, his best chance was that Kamanski would appear to save him.

The monster knew he had him then. What he didn't know, *couldn't* know, was that the Ferryman had been trained to use pain, to make it work for him when there was nothing else left. The monster was going to try for his neck again; he counted on that, because it would bring his adversary close.

The giant's hands came up boldly for his neck, and Kimberlain felt himself locked in an iron grasp. He backed up to a rack of meat cleavers and felt for one blindly before snatching hold with his right hand. The monster had already started to twist, and it was difficult to say where at that point the pain was greater for Kimberlain. Before it could grow any worse, he swung the cleaver forward with a shrill scream.

The monster wailed horribly, then staggered about, trying to free the cleaver from its position between his collarbone and neck. Blood pumped fiercely from the wound, but the Ferryman knew he was still dangerous, a wounded animal.

Using his own pain as a source of strength, Kimberlain feigned going for the pistol that was now halfway between them. The monster managed to work the cleaver free with a throaty scream and had no choice now but to try to cut Kimberlain off from the gun. The Ferryman had anticipated the reaction perfectly. His arms were useless now, but he still had his legs. He unleashed a vicious onslaught of kicks that reduced the giant to a gasping pulp on the blood-wet kitchen floor. The monster made one last effort at Kimberlain, but the Ferryman's reserves carried him to the gun and then to a moderately safe distance from the bleeding animal.

Kimberlain got the gun up but didn't fire as he heard Kamanski's men charge through the entrance to the bar.

Fire, he told himself.

Shoot me, the monster's sagging eyes seemed to beg.

The Ferryman held the gun rigid, and then Kamanski was by his side. His men circled the giant, their pistols and rifles ready as though he were a wild beast finally cornered in the jungle.

The trial didn't start until Kimberlain's two-month stay in the hospital had ended. He emerged still in a neck collar, part of a kidney ruined, with a staple in his shoulder and a pin in his wrist. All told there had been four operations, with another two in the offing. The Ferryman took the stand and eyed Winston Peet the whole time he spoke; Peet was chained and under armed guard even in the closed courtroom.

Kimberlain testified as an expert witness that Peet was the most malevolent criminal he had ever encountered, his capacity for violence exceeded only by his willingness to commit it. His testimony mesmerized the court but did nothing to sway the judge. The judgment of the court was that Winston Peet was totally incapable of distinguishing between right and wrong, and he was sentenced to The Locks until such time as he was deemed fit to stand trial again or reenter society a cured man. One day Winston Peet could conceivably be released, and the Ferryman knew the killing would start again. But they would never catch Peet again because he wouldn't let himself be caught as he had before, and it would be Kimberlain's fault because he hadn't shot him.

And now, three years later, he found himself facing the monster again from six feet away.

"I've been expecting you, Ferryman," Peet said. "You've come about the murders."

CHAPTER 6

"I KNEW THE LETTERS WOULD DRAW YOU HERE," PEET SAID. "I knew you couldn't turn your back."

Kimberlain wondered how David Kamanski might have accepted the news that he had actually done his research into Turan and Rand after Peet's letters had called attention to their killings. The giant had sensed something in the murders before anyone else. Perhaps Peet was sensitive to the trail of another so much like himself. Or perhaps he was jealous and desperately wanted the perpetrator to be found. Why else would he have contacted Kimberlain?

"There's been another murder," the Ferryman said.

"I know. Jordan Lime. The details were sketchy."

"A step beyond the others. I want to know what you think about this. I want you to tell me where you think I should look."

"What's the weather like outside?" Peet asked suddenly.

"Cold and snowing."

"First snow of the season?"

"Maybe."

"Rebirth, Ferryman. Virgin white coating a land in need of renewal."

Peet rose to his feet. He was naked to the waist and wore khaki pants that barely touched his sandaled feet. His huge muscles rippled with every breath, fleshy bands pulsing even through his neck. Kimberlain couldn't help but gawk. Memory didn't do the monster justice.

"I believe that men lie in wait of similar renewal, Ferryman."

"Dr. Vogelhut seems to think you're well on your way to yours."

"He is easily fooled."

"And is that what you're doing to him?"

"Only in letting him believe his therapy is to blame for my renewal." There was a pause in which Peet eyed Kimberlain with naked intensity. "It was you, Ferryman, back there in that town. That was where *my* rebirth started." He looked over at the huge stack of coverless philosophy books against the back wall. "My friend Nietzsche wrote that a man has much to learn from his enemies. You didn't kill me in Kansas. I found that interesting."

"We all make mistakes."

"I won't praise you for your compassion, since I know that had nothing to do with it. The trophy was more meaningful when brought in alive. Killing me would have reduced the pleasure of your victory, so you spared my life. It was then that I realized we were the same, you and I."

"Your wounds must have made you delirious."

"Denials are pointless. Your soul is no stranger to me. But still I found the fact that you spared my life upsetting. New thoughts were spurred. I began to see that fate had spared me for a reason."

Peet held his eyes closed as if meditating, and Kimberlain used the time to gaze around his cell. Everything was neat, ordered, precise. A plastic sink and toilet, a one-piece cot lacking springs, and piles of books, with Nietzsche on top. Nearer the bed were stacks and stacks of newspapers, piled so precisely they seemed unread. So that's how he came to know about the murders, Kimberlain realized, and then turned his thoughts to the array of potential weapons the madman had assembled. Even newsprint, peeled off by fingernails and properly aged, made a volatile poison. And what of the pens with which he had written the letters? They were of the felt-tip variety and thus less dangerous, but with Peet the element of danger could never be ruled out.

"Is it one man behind the killings or more than one?" the Ferryman asked him.

Winston Peet's eyes opened again. "It is one man *and* more than one."

"Is that a riddle?"

"It's no ordinary killer you're after."

"Then who might it be?"

"I've been studying the cases. I read the papers avidly, Ferryman, always in search of a man whose own skills rival mine."

"Does this one make you jealous?"

"Hardly."

"Any ideas?"

Peet considered the question only briefly. "Dreighton Quail, perhaps."

"The Dutchman's dead."

"Did you kill him?"

"No."

"Then he's not dead."

"You're not helping."

"As I said in the letters, to be of service I require your help first."

"Excuse me?"

Peet stepped closer to the bars. The armed guards six feet on either sided of the Ferryman clutched their rifles tighter. The giant slid his hands up the steel. "Why don't you step in here with me?"

"Because I'm too old to spend another three months in the hospital."

"You still have pain?"

Kimberlain didn't bother saying he did.

"I as well." Peet indicated the jagged scar that cut diagonally across his collarbone and stretched toward his bulging neck. His hands squeezed the bars tighter. "I could rip these out quite easily, you know. I'd be on you before they could shoot, and force you to finish the job you started all those years ago. But I won't, Ferryman, because I'm not the same man anymore. My soul is like the earth's: reborn.''

''We were talking about the murders.''

''I still am. Between good and evil actions there is no difference in kind, but mostly one of degree. The standard is constantly changing.''

''No standard gives you the right to kill seventeen people.''

''Each man has as much right as he has power. Would you not admit to killing more than seventeen yourself?''

Kimberlain didn't respond.

''Was it any more right for you? Or wrong? I think not. The deed is not judged in its own context, it *is* its own context. The beast in us wants to be lied to, and judgments form these lies. But my renewal began when I stopped judging myself or letting myself be judged. Was your killing any more justified because it was for a cause? I see in your soul much of what I see in my own. I see both of us striving to provide balance for our actions. We are held prisoners in a moral cell of our own making, and its bars are much stronger than the ones I'm holding now.''

''So you've seen the light. Is that it?''

''We both have. But you are free to seek your renewal, while mine must remain a state of mind rather than being. My renewal has cast me as the master of myself. My mind has sharpened. I was punished for my crimes, and now I am being punished for my desires. He who deviates from the traditional falls victim to the extraordinary; he who remains in the traditional becomes its slave.''

''Nothing human is worthy of being taken very seriously, Peet.''

The giant smiled for the first time. ''Plato. I'm impressed, Ferryman. But the man who has overcome his passions has entered into possession of the most fertile ground for ripening thoughts. These killings are a sign.''

''Sign of what?''

''That the time for my reentry into the world has come. You can't win alone this time. You are fighting forces you cannot possibly comprehend.''

"I don't believe in monsters, Peet.'' And, eyeing him tightly, "Not anymore.''

"Not monsters, Ferryman, causes.''

"A cause didn't mutilate Jordan Lime.''

"But it unleashed the energy which did. Raw and untempered.''

"One man and more than one,'' muttered Kimberlain, repeating Peet's earlier words.

"The force behind what you are pursuing cannot be adequately measured. Alone you're no match for it.'' Peet's tone became almost pleading. "Release me from this prison so that I may purge my final demons and conquer the enemy by your side.''

"I couldn't do that even if I wanted to.''

"Then why did you come here, Ferryman? Was it to question me about the murders, or was it for a different reason? Have you avoided the mirror for so long that you needed to see what your reflection looked like? Have you lost touch with the side of you I represent?''

Kimberlain held the giant's stare while he backed away. "Have a great life in there, Peet.''

"That which does not kill me, Ferryman, makes me stronger.''

Before leaving The Locks, Kimberlain received a message that Captain Seven wanted very much to see him at the Lime estate. He was glad for that, as much as anything because it took his mind off his strangely unsettling encounter with Peet. During the boat ride back to the mainland and the long drive south, he searched for reasons to hate the man who had almost killed him, but his search came up empty. He wanted to feel as he had in the courtroom when he testified, wanted to feel as he had when the judge announced the sentence and his first thought had been to grab one of the guard's guns and pull the trigger, as he should have in Medicine Lodge. Today, though, he could find no hate in him for Peet. He wondered if indeed this was a different man from the one he had captured, and if so, how different might he himself have become without realizing it?

Back in Greenwich, Kimberlain found Captain Seven seated in the middle of the Lime mansion's huge center staircase. He had just started munching on a collection of salad greens packed into a pita pocket. A bottle of natural soda stood by his side.

"Woulda brought one for you if I'd known you were gonna join me," said Seven.

"Some startling revelations would more than make up for it."

"If you're talking about what went down here, I'm not ready yet. Close, but not quite. By the way, think you might be able to get your friend Herman off my back?"

"Herm*es*, not Herm*an*. As in the messenger of the gods."

"I don't give a fuck if he runs Western Union, he's a royal pain in the ass. I work a certain way. Make sure he knows that."

"I'll make the point again. I assume your computer turned up some insightful info."

The captain nodded. "Had a good day. Your three victims were connected all right—through the military."

"Sounds like too easy a connection for the traditional authorities to have missed."

"Not when you consider the dumb asses never read between the lines." Seven continued from memory, as if reading the material straight off his computer monitor. Alfalfa sprouts slid from the corners of his mouth. "Benjamin Turan's plastic steel will soon revolutionize missile production. Its composition has been estimated to quicken delivery time by up to fifty percent and set radar back fifty years. Adam Rand's discovery of that hypersensitive transmission will similarly revolutionize tanks and other direct-drive battle vehicles. Speed can be increased on the order of sixty percent." Captain Seven took another hefty bite from his pita pocket and spoke on through chews. "Jordan Lime's transistor coupling which resists burnout will soon be state of the art when it comes to weapons systems. It eliminates breakdowns and renders such systems safe from the electromagnetic pulse caused by the detonation of nuclear weapons in outer space. Might not be the most colorful of the three, but it's the one I'd wager Washington is hottest for.''

''Any of this public?''

''Not on any file the normal mind can access.''

''So our boy is knocking off the heads of companies who've recently closed or are about to close major deals with the military,'' Kimberlain concluded.

Seven nodded. ''Focusing on state-of-the-art discoveries and futuristic technology. Like I said, in none of the cases is the product even close to being on the market yet, so whoever our killer is, he must have a hell of a pipeline. This is strictly deeply buried stuff.''

''How many victims, Captain?''

''Ah, I was hoping you'd raise that issue. At least eleven in addition to the three we know about in the past eighteen months, all industrialists with some kind of military connections eliminated as follows: two shootings, one stabbing, three car accidents, one accidental poisoning, two killed in the process of a robbery, one executed by a terrorist group after being taken hostage, and one who didn't make it through routine surgery.''

''Then it's escalating,'' Kimberlain said. ''The killings are becoming more complex, more technologically oriented. Our boy has faced increased security as he's gone on and has overcome it with ease. He's loving this, Captain, I can feel it. What about the next victim I asked you to pin down?''

''Found maybe three hundred potentials, keying off variables pulled from the pattern. I was able to eliminate two hundred and fifty pretty easily and then ran probability factors on those remaining.''

''Who drew the highest?''

''Chick named Lisa Eiseman, president and chairman of the board of TLP Industries, based in Atlanta.''

''TLP Industries. Don't they make—''

''Yup,'' broke in Captain Seven. ''Toys. Pioneers and holders of the patent on the interactive memory chip. Made a fortune with their line of the Powerized Officers of War—the POW! dolls.''

"Dolls?''

The captain nodded. "So to speak. TLP's specialty is toy soldiers.''

CHAPTER 7

THE PHOTO SHOP WAS LOCATED ON GEORGETOWN'S M STREET, three blocks from the Four Seasons Hotel. Squeezed between an ice cream shop and a record store, it looked innocuous, right down to the bold sign assuring customers of same-day service on their color prints. On this day, though, the CLOSED sign dangled from the window a full hour before the shop's advertised seven P.M. closing.

In one of three dark rooms located in the rear, a man with thick glasses looked up from a developing machine. Switching the developed material to a hypersensitive computer-keyed enhancer, he took another look and then turned his stare through the red half-light at Danielle.

"There it is," he announced. "Not terrific, but the best I can do."

Danielle moved her eye to the lens to see whatever he'd been able to reconstruct of the burned pages. She had left for Washington as soon as the preliminary results had been revealed to her. During the long flight across the Atlantic she tried to sleep, but every time she dozed off she was seized by a fuzzy dream of her parents, seen only from the rear since she had no real memory of them. The dreams always came at times of maximum stress, as if to remind her of the path that had brought her to where she was. Her parents were mere shadows in her memory, dark and without definition. More vividly she remembered an endless succession of refugee camps in Lebanon. In each she was given a different name, but the real hell did not begin until she was twelve. Thin and frail, yet mysteriously attractive, she was lighter-skinned than the other girls but with the darkest eyes of any.

The first man to force himself upon her smelled of liquor and sweat and drove a pain through her like none she thought possible. And when he was done, he had dragged her bloodied body into his tent, where more men were ready to take their turn. As the first of them mounted her she felt the pain even worse than before. She wanted to scream but lacked the strength; she thought of holding her breath until she was dead.

Suddenly three well-dressed men stormed into the tent. The savage on top of her was yanked off and his throat slit as guns were drawn on his fellows. Then a concerned-looking man who smelled good gently lifted her from the floor as she passed out.

When she came to, it was daytime and she was being led out of a car with vague memories of flying in a jet larger than those that buzzed the camps constantly. She was wearing clean, fresh-smelling clothes that were almost her size. Before her was a camp not at all like the others. It had gardens and buildings instead of tents, and there were spacious grounds and woods. The compound was enclosed by a waist-high stone fence rather than the barbed wire she had grown up staring at. The buildings contained rooms laid out in dormitory fashion with six children in each. By the time she was escorted to hers, more fresh new clothes had been stacked neatly in a chest of drawers, and still more hung in her closet. Dinner that night was the greatest meal of her life, the food hot and plentiful, and Danielle—though she had not yet come to be called that—almost cried with happiness.

There were fifty or so other children present, and she was among the oldest. Many of the others looked to be no more than five or six. Danielle watched as a new world began to open up for her. She had never seen so many different kinds of people with different skin, hair, and eyes. All seemed happy to be there.

The lessons started almost immediately. Danielle had had virtually no schooling up to this point, and the work was hard, including courses in math, science, and a variety of languages including French, English, and German. She learned fast, completed her work diligently, and often had to be prodded to go outside to play with the others in the neatly sculptured gardens. Her world began at the stone fence and ended in the woods. Still, it was a massive world compared to what she had been used to for as long as she could remember. The children were encouraged to run free in the rolling expanse of wooded land at the back of the compound. Hide-and-go-seek was the favorite game, and it grew more elaborate as the months passed. The children's training had begun though they didn't know it, even as their numbers slowly dwindled. Occasionally at night a child would disappear without question or explanation.

For her own part Danielle was too engrossed in her studies to notice. She thoroughly enjoyed the new challenges presented her almost daily, and she began to thrive. She mastered the languages with ease, along with other complex subjects such as world currency tables and various laws for entry and exit visas. Here again she did not question; she simply learned.

The years passed and Danielle grew taller and more ravishing. Of her original batch of children, barely a third remained. Friendships were not encouraged, and she had made none. She knew she was being singled out by the men who were her instructors, knew she was excelling in the complicated field games added to the classroom work. Drilling in hand-to-hand combat and weaponry had started, and the remaining children accepted this as easily as everything else. After all, the one thing that held all of them together was that before coming here they had all lived with violence. With such a perspective, nursed almost from birth, there was no resistance to the training they were now required to undergo. It was simply a part of life.

Danielle excelled at the training. She approached the drills and practice sessions diffidently yet with the same precision with which she attacked her studies. The ones who failed, both boys and girls, seemed to be trying too hard. For her it all came easy. In the camps she had known neither failure nor success, just depression and destitution. Her new life taught her that failure need not exist at all. Everything depended on attitude, and she learned to become the master of hers.

If only she had known, then . . .

Then what? That night in the woods when the second phase began, when she became Danielle, maybe she would have let herself die. But they had pushed the right buttons to activate the desired response. They had made her in the image they desired, and she had become *their* prisoner, instead of a prisoner of the camps. That night in the woods had accomplished the final forging of her persona, determining her shape through years to come until . . .

". . . so I couldn't make any sense of the contents of the pages under standard infrared or ultraviolet," the man with thick glasses was explaining. Danielle realized her mind had drifted while her eye had been pressed to the lens. She looked up from it. "So what I did," the man continued, "was I retreated the pages entirely. Risky business since we mighta lost everything in the process, but I laid the overcoating on by hand to assure the smoothest impression, and"—dramatically now—"*voilà!*"

Danielle returned her eye to the lens and spun the focusing wheel. The picture that sharpened was the government seal that had drawn her here in the first place.

"Yes," she commented. "I told you about that."

"You told me it was just government. Actually it's a Defense Department seal reserved for the touchiest documents. Top secret, highly classified, and all that sort of stuff. Anyway, you actually brought me fragments of two separate documents, from what the salvaged excerpts indicate. The one you're looking at now was the most damaged. It was probably lifted off microfilm which would have meant loss of resolution even without the fire. Best I could do was that one seal and a single word noteworthy for its repetition.''

''What word?''

''Spiderweb.''

''That's all?''

''That and the fact it was under what they call ULTSEC for 'ultrasecret.' The second document wasn't as badly burned, and it was infinitely more interesting.'' The man carefully slid the piece of retouched Kodak paper aside and placed another sheet beneath the computer-keyed lens. ''Here we go. Have a look.''

Danielle rotated the lens. What she saw was a mass of lines, measurements, and notations that were meaningless to her. ''Plans,'' she said simply.

''Yes,'' the man acknowledged, and he slid the page to place a specific section under the lens. ''Now look.''

Danielle's vision sharped to recognize a pair of letters. ''EB . . . Electric Boat?''

''The very boys up in Groton, Connecticut, who make some rather impressive subs.''

''Then these are plans for a submarine?''

''Fragments of them, yes, and not just any sub either. From what I can gather, you're looking at the midship of the new Jupiter class of super-Tridents. Soviets would pay a fortune to get their hands on these.'' He paused. ''Is that what this is about?''

She looked down through the lens again and then back up at the man. Her eyes hardened.

''Okay,'' he said fearfully, ''just forget I asked.''

Danielle went back to the lens, mostly to keep the man from seeing any fear in her own face.

The plans for a new class of Trident submarines.

Something in the Defense Department called Spiderweb.

And somewhere a connection between the two.

CHAPTER 8

COMMANDER MCKENZIE BARLOW LAY TWISTING ON HIS COT fighting against sleep. The battle was between a body that craved rest and a mind terrified that more hours lost would make more distant the awesome task still ahead.

Seventeen days now. Seventeen days of confinement and disgrace aboard his own ship. Seventeen days. In that period Mac had been allowed out of his quarters on only five occasions and then only to transmit a code signaling that all was well on board the *Rhode Island*.

A lie. A great big fucking lie.

The *Rhode Island* was the prototype for a new class of super-Trident submarines, twenty percent larger than the last generation and at least that much faster. She could remain submerged indefinitely, and the transport of her deadly cargo of twenty-eight nuclear missiles was totally at the discretion of her commanding officer.

At least it had been.

Those missiles, with more than ten thousand times the explosive force of the bombs used on Hiroshima and Nagasaki, were deadly accurate, thanks to the wonders of microchip technology. The *Rhode Island*'s Jupiter-class missiles alone made her the third-greatest nuclear power on Earth, capable of knocking out seventy-three percent of the Soviet populace on her own. But aside from her power and speed, the *Rhode Island*'s greatest feature was that she couldn't be tracked—not by Soviet forces, and not by her American counterparts. Even her routine messages were bounced off so many beacons that only a rough estimate of her position could be gained. In fact, one of the major purposes of the *Rhode Island*'s maiden voyage was to see whether SOSUS (sonar surveillance system) could come close to tracking her. The system, composed of hundreds of powerful sensors lodged on the bottom of the sea, was designed to follow the paths of Soviet Victor and Charlie subs. It was the most sophisticated in the world, and if the *Rhode Island*'s silent running could evade detection by it she could evade detection by anything.

In actuality, no sub as fast as the *Rhode Island* could operate silently. Instead of trying to, she sent out contradictory signals that sensors normally read as schools of fish. Electric Boat had set out to build the perfect warship, and the feeling on the eve of the *Rhode Island*'s maiden voyage was that they had come very close.

Mac heard footsteps approaching, then a key being turned in his door. It wasn't mealtime, so he must have miscounted the days. Today must be the eighteenth, not the seventeenth, time for his three-day signal pass to COMSUBLANT—Commander of the Submarine Force in the Atlantic. No matter, for he'd already composed in his mind the masked message he intended to send to advise COMSUBLANT of what was really going on aboard the *Rhode Island*.

At fifty-three he had considered himself too old for such a command and had let himself be talked into it against his better judgment. If the Jupiter class of super-Tridents was to be utilized to its utmost potential, he was told, it needed men of Mac's savvy and stature at the helm.

That stature might have been defined by many things, but size was not one of them. McKenzie Barlow stood barely five and a half feet tall. He had been christened "Mighty Mac" back in his early training days when he fought to join the SEALs, the navy's elite commando company, against concerted antagonism from those who believed he didn't fit the image. Mac had proved them wrong then and later in Vietnam, where his specialty was underwater demolitions. Though records weren't kept, he had probably spent more time behind enemy lines than anyone else serving with Navy stripes.

On one mission the Cong locked on to the gunboat transporting him and a team out of a fire zone, and Mac had risked capture and death by venturing back into the flames on four separate occasions to carry out the rest of the crew. The incident left him with multiple skin grafts on his arms and permanently damaged shoulder joints from the pressure of carrying two of the men for three miles through enemy jungle.

That was the last combat Mac ever saw as a SEAL, but his subsequent rise though the Navy chain of command was swift, culminating in his holding the con of the Trident sub *Florida* for six years prior to his retirement. They had lured him back into the command chair to take the *Rhode Island* only after assuring him that this maiden voyage would be strictly window dressing: in other words, no nuclear armaments on board. The order of business was thirty days at sea just to check out the silent-running systems and give the press something to write about. Mac even agreed to participate in the christening ceremonies at Electric Boat in Groton. He was on board running systems checks when sealed orders arrived from the vice-admiral of COMSUBLANT to steam out of Groton for Newport News, Virginia, to take on a full complement of twenty-eight Jupiter-class missiles prior to deep-lie mission. If he had known . . . But who was he kidding? He was Navy all the way; he would never have said no to them, no matter what. He was miffed that they had kept him in the dark, but he knew it was nothing personal, just a matter of security. The very existence of the Jupiter-class missile hadn't been made public yet, and a leak prior to the *Rhode Island*'s maiden voyage could sink her faster than any charge from a Victor or Charlie.

Mac fumed until the first hours at sea refreshed him and he lost himself in his command. The first two days out of Newport News by way of Groton were totally without incident. The *Rhode Island* drove like a sports car, and Mac treated her as such, airing her out beneath the sea that to him was like one giant superhighway without a speed limit. As a boy he had loved driving his bike through the back roads of Wisconsin, turning and twisting until he was hopelessly lost. Deciding on a course for this Jupiter-class prototype was much the same, except the instruments were always there to tell him where he was. Took some of the fun out of it, if you asked McKenzie Barlow.

But all the fun disappeared seventeen, no, eighteen days ago. Commanders generally allow themselves little sleep, and even at fifty-three, Mac was no exception—four hours at most per day, and often not even that much. Without the guidelines of night and day, sleep seemed less important anyway. He was just coming out of a rare dream when the alarm bell chimed and drove him up like a bolt. Mac recognized the ring as that of an on-board systems failure, and the darkness in his own quarters, broken only by a single emergency lamp, told him the damn power had gone out all over the ship. He stumbled for the door and was immediately thrown against the wall by the force of the sub heaving herself nose-first for the surface like a swimmer who knows he has reached his underwater limit. Since a similar power failure had destroyed the *Thresher* more than twenty-five years before, all Trident, attack, and 688-class subs had been built with an automatic surface feature that was triggered in the event of a power failure.

The *Rhode Island* was halfway up when Mac finally finished his climb to the bridge.

"Status?" he asked the officer of the deck.

"Source of failure unknown, Commander."

"Two thousand meters," from sonar.

"Damage?" Mac wanted to know.

"Structure is tight and sound. It's electrical. Computer should have it pinpointed by the time we reach the surface."

"Fifteen hundred," sonar announced.

"Damn," Mac muttered to himself. Something felt wrong about

this. Maybe he was getting old. "Check vertical sonar. Anything above us?"

"Negative, sir."

Mac told himself to relax. They would surface, pinpoint the problem, and be under again before even the currents knew the difference.

"One thousand," sonar reported.

"Sir, I'm showing something on vertical," said the man seated next to him.

"Coordinates?"

"Directly above us. Small patches, like several oil spills. No movement, no confidence of engine."

"Five hundred meters."

Mac's mind was working feverishly. "Helm, can you give me anything?"

"Sir?"

"Steer us away from those patches, man!"

"Two hundred and fifty meters."

Helm tried some buttons. "Negative, sir. She's coming up too fast."

"One hundred meters," said sonar.

A sudden thrust shook the *Rhode Island* as she crested nose-first through the surface and her vast bulk began to settle.

"Get us back under!" ordered Mac.

"No response, sir. Power's still down, still . . ."

Already the voice was sounding faraway, words shrinking into darkness as Mac slid to the floor. The last thing he felt was the rhythmic bobbing of his ship.

When he awoke in his quarters, a stranger was standing over his cot. The man wasn't much taller than he and was dressed all in black. His eyes were cold and dark, and his hair was long on the sides but showed a dome on top. A pair of larger men stood back by the door as deterrents against Mac's first impulse.

"Your ship is mine, Commander Barlow," the dark man said flatly.

"I guess we're past the name, rank, and serial number stage."

"Quite."

"You have the advantage of me."

"The name is Jones," said the stranger.

"Really?"

"Smith if you prefer." He smiled, very much at ease.

"Where's my crew?"

"They're being held prisoner, but they are all safe. They are no longer on board."

"*What?*" Mac sat up so suddenly that the deterrents started forward.

"We're already underwater again, riding smooth," Mr. Jones said. "All necessary personnel have been replaced with my men. Fear not. They're well schooled in the operation of this vessel."

"And yet I'm still on board."

"Because we need you. You're going to help us."

"Am I?"

"Oh, most definitely." The stranger in black slid a chair closer to the cot and seated himself. "I foresee no problems whatsoever."

"You got bad vision, pal."

"Let's say there are things you haven't seen yet, Mac. May I call you, Mac? I understand under some circumstances even enlisted men address you that way."

"You got a commission?"

"Better—I've got your ship."

"Terrorists?"

Jones looked insulted. "Please, Commander." He moved his chair still closer. "I represent a totally unaligned party who requires this vessel for nonmilitary reasons."

"You don't hijack a super-Trident in the name of peace."

"I assure you there is a plan."

"Excuse me for saying your assurances aren't worth a hell of a lot."

The man remained deadly calm and even friendly. "You're wondering how we accomplished all this, no doubt."

"My head hurts a little too much to think about it."

"You'll experience no long-lasting effects from the gas, Mac. We shot high-pressured darts through your hull just behind the sail. The darts were attached to hoses which instantly began pumping the gas into your air supply. Remarkably potent stuff. Explains why it took so little time to knock your whole crew out. Don't worry, we plugged the holes before diving again."

"The blotches that were identified as oil spills—rubber rafts?"

Jones smiled. "Very good, Mac. You're as good as I was led to believe."

"The rafts were drifting in the water with the currents, so vertical sonar couldn't have picked them up before—"

"Before the power failure—is that what you were going to say? Of course you realize now that that was our doing. A circuit in your main console board shorted out, and the whole system would have overloaded if not for the automatic shutoff device. Under normal circumstances, a simple matter for you to pin down and rectify on the surface."

Mac was confused now. The dark stranger was describing a type of sabotage that had been explicitly ruled out in a super-Trident.

Jones seemed to read his mind. "Yes, all the computer chips that could arrange the 'appearance' of such a short circuit are tested for tampering dozens of times before implementation, and all have backups. But no amount of tests can guard against the use of two such chips, and both their backups, working in tandem, one useless and thus undetectable without the other."

"My God . . ."

"Everything was on timer. Quite brilliant."

"But you knew where we were. You *tracked* us."

"A homing beacon of sorts, Mac. We've followed your progress almost since you left Groton. Of course we already knew about your stop in Virginia, so there was no reason to pick you up until you were well at sea."

"The ship was swept. Everything. I supervised the process myself."

"The storage cupboards in the galley, Mac?"

"Yes."

"But not the condensed milk itself. When mixed with water, a radioactive isotope was activated. It was a very mild dose, but with five days' worth in each man's system, well, let's just say that for anyone who knew what to look for, you weren't hard to find."

"All carried out for nothing, I'm afraid," Mac said. "As you said, I'm still on board because you need me, except there's nothing you can do or say that will make me cooperate."

"Then I suppose I'll have to show you something instead."

"I think you'll find this interesting," Jones said after they were seated before the television in the ship's rec room. The super-Trident's expanded size allowed for a number of luxuries not included in the earlier models, including a quarter-mile running track and a workout center complete with free weights and Nautilus equipment. There was even a racquetball court adjacent to the rec room. Jones signaled to one of his men to insert a cassette into the VCR.

There were a few moments of flutter, and then the picture sharpened to reveal Mac's wife and two surviving sons, who were both in high school. The three of them were seated in chairs in a room he had never seen before. They were obviously frightened. The camera backed up, and the four men standing behind them became clear. Two held rifles.

"Just for show," Jones explained, following Mac's eyes. "I was against it. I loathe even the suggestion of unnecessary violence."

"You fucking *bastard*!"

Jones nodded almost sadly. "To you, I suppose I am. Maybe even to myself. But I promise that nothing will happen to your family so long as you cooperate. They are safe and sound and will be released just as soon as we are finished with you and your ship. I know it's probably not worth much, but you have my word on that."

Jones froze the picture, and there it was, Mac's whole life right before him, and this bastard held it in his hand. Mac looked at his wife and kids and felt the conflict inside himself: his ship and country on one side, everything else he loved on the other.

"This is about the missiles, isn't it?"

"I'm afraid so, Mac."

"Then you're out of luck, mister, because I can't fire them alone. Four keypad combinations are required, and unfortunately you have removed the other three from the ship."

"Four to fire," Jones corrected. "One to enable. You and only you, Mac."

"What the hell good is enabling the warheads if there's no way you can fire the missiles?"

"All in good time, Mac, all in good time."

"Where are we heading? Can you tell me that much?"

"South," Jones replied. "Our journey will take approximately twenty-four days. When we reach our destination all you need do is supply the enabling codes and your family will be released."

"And I'll be freed to join them?"

"If you wish, yes."

"After seeing your face and the faces of all your men?"

"It won't matter. Believe me."

Mac felt chilled by the grim intent in Jones's response. "Who are you?" he demanded.

"A man charged with helping to remake destiny. I'll explain it all to you in time. I promise. I owe you that much, and when I explain you'll understand, though I'm sure you won't agree."

"You can bet on that."

"I'm sorry we had to take your family, Mac, I truly am. A man's family is sacred. A man's family is everything until . . ." Jones stopped himself just as emotion began sneaking into his voice. "Please realize I could have used drugs on you, or torture. But you are not my enemy, and if I violate your dignity, then what is mine worth?" The emotion crept in again. "Too much of that very commodity has been lost, necessitating this mission."

Mac just looked at him. He had the presence of mind to realize that there was no way for Mr. Jones to get word off the *Rhode Island* about anything to anyone, including the captors of his family, without risking betraying their position. So he had—what was it?—twenty-four days to try something.

But now eighteen had passed and he hadn't done a thing. Five times now he had been brought by Jones to the ship's com center to provide the rotating status code to COMSUBLANT, and on each occasion Jones had made it a point to show him the videotape again. He knew it by heart now. The camera stayed on each boy for eight seconds, then lingered for twice that long on his wife. The final shot pulled back to include all of them sitting there side by side in a grotesque family portrait, holding just long enough to ensure Mac could see their frightened faces.

On days when he was not taken from his cabin, Mac spent much of the time replaying the tape in his mind, using the image to fire his courage. Strangely, the effect of watching it seemed just as great on Jones. After the third viewing or maybe the fourth, Mac could have sworn he saw tears welling in his captor's eyes and thought, *I know this man. Somehow, somewhere, I've seen him before.*

But none of that mattered. Nothing mattered except the fact he now had a plan along with the courage to implement it.

Today.

The door to his cabin was opening, and McKenzie Barlow made sure his face was impassive and his body relaxed so he would not betray his intentions.

"Ready, Mac?" Jones asked as he stepped through the doorway with the ever-present deterrents just behind.

"Absolutely."

THE THIRD TRUMPET

TOY SOLDIERS

THURSDAY, NOVEMBER 19; 10:00 A.M.

CHAPTER 9

KIMBERLAIN SPENT THE FLIGHT FROM NEW YORK TO ATLANTA familiarizing himself with the dossier Captain Seven had compiled on Lisa Eiseman. He lingered over her picture, trying to supply color to the black-and-white head shot. She was beautiful, but was her hair dark brown or black? Her eyes were dark, and she seemed to be olive-skinned. The file said that although she was now the chief executive officer of a $500 million corporation, she still drove herself to work every morning. The Ferryman liked that.

He went over parts of her dossier a third time toward the end of the flight in an attempt to keep his mind from wandering to thoughts he liked to keep shelved high and out of reach. But sometimes they toppled and needed to be restacked.

Lisa Eiseman, age 29. Born in Atlanta. Father was Burton Eiseman, founder and owner of TLP Industries. Specializes in toys and games for children and adults. Company enjoyed banner success in the early through middle '70s, then floundered gravely in the early '80s. Bankruptcy considered. Burton Eiseman died in 1980 at age 52. Circumstances sketchy. Official verdict was heart attack, but suicide suspected.

Kimberlain felt his thoughts start to veer and let them go. Lisa

Eiseman had been twenty-two when her father died, just one year younger than he was on the day that had changed his life. He had finished training with the Special Forces and been accepted for a tour with the anti-terrorist commandos of Delta Force. At the time it was the high point of his life. He remembered how excited he had been making the phone call to his father, a career officer who had recently retired with the rank of sergeant major. The senior Kimberlain had always stifled his enthusiasm but couldn't on that day, for he knew the appointment meant his son was the elite of the elite.

The phone call was a long one because once training began at Fort Bragg, members of Delta Force were allowed no contact whatsoever with the outside world for three months. Security was paramount. Everything about Delta Force was secret, including the identity of its commandos.

So it was with considerable surprise and concern that Kimberlain found himself called to the commander's office to receive a message some weeks later. None of the men knew the commander's name, only that he was a short, powerfully built man who never smiled or gave slack. That day was the first time Kimberlain had seen any expression on his face.

"There's been some trouble," he reported. "I'm sorry to have to tell you this. Your parents were killed."

Not "are dead," Kimberlain remembered noting in his mind. "Were killed."

"I can arrange for you to attend the funeral."

"Thank you, sir."

"Normally, leaving base would mean the end of Delta Force duties, but, damn it, I knew your father. The Army owes him enough to arrange an exception."

"I'd appreciate that, sir."

Of course his father wouldn't have wanted any such exception for him, would have preferred that he not leave the base at all to attend the funeral. His father was not a sentimental man. Duty first and foremost; duty always. But Kimberlain knew he had to leave the base to find out what had really happened out there in the California desert where his parents had died.

Were killed.

The phrase stuck in his mind. Kimberlain found out the truth little by little, piecing together fragments of the story. Apparently his parents were touring California in their recently purchased RV when mechanical problems forced them to pull over. His father must have stubbornly insisted he could fix it himself, and the problems had dragged on past nightfall, when the aging couple became prey to a gang of bikers who decided to expropriate the RV for themselves. Shots were exchanged, and by all accounts his father had put up an incredible fight. But in the end the sheer number of the bikers had won out, and both his parents were killed. The bikers left the RV behind.

Kimberlain had been given the day of the funeral plus two additional days leave from the base. At the grave site he ignored the clichéd phrases of the unknown minister and focused his thoughts instead on what had consumed him since he first heard the story back at Bragg. There had to be a fitting retribution here.

A payback.

At the end of the funeral the local sheriff asked if there was anything he could do.

Jared said as a matter of fact there was.

The sheriff was a flabby man whose heart showed on his face. He told Kimberlain that the bikers were based in Barstow and hung out in a bar only those meeting their approval could enter. Kimberlain had smuggled a .45 off Bragg in his duffel, and if he needed more than twelve bullets to finish the job, he deserved whatever fate awaited him.

The plan he would use developed quickly. He remained in the civilian suit he had worn to the funeral and pulled a cap over his standard Army haircut. He rented a huge Lincoln at the nearest Hertz, paying cash for the monster that was necessary for his plan. He drove to the bikers' bar on a recon mission and from the outside found it packed with an unruly crowd of leather-clad drunkards and roisterers. Judging that it would be at least midnight before the crowd began to disperse, Jared bided his time.

He left a half hour ahead of the first group and drove south. All the bikers lived in a housing development just off Route 15, and Jared picked a spot in the meager spill of a streetlight to pull over and jack up his car, yanking a rear tire off as if it were flat.

Dozens of bikes flew by him without stopping. A few slowed. Obscenities were shouted. Kimberlain started to consider what he might do if the night finished this way, but he didn't have to consider long when seven of them pulled up. They had driven by initially, then circled back.

"We help ya any, mister?" a big, bearded biker offered.

In the darkness Kimberlain made himself look uneasy. "No, it's okay. Just about finished." And he started to roll the tire back onto the wheel.

"No," said another, moving forward to hold it in place. "We gotta insist. See, it's part of our code to help strangers. Kinda gives us a good name in the town."

"Oh, well . . ."

The biker slid the tire from his grasp, while the others rested their bikes on kickstands. Kimberlain moved slowly away. A big man can conceal his quickness more easily than a small one, mostly because looking at him you don't judge him to be quick. He looked about warily, sure to place the right amount of fear and uncertainty in his eyes.

The bikers were smiling at him. Two of them were twisting the lug nuts into place now, belching regularly.

Kimberlain felt the biggest one of all coming up on him from behind. He knew the biker was going for a grasp and let him.

"Okay, fucker," a beer breath voice rasped in his ears. "You're ours."

Kimberlain kicked his legs and thrashed a little. The other bikers stalked forward, led by an acne-scarred one with sunglasses and a ring dangling from a chain around his neck.

"What you reckon this car's worth, Mo?" the big one holding Kimberlain asked the acne-scarred one.

"Don't know for sure. Twenty maybe, Ax."

"Bet we could get fifteen no questions."

"Make up for the weekend," another said, but that wasn't what spurred Kimberlain into action. It might have before too many more seconds were up, because it was on Saturday that his parents had been killed. But his eyes had focused on the ring the ugly one named Mo had on his neck chain, and a chill like none he could ever remember went through him.

It was his father's wedding band.

What happened next must have seemed impossible to the bikers, because there was Ax, the biggest of them all, being hoisted up and over the stranger's shoulders and hurled onto the Lincoln's roof. The thud hadn't even sounded when the stranger's hand lashed out toward Mo, who was backing up. Mo saw the blur and felt his air choked off as his neck chain was twisted round his throat and knotted so he couldn't untangle it.

As Ax slid unconscious from the dent he'd left in the Lincoln's roof, the others went into motion. But they'd already lost one step to hesitation and another to beer, facing a crazed whirlwind who was never in the same spot long enough to see.

Kimberlain killed the next two with his bare hands, using Special Forces techniques that had always impressed him with how easy it was to bring on death. He didn't draw the .45 from the holster on his hip until he saw the first of the bikers show their pistols. A single shot for each, and then two for the one staggering for the sawed-off shotgun strapped to his bike.

He left Ax there on the road to wake up and find the bodies of his fellows. There had to be someone left to tell the story of what had happened. The best paybacks were the ones that didn't stop paying back.

And on that night, Kimberlain supposed, the Ferryman had been born.

He drove off without giving the bikers another look, frightened not of the consequences he had been resigned to face from the start, but of the feeling that had surged through him during this first payback.

He had enjoyed it. And later perhaps, after his encounter with Peet in the hospital, it was the memory of that feeling that had brought him back to the paybacks and kept him there.

He had proceeded to drive the Lincoln straight to Fort Bragg, where he turned himself in to the MPs and confessed. Military jurisdiction won out, and he was placed in the stockade to await summary court martial. Hanging was a very real possibility, or life in the stockade at the very least.

He made himself endure those first weeks prior to the trial, but the pain of it eliminated any question of his accepting Kamanski's offer. He was being given a second chance, and this time he would make it work. He would lose his emotions in his deadly skills and abilities.

As one of The Caretakers.

He liked the anonym "Ferryman" and promised himself to live up to it. His first two years were not marred by a single mission failure. He lived and breathed on raw, animalistic action. Each Caretaker had a specialty, and his was killing. He was ruthless and obsessed with the assignments that Hermes brought him from Zeus. All those chartered for passage across the River Styx completed their journey. He knew the other side very well and enjoyed returning from it alone and successful.

Like Charon in his passages.

A comment from a stewardess brought Kimberlain out of his musings, and he went back to the file opened on the tray table before him.

Upon his death, Burton Eiseman's struggling TLP Industries was inherited by his three children. Two sons, Thomas and Peter, and his only daughter, Lisa. Company was named for first initials of his children, from youngest to oldest. The sons had no interest in taking over the business, so Lisa took charge.

Her first task was to deal with a hostile takeover attempt by the

Wally Toy Company, then the nation's largest. TLP board of directors was split on the decision, resulting in a boardroom struggle. By quirk of company charter, Lisa Eiseman was able to dissolve the board and appoint herself acting president and chairperson. Risked financial ruin and almost certain bankruptcy. Cash flow was reduced to nothing. Strikes were threatened, initiated, then quickly and miraculously resolved by Lisa Eiseman personally. Details not available. Shortly thereafter financing was received from an unknown source for interactive POW! project. Discovery perfected and patented. With buy-out of Wally Toys, TLP Industries has emerged as the most successful toy manufacturer in the country.

Kimberlain struggled to read on, but once again he found his thoughts wandering.

Something had changed during his final year with The Caretakers. It had happened gradually, and slowly became something much more complex than burnout. It started, he guessed, with his discovery of the existence of a network of assassins called the Hashi. Despite the evidence Kimberlain brought to him, Zeus refused to sanction their pursuit, and that refusal had started Kimberlain thinking. What came into his mind wasn't pleasant.

He had survived and excelled as the Ferryman because he was able to tap into the same raw reserves called upon that night against the bikers in Barstow. He was the master of his emotions, and he used them as he did any other weapons. Pursuit of the Hashi seemed an extension of his role. When Zeus failed to see it that way, Kimberlain realized the truth: he was a hired killer and nothing more. His performance was unaffected, but inside he began to seethe.

His final assignment ended in the confirmation of all his fears. After a successful mission in the jungles of Central America he was abandoned: Zeus opted not to send in a retrieval team, leaving him stranded, and he emerged from the jungle three weeks later more animal than man. His three-year term was up, but the Ferryman wasn't finished. His own abandonment led to further realization of the folly of his pursuits. To destroy evil he had become evil. Moreover, it was clear that Zeus was escalating his projects and his power. The Caretakers had become dangerous. By alerting the proper authorities, Kimberlain forced the issue. Having their existence revealed in the wrong Washington quarters was more than The Caretakers could take. They were dissolved as quietly as they had been formed. Zeus was plugged into an innocuous security position so the government could keep him under its thumb.

As for Kimberlain, Kamanski's assurances that he would never have to worry financially turned out to be true enough, but that was the only area in which he felt secure. He found himself tense and uncomfortable in the presence of others. His paranoia drove him to the woods, where he built cabins to pass the time. With a pair constructed, he started up his hobby of restoring old weapons. Perhaps he could restore the feeling of more civilized times by absorbing the energy of the noble warriors who had wielded them.

None of it worked. He couldn't sleep at night and spent long lonely hours seated in a totally dark room watching the same movies over and over again on television. He desperately missed the action of the field and the purpose it provided him. Despite its falseness, it had at least provided a center for his life, and without that center he felt useless. He needed to feel worthy again; he needed to matter.

The initial solution came to him quite by accident. A former Caretaker he had worked with had become a sheriff in Southern California. His Orange County district was being plagued by a series of stranglings, and he asked for the Ferryman's help. Kimberlain was reluctant at first, but taking up the chase enabled him to employ the skills he so sorely missed. Now *he* was in control. His work resulted in the strangler's capture, and his reward was a deeper understanding of himself. He was a hunter, and a hunter needed to hunt. He began working on his own, uninvited, to track down the most loathsome and offensive of criminals. By the time Kamanski came to him about Peet he had been successful in all but one of his pursuits—finding the man who was doubtless the most devastating killer of them all. A man named Dreighton Quail, known better as the Flying Dutchman.

Kimberlain had stalked the stalker of the nation's highways and gotten close—but never close enough. Quail, the giant with no face, was still out there. The fire that obliterated his face had started a rampage that ultimately claimed over a hundred lives.

And Peet too might still have been free if not for him. To track down these most monstrous of criminals he had to enter their thoughts, and even before Peet, the hate was telling on him. He had thought that tracking them down would somehow vindicate him for his actions as a Caretaker. Yet their victims were just as dead as his were. He lay in the hospital those long weeks after his encounter with Peet and considered the track his life was on, no longer satisfied with it. Everything was death; his entire existence was defined by it. Nothing had changed and nothing would until he found a way to breathe life back into himself. Through others who lacked a vent for their own hate.

And the paybacks began. Slowly at first, until word leaked out and he was flooded with more requests than he could fill. There was no way to reach him except a post office box. But word continued to spread. People with a need for his services always seemed able to find him, and he helped them because the process allowed him to help himself. How many lives had he taken or destroyed as a Caretaker? Kimberlain hadn't counted back then, just as now he didn't count the specific number of people helped by his paybacks. He knew there was a balance to be achieved, and he would feel it when it was reached. Until then, the paybacks would continue.

But for now there was Lisa Eiseman and a stubborn resolve to keep her alive. From the first of Peet's letters he had begun to feel there was something here that would lead him to the greatest payback of all.

Beyond the window, Atlanta's Hartsfield International Airport sharpened in view.

CHAPTER 10

"IF THERE'S NOTHING ELSE, I'LL SEE YOU ALL AT THE DEMonstration in one hour," Lisa Eiseman said to close the meeting. "Thank you very much, ladies and gentlemen."

The eleven department heads who reported to her waited for the chief executive of TLP Industries to rise before easing their chairs back. The gesture was born out of respect for a person they could call a friend as well as an employer. In fact, everyone from the workers at the company's Atlanta headquarters to the assemblers in four factories across the country to the drivers who trucked the finished products felt the same way. Lisa Eiseman had at one time or another shaken the hand of everyone who worked for her, and in that moment each had felt more than a simple grasp.

They felt that she cared. About them. And in return their loyalty to the woman who sat in the president's chair high within Peachtree Towers was fierce.

It was into that chair she now settled after moving through the connecting door from the conference room to her office. She was exhausted. Weekly staff meetings were a necessity, if for no other reason than to reassure her department heads that she continued to maintain a keen interest in the goings-on within their individual domains. But these days that chore did not come easily, with so many other concerns before her. She had never dreamed that success would bring the kind of complications she faced daily. Rising to the top had been great fun, a challenge at every step; but then the real work had begun. Finishing the day with a sense of accomplishment had always been something she treasured. Lately, though, she would leave the office too close to morning and bed down with the realization that far more had been put off than had been completed. The work just kept piling up, and her refusal to delegate authority allowed only the smallest dents to be made in the vast heap.

Her intercom buzzed.

"Yes, Amy?" Lisa said into the speaker built into the phone.

"Mr. Kimberlain called again while you were in the meeting," her secretary said.

"Did you give him my message?"

"Yes, and he said he was heading over here anyway."

"You mean he came down? To Atlanta?"

"He called from the airport."

"Damn. I want you to leave word with security that he is not to be allowed entry to the building," she said firmly. "Is that clear?"

"Absolutely. I'll call downstairs immediately."

Lisa leaned back again, upset she had been so terse with her secretary. Amy wasn't to blame for her problems, the most recent of which concerned the strange claims by this man Kimberlain, which angered more than frightened her. She had no time for fear.

She looked around the room. This same office had been her father's, and she had made no changes in it whatsoever since taking over the business. The oversized soft leather chair, which seemed ready to swallow her frame at any moment, the mahogany paneled walls with matching bookshelves and desk, the imported hardwood chairs and tables, even the paintings on the walls were all too masculine to suit her tastes. But they symbolized something she felt she needed to keep in touch with: her father's life, and the business he had built and then allowed to tumble.

Lisa recalled those early days following his death. He had left a mess behind, and the soundest advice the lawyers and bankers could give her was to sell off all assets, including the business, in order to settle the estate. Her two brothers were all for it, but Lisa would not hear of it. A strange addenda to her father's will stated that all decisions relating to the sale of the company required a unanimous vote by his children. Accordingly, since another stipulation named her chief executive officer, by casting her vote against selling she effectively gave the business to herself.

Lisa believed that that was what her father had wanted.

Her first move was to dissolve the board of directors when they refused to back her plans to rebuild TLP and make it solvent again. Dissolution proved costly, and almost fatal, for litigation froze Lisa's operating funds. Then the unions called a strike at all her factories and warehouses the day after the first paychecks weren't available. Lisa bypassed the union hierarchy totally and went straight to the workers her father had treated like family. She visited all four factories in a two-day whirlwind tour. She reminded the workers of the various innovative plans TLP had provided them, including low-interest loans for emergencies. She told them that this strike would destroy the business and their jobs. She pleaded for just a little time to get things settled. In return, she would institute a profit-sharing plan: the better TLP did, the better its employees would do. She was going to make the company the largest of its kind. She was onto something big, she told them, and it was her only lie.

After they returned to work, Lisa scrambled to put the pieces of the company back together. Every day was worse than the one before, turning up more and more debts that bled TLP's meager assets dry. Additionally, the dissolved board of directors had joined with Wally Toys in a hostile takeover effort that Lisa was powerless to prevent.

Unless she found that something big.

She turned her attention to the research and development files and discovered an intriguing report by a pair of recently hired young computer whizzes concerning high-tech toys of the future. They were called "interactive" and were capable of accepting commands from an outside source such as a television program. Her father had rejected the proposal because of its huge costs and controversially violent aspects. Lisa read the preliminary report and was fascinated. She had found what she needed.

The price for bringing the program from the research stages into the marketplace would be in the area of $50 million. Even by selling off all liquid assets and subsidiaries of the company, Lisa would barely be able to come up with a tenth of that, and in so doing would leave herself wide open for the Wally Toys takeover bid. She went to the bank her father had dealt with for years and a dozen more after it. The results were always the same: no one wanted to do business with her failing company.

But Lisa was determined to find the money. For a time her father had been part of a golf foursome that included an old Mafia don named Victor Torelli, head of perhaps the most powerful family in the South. As a child, she had often played with Torelli's son Dominick, and in later years she was continually turning away his overtures. His father had died several years back, and Dom was running the family now. She hadn't seen him in months, and she hesitated before calling him. But he was her last resort.

"I assume this isn't a social call," he said after pleasantries were exchanged and before lunch was served on the terrace outside his office.

"It isn't. Remember all those swimming lessons I gave you years ago? I think it's time I was compensated."

He laughed. "With interest, what's the tally?"

"Thirty-five million dollars."

He stroked his chin dramatically, showing no surprise. "I understand you were after fifty from the banks."

"I've scaled down my plans."

"Why? You don't want to enter a brave new market without going all out, do you?"

Her eyes brightened. "You mean you also know about—"

"Of course. Somebody's gotta look after you, right? I think the idea's brilliant. I'd like nothing better than to get in on the ground floor. But fifty million dollars . . ."

"In exchange for twenty-five percent of all company profits for the next fifteen years."

"I was thinking closer to fifty percent."

"Look, Dom, I could have come in here and said ten, you would have said fifty, and we would have settled on twenty-five. I'm just trying to spare you some time."

He laughed again. "Assuming I go along with this, you know where the money will be coming from. Are you sure it won't bother you?"

"I'm absolutely sure."

All that mattered to Lisa was saving her father's company. TLP gained a patent on the interactive toy, and the company's stock more than quadrupled in the next nine months. The profit-sharing plan was already making rich men and women out of many of the employees who had stuck it out, and Dom Torelli earned four times his initial investment. In another move, more Torelli money was used to finance the buy-out of Wally Toys. Lisa harbored no guilt over the fact that organized crime had played such an important role in TLP's survival and subsequent flourishing. She had tried to make things work through the system, but the system wanted no part of her. Her father had entrusted her with a duty, and that duty was all she was concerned with.

Lisa herself had not grown nearly as rich as many people believed over these last few years. The profit-sharing plan drained much of her cash flow, and payments to Torelli through what amounted to an elaborate laundering operation took much of the rest. She didn't care, because she knew her father would have been proud of her. It was strange how close they had been. Though he had a son on either side of her, he had nonetheless chosen Lisa to be the one he would cart to the office with him on school vacations. Most of this was due to the fact that when the boys did come, they chose to spend their time within the TLP display areas fiddling with the latest creations, while her greatest pleasure was sitting with her father in his big office. At important staff and board meetings he would sit her right by his side and give her a steno pad she could doodle on while pretending to make important notes.

"Better take that down," he would say to her occasionally, and that became a signal to the underlings gathered before him that a report had particularly pleased him.

When he died, it created a void in Lisa that she filled by hard work and intense dedication to the company he had founded. The world had to know that Burton Eiseman had been the best at what he did, even if it was left to his daughter to demonstrate that. And yet such a relentless pursuit had led to so many complications, the most recent of which was the bizarre claims made by this man Kimberlain.

Her intercom buzzed again.

"Yes, Amy?" she said into the speaker.

"Miss Eiseman, er, Mr. Kimberlain is here to see you."

"Just tell them downstairs not to let him up."

"That's just it. He's not downstairs. He's here. In the office."

"I thought I told you—"

"I did. I informed the guards to deny him entry, but he's standing right here . . . Wait a minute, he's gone. He was right here a second ago but now he's . . ."

It was then that Lisa felt the motion behind her, which was strange because she had no sense of someone having entered the room and her eyes for much of the time had been aimed straight through the open door.

"You must want to die awfully bad, Miss Eiseman," said the Ferryman.

"I've been fed better lines," she replied.

"Allow me to introduce myself."

"Don't bother. Your reputation precedes you."

"Excuse the intrusion, but I got the feeling I wouldn't have gotten in to see you otherwise."

"Orders were to deny you entry. Apparently they didn't do much to impede you."

"Not the orders, your security people. Terribly lax. Might as well fire them all if someone can get to you this easily."

"And that's what brought you here, isn't it? The fact that you believe my life will soon be threatened."

"The indications are there, Miss Eiseman."

A pair of green-clad security guards charged through her office door with guns drawn.

"It's all right," she told them. "Mr. Kimberlain will be leaving soon. I've granted him a few moments of my time first."

The security guards backed warily out. One of them closed the door behind him.

The Ferryman moved around to the front of the desk so the woman would be more comfortable. "I appreciate the few moments."

"What would have happened if I had ordered the guards to escort you out?"

"I suspect they would have been injured."

"And if I had ordered them to use their guns on you?"

"I suspect they would have been even more injured."

"You seem quite sure of yourself, Mr. Kimberlain, or would you prefer I call you Mr. Ferryman."

"I see you've done your homework."

"You weren't a difficult man to research." Her stare turned contemplative. "I suppose you would best be described as an avenger, wouldn't you say?"

"No, but go on."

"A Lone Ranger without the mask. The three years of your life for which there is no record, I assume you were working for the government in some capacity."

"Some."

"Your story becomes quite an interesting one not long after that gap. Rescuing kittens from trees, walking old ladies across the street—you are one for good deeds, aren't you?"

Kimberlain showed two fingers. "Scout's honor."

"You'd be more comfortable sitting."

"Wouldn't be able to move as fast."

"And you think you might have to."

"There's always that possibility."

Lisa paused. "I didn't see you come into the office."

"I kept myself where you weren't looking."

"Neat trick."

"I have my moments."

"This isn't one of them, Mr. Kimberlain. I have no need for your rather unique services. Nothing to avenge on my account." Then, softer, "I've handled that myself."

"Do I detect a note of disapproval in your voice?"

"Only for your presence here, not for your chosen profession."

"It's what I am, not what I do."

"Very profound, but I'm still not clear on what you're doing in my office."

Kimberlain looked at her closely. Her strength and vitality made her beauty even more radiant. She had clear brown eyes and auburn hair. She wore little makeup and was dressed in a fairly simple suit that cast her as anything but the Joan Collins type of female entrepreneur.

"All you have to be clear on is that your life may be in danger."

"But I didn't call on you. I mean, that's how it works, isn't it? Someone calls you as—how would you describe it?—a last resort? And never a penny earned for your efforts."

"I like helping out my friends."

"Like the woman whose husband was killed by the youth gang in Detroit? I understand the police couldn't find enough evidence for an arrest but that the gang mysteriously dropped out of sight two months later and hasn't been heard from since."

"She sends me Christmas cards."

"What about the owner of that housing project who was found suspended from the ceiling in one of his apartments with rats just out of reach of his honey-coated fingers and toes?"

"The same rats had already eaten a couple of kids."

"You're a busy man, Mr. Kimberlain. I'm surprised you could fit me into your schedule."

"It's off season."

"I don't need you."

"I think you do." The Ferryman sat down at last, and somehow it made him look more menacing to Lisa. He seemed too coiled to be able to keep from springing for very long. "There's a pattern to a series of killings that have been occurring all over the country. Heads of companies either directly or indirectly involved with the military are being systematically eliminated."

"Then you've come to the wrong place, Mr. Kimberlain. I have nothing to do with the military."

"But you've been approached with regard to the POW! toy line."

"By the government, *not* the military."

"They don't advertise themselves that way, Miss Eiseman, because it makes them seem too eager and presents too much of a security risk if they decide to go ahead with the purchase. The man who visited you is known as a procurement officer. He evaluates new discoveries that have potential military benefits, and if his evaluation is positive, his job is to obtain the discovery at the lowest possible price. Then he makes recommendations as to which military branch can best utilize it."

"And now the military is interested in *toy soldiers*?" Lisa said incredulously.

"It's the interactive principle that interests them, I'd guess. A kid turns on his television and, *zap!* the figures on his table or the floor start playing out the actions going on on the screen, thanks to signals decoded by chips in your toys."

She was nodding, as impressed with his research as he had been with hers. "The commands you're referring to are hidden as rasps, barely audible computerized noises on the sound track. The decoder box sends these sounds through the television to a computer console. The console translates the sounds and transmits them through a small attached antenna to the individual figures."

"Wires?"

"Not anymore."

"Then look at it from the standpoint of the procurement office. They look into the future and see us shipping a toy soldier to some Soviet spy. Then send the right signal and, *bam!* the toy shoots the poor dumb bastard."

"You're stretching things."

"I'm just getting started, Miss Eiseman. How about a division of life-size toy soldiers programmed like your plastic monstrosities on Saturday-morning television? Give them titanium shells and equip them with the latest weaponry and they could take over your average Third World country within days."

"Hardly cost effective."

"When it comes to new toys for the military to play with, other balance sheets come into play."

Lisa could feel herself weakening. Fear began to rise in her like a dull ache. She gazed across the desk and saw Kimberlain in a different light. He looked far less menacing, in spite of the piercing blue eyes which seemed able to delve deep inside her.

"Why me?" she wanted to know. "There must be others this procurement office deals with. Dozens, hundreds."

"Yes, but you fit the pattern of the more recent victims. Each one has been responsible for a more attractive discovery than the one previous. Yours has the greatest military potential so far, in my humble opinion."

"What would you suggest I do?"

"For starters, you stay alive."

"And that's your job?"

"Until I'm convinced you're safe it is."

She made herself look brave, though her father's desk and chair seemed bigger than ever. "I don't scare easily, Mr. Kimberlain."

"But you'll die just as easily as the other victims. Maybe more easily. Most of them had better security."

The phone buzzed, and Lisa lifted it this time, hand trembling slightly. "Yes, I know. . . . Tell them I'll be right down." She lowered the receiver and said to the Ferryman, "I'm late for a demonstration of our latest POW! line. Since that's what might be about to cost me my life, maybe you should see it in action."

CHAPTER 11

"**T**HE INTERACTIVE TOY MARKET REPRESENTS THE WAVE OF the future,"" Lisa Eiseman explained as they stepped into the private elevator that would take them down to TLP's research and development department. "Kids want more from their television programs and more from their toys. POW! brings the two of these together."

"Sort of takes the imagination out of playing, doesn't it?" Kimberlain said. "I mean, all the kids do is flip on the set, tune in the right channel, and their toys play all by themselves. Regular toy soldiers are more to my liking."

"I'm not surprised," she snapped, intent clear. "But your comment about imagination doesn't hold. Television has become such a crucial part of children's lives, it was only natural that eventually they would expect more from it. The next generation of POW! toys will allow children to control their army against one being controlled by a chip interpreting signals from the television."

Kimberlain shrugged, not convinced. "I've got a friend who designed a multidimensional television for me. He knows I love movies, and now when I watch them I'm right in the middle of the action."

"Same thing."

"Not really. I'm just a spectator, and I know it. No signals from the system telling my pots and pans to do swan dives into the kitchen sink."

She looked at him harshly as the elevator stopped at their floor. The doors slid open to reveal a long empty corridor. Forty yards ahead a steel fence ran from floor to ceiling.

"This floor isn't listed on the standard building elevators," Lisa explained. "You need a special coded pad like the one I inserted upstairs to gain access."

They stepped out and walked side by side down the corridor.

"It might seem overdone," Lisa continued. "But industrial espionage in the toy business is a way of life. If you can't do the research yourself, the maxim goes, steal someone else's. My father built this wing. I've updated it a bit to handle the POW! line."

They reached the steel gate and Lisa greeted the pair of guards on duty.

"Decent security against industrial espionage," Kimberlain told her. "But right now that's the least of your worries."

"So you say."

Once they'd been cleared for entry, a guard unlocked a gate carved out of the security fence and they went through and then straight down the hallway beyond. A left turn headed them toward another door guarded by a second pair of uniformed men. Kimberlain thought there were five at first until he realized that three of them were actually life-size models of futuristic soldiers from the Powerized Officers of War collection. All three had square wheelbases for legs and stood about six feet tall, not including the small antennae that sprouted from their heads.

"Each represents a different entry in our latest line," Lisa explained.

Kimberlain noted that each of the figures was different in structure and features except for the square wheelbase required for motion. The only one that looked even remotely humanoid stood closest to the door and was called Megalon. His upper torso was framed in steel and shaped into huge bands of muscle worthy of a Mr. Universe candidate. His head was an angular robot top that looked like a helmet, with a pair of red eyes beneath a flat forehead. His arms were encased in black; one of his hands was shaped in the form of pincers, the other as an adapter for a variety of weapons attachments. At the moment it held a spear capable of shooting outward and then retracting again.

No wonder the POW! soldiers had aroused so much controversy among parents groups.

Megalon's two companions were similarly impressive. One stood on the other side of the door in a perpetual hunched stance and featured a lizard-like head that extended straight from its torso. Its arms, black like Megalon's, ended in pincers. This one was called Armagill, and Kimberlain could almost imagine a skinny tongue swishing inside its mouth, which had a hole in its center.

The third life-size POW! was known as Neutron because of the laser beam it claimed as its major weapon. Standing almost directly across from Armagill, it was the shortest and least impressive of the figures but in many ways the most functional. It had no torso as the others did, just a huge head mounted atop the wheelbase. It had black, slanted eyes and a barrel where its nose and mouth should have been. Kimberlain noted that it was the only one that could rotate a full 360 degrees on its base, and he would have bet this was the one that most interested the procurement officer for its easy adaptation to weapons.

"These are fully functional models, scaled up to use on an upcoming holiday float," Lisa explained as one of the guards opened the electronic door for her.

"Might make a nice incentive contest prize," Kimberlain told her. " 'Hey, kids, send in the back of a POW! box and you might win a machine capable of ripping your parents' heads off. Enter as often as you like. Batteries not included.' "

He followed her through the door into a small circular auditorium. The seats ringed the room in escalating rows accessible by aisles set at regular intervals, all situated so as to provide a clear view of the staging area located to the right of the door. The seating construction left the front wall free, to allow for placement of a large screen.

Today's demonstration, though, was going to be live. Situated a bit off center toward the empty front wall was a fifteen-by-thirty-foot terrain setting placed atop a number of squeezed-together tables. The terrain was part jungle, part hills and mountains, and part desert. Various ten-inch-tall versions of the life-sized models Kimberlain had seen in the hallway were arrayed for battle, with a few behind positions of cover to add to the effect.

Kimberlain followed Lisa to their seats in the eighth row. A bearded man in a white lab coat waited until they sat down before stepping up to the podium located between the empty front wall and the display tables. The raised circular tiers around them, Jared noted, were sparsely occupied by not more than fifty people, who were clustered mostly in the first ten rows. A few of these had their notebooks open and ready.

"Thank you all for coming," the bearded man said without benefit of microphone. "What you are about to see is a demonstration of the next generation of POW! interactive toys, which is far advanced from the last and promises to propel us to even greater heights in our industry."

A soft murmuring passed through the crowd. Kimberlain noticed that the two guards were standing inside now on either side of the electronically sealed door. Their guns bothered him, and just to keep a closer eye on them, he slid from his chair and took up a vigil against the near wall.

"The various terrains you see depicted," the bearded man continued, "will all be available soon and sold separately from the POW! action figures." He tilted an open palm behind him in the direction of a television perched on a raised, movable stand. "As you will soon see, many of the battlefields depicted on the display boards are exact replicas of the battlefields in the POW! action programming. The child turns on his television, and the designated figures respond to signals carried over the air. The child, meanwhile, manipulates his figures with the joysticks and buttons on the console as shown in your brochure. The result is that he or she is able to play along as the action unfolds on the screen. Each battle is made different by the computer's interpretation of the figures' positions on the game board.

"Of course, the child does not have to wait for the program to air to use his figures." He held up a thin wafer cassette game cartridge. "He or she can purchase POW! program tapes separately and plug them into the game computer, which will allow the designated enemy figures to move about and interact with the ones controlled by the child. This is where our greatest strides have been made, for now no single tape will provide the same scenario twice unless the action figures are placed in identical relations to each other. Otherwise, the game board's built-in computer will program the changes as it receives commands from the cassette, with the figures' respective positions taken into consideration.

"Children will also be able to create their own programs for the toys and expand them as they grow older. The upshot, of course, is that they will be influenced to buy more and more game board pieces and POW! action figures to increase the scale and intensity of the interaction. I like to think of this like the old Lionel train sets which could be expanded yearly with tunnels, bridges, additional cars and track, until an entire room of the house would be taken up by the toy. In essence, expandable toys allow children to grow with them. They never become outdated. The child will continue adding to them, and all future systems will be designed to accommodate past, less elaborate figures to mix with the ones we will no doubt be creating in the near future."

He stepped away from the podium, now holding a television remote control device in his hand, and moved toward the huge game board. Many of those farthest away from the game board rose to get a better view.

"To illustrate our latest breakthroughs, my department is pleased to present a pair of demonstrations, starting with over-the-air transmission via the television signals received from our broadcast."

He switched on the television and the POW! logo filled the screen briefly. Then he slid his hands to the console attached beneath the game board.

On the television screen Megalon was faced with an ambush by troops of Armagills and Neutrons.

"Please notice," the bearded man went on as he deftly manipulated the joysticks and buttons controlling the Megalons, "that the action occurring on the game boards does not exactly mirror that happening on the monitor. Placement of the figures, as I said earlier, is the key."

He let the scene proceed for several minutes, long enough for an ample number of televised and live figures to perish, before switching the television off. The figures on the game board stopped instantly. He then popped the wafer cassette he'd been holding into a computer terminal hidden beneath the central game board.

"The cassette's signals will be interpreted by the computer solely on the placement of the figures," he explained, "thus taking the place of our over-the-air signals and allowing continued interaction." He pushed a button and returned his hands to the controls of his figures. Kimberlain watched the motorized figures rush about, seeming more alive than before, more animated, as if released to a will of their own. The Armagills and Neutrons controlled by the computer were again battling the lab man's Megalons. The Megalons fought bravely, thanks mostly to the superior position they had been provided with, but their numbers were falling so fast there was no hope for victory.

The figures darted about, actually utilizing available cover and appearing to set ambushes. They seemed to be thinking and plotting. The people in the audience were all standing now, clustered together as close to the action as possible, responding enthusiastically to especially colorful sequences of the battle.

"And remember," the lab man reminded them, "it's never the same twice. Let's look at another cassette."

His hand glided to the slot. He looked a bit puzzled and steadied himself to reach deeper, his head leaning slightly over the jungle part of the game board to better his angle. Kimberlain saw one of the Neutron figures roaring toward him but paid it little heed until the bearded man's face registered confusion.

"Hold on just a second. I'm having trouble ejecting the—"

The torsoless Neutron blasted away before the man could finish speaking. Along with the familiar sound effects, something seemed to shoot out from its barrel. The effect might have been comical if the bearded lab man hadn't staggered backwards with hands clutching for his face. They fell back down as he started to crumble to the floor and Kimberlain noted the small splotch of blood in the center of his forehead, a dart probably, and almost certain to be poisonous.

Kimberlain sprang into action instantly, rushing toward Lisa Eiseman and bashing into a number of chairs en route, as the POW! figures commenced their assault. The Neutrons seemed to be in charge, forming the first wave, with their center-placed guns rotating at anything that moved. The first barrage was fired toward the door to discourage a rush for it, while a wave of ten-inch-tall Megalons dropped to the floor and began cutting a straight line forward to cut off access to it, firing at any motion before them. Kimberlain already knew the darts were small enough for each of the sabotaged figures to have a complement of at least six to eight.

He had reached Lisa Eiseman by then and was shoving her beneath him as one of the two armed guards dove low across the floor, going for the console in which the tape controlling this assault was in place. The computer was still in command; the murderous figures were incapable of independent thought. The guard reached the console and was going for the eject button when a pair of Armagills fired at him through the spouts where their mouths should have been. The guard raised his hands to his pierced face, screaming, and tumbled back dead before the armed toy army reached him.

The second guard had drawn his gun and was fighting to steady it with both hands while the only occupants of the room with the composure to move joined ranks behind him, with the deadly toys blocking their route to the room's only exit. A Neutron rotated on its base toward the guard as he got off a shot that flew wildly astray and struck a sales rep seeking cover against the far wall. The guard tried three more shots, none of which came even close, and by the time he was trying for a fifth another Neutron had locked on to him and fired its dart home.

By then Kimberlain had raised himself into a crouch, with Lisa Eiseman supported behind him. He palmed his fifteen-shot, nine-millimeter Beretta and noted that the POW! figures had managed to cut off all other possible routes to the single door. He and Lisa were alone in this section of the ringed platform as around them TLP employees continued to scatter for cover and safety. Kimberlain listened for the mechanical grinding of the figures' wheels against tile. They drove in directly from the front for the kill, using built-in levelers to negotiate the steps. But toy after toy was blown into bits of shattered plastic and stubbornly spinning rubber as Kimberlain responded to the grindings by whirling and blasting away.

Somehow they had managed to lock on to Lisa specifically and were circling around to attack from the rear as well as the front. A Megalon figure led the charge from behind, and the Ferryman's bullet tore its entire torso and head clean off. A pair of Armagills roared at him from the front, close to each other but just far enough apart to require two separate bullets.

They're sacrificing themselves, damn it! They're trying to wear me down!

Kimberlain tucked Lisa beneath him. He couldn't believe what he was seeing. Virtually all the figures from the game board had tumbled down now and were in the midst of a superbly orchestrated all-out assault. They had been programmed by someone who knew the layout of the room perfectly and had anticipated exactly what the reactions of the people would be.

That someone could not have anticipated Kimberlain's presence, of course, but he was running out of bullets and carried no spare clip.

The Ferryman watched as another of TLP's employees scattered the mechanical monsters with a chair and rushed down a cleared path toward the door. The Powerized Officers of War he had managed to upend lifted themselves back to their bases just as the man was reaching for the button that would have slid the door open. A dozen darts pierced him from behind all at once. His spine arched. A single spasm followed as he died.

The rest of the windowless auditorium was filled with whimpers and screams. The POW! figures continued to stalk all those who had moved to take cover. The braver men and women were fighting as best as they could, tossing whatever they could find at the attacking figures. But the toys rallied, forming into another wave that rolled up the aisles toward the barricades erected by their targets.

But their primary target remained Lisa. Kimberlain spun around just as four of the POW! soldiers neared killing range for their darts. A pair of bullets felled the four, leaving him with just three in his clip. The mechanical whirl of the many miniature tires propelling the attacking forces told him he was going to come up woefully short. Beneath him, Lisa, her eyes filled with terror, seemed to be searching for a weapon of her own.

As more of the creatures circled, the Ferryman turned his attention to how they could be focusing so much on Lisa. How could they know she was their primary target? It had to be more than position; it had to be!

Kimberlain shattered two more with one bullet and used another to fell a single attacker. With just one shot left he wondered if the damn little monsters were keeping count. His eyes fell to Lisa's neck and noted the locket dangling from a silver chain. In the instant of realization that followed his hand swiped forward to tear it free.

"What are—"

Kimberlain wasn't finished. Her watch was next and then her jewelry. He would never know for sure which held the transmitter the deadly toys had been programmed to home in on, nor did he care. All he knew was that the wave of attacking figures began

spinning crazily, suddenly unsure of their motion and firing at random toward anything in motion, including their counterparts around
the room.

They're like a goddamn army!

A TLP employee who had made his defense from the center of
the rows had managed to set fire to a sheath of notebook pages tied
tightly to a stripped-off belt and was rushing for the door swinging
the makeshift weapon madly at the POW! robots. He tripped at the
bottom of the steps and they swarmed over him, bases rolling over
the flames as if to extinguish them.

That sight gave Kimberlain an idea, and he was starting to search
the front wall when a pair of Megalons and a single Armagill leaned
their torsos over the level three above his. Kimberlain went for the
one in the center, angling his shot so at least one of the others
would be taken out in the explosion of debris. He squeezed the
trigger and the single Armagill blew apart.

Enough of its fragments found both Megalons to topple them
temporarily as well.

Kimberlain's next action was to yank Lisa down toward floor
level, in the direction of a trio of Neutrons on the first tier. The
Ferryman stripped off one of his shoes and hurled it at them. It hit
solidly enough to topple all three in a heap he and Lisa leaped over
before the trio could recover their balance. With his attention still
on the front wall, Kimberlain pulled Lisa down to the floor with
him and pushed her beneath the tables supporting the various terrains.

"Don't move," he ordered her. "Movement attracts them!"

The Ferryman pushed himself backwards and turned to see a
Neutron aiming its barrel at him. He swiped at it with his left hand
and the miniature monster went flying. Afraid to rise all the way to
his feet, Kimberlain crawled around the tables, recalling the position of the bearded lab man when he had reached under for the
control panel. His target for now was lodged on the front wall a
good ten yards and at least that many mechanical killers away. Their

range seemed most limited when firing upward, and he knew this weakness was what he had to exploit.

Wasting no further thought, he rose and leaped in the same motion. He threw his arms up and out so they grasped the ledge of the speaker's podium. His arms supplied sufficient thrust to pull him atop it, but his balance wavered, and a tumble now would assure his death. The wood trembled beneath him, and, as he felt the base listing, he gave another great leap upward and out.

He landed a foot from the far wall and reached up for the heavy-duty fire extinguisher as the nearest POW! figure turned toward him. By the time they were rolling his way, he had torn the ring free and was squeezing the trigger that sprayed clouds of white foam from its nozzle. He aimed it in a wide spray at any of the motorized killers he could find, starting with the closest. The extinguisher's range of spray was twenty feet, and he used all of that.

Then, continuing to squeeze the extinguisher's trigger, the Ferryman headed for the computer console. The POW! figures spun crazily, some ending up on their backs or sides in the spasms of mechanical death as the white foam clogged their works. The extinguisher had sissed empty just as Kimberlain located the eject button on the control panel. A press inward popped the tape out onto the floor, and those figures that were somehow still moving stopped abruptly. Kimberlain paused to take a deep breath and then hurried back to help Lisa out from her hiding place.

"It's over," he soothed, holding her arm tight. "It's over."

She was trembling badly, squeezing her eyes shut while she fought to make herself strong. He drew her close, putting an arm around her shoulder for support, and together they moved toward the sliding electronic door. The other surviving employees rose tentatively to follow, as if expecting another attack any second.

"Oh God," Lisa was muttering to no one in particular. "I'm sorry. It's my fault. This is all my fault!"

Still alert, Kimberlain moved his finger to the button that would at last open the door. A quick sprint down the L-shaped corridor from there and they would be at the steel security fence, with the nightmare behind them. As the door slid open, the Ferryman advanced ahead of Lisa. He turned into the corridor.

And the life-sized version of Megalon shot a metallic fist straight into his face.

CHAPTER 12

THE BLOW STUNNED HIM ALMOST SENSELESS. HE LOST HIS LEGS and felt himself fall backward and land on his buttocks. In the end it was the screaming that revived him. As he came to, he saw the six-foot-tall Powerized Officer of War reach out to grab a shrieking Lisa with its pincers.

The other TLP personnel were stumbling back into the hall of death they had so desperately sought to flee as Kimberlain struggled to his feet. He saw the razor-sharp blade snap out of the slot in Megalon's other metallic arm, and he threw himself into motion as its pincers continued to snap toward Lisa, who was pressed helplessly against the wall. The Ferryman crashed into the life-size figure with all the force he could muster. The collision sent a bolt of pain through his entire side, centering in his bad shoulder, the one Peet had nearly ruined three years before.

Megalon tilted backward on its base and rolled hard into the wall across the hallway.

Kimberlain staggered sideways, eyes on the spear that was an extension of the thing's left arm. Megalon's wheels touched tile again and it rotated its metallic head toward him.

A pair of workers started out the door again, their intent to risk a dash past the POW! robot.

"Get back in there!" Kimberlain screamed at them.

Megalon wheeled toward Lisa again, but its sightless red eyes stayed on the Ferryman. Lisa was sliding her way down the wall sideways, trying to keep herself between Kimberlain and Megalon as she negotiated the corridor. She reached the Armagill replica and started to slant around it when a cold metallic hand grasped her thigh and pulled down hard.

"No!" Lisa wailed, terrified.

The hand pulled down as it held her tight. Lisa flailed futilely, and the motion stripped her of her remaining balance. On the floor now, she tried to kick free.

Armagill's mouth parted to allow a spear to shoot out and lock. Mechanically, it bent over at the head and lowered the promised death toward its victim. Kimberlain saw what was happening and tried to lunge forward, but Megalon's pincers shot out toward him, working in tandem with its spear hand. Kimberlain sidestepped and maneuvered to grasp the pincers so he could remain out of range of the spear.

Lisa shrank lower to avoid Armagill's spear, which looked obscenely like a tongue. The creature kept poking at her, trying to lift her slightly with its arms, which were linked to its shoulders by rubberized tubing to promote flexibility. Once more Kimberlain tried to reach her, but Megalon's spear whipped forward again.

"Help her!" the Ferryman yelled to a trio of men emerging from the auditorium.

The men hesitated only slightly before bolting toward the creature holding Lisa with its back to them. Their path brought them by the Neutron replica standing on the other side of the hall. They never saw the gun barrel extended beneath its empty eyes begin to rotate and the bullets start to spew outward.

The screams were awful, and the rapid bursts continued well after they had stopped. Blood splattered against the wall; some reached Kimberlain and still more splashed against Lisa as she cowered in Armagill's death grip.

Neutron rotated his barrel toward the doorway the men had emerged from and fired a spray to discourage further attempts. Motion again, Kimberlain realized, it had to be. The specifics of the program eluded him, but it was obvious that each of the replicas' computer chip brains had been programmed to initiate a specific assault when a certain set of conditions was met. If he could make those conditions work for him, maybe, just maybe . . .

Lisa was losing the fight against Armagill. Its razor-sharp spear lowered toward her throat. An alarm bell had begun to screech. Obviously the gunfire had alerted security to the battle going on. But where were they? What was taking them so long to respond?

Kimberlain readied himself to move toward Lisa, avoiding consideration of the risks. He let go of Megalon's pincers and the figure whirled on its base and jabbed at him with its spear. The Ferryman spun sideways and the spear dug straight into the wall. As the creature yanked its weapon free, he ducked low under the motion. In that instant, Neutron's electric eye could not distinguish his motion from that of Megalon's when it started to roll on its base toward him. Neutron started firing again, with Megalon directly in the path of its bullets and Kimberlain hugging the floor beneath the line of fire. The bullets carved jagged lines into Megalon's head and torso, making it twist and turn crazily. It spun on its base and snapped its pincers together as if in desperation.

Armagill's programming must have lacked the capability to perform two operations at once, because it never wavered from its attention to Lisa while Kimberlain tore the fire ax down from the wall not far from it. His first strike obliterated the top of its head just as its spear was about to graze Lisa's flesh. His second blow shattered the creature's torso, wedging tight into rubber and plastic and metal.

"Stay down!" Kimberlain yelled to Lisa as Neutron whirled toward them, their motion having drawn its attention. "Stay still!"

He dove and rolled across the hall to draw the creature's attention from Lisa.

The bullets came mechanically, like the tracer fire in the deadly obstacle courses he had been trained in. It was a simple matter to stay ahead of until he ran out of room, moving down the corridor beyond the entrance to the auditorium to ensure that the bullets would hit only the walls. The other key for him was to time his circle rush past Neutron in a way that would close the gap faster than the creature was capable of adjusting its aim. He counted the seconds, basing his strategy on the fact that the first two bursts had both lasted just under five seconds—probably the limit for each clip stored somewhere in the creature's innards.

The bullets stopped as quickly as they had started. Neutron whirled its torso about, believing itself to be still firing. Kimberlain rushed by close enough to get a mouthful of bitter cordite and pulled Lisa to her feet. They had seconds more at best to flee down the corridor to the steel security fence. The piercing alarm continued to wail as they picked up speed, but still there was no sign of help from the guards. And when Kimberlain led Lisa around the corner of the hall he saw why.

The electronic gate had somehow been sealed, and security personnel were working frantically to get it open. Two men were slicing a hole in the steel links with bolt cutters, and as Kimberlain and Lisa started their charge down the remaining thirty yards a thin guard managed to slither through brandishing a shotgun. He was just getting to his feet when Kimberlain heard the now familiar grind behind him and shouted a warning to the guard. He took Lisa with him to the floor just as Neutron's wheelbase cleared the corner and it began firing.

The security guard had just steadied himself when the bullets tore into him and catapulted him backward into the fence. The motion of his fellows drew all of Neutron's fire, and it continued to spray bullets, killing or maiming a half-dozen men on the other side of the fence. Their screams rose above the wail of the alarm.

The vibrations turned the last of Neutron's fire toward the ceiling. Electric wires and conduits, coughing sparks and smoke, dropped down like tentacles and touched the steel links. The electronic gate sizzled.

The guard who'd made it through the hole in the fence had lost his shotgun when Neutron's burst cut into him, and it had slid across the floor. As Kimberlain maneuvered close to it, Neutron spun toward his motion. He was prone while he brought it up, looking into the dark face of his own death when he fired, pumped, and fired again. Neutron's head was mostly gone by the second shot, and the third obliterated the rest and took the gun barrel along with it. The giant toy was still struggling to rotate as it crashed to the floor.

Kimberlain discarded the shotgun and climbed back to his feet, then moved to help Lisa. She was shaking again, and he wrapped his arm tight around her shoulder for comfort. As they approached the gate, Kimberlain saw the dangling live wires that had electrified it and understood why the surviving guards were keeping their distance. It would probably be several minutes before all power in the building could be shut down to allow them to pass through safely.

"Somebody cut off that damn alarm!" the guard closest to them ordered. Neutron's bullets had reduced the sound to a dull clicking, but it kept up. In the next moment the guard's eyes filled with terror. "Oh my Jesus . . ."

Kimberlain swung to follow the man's stare. Megalon, torso punctured and splintered, was coming forward down the last stretch of the corridor. Its motions were jerky and spasmodic, and a grating sound indicated that one of its base wheels had seized tight. But its pincers were still operative, as was the spear extension which was swiping back and forth even now.

The Ferryman had no time to do anything but lunge in front of Lisa, who had drawn as close to the electrified fence as she dared. He locked one hand on the thing's pincers and the second on the metallic arm where the spear began its extension. Megalon spun to better its position, and they grappled like wrestlers feeling each other out at the start of a match.

From the corner of his eye, Kimberlain saw a guard steady a rifle and readied to duck.

"Now!" he screamed, and the man fired.

Most of Megalon's head exploded, but its appendages still gripped the Ferryman. As if clinging to its twisted life, the creature turned so that Kimberlain was between him and the guards. When the Ferryman had ducked, it had allowed the thing's pincers to close on his wrist, and now Megalon began to squeeze. What with the monster's superior position, it was all Kimberlain could do to hold the spear extension back with his single available hand.

"*Shoot! Shoot!*" he called to the guards, but no one trusted his aim enough to chance it.

His eyes recorded motion as Lisa threw herself at him, swinging the shotgun around, with the butt coming hard and fast. It connected squarely against what remained of Megalon's head. She drew it back for another strike.

Megalon turned sluggishly while maintaining its hold on Kimberlain. It lashed out at Lisa with its spear, and the Ferryman used that to his advantage by suddenly pulling free of the thing's pincers. Megalon lashed out at Lisa again but missed by even more. This time the motion placed too much pressure on its jammed wheel, and its balance wavered long enough for Kimberlain to grasp the pincers as they spasmodically snapped open and closed. What remained of Megalon's head turned back toward him, but it was too late. The Ferryman yanked the pincers over him and up toward the fence as he pulled and shoved the thing forward. Steel met steel, and smoke and sparks began pouring from the many punctures in Megalon's body as Kimberlain rolled free.

"Fry, you son of a bitch!" he called up to what remained of the life-size POW! robot.

* * *

Kimberlain reached David Kamanski minutes after the guards had finally managed to cut the power and work the gate open. Dried blood and sweat covered his clothes and flesh.

"Jared, where the hell have you been? I've been trying to reach you for—"

"I've been busy, David. Lots of people are dead down here. It's right up your alley."

"Is Lisa Eiseman one—"

"No, she's alive, but not by much. The weapon was murderous toy soldiers this time. Our boy just keeps getting better. This was beyond even Lime's murder, way beyond."

Kamanski sighed. "Exactly why I've been trying to reach you. Your friend Captain Seven claims our mystery up here's been solved."

CHAPTER 13

IT WAS THURSDAY AFTERNOON, AND DANIELLE SAT WAITING. Waiting was nothing new to her; she had spent much of her life doing just that and had somehow never grown used to it.

Before leaving Washington the day before, she had used a false identity card to gain access to the computer terminals at the National Registry. As a key national processing center, it contained virtually all pertinent information relating to every sphere of governmental budget, but it was available only to those with the proper access codes. She had managed quite easily to patch into Def-Net, the Defense Department's data base, and request a call-up on Spiderweb. A few seconds of nothing followed, then:

ACCESS DENIED. MESSAGE TERMINATED.

Danielle tried a different access code and waited.

ACCESS DENIED. MESSAGE TERMINATED.

She wasn't surprised. Spiderweb must lie under an ULTSEC seal that would deny access to the file to anyone not specifically cleared to see it. This closed the front door for her but left the slightest of cracks in the back one. She typed in an emergency outreach code designed to bring up a list of those who were cleared to view the Spiderweb file. Her plan was to obtain the information she sought from a man now instead of a machine, providing that all those listed weren't too high up in the government and thus too risky to approach.

At last the screen began displaying names, one per line. The first four were totally expected and not accessible. The fifth was . . .

JAMES ROBERT STANTON STONE.

What in hell was *he* doing on this list?

She checked her watch. She'd been on line too long already. If her invasion had been noted, Defense Department authorities might already be on their way. She rose cautiously and moved to the elevator. Back outside in the cool fall sun, she turned her thoughts to the fifth name. James Robert Stanton Stone was one of the richest men in the world, thanks mostly to oil. Somehow he was connected to Spiderweb, which was connected to the stolen plans for a Jupiter-class super-Trident submarine. Her next move was clear: she had to learn what she needed to from Stone.

Toward that end, she now found herself waiting in a Fort Worth, Texas, parking garage for his expected arrival. Seconds, minutes, hours; as always they had already become indistinguishable from one another. Patience was the key. But patience allowed time to think, and thinking meant remembering, which was where the real pain lay.

She had been fifteen when the games in the wooded compound the men had brought her to began to grow more complex. The number of children remaining had shrunk drastically, to barely more than a dozen. Danielle had a room to herself now. She was comfortable being a loner and preferred her own company to that of others. She had started to notice the lingering stares the boys in the compound were giving her, especially an inseparable pair she knew as Jack and Jules and whom she did her best to avoid.

One night she was sent into the woods on what the instructors told her was the first step of survival training. She went in with no weapons and skimpy clothes which exposed her to the elements. She was to see how well she could transfer practiced skills into a real arena. Danielle accepted the task with the same commitment with which she approached everything else.

Dawn was streaking the sky when she heard a rustling on the path behind her. Sleep had refused to come all night, and, ravenous, she was on her way to the stream to catch a fish for breakfast. Now all her hunger pangs vanished. She was being stalked, and she knew it. First she had to get off the path and find cover. Then she would need a weapon.

She had started off the path when her foot lodged in a soft patch in the ground. She realized what was happening but leaped too late. The noose tightened around her ankle, she was hoisted feet-first into the air, and she dangled there above the ground. She fought to kick free and her head slammed into the huge tree supporting her. Dazed now, she felt the warm spill of blood on her scalp and swiped at the wound. Her fingers came away sticky with blood. She struggled to steady herself. Then her ears caught the rustling sounds more clearly, and from her upside-down position she recognized Jules and Jack proudly prancing toward her down the path.

So it was a game and they had won. Fine.

"Cut me down, you bastards!" she yelled, still swaying.

"Gag her," Jack, the taller boy, ordered.

"You gag her," returned Jules obstinately. He was almost feminine-looking, with long hair that hung down past his shoulders.

Jack cast a mean stare Jules's way but yanked a filthy bandanna from his pocket and started forward. When he was almost upon her, Danielle altered her swinging to be able to flail at him with her arms. Several of the blows connected. Jack backed off. Jules giggled sheepishly.

"She's just a girl," he chided.

"She's good. I've seen her. Grab hold of her arms."

This Jules did after a brief struggle, binding her hands while Jack strapped the soiled bandanna around her mouth. Next they lowered her to the ground hard. They left her legs in the noose but cut away the extra rope. Jack turned her on her back and smacked her hard in the jaw with the back of his hand, making sure his knuckles ground home. Danielle felt blood swirling about in her mouth. She thrashed frantically to free herself.

"Hold her legs while I get these off," Jack instructed.

Jules fastened his hands on her legs as Jack yanked her thin shorts down past her hips. She wasn't wearing any undergarments because she hadn't been issued any. Jack smacked her three more times hard, and she wavered toward unconsciousness.

"Let's stand her up."

Danielle was conscious enough to realize what was going to happen and be terrified by it. Once again she was a helpless child about to be violated. She screamed silently inside her gag and nearly swallowed it. She imagined that death would be better than what was coming. She remembered years before trying to hold her breath when the foul-smelling man had mounted her and made her bleed.

But why were these boys doing this? It had to be a game, another exercise. She was being tested. In a few seconds the boys' victory would be obvious and it would be done. Unless they were acting on their own, or, worse, had interpreted their instructions to mean precisely this.

"I want front," Jack was saying, and Danielle felt Jules stiffen while holding her upright from the side.

They shoved her back against the tree long enough to pull down their pants. Then they jammed her forward again until she was standing between them with their hands laced over her shoulders. Soft, level brush lay beneath her feet. The fear made her heart lunge within her chest.

Stop! Stop! she pleaded, but grunts were all that emerged through her gagged mouth.

Jack penetrated her from the front first, hot and pulsing, motions as rapid as they were uncertain. It wasn't as painful as it had been with the man in the camp, but it was just as revolting, and Danielle threw all her efforts into the rope binding her from the rear. The training had taught her how to slither through even the best of knots. She had to be patient and keep her motions slow. Focus on the hands, see the fingers sliding against the rope now, the knot weakening, weakening. . . .

She lost her concentration when Jules finally pushed himself inside her from behind. The agony rocked her. She cried out, forgetting the gag, and bit into her tongue. The motions of the two boys were erratic. She could hear them panting—Jack in front, Jules behind. Both having invaded her. Both inside her now. Both causing her pain.

Make it stop!

But she was the only one who could heed her plea. She focused even more on the hands that were gradually working the knot loose, as a hate surged through her that took her far away from this place, to where she felt nothing at all except the certainty of what she had to do.

Almost free . . .

Jules was panting horribly now, arms laced high on her shoulders just above Jack's, where they linked behind her. She felt one of her hands ready to come free, and her eyes locked on the knife still sheathed on Jack's belt. There was no question of what she was going to do. The rage within her was contained, controlled now, held like an attack dog under leash until just the right instant.

Jack was moaning now, lost in his passion. She feared him more, which made the time right. She tore her left hand from behind her and whipped it around her body low toward Jack's belt, which was on his pants around his ankles, stooping slightly to ease the motion. Both boys sensed what was happening, must have realized what she was trying for, but by then the knife was in her hand and it was too late. Jack had pulled himself out of her, and he had reeled back when it slid into his stomach all the way to the hilt. His eyes bulged and he gasped, mouth dropped open for a scream that never emerged.

Danielle had the knife out and was swinging it around in the same motion. Jules had actually withdrawn from her first, which meant he had had more time to locate a weapon. Sure enough his knife was sweeping upward as he backpedaled, stumbling on the pants that had fallen past his knees. Danielle realized that she didn't have to kill him, but by then her motion was already committed. Her blade sliced across Jules's throat, and his blood jetted out on her as he spasmed over, writhing and twitching.

She collapsed not long after he did, sank to her knees and watched death come to him. She wanted to be sick but couldn't. She wanted to feel guilty but couldn't. She felt nothing—neither remorse nor satisfaction, but just an acceptance of the task and the necessity of it. She did not realize then that the boys had merely been acting on precise orders, that the men in the compound had orchestrated the entire incident to truly test her. Nor was it clear to her then that they had saved her in order to create her in the image they desired. They had known all along the proper buttons to press to release the hate she would need, and now they had proven to her what she was capable of.

After that night her training intensified on an individual level. She trained with virtually every weapon imaginable, became familiar with any and all firearms on the market. Document forging was studied and later the ways to manipulate computers, to make them allies when needed.

Not much later she was sent on her first mission, and before she had taken part in many more they became as much a blur as her past. One followed another. Sometimes she was around to witness the results of her handiwork, sometimes not. On a few occasions she wasn't certain of success until a radio or television bulletin or a headline in a newspaper alerted her. Just as she had seen no beginning, she could see no end. There was simply the perpetuation of what she was, what they had made her.

They had saved her in the camp only to kill her a thousand different ways. Fate, though, in recent months had granted her the purpose she needed to overcome the indifference hammered into her during the training. Now she had a reason for what she did.

Through the limousine's darkened window she saw the garage's elevator doors slide open and James Robert Stanton Stone emerge.

* * *

Jim Bob, as he was known to anyone who knew him and plenty who didn't, had been born rich and made himself a whole lot richer, but never at the expense of restricting his own life or damaging the lives of others. Over a period when most others in the oil business were losing their shirts, Jim Bob was sewing more of his own. Buying up others' discarded wells for what he knew was the inevitable price rise drove his stock through the roof when it came. He was richer than he cared to be and made up for it somewhat by holding his prices down so the poor guy would get more for his ten bucks' worth at the pump. As for himself, Jim Bob always had his chauffeur pull up to the self-service aisles. He liked the smell of gasoline on his hands. Made him feel like he was worth more than money.

The meeting in Fort Worth over new drilling rights had gone on longer and accomplished less than it should have thanks to men who could barely take a breath without authorization in triplicate when a handshake was plenty enough for Jim Bob. A pair of security guards escorted him down in the garage elevator and started back up only when he got the rear door of his stretch open. Jim Bob had thoughts of propping his feet up on one of the extra seats and pouring himself a Jack Daniel's.

Jim Bob was halfway in when he noticed the woman.

"On the rocks with a twist, isn't it?" she asked him.

Jim Bob saw the glass in one hand and the gun in the other. "Got that right," he told her, freezing in place. "Suppose you want me to get in and close the door."

"Please," Danielle said.

Jim Bob did so, eyeing the darkened partition behind the front seat. "My driver, ma'am, is he . . ."

"Fine. Just incapacitated. In the trunk. I made sure he could breathe easily."

"Right nice of ya."

Danielle tapped the glass divider. Her driver started the big car and eased it toward the garage exit.

"Kidnappin', I suppose," Jim Bob said surely, sipping his liquor.

"Not at all."

"Well, it ain't no social visit."

"There are questions I need answered, Mr. Stone."

"Call me Jim Bob. All my friends and kidnappers do. What are you, some kinda reporter desperate for a story? Hell, you coulda made an appointment, you know."

"It isn't like that."

"Why don't you tell me what it *is* like, ma'am?"

"I'm not a reporter."

"But you still got questions. So ask away. Just get me to the airport in time to make it home to catch my son's football game."

"Division championship," Danielle noted.

"For someone who ain't a reporter, you've done some pretty deep research."

The limo was cruising the city streets now, moving toward the Airport Freeway. Danielle's free hand crept into her pocket and came out with a syringe.

"Ma'am, I'm not much for needles. 'Sides, I can't answer your questions asleep."

"It's sodium amytal," she explained. "Truth serum."

"Hell, I don't need that shit to tell the truth. Just ask away. Cross my heart and all that stuff."

Danielle shook her head. "It's for your own good. You won't remember any of the questions or answers this way."

Jim Bob Stone started to roll up his sleeve. Turning away from her, he squeezed his eyes closed, muttering, "Damn, damn, damn . . ."

An instant after she injected him, he went limp. A minute later she turned his head toward her. His eyes opened, glassy and barren.

"What's your name?" she asked him.

"James Robert Stanton Stone. Friends call me Jim Bob."

"Mr. Stone—"

"Jim Bob."

"Jim Bob, what is Spiderweb?"

His voice emerged in a slow drawl, like a tape recording being run on low batteries. "Operation undertaken to assure future oil reserves when everything else is gone."

"What kind of operation?"

"Mining the largest oil reserves left on earth. Much as all them Arab countries combined."

"Where?"

"Antarctica."

Danielle leaned closer to him. "What is the significance of the word 'Spiderweb'?"

Jim Bob Stone started to speak again, with his eyes fixed blankly ahead. "Finding the oil and bringing it up ain't the problem. Problem was what to do with it thousands of miles from anywhere. Solution was to build a pipeline linking all the wells together at a central pumping station. Called Spiderweb 'cause of the way the lines run through the landscape."

"When will the pumping start?"

"It already has. Been goin' on for years now. We're stockpilin' oil in underground containers to ease the import pressure. More crude than we know what to do with."

Danielle stopped to collect her thoughts. This entire operation had been carried out in total secrecy, unknown to the press or the public. It wasn't hard to believe. After all, the Antarctic continent was in many respects the last wilderness on the face of the world. Engineering crews would be able to work unbothered and in secret. But what could that have to do with the stolen plans for a Jupiter-class super-Trident? There was only one possible link.

"Why is Spiderweb on Defense Department data tapes?" she resumed.

" 'Cause oil is the best defense of all against future economic dependency on less than friendly nations. Spiderweb's like a giant life preserver ready to be tossed out to the country in case we start sinkin'."

The enemy possessed not only the plans for a super-Trident submarine, but also the schema for this Spiderweb installation Stone was describing. Obviously they were connected. But how?

"Tell me about the central pumping station you referred to. What's it called? Where is it?"

"Outpost 10," Jim Bob answered emotionlessly. "Located beyond the Ross Ice Shelf and Transantarctic Mountains, sixty miles due northwest of the Shackleton Icefalls. Almost exact center of the South Pole."

"How was such a massive operation hidden from the public and press?"

"Army Corps of Engineers used for almost all the work, and all coordinating left to small panel of businessmen composed of me, Benbasset . . ."

Danielle could tell the sodium amytal was wearing off, and she didn't dare risk another injection. "You said almost. Other parties must have been involved as well. Who?"

"Problem was ice: drilling through ice and frozen tundra to lay the pipeline. Kept us stuck for months until we got hold of Cyberdine Systems, 'cause of a new process they'd invented. Incredible. Gained us back the time we lost."

Stone's head slumped to his chest. Danielle lifted it back up and pinched him at the chin to force him alert.

"Who was your contact at Cyberdine?" she demanded. "Who did you work with?"

"Mendelson," Jim Bob said with the last of his voice. "Dr. Alan Mendelson."

Then he faded off and started snoring.

THE FOURTH TRUMPET

THE FLYING DUTCHMAN

Thursday, November 19; 10:00 P.M.

CHAPTER 14

THE BED WAS SURROUNDED BY A BLACK PLASTEEL CURTAIN THAT swallowed even the shadows. It ran the full length from floor to ceiling, creating a void that was penetrated only by the dozens of cords and wires that ran beneath it.

Beep . . . beep . . . beep . . .

The regular sound of medical machines and monitors was maddening until the ear grew accustomed to it, though it was impossible to get used to the breathing. A gurgling rasp was more the sound of it, an asthmatic in the midst of an attack no inhaler could ease, the noises amplified by the various life support machines that permitted any breath at all.

Quintanna had never been inside those curtains, not once. Yet his dark features and equally dark clothing suited the surroundings perfectly. He was a tall man, his gaunt frame layered with long bands of sinewy muscle. He approached the black curtains cautiously, aware that his progress was being followed the whole way from the elevator by the video camera mounted atop the curtain that broadcast its picture onto a monitor inside for the man, or what was left of the man, to see. Quintanna stopped at his usual spot and waited with feigned reverence for the voice to address him. He was adept at playing up to those who could help him, and the man within the curtain was helping him achieve the goal of a lifetime's work. It was a noble goal, even a *holy* goal, one his brethren from years past would have been wiser to pursue. At that time they had served as instruments of power instead of pursuing that power for themselves. But fortune had not dealt as kindly with them as it had with him. Fortune had brought him to the man behind the curtain who possessed the vast resources he needed for achieving his goal.

Quintanna stood there and waited. When the voice came, it knifed through him as always—not a voice so much as syllables squeezed together on borrowed breaths, as if the speaker could not separate the independent actions and had to combine them instead. There was never any cadence of tone to the words, no rhythmic balance or intonation. It was all mutters and half-formed utterances, the shadow of words but not the form. It emerged through a small speaker as black as the curtain it hung from.

"Mr. Quintanna," the box said, "you have more to tell me?"

"We have received additional information concerning our failure in Atlanta," Quintanna replied in a voice formed of so many accents that its origin was unidentifiable.

"Why refer to it as 'our' failure when you mean yours?"

"Whatever you wish."

"What I wish is that your people simply fulfill their side of the bargain. You and your group were retained to avoid such complications."

"It is merely one woman."

"Not just a woman!" The voice came out as a whispery shout. "A cog, a vital cog in a machine that must be rendered impotent before the rest of my operation can begin. You are failing to live up to your part of the bargain. Perhaps I should consider failing to live up to part of mine."

"The woman will be eliminated. The situation is under control."

"Really? Then what is this additional information you came up here to pass on?"

"The Eiseman woman's life was saved by a man who has apparently discovered our pattern."

"This man, who is he?"

"His name is Jared Kimberlain."

More awful breathing. "You mentioned his name earlier, Mr. Quintanna. Now I wish to know *who* he is."

"Many things, all of them dangerous." And Quintanna proceeded to provide a capsule summary of Kimberlain's rather extensive file. When he was finished, the breathing filled his ears for long seconds before the voice emerged from it.

"Spoken from memory, Quintanna. Apparently you know much about this . . . Ferryman."

"He came close to us during his tour with The Caretakers."

"And yet you didn't kill him. Why? Were you frightened? *Are* you frightened of him?"

"It is often better to avoid a problem than to confront it. Kimberlain is a powerful adversary and one it is advisable not to cross."

The breathing filled the air beyond the black curtains.

Beep . . . beep . . . beep . . .

"Mr. Quintanna, I do not approve of you or what you stand for. You were chosen to fulfill a purpose for me, and I realize I fulfill a purpose for you as well. Fine. We serve each other, and when my work is done, I care not in the least what you make of the remains. But I will have my work done as I wish it until the time that final moment comes. We cannot permit this Ferryman to become a hindrance to us. I must see my operation finish as I have planned it. I must see the dawning of tomorrow."

"Kimberlain has only pieces, fragments, nothing to alert him to the true shape of our plan."

" 'Our' again, Mr. Quintanna?"

"Figure of speech."

"You will kill the Ferryman. Do it any way you choose, but I want him killed. Is that clear?"

"Yes."

"The woman too, only sooner. Immediately." Quintanna could

feel the man watching him on the monitor. "You're hedging, Mr. Quintanna."

"We know where she is, but she is extremely well protected. It can be done, but it will take time. A day at least."

"Then get started, and see that she is disposed of."

"Using our resources for such a risky venture seems senseless at this stage of the operation."

The sounds of the monitor quickened. The breaths emerged thicker and wetter until the voice resumed.

"It is my lot to make sense of this, Mr. Quintanna, not yours. You still do not understand. You still do not see that the individuals must be made to pay separately. These tycoons of technology were responsible in themselves for this world of terror and death and must accordingly be torn from the planet like so many trees that no longer fit in the landscape—the landscape I am crafting and you will inherit when my work is done. The woman must be made to pay as the others already have been. You will see to it, Quintanna. Whatever it takes to reach her, to kill her."

"Yes," Quintanna acknowledged, burying his reluctance in the thought that it wasn't a "what" that was called for, but a "who."

The old Chevy rattled down Alabama's Route 59 in the general direction of Birmingham, though it would turn off well before nearing that city. Night had come hours before, and the lights of cars streaming in the opposite direction were the only things that told Dreighton Quail anyone else was alive.

The night was his time. It belonged to him.

He slept the days away, and he liked the winter best because then they were the shortest. He pulled off the road and slept in whatever old car he was driving at the time. He was always able to find a spot no one could see while driving past. Old, lonely roads were best, because then if he was seen it would be by a single driver in a totally secluded setting. If the person chose not to approach, that was fine. If he chose to approach, that was fine too.

He'd been branded with many labels over the years of his travels:

the Freeway Killer, Dormitory Slasher, Vampire, Gemini, and others. In at least three of the cases other men had been caught and convicted of serial murders a majority of which had been committed by him. Quail's secret was to sniff out a serial killer in the papers and follow the other's pattern for a time. Worked like a charm. He could kill all he wanted, safe in the knowledge that someone else would be caught and blamed.

Quail was without peer, unless of course you counted Winston Peet. Quail had almost cried with joy the day Peet had been caught, because it left him alone to cruise the dark underbelly of America with killing on his mind. He feared no man except maybe Kimberlain, and Kimberlain was out of his life now, just a shadow from the past like so many signposts on the many roads he had traveled once and would never travel again.

But the past had many shadows, slippery and dim and clinging to the dusty corners of his mind. He had been beaten as a child in Pennsylvania, beaten bloody by both parents, who felt they were exercising the will of God. He was reduced to a cowering shape that slept under the bed instead of on it. But when he was taken from his parents by the welfare people and adopted by another couple, in another part of the state, what had started out bad got plenty worse.

A few months past his twelfth birthday, they'd caught him fondling himself. The Devil's work it was. *Jesus God, save our boy, save him; show us the way, O Lord, show us the way . . .* It was the hands that had touched and stroked, and thus the hands would have to pay.

Oh yes.

So they dragged him kicking and screaming to the wood stove, with the full intention of forcing those cursed hands into the raging flames. Quail kicked and fought, and, with the hearth doors open, one of his kicks struck a gasoline keg his father used to quicken the fire. It splashed up at him just as the flames reached out. Yes, these shadows still brought back the pain, so awful and unrelenting, along with the screams that followed him to the hospital and beyond.

He had been burned over ninety percent of his upper body, all his hair gone, an ear, his lips, part of his nose. And his face, oh, his face! It simply wasn't there. Skin grafts did little; the pain was hardly worth it. He didn't die, and for a long time Quail didn't understand why that was so.

Months passed and the couple that called themselves his parents took him home. The beatings were replaced by their total avoidance of him. They moved him into the basement behind a locked door, and that became his world. He grew to hate the light and love the dark, because the dark spared him his own reflection. Quail lost track of time, of the months and years passing. But the pain was always there. He grew bigger than the damp bed they gave him and had to curl his knees tighter and tighter to squeeze under the blankets on frigid nights. If he listened hard enough, he could hear them praying for help upstairs, for forgiveness, for salvation.

Quail hated them.

He knew even without the company of others that he was different. It was more than just the hideous features hidden behind the chalk-white masks the doctors had given him. There was wood for the stove in the basement, and Quail could crush fist-size fragments in his hands. There were layers of thick steel piping, and these he bent, then twisted, then ripped apart.

He wasn't sure why he ventured upstairs that one night in particular; he was sure only that there was something for him beyond this door and the next, something that remained unfinished. The locked cellar door was a simple matter to negotiate: barely a nudge of his shoulder splintered it open. He slid through the house in utter silence, making sure all the doors and windows were locked and tied down. Then he soaked the floors with gasoline from the same keg that had burned him, and tossed one match on the second floor and another on the first. Outside he stayed close enough to the flames to feel their heat in order to make sure he would hear the awful shrieks of the man and woman who had made him what he was.

And just what was that?

He was a traveler of the night who trembled with happiness to hear screams of pain. Not his pain: he had survived all that, he realized, because it was his lot to bring it to others, to grow stronger with each wailing gasp, each final breath of life. Quail barely noticed his huge size—then or now; he only realized there were plenty of doorways he had to duck to pass under and driver's seats it was impossible to be comfortable in.

He used that first car to start his cruise of the nation's freeways and back roads, driving by night and sleeping mostly by day, avoiding the sun as much as possible. The flaming corpses he left behind taught him that he had been nothing for so long that he had become nothing. He was starting from scratch, then, on his way to becoming something greater and better. It was killing that made him feel good for the first time, so killing must be the answer he sought, and Quail embraced it. At night, when the lonely and vulnerable were out, walking the highways and huddled in the dark crevices in search of a ride or a friend, Quail would appear. There was never a pattern to the killings besides those that others had begun. He had long lost track of how many had perished by his hand; he knew only that he grew stronger with each death. He couldn't visualize life without the killing. It *was* life.

There had been four sets of perfectly imitated random killings before the Ferryman caught on to his existence and took up the chase. Not only had Kimberlain caught on, but he had even traced Quail back to his Pennsylvania Dutch origins and had found out about the terrible fire that had started it all. And when "the Dutchman," as he came to be called, continued to elude capture in spite of the killings left in his wake, the word "Flying" was added to his title naming him after the mythical Dutch mariner doomed to sail the seas forever. The roads of America were Quail's seas and the idea that one man could be responsible for a nationwide reign of terror devoid of pattern or motive was bizarre enough to keep Kimberlain virtually alone in his pursuit. But the Ferryman drew closer and closer. Quail began seeing him in every hitchhiker, in every car he passed or that passed him.

Their confrontation seemed inevitable, and Quail thought it had come when the roadside diner he had entered just before a dawn many months ago was flooded with well-dressed men. He left a number of them broken and unconscious, but the rest overcame him and took him to another town and a motel room where a dark man waited in the shadows. The man told the others to leave the two of them alone. This impressed Quail even before the dark man lauded his skills, his brilliance, said they were things that deserved to be recognized, utilized, rewarded. The dark man said that Kimberlain could be thrown off the track and arrangements made to ease Quail's cross-country sojourns. Money when needed, refuge if required. There would be a number to call anytime he wanted to. In return there were jobs the dark man would want done for him, tasks deemed impossible by others who had considered them.

Quail didn't believe in the impossible. And the dark man was offering him a chance to prove he was far, far more than nothing.

Since the first job he had done for the dark man, every other day the Flying Dutchman would make a call to an answering machine. If his services were required, he was referred to another number where the assignment would be detailed. Quail loved the legitimacy the dark man offered him along with much-deserved recognition of his special powers. His anonymity bothered him only because it kept Winston Peet as the most renowned, and thus the greatest, in his field. How unfair. Peet had killed seventeen at most, Quail as many as ten times that number. He carried the news clippings of his killings in the glove compartment of whatever car he was driving at the time the way a young boy stuffs baseball cards into the pockets of his jeans. Since Kimberlain no one had dared believe a single man could be responsible for it all. In that respect, the Dutchman had fallen victim to his own expertise.

Quail figured the time had come for a phone call, so he pulled over at the next gas station he came to and stepped into the phone booth, keeping the door cracked open to keep the light off.

The phone rang twice as always. The answering machine picked up.

Quail smiled. The dark man had work for him again.

CHAPTER 15

ON THE PLANE BACK TO NEW YORK, KIMBERLAIN DIDN'T BOTHER to hide his surprise when a stewardess handed him an Airophone he thought was reserved for outgoing calls.

"Mr. Kimberlain," she said, as surprised as he was, "it's for you."

Up to that point he had busied himself with considering the aftermath of the attack on Lisa Eiseman by her sabotaged creations. Clearly she needed protection, and just as clearly he was in no position to provide it himself. It was Lisa who suggested the solution.

"Dom Torelli," she said, and he proceeded to explain who Torelli was and how she knew him. "Torelli's a king down here," she finished. "Nobody would ever dare cross him."

"Whoever's after you isn't from down here, and I doubt very much they're afraid to cross anybody."

"But Dom has his own island off the coast. It was built as a fortress for his family by his father, and that's just what it is."

"Been there often, have you?"

Lisa thought she caught a note of jealousy in Kimberlain's voice.

139

"Never, but he talks about it plenty—all those times he tried to convince me to go out with him."

"You're trying to tell me you never did?"

She nodded. "And I won't be a hypocrite and say it's because of what he is and does. He's a businessman, Jared, and to tell you the truth he reminds me a little of you."

"You know me that well already?"

"The few hours we've shared have been rather intense." She sighed and forced back a shudder. "Those people who died were my employees, my friends, and the only thing stopping the guilt from setting in is the reality that if it weren't for you I'd be dead too. When you're indebted to somebody, you feel you know them better."

"There's some truth in that."

Kimberlain also found himself agreeing with Lisa that Torelli was the best option available. He placed her personally in the young don's hands, and although he couldn't say he liked Torelli at first, neither did he dislike him. His interest in Lisa appeared to be as genuine as Kimberlain's.

The Ferryman accepted the Airophone from the stewardess.

"Yes?"

"How good to hear your voice again, Ferryman." It was Zeus, and suddenly everything became clear. "I understand you ran into some complications in Atlanta."

"Calling to claim credit?"

The blind man laughed. "Not this time. But I'm still worried about the loss of five hundred pounds of C-12 plastic explosives. In case you've forgotten, that amount could quite easily level a large portion of a major city."

"They're about to serve dinner, Zeus, and I really am hungry."

"I'm surprised the surfacing of the Hashi hasn't spoiled your appetite." Zeus paused, then spoke urgently. "Come back to us, Jared."

"You're sounding desperate, Zeus."

"Just trying to do you a favor. Conscience is what your life is about now, these paybacks. I'm merely trying to save you the pain of partial responsibility for the millions of dead when those explosives are set off.''

"Don't bother trying to pin this on me.''

"You can stop it, Ferryman. You can stop *them*. It wasn't like the Hashi to take such a risk; to come so far over the surface. The risk must be worth it, and if you don't try to at least find out why, you'll be as guilty as the rest of us, who shouldn't have allowed the theft in the first place.''

"Go to hell, Zeus,'' Kimberlain said and switched the phone to OFF.

"This is where the murder happened,'' Captain Seven explained to Kamanski and Kimberlain. The three of them were standing in the gazebo located direcly opposite Jordan Lime's bedroom on ground level.

"In case you've forgotten, Lime was killed in his bedroom,'' Kamanski snapped.

Captain Seven shook his head. "All those negative ions you're pumping will ruin your liver, David. Chill out and pay attention. He died in his bedroom, but this is where he was killed from.''

"The gazebo was sealed. No one could have gotten inside.''

"*Electronically* sealed, Herman, and easily bypassed by a dude who knows the how of it, which obviously you don't. Here, look.'' Captain Seven shuffled his sneakered feet across the gazebo's tile floor to its single entrance. "Basically the only seal you've got on this door is this switch,'' he said, opening it and pointing at a small piece of plastic wedged against the frame. "Door breaks contact with the switch and, *boom,* alarm bells start chiming. Correct?''

"Of course. So what?''

"So tell your man to switch on the alarm system after I'm outside and watch. And put a hold on those negative ions, man.''

"Make it fast,'' Kamanski said and reached for his walkie-talkie as the captain slid out the door and closed it behind him.

"All set,'' Kimberlain called to Seven moments later.

With Captain Seven outside, they heard a slight scraping noise, then the door latch began to jiggle. At last it opened ever so slightly, and they moved close enough to see Seven, still on his knees, pressing something against the plastic switch on the hinged side. Next the door opened enough to let him slither through. The alarm had not sounded.

He crawled inside while what looked to be a very thin steel file stayed pinned against the switch. Then he closed the door again with enough care to trap the file as it was. He rose to his feet and brushed the dirt and dust from his knees.

"No bells," he said, smiling.

"Okay," Kamanski granted. "So somebody could get into the gazebo, but they couldn't get to it over the grounds. Not with our surveillance cameras sweeping constantly."

"What are they trained for?"

"Motion. If a stray one is found, they automatically search for a security medallion keying them that it's one of our men. Otherwise the alarm would sound instantly. And don't try telling me this phantom of yours made off with one of our medallions or made one of his own. Neither is possible."

"Don't worry, my phantom wouldn't have needed a medallion." Captain Seven paused long enough to wink at the Ferryman. "Your alarms go off every time a bush blows in the breeze, Herman?"

"Of course not."

"Why? What stops them?"

"The lenses pick up the lack of a heat pattern given off by the needles, leaves, and branches."

"So a stray bush getting pushed around in the wind wouldn't make bells."

"I just told you no."

Captain Seven got down on his stomach and began to shimmy across the gazebo floor with his elbows supplying the thrust. "Ain't done this since Nam," he moaned. "Brings back great memories, let me tell you."

"Get to the point!" Kamanski ordered.

"Get to your doctor, dude. I'll take my time." He gazed up at Kimberlain, who didn't bother to hide his smile. "Picture me, the back of me anyway, covered in a light coating of natural greens. Maybe it's even part of my clothes, like sewn in. It's night here at the Lime estate, and nobody's home except you weirdos. So I dig myself a hole, not much of one, just enough for me to slide under the fence to the other side and then fill everything back in so it won't be noticed. Are you picturing this, Mr. Negative Ions? Okay, so I'm in now and disguised in a way that'll keep your cameras from locking in on me. My victim isn't on the grounds yet, so your guards' attention is low enough to miss me. I've done similar stuff before. I know all the tricks."

Kamanski was listening now.

"I reach the gazebo and make my way inside as demonstrated a couple of seconds ago. The toughest part is over."

"You're still not even close to Lime."

"I'm as close as I need to be." Captain Seven climbed back to his feet and moved to the front window of the gazebo, which looked up at Lime's bedroom. "The killer opened this window just like he opened the door. Everything was in place."

"For what?"

"Let's head into the mansion and I'll show you."

The two Pro-Tech guards were standing before Jordan Lime's bedroom when they got there.

"Wanted everything to be just the way it was four nights ago," the captain explained. "Let's go inside."

After they did, Kamanski's eyes swept about him in shock. "What the hell did you do in here?"

"Made some changes. Like I said, I wanted everything to be just like it was the night of the murder."

"You disturbed evidence, you ass. Evidence!"

"Put a hold on it, Herman. There was no evidence to disturb, nothing worth anything to the police or the FBI . . . except what they missed. Let me show you something." He moved to the win-

dow, which was open just as it had been the night Jordan Lime had
been killed.

Seven had made sure the bulletproof glass curtains were drawn,
and they fluttered slightly in the wind as they had Sunday night.
The captain pulled a small container of talcum powder from his
pocket, twisted it open, and squeezed the nozzle against the back
of the curtain. White dusty particles danced into the air of the room.
Seven squeezed the container again, and more joined the first batch.

"You notice these holes and slight slices in the curtain?"

"Normal wear and tear, we thought," replied Kamanski. "No
evidence of any weapon as the cause."

"Meaning any weapon you're aware of. Let's take it by the numbers now. Lime's lying in bed. He hears a crash."

"Glass breaking," said Kamanski. "It's on tape. We figured it
was the painting falling from the wall."

"It was. The most subtle yet the most important part of the entire
plan."

"Because it made Lime sit up and turn the lights on," the Ferryman guessed. "With the right equipment, his shape would have
been clearly visible from the gazebo even behind the curtains."

"And a shape was all our killer needed to focus on." Captain
Seven separated his hands by about a foot and imitated holding a
weapon. "It would have been the size of a small bazooka, easily
concealed beneath his jacket while he crawled across the lawn
toward the gazebo."

"What would have been?" asked Kamanski.

"A water cannon," Captain Seven said without missing a beat.

"A water *what*?"

"You won't find it in any of your old *Soldier of Fortunes*, Herman, because technically it doesn't exist in the form I just described. What exist are high-speed water jet drills that can slice
through anything from titanium to taffy. Heart of the system is a
pair of pumps: a standard motor-driven hydraulic piston pump
which drives a plunger type called an intensifier. Hydraulic oil is
delivered to a large piston in the intensifier, driving it back and

forth in a tubular housing—that's what I meant by bazooka. Connected to the large piston are two smaller piston plungers which pump the water through the system under extremely high pressure. By the time the water emerges from the nozzle it's traveling at least three thousand feet per second at sixty thousand psi.''

"Wow," said the Ferryman.

"Yeah, but like I said, it don't exist, at least it didn't used to. See, the problem with utilizing the water jet principle as a weapon is that air dulls the jet's cutting abilities. Less than a foot of travel in open air reduces effectiveness to practically nil, and the gazebo is a full fifty feet from the bedroom window, making things even more difficult.''

"So where does that leave us?" asked an exasperated Kamanski.

"Somebody made modifications. Increasing power of the pistons would be the key to generating a faster pace for the water. You'd also need more molecules packed into the same size stream, which would actually require a slightly bigger tube. Get the speed of the jets up to around fifty thousand feet per second and mix in sufficient levels of abrasive particles like garnet or silica and the jets'll cut through damn near anything from up to maybe a hundred feet away.''

"For how long?" Kimberlain asked.

"Depends on the size of the tank. Six seconds would be a pretty fair guess, like a single clip from a machine gun." Captain Seven paused to collect his thoughts. "Picture it all now. The shooter down in the gazebo eases his water cannon onto the window ledge. He's got the layout of the bedroom memorized, and it's a simple problem of mathematics to figure out the necessary angle to send the picture crashing to the floor and sever your video feed line in the process.''

Captain Seven stopped suddenly and dove onto Jordan Lime's freshly made bed. "Lime hears the crash, bolts up instinctively, and turns on the lights." He sat up and mocked turning the lights on from the switch above the headboard. "The light goes on and that cues the shooter to Lime's position. The shooter takes aim, fires, and the water jet slices through the glass curtains in part of the pattern I showed you, and enough of the first spray finds Lime sitting up in bed or . . .'' Captain Seven threw his legs over the side and feigned shaking himself alert. ''Or maybe he was starting to get out, something like this. Either way the jet finds him. We're talking about a weapon with the same cutting power as a laser beam here. But the jet itself has a diameter only about the same size as a pen point. Whatever it touches, it slices clean through and off. Totally clean. No burned or jagged edges.'' The captain spun himself around for effect. ''The first burst tears Lime's arm off, and the shock straightens him long enough for another spray to catch him. The shooter would have had to maneuver the cannon only slightly down in the gazebo to achieve what happened to the rest of Lime. It would have been over very fast.''

''Incredible,'' was Kamanski's only comment.

''We're talking high-tech murder here, Herman.'' Captain Seven staggered from the area of the bed. ''All those screams indicate Lime must have been alive through most of it. The blood keeps spewing as the jets continue to tear him apart, scattering the pieces all over the room.''

Kamanski was nodding. ''The blood that was all over the walls— we couldn't figure out how it got there. It must have mixed with the jets and splashed.''

''On the money, David. And the jets didn't carve the walls to shreds because penetrating Lime's body had slowed them up.''

''One last thing, Captain,'' said the Ferryman. ''When the alarm was sounded, the estate was sealed from bottom to top, including the area around the gazebo. How'd the shooter escape?''

''Dudes running everywhere?'' Seven asked Kamanski.

''Of course.''

''Police too?''

''All over the grounds in a matter of minutes.''

''Then you had to turn off your special cameras that key off those medallions.''

''Yes. Why?''

"Simple." And with that, Captain Seven pulled back the buttons of his denim work shirt to reveal the uniform top of a Pro-Tech guard beneath it. "Ta-daaaaah!" he exclaimed. "Presto-chango. In all the confusion, our killer just mixed in and walked off into the darkness."

"Unbelievable," Kamanski said.

"Can I keep the shirt?" Captain Seven asked.

"Only if you tell us how to find where this water cannon came from," Kimberlain told him.

"That's easy. Only one place got the tech background to build one, boss. Cyberdine Systems in good old Boston, Massachusetts. Ask for project director, Dr. Alan Mendelson."

Kamanski was about ask more when his walkie-talkie started squawking. He raised the small apparatus to his ear.

"Kamanski. Go ahead."

Kimberlain caught a garble in return and just barely noticed Kamanski's eyes seek him out as he lowered the walkie-talkie from his ear with the garbled voice still going strong.

"We just got a call from The Locks," he told the Ferryman. "Winston Peet's escaped."

CHAPTER 16

" . . . **O**NCE AGAIN WE THANK YOU FOR CHOOSING THE
Eastern shuttle and hope that . . ."

Kimberlain came out of his daze after most of the stewardess's standard speech was completed and realized he hadn't fastened his seat belt for landing at Boston's Logan Airport. Dr. Alan Mendelson would be expecting him in less than an hour, but Kimberlain had spent the short flight as he had spent the night before, with thoughts of the now free Winston Peet. Sixteen hours had passed since his escape, enough time for Peet to cover lots of ground.

"He faked choking on his dinner," Kamanski had explained Thursday night after the facts became clear. "Guards waited until two minutes had passed before entering the cell. Peet's features had gone blue, and all respiratory function seemed to have ceased. They had rules to follow too, Jared. They waited as long as they could."

"Apparently not."

"A pair of them entered the cell to revive Peet, with a half-dozen armed reinforcements standing outside. The two who went in did so weaponless. Everything was by the book."

"Peet kill them both?"

"No. Used them as hostages. The guards were planning to lock

148

themselves in while they tried to resuscitate Peet, but he lunged on them from the floor before the cell door was all the way locked. The guards outside held their fire out of fear of hitting their fellows.''

"Go on.''

"Peet made straight for the shoreline, hostages in tow. Night had just fallen, and the darkness made it impossible for anyone to get a clear shot. Peet used his shields right up to the water's edge, when he shoved the guards aside and dove in.''

"Wearing?''

"We're on the same wavelength, Jared. He was wearing his usual pair of khakis and was naked above the waist. Nothing else on but sandals. It was fifteen degrees outside; the water wasn't even forty. It's a two-mile swim in any direction to reach land from The Locks. No man could survive it.''

"Peet's not a man." Kimberlain shook his head in disgust. "After all these years you still don't see that, do you? Sure, he breathes and bleeds like the rest of us, but that's where the comparison stops. People like him and Quail aren't like everyone else. The difference is that their abilities mirror their desires, and the mistake we make is in not recognizing that. It's how they're able to thrive in the world for as long as they do.''

Kamanski didn't look convinced. "Vogelhut put an alert out, and the shores were crawling with cops within minutes. None of them reported any sign of Peet.''

"Was a body found?''

"With the currents this time of year, I wouldn't expect one to be.''

"He's alive, David. He's alive because you didn't make sure he was executed when you had the chance, and now he's going to come looking for me.''

"Even if he survived, you really think he'll come after you?''

"It's what drives the bastard. You didn't see him two days ago. I defeated him, the only man who ever did. Life and death don't

mean a damn thing when measured against evening that score. He's
alive, and he'll be coming. You can count on both.''

That certainty had tempered the first breakthrough they'd made
into the investigation of this latest serial killer. If Captain Seven's
assertions were correct, then the killer at some point must have
obtained equipment and knowledge from Boston's Cyberdine Systems. A former employee maybe, or perhaps a friend of a present
employee. Kimberlain intended to have all possibilities checked
out.

The taxi pulled to a halt on Congress Street in front of the mod-
ernistic First National Bank of Boston Building. The Ferryman
climbed out after paying the driver and eyed the structure before
him. It was made of elegant brownish marble and was shaped
somewhat like a peg driven into the landscape, with its middle
seven stories protruding symmetrically out from the four beneath
and nine above it. Cyberdine Systems occupied these middle seven,
and Kimberlain took the elevator up to the tenth floor, where Alan
Mendelson's office was located. A receptionist buzzed Mendelson's
secretary to announce his arrival. The meeting had been set for
eleven A.M., and fifteen minutes remained until that hour.

Mendelson's secretary, a tall, dark-haired woman, appeared moments later and escorted him down a long, twisting corridor which
had the feel and look of something from a futuristic space craft.
The corners were rounded instead of square. The doors they passed
were of the mechanical, sliding variety; nothing as old-fashioned
as knobs and latches.

''Dr. Mendelson is expecting you,'' the secretary said when they
reached the last door. She pushed a button on the wall and the door
slid open. The secretary smiled artificially and told him to enter.

''Mr. Kimberlain, I presume,'' came a voice from the large
office's far end. ''Please come in.''

With the door closed behind him, Kimberlain found himself inside the most modern office he had ever seen. The carpet was blue-
gray, the walls cream white and lined with nonobjective paintings.

The entire rear wall, before which sat a semicircular white desk, was formed of windows that drenched the office in sunlight, providing life to a myriad of plants and small trees scattered about. Attached to each plant was a tube that disappeared through the carpet to provide what must have been an automatic watering system.

"Water systems are my specialty, Mr. Kimberlain," the voice said, and Jared had to squint into the bright late-morning sun to see the speaker. Alan Mendelson stepped out from behind his desk, and now Kimberlain could see him more clearly. "Sensors in the soil alert the pumps to dryness and automatically activate the hoses. We're testing this system in a much larger scale at farms in the Midwest. Could save millions, in man-hours as well as dollars."

Kimberlain had reached him by then, and the two men shook hands. Mendelson's eyes bore into his, looking fearful and hesitant. The scientist led him toward a trio of chairs set immediately before his desk but didn't offer one. The chairs looked to be made of the same material as the carpeted floor, like an outgrowth of some hybrid plant. The same could be said for the rest of the office furniture—a table and a pair of couches in a sitting area. None possessed any identity of its own, just growths in a landscape dominated by the jungle of plants and trees.

Mendelson's eyes were quivering now, blinking rapidly. "The man who called was vague. Are you, what I mean is, are you a part of the government?"

"I have been."

"What I mean is . . ." The words were obviously coming hard for Mendelson, and his fear was growing. "What I'm trying to say is do you represent anybody in a position to provide, I guess you'd call it protection, in return for cooperation?"

Kimberlain grasped his meaning and felt his pulse quicken. "A phone call away, Doctor."

"I need help. I didn't know what I was getting into. They had the right credentials. I thought their request was an extension of the previous work. I was simply filling an order."

"You're talking about the water cannon."

"Not a cannon! The potential was there, yes, due to the modifications in design, but I never dreamed that was the purpose until I received that phone call last night. I swear it!"

"What modifications in design?"

"A drill—that's what it was originally. That's what it was supposed to be, what Benbasset paid a hundred million dollars to have developed seven years ago."

"Benbasset?"

"The billionaire industrialist. It was his project, but the government had a substantial interest as well. That much was obvious."

"A substantial interest in what?"

"It doesn't matter now. I completed the new design just four weeks ago and delivered it just as they specified."

" 'They'?"

"They had the right credentials, I tell you! But I should have known by how they wanted it delivered that something was wrong. I should have suspected."

"Details, Doctor, I need details."

"No!" Mendelson came closer still. "We've got to get out. I'll take you at your word. Protection in return for everything I know." He lowered his voice to a virtual whisper. "There's a private elevator in the closet behind that door across the room. We'll take it downstairs. Then you'll get me safely out of the building."

With no other choice, Kimberlain followed Mendelson to the door. His pulse was racing, but he kept himself from considering the implications of what Mendelson had said until the opportunity came for him to elaborate further.

They had the right credentials. . . .

Plural, not singular. Suddenly the search for a serial killer seemed about to become extremely complicated.

Mendelson reached the closet door and started to open it. He was breathing hard; even the simplest motion seemed to tax him. The door eased inward and he started through it.

The figure that lunged from the darkness Kimberlain recognized as the long, leggy shape of Mendelson's secretary. He was going for his gun even as he saw her bringing hers up. It was a gun like no other he had ever seen.

"No!" Mendelson screamed and brought his hand up before his face.

The secretary fired the squat, rifle-like weapon. A hiss followed. Mendelson screamed. His severed hand struck the blue-gray carpet, splattering red as waves of blood pumped from the gaping wound.

Kimberlain dove to the floor, realizing that the weapon he was facing was the one that had torn Jordan Lime apart. He had his gun steadied as he rolled after landing, aiming at the secretary and firing, but she moved the fraction required to save herself, and his bullet hit the wall where her head had been. Mendelson was still shrieking, staggering, but the woman's attention was on Kimberlain now as he sighted for another shot.

He got it off, dead on line with her chest, for a certain kill. It thumped home and the woman recoiled, but when no spurt of blood emerged, the Ferryman knew she was wearing some sort of body armor and he'd better move now—and fast.

A jet hissed out of the barrel as he twisted across the carpet just ahead of the dark, scalpel-like incision sliced through the blue-gray piling. He was square in the open, and the woman had him in her sights, when, screaming, Mendelson charged at her with blood still pumping from where his hand had been.

She brought the gun around, firing, and Kimberlain saw a wave of blood gush from Mendelson's chest and back simultaneously as the water jet sliced in and through. Mendelson reeled backward, writhing and spasming, searching for the breath needed to scream. He had bought Kimberlain time, though, and the Ferryman grabbed for it, going for a head shot that missed when the woman swung back. The bullet grazed her unprotected shoulder at the clavicle joint and spun her around as she wailed in pain, her water jet weapon ripping a crevice in the wall.

From his prone position, Kimberlain steadied his gun once more.

The woman was still in motion when she fired next, and in that instant Kimberlain was certain he could see the dark blur coming at him. As he instinctively raised his arm for protection, the water jet sliced into his pistol and turned it scorching hot in his grasp. As he dropped it, another jet cut flesh from his left side.

The agony rocked him all the way to his feet and sent him into motion, not toward the woman but toward the thick leather couch that seemed to be growing out of the floor against the far wall. Mendelson, meanwhile, was clawing for something on his desk. He reached up and spilled the contents of his blotter to the rug.

The woman fired her weapon again just as Kimberlain threw himself behind the couch. The water jet hissed through the fabric and singed the air above him as he hugged the carpet.

Kimberlain realized his best chance, his only chance, was to keep moving. He darted from the cover of the couch and dove behind Mendelson's desk. Again the water jet traced his path, the last edge of it slicing open his other side with a feeling of ice sliding down his shirt. Kimberlain twisted the other way, and the motion brought him next to Mendelson, still alive somehow, with his eyes twitching and focusing on a piece of paper beneath the hand that remained attached. Another burst from the water-jet gun forced the Ferryman even lower. Warm blood soaked his shirt on both sides. He felt himself weakening and began to wonder how much more spray the gun could hold. Captain Seven had guessed six seconds' worth, but obviously that estimate was low.

He heard its wielder coming and grabbed reflexively for some damp earth from the nearest potted palm. As the woman's shape lunged over the desk with the deadly barrel leading, Kimberlain tossed the dirt upward into her face. Her weapon tore a chasm from the floor where he had been, and before she could recover, Kimberlain threw himself on her and grabbed for the water-jet gun.

Their fight for control of the weapon twisted and turned the length and breadth of the room. In the course of their wrestling, the woman compressed the trigger. An entire wall split in two, followed by fragments from the ceiling. At last the conference table collapsed, with its legs severed. The woman was good with her feet and used them effectively against the Ferryman's knees. He could feel himself weakening considerably from loss of blood. His concentration on the weapon left his groin exposed, and she rammed into him with something that felt like a brick. He bit his lip to cling to consciousness while his feet wavered beneath him. He felt himself slipping away and knew his next move was the only one that mattered.

The Ferryman changed his strategy and went with the woman's move instead of against it; he let her have the gun, let her think she could fire it. And when she brought it up, Kimberlain grabbed the bore at the absolute last instant and forced it hard into the dirt of a potted plant just as the woman pulled the trigger.

The dirt clogged the barrel and jammed the mechanism. That, Kimberlain had anticipated. The rest he hadn't.

The charge of water going down at fifty thousand feet per second and jammed with an incredible suddenness sought the only other possible route of exit: the other end of the gun. The jet blasted upward in a single stream and exploded at peak velocity from the opposite side, the entire weapon shattering as it shot out. The jet sliced through the woman's body armor and penetrated her flesh. Her mouth gaped with an awful soundless scream. The impact smashed her backwards against the far wall, and she left a trail of red on it as she slid down, hate-filled eyes clinging to life as they locked with the Ferryman's.

"You will pay," she rasped through the gurgling of frothy blood in her mouth. "You will all pay. One million will die before fifty million. The—"

That was as far as she got. A spasm shook her, and her eyes locked open.

Kimberlain sank to his knees in pain and exhaustion. His eyes were level with the dead woman's shoulder, exposed now since the rupturing of the water-jet gun had shredded her blouse. He wiped his eyes and squinted, not believing what he saw imprinted on her flesh. But it was there. *It was there!*

A tattoo of a smiling death's-head with a spear running through it from temple to temple.

The woman was a Hashi!

The Ferryman moved back toward Mendelson with his thoughts in a frenzy.

The Hashi! Here, now, a part of this! What had Zeus said about explosives? Could there be, might there be a—

Mendelson was dead, but he had managed to scrawl something in his own blood on the piece of paper beneath his hand. Kimberlain started to reach for it, eyes already taking in its message. Three numbers, followed by two letters: 719, 720, 721 PS.

He heard the door slide open and tried to swing fast. But the wounds to his sides drove pain through him, and he nearly toppled over.

"Don't move," ordered a tall blond woman after the door had closed behind her. She was wearing black jeans and boots, and she was holding a gun. The pistol looked too big for her, but she held it confidently. It seemed to Kimberlain that her eyes too had focused on the dead woman's shoulder, on the Hashi tattoo. "Slide the piece of paper over to me," she ordered next. "Use your left hand."

The blonde came closer but kept enough distance to assure him she was a pro and a good one. Yet if she was another Hashi, a backup for the secretary, he would have been dead already. So who was she?

Kimberlain did as he was told. The blonde leaned over and lifted the bloodied sheet of paper from the carpet. Before he could contemplate moving, the woman had backed up well out of range, still showing her pistol. Without speaking again she retreated through the door, which closed again instantly.

Fighting down his pain, Kimberlain lunged to his feet and bolted forward. He pushed the button that should have opened the door again.

Nothing. The woman must have shorted it out on the other side, thinking she had left him trapped. But he could still make use of Mendelson's private elevator in the closet. If it whisked him down fast enough, he might find the woman and give chase. A moment later he was in the small compartment, descending, pressed against the wall for support.

The doors opened at the far end of the lobby level, apart from the main congestion of those coming and going. The Ferryman tried to move quickly toward the nearest exit, but he was too weak. He had lost more blood and was feeling extremely dizzy as he emerged at the side of the building and started around toward the front. He was dimly aware of his heels clicking against the layered brick and cement inlay design, color-keyed to mesh with the brown marble of the building. It looked rusty to him, almost like blood.

At the front of the building, the lunchtime crowds of Congress Street swallowed him up. His eyes probed ahead as he wavered through the mass, searching for a blond head while holding his arms pressed to his sides to keep the blood hidden by his jacket. He caught a glimpse of a black sweater and boots beneath a blond head twenty yards ahead and started to run.

Hardly into his dash, everything turned slow. The world started spinning.

And the Ferryman tried to grasp the air so he wouldn't fall off it as he tumbled to the ground.

THE FIFTH TRUMPET

ST. ANDREW SOUND

Friday, November 20; 7:00 P.M.

CHAPTER 17

"A PHONE, DAVID. JUST GET ME A GODDAMN PHONE!"

Kimberlain slammed his fist against the hospital bed in disgust, bolts of pain searing through him from the motion.

"Careful, Jared. Might strip your sutures off."

Kimberlain felt a rush of cold replace the pain. "I remember reciting Mendelson's message. Did you write it down?"

"Right here," Kamanski told him, turning his eyes to the night table. "Don't waste your time. It's just gibberish."

"The fuck it is," the Ferryman came back, remembering now. "Numbers," he muttered. "In sequence."

"719, 720, 721, followed by PS."

"What about the woman? I gave you a description."

"Sure, of a blond woman in black. Only maybe ten thousand of them in the city. I put out an APB."

"She was there to see Mendelson too. She must be part of what's going on, maybe a different part we're not even aware of."

"Which part, Jared?"

"Look, Hermes, there's something you'd better get through your bureaucratic skull, and fast. We're not facing a single madman here. What we're facing is a whole *society* of killers called the

161

Hashi. Sound familiar? They wear a certain tattoo on their right shoulder, and they're utterly ruthless.''

''Hold on a—''

''No, Hermes. There's more. That secretary was there to kill me, not Mendelson.''

''That's absurd.''

''Is it? Well let me tell you something else. Mendelson said 'they,' the people who ordered the weapon, had the right credentials. He believed he had worked with them on something else that was probably legitimate that had also utilized the water-jet principle. So Mendelson was a risk to them all along, but they could have eliminated him at anytime. Instead they waited until I met with him.'' With that Kimberlain felt even colder. ''Which means they knew I was coming. Somehow they knew I was coming.''

''You've got more immediate problems to worry about. Just so you know it, there's a pair of Boston police officers outside your door. Technically you're under arrest, though they're still calling it protective custody. The police have two dead bodies in a downtown office building and a wounded man unconscious on the street they've already pinned to the scene. And there's not a damn thing I can do to help. We're both just private citizens now.''

''You let me worry about my pending incarceration. That way you can go home with a clear head and bring me everything you can on Jason Benbasset tomorrow morning.''

''Jason Benbasset, the billionaire?''

''The only one I know of, Hermes.''

''Anything else?''

''Yeah. Even if I was under arrest, I'd be allowed a phone call. Now bring me a damn phone!''

Kimberlain's second call was to Dominick Torelli's private number. Actually it took the dialing of two others to track down the don at his favorite Atlanta restaurant.

''What can I do for you, Mr. Kimberlain?''

''Lisa's not safe, Mr. Torelli.''

"I told you to call me Dom. I just checked in. Everything's fine."

"Double the guards, hire an army. That's what you're up against."

Torelli sighed. "You've learned something new."

"Not much that would mean anything to you. Just the name of the group that was probably hired to kill her and the others in the first place. They don't miss very often, and almost never twice."

There was a pause on the other end of the line, and the tension spoke for itself.

"I checked you out, Mr. Kimberlain," Torelli said finally. "Lots of people speak quite highly of what you stand for, what you do. Lots of them are scared. I also understand our paths have crossed before, not directly but through an intermediary of mine in Chicago."

"I sent flowers and candy. Should be up and around by now."

"Oh, I know he deserved it. What I don't understand is why you agreed to involve yourself. I like that in a man, Mr. Kimberlain. It's something we don't see enough of anymore."

"We were talking about Lisa."

"I'll get more of my personal soldiers to her within hours. Fly down myself as soon as I clear up a little business. Make you happy?"

"Close enough."

"Good night, Mr. Kimberlain."

Beep . . . beep . . . beep . . .

Quintanna stood before the black plasteel curtain, waiting for its occupant to respond to his report.

"You assured me that matters were under control, Mr. Quintanna. You assured me that Kimberlain would be eliminated at the first available opportunity, and now you say that opportunity has passed with failure."

"One attempt has failed. The next one will not."

"And what if Mendelson passed on information pertaining to the substance of my plan?"

"He knew nothing of the substance."

"But Kimberlain now knows of your people's involvement and can only conclude there is far more to the plot than he originally believed."

"I am more concerned about the presence of this woman at Mendelson's office," said Quintanna. "Her description matches that of a commando who single-handedly destroyed our stronghold in Nice. That same stronghold contained the plans for Spiderweb and the *Rhode Island*. If she managed to salvage them somehow, if that was what brought her to America on a trail that eventually led her to Mendelson, then, yes, we must face the fact that crucial elements of the plan are no longer secret."

"You knew Kimberlain. Do you also know this woman?"

"Not specifically. But the Hashi are not without enemies."

"And now your enemies have become mine, Mr. Quintanna. What would you have me do about that?"

"Postpone the operation until we have a chance to bring the situation under control."

"It appears you are moving in quite the opposite direction, though, doesn't it? You fear Kimberlain and you fear the woman. I can sense it in your voice."

"I fear the possibility that they will eventually join forces."

"According to your words, then, everything I have done is now in jeopardy thanks to the bungling of your people. I came to you with the plan already set. You had merely to plug in the proper pieces, and even that task has proven too much for you."

"There were things I couldn't foresee."

"And my operation is what suffers for your oversight."

"It doesn't have to. Postponement means the choice of another event, that's all."

The black curtain fluttered in rhythm with the life-support machines within. Quintanna could hear the breathing grow more labored—thicker and wetter.

"You still do not understand, do you?" accused the voice. "There is no other event. All this must go forth as I have planned it. The circle must close as it began. There is no alternative. If we abandon one stage of the operation, we abandon it all.''

"I didn't mean—"

"It's clear you don't know what you mean. You allow yourself only a narrow view of what I am trying to accomplish. You are a scavenger, Quintanna. You wish to feed off the corpse of the world when I am finished with it, and nothing more, so of course the timing and means are of no interest to you. But the end must come as *I* direct. You think I have lain here and plotted at whim, accepting what is thrust at me the way a scavenger like yourself might? No, no! Man had his chance at progress, at technology, at developing civilization, and all he accomplished was wanton murder, famine, destruction, a society powered by hate instead of love. Your kind of society, of world, Quintanna. Fine. I leave it to you. I *will* it to you. The two of you deserve each other. In six days' time the dawn of what is usually a happy time of year will in this case prove the dawn of something else. It will come to pass on the day I direct, because only by that means can justice be done for all the wrongs committed.''

"Then I shall find a means to deal with the Ferryman.''

"And the Eiseman woman, lest you forget. I am forced to rely on you, Mr. Quintanna. For now, just leave me.''

Wordlessly, Quintanna turned on his heels and started for the elevator.

Commander McKenzie Barlow was sitting behind the small desk in his quarters when the lock turned from the outside and Jones entered, looking frazzled.

"We've just had a communiqué from COMSUBLANT requesting an update,'' he said. "That's not procedure. They know something's wrong. Tell me what you did.''

"Might help, Mr. Jones, if I saw the message.''

Jones handed over a slightly crumpled bit of paper. Mac unfolded it and smoothed the edges. Its contents were simple: "Request repeat status grade.''

"What's it mean?" Jones demanded.

"Nothing to worry about. They just want us to send another status report over main line instead of bouncing it off beacons. The beacon system hasn't been updated to allow for the deep lie of a super-Trident," Mac lied, "so that message I sent must have come through garbled."

"The others didn't."

"We were closer to the States then, weren't we? It wouldn't have bothered them ordinarily, except in this case I was given some parameters that you've broken. If we're straying, they'd be concerned the navigational gear is to blame. Thus, the request for an update."

"What else? Don't forget your family, Mac. Don't make me do something I don't want to."

"Main-line status grade requires a listing of coordinates."

"But even main line will give them only a rough estimate of our coordinates."

"Right, so we can lie and they'll have no way of checking up. Just gotta make sure what we give them jibes somewhat with what they already suspect."

"Then let's get to the com center, Commander."

Mac nodded routinely. The crucial part of the message his last status grade had created the need for was ready in his mind as Mr. Jones led him from his quarters.

It was four hours past nightfall and Kimberlain was dozing when the door eased open to allow a trio of figures to enter, the middle one dwarfed by the ones flanking it.

Tap . . . tap . . . tap . . .

The sound of a cane marking the blind man's path forward reached Kimberlain's ears. The darkness of his hospital room was broken only by the spill of street lamps sneaking through cracks in the blinds.

"I could come back in the morning," Zeus said, after the Ferryman had reached above him and switched on the light.

Kimberlain sat up. "I think I can stomach you better after my evening pain shot."

The old man gave him a knowing grin as his two giant body-guards went to stand by the door. "Ah, but this time it was you who called me."

"Because we seem to have something in common. That doesn't change the way I feel."

"Necessity heals all wounds."

"Not the old ones, Zeus, not the old ones."

"You mentioned the Hashi when you called, Ferryman."

"Somehow they figure into what I've been working on."

"The murders?"

He nodded. "They're almost certainly behind them, and with the theft of those explosives fitting in so neatly in terms of the timing . . ."

"You sense a connection, eh, Ferryman? Never were one to pass anything off to coincidence."

"I think the C-12 *plastique* might have plenty to do with something I've stumbled on accidentally." And he proceeded to relate to Zeus all the day's events, repeating in the end the threat rasped at him by the dying Hashi killer.

"The contradiction in terms is interesting," Zeus told him. "One million will die and then fifty million."

"No, Zeus, you're interpreting the words wrong, specifically one word: 'before'."

"Of course! In front of."

"So it could mean one million will die *in front of* fifty million witnesses."

"Television?"

"Yes," Kimberlain acknowledged. "A huge event of some sort, with one million people on the scene."

"And these one million are to be murdered then and there. The explosives! Of course!" The old man didn't bother to restrain his smile. "A challenge for us, Ferryman, requiring our best efforts if it is to be successfully overcome."

"This isn't a game, Zeus."

"We need to be allies here, Ferryman. The past must be put behind us. What forced us apart in earlier times were errors in interpretation, not intention. You believed I left you in the jungle to die because of my fear of what you might do, and, accordingly, my actions forced you to make the very move I feared the most. Ironic, isn't it?"

Kimberlain said nothing.

"After the dissolution of The Caretakers, I was transferred to another role that was important but infinitely less rewarding. Security for a collection of secret installations. They made me a night watchman, Ferryman, however glorified. You see, we've both had to make adjustments in our lives."

"Let's get back to the subject at hand."

"Fear not, Ferryman. The best minds in the network will be on this by midnight." Zeus smiled. "You'll also be pleased to know that all charges against you have mysteriously vanished and the file containing the investigating officers' report has disappeared."

"Sounds like you're not entirely helpless after all, Zeus."

"We'll talk in the morning."

But it wasn't morning when Kimberlain awoke next. And by all rights he shouldn't have awoken at all. The room was just as it had been when Zeus had left. Nothing to raise him from his slumber except . . .

A shape stirred, straddling a pair of chairs at arm's distance from the bedside, a monstrous silhouette set against the room's darkness.

"Hello, Ferryman," said Winston Peet.

CHAPTER 18

I'M STILL ALIVE, KIMBERLAIN THOUGHT. THAT'S SOMETHING, BUT it might not be much.

He stifled the instinct to reach for the call button, knowing that would only summon more victims for Peet.

"I didn't want to wake you," the giant said, moving not an inch.

"That's considerate."

"I owed you that much." Peet shifted and the chairs creaked.

"How'd you find me?"

"At The Locks you mentioned the messenger man had brought you in on this just as he brought you into the chase for me. Finding him in New York was simple. He led me to you."

"Good old Hermes."

Peet regarded him calmly. "You don't have a gun, Ferryman. If you did it would be out by now."

Kimberlain just looked at him, fighting with his mind to regain control of his body. If Peet lunged, he had to be ready. If he could fend off the giant for a few moments, the commotion would attract help. He found himself wishing Zeus hadn't dismissed the police posted by his door.

And then Peet stood up, just a foot separating him from the

169

ceiling. Kimberlain flinched and drew back. A pair of IV pouches smacked against each other.

"Back in the dark times, Ferryman, I thought I had come to grips with what I was and wished to be. The killing beat back the great flames that raged inside me. But then, on the day of my rebirth, you stood over me with gun ready. The traditional bullet never emerged, but a spiritual one did. The dark part of me was slain, and for that I owed you a debt I waited all those years in The Locks to repay. I knew the time was coming when I wrote you the letters, and I knew the time had come when you visited. I saw death in your eyes, Ferryman, your own death, and I alone can prevent it."

Then you're not going to kill me. Kimberlain might have said it out loud if the giant hadn't continued, bald head glistening in the thin light.

"I could have escaped anytime I chose; a dozen different ways were available. But until you came and I saw your eyes, there was no reason. You gave me reason, just as you gave me life with your spiritual bullet. I must save you because it is through this that my final cleansing will take place."

Peet smiled, and the gesture sent chills through Kimberlain. He wanted to pull the bed sheet up high over his eyes like a child hiding from imagined monsters.

"Back in The Locks, Ferryman, I said we were the same because we can feel disturbances in the great field of energy that surrounds and binds the world. In the jungle, the hunter is alerted by the trail. In our world, the hunter is alerted by vibrations that don't belong, neither good nor evil but simply anomalous. All those years ago, you felt me in that town, knew I was there, didn't you?"

"Yes."

"And when you tracked Quail you knew he was out there too. You had no evidence of his existence, no less his true identity, but you felt the truth and nearly caught him."

"Where is this leading?"

"He's a part of this now."

"The Dutchman?"

Peet nodded. "Out there as we speak. The disturbances in the layers of *ki* I am attuned to alerted me, and I must be the one to stop him."

"This is starting to sound very personal."

"For me there is no personal, Ferryman. My soul and spirit have been given up to something much greater. All the personal died back in time to your spiritual bullet. It is more that my reborn soul cannot rest peacefully so long as he is out there; the part of me I seek to be rid of clings to life in his person. Just because I vanquished it in myself does not mean it is gone. It merely fled into another soul, which must be crushed if I am ever to end the flux within me. That my path will cross Quail's is our certain common fate. Either he will kill me or I will kill him. If I don't try, then your life will end by his hand." Peet backed up a step, drawing a hard swallow from Kimberlain. "I will leave you the phone number of the room where I am staying."

"I could give it to the authorities," Kimberlain said, trying to sound as though he meant it. "Have you picked up."

"But you won't," Peet told him. "Because you're going to need me."

Danielle accepted the report without surprise.

"We can make no sense of the note," came the voice from across the ocean. "The man is something else again. Are you sure it was—"

"Yes, I'm sure. The Ferryman."

"And the Hashi tried to kill him in Mendelson's office?"

"*Along* with Mendelson."

"Then whatever the Ferryman is pursuing led him to Mendelson as well."

"His pursuits have somehow intersected with our own," Danielle added. "There is more involved than he expected, just as there must be more involved than we did."

"If your conclusions about the submarine and the Antarctic oil installation are correct . . ."

"The Ferryman may know nothing of them; he probably doesn't. But he does know something else, another part—a different part— perhaps the one that will make sense of what we have uncovered."

"To understand the whole," the man said, "we must have all the parts."

"Then we need Kimberlain."

"Can you find him?"

"Finding him will hardly be sufficient."

"All our resources are at your disposal."

"Against the Ferryman, they might not be sufficient either."

The special reinforcements sent down at Kimberlain's request to St. Andrew Sound by Dominick Torelli arrived on the mainland at Crooked Bluff at eleven P.M. As ordered, the island's cabin cruiser had been sent across to pick them up. A patrol launch would have been a more logical choice, but no two were large enough to comfortably accommodate all twelve of the extra commandos necessary to double the guard around Lisa Eiseman.

Crooked Bluff was located thirty miles down a lonely road off Route 95 as it cut through southern Georgia. The name was fitting, since the bluff was actually a ragged peninsula jutting out toward the islands in the sound like a set of gator teeth ready to close. Torelli's island lay apart from the others, invisible from the mainland. For two generations the Torelli family had utilized its easily defensible position as a refuge in threatening times.

The island enjoyed a natural fortification of powerful rocks reaching out from beneath the surface to slash boats attempting to land on its shore. One the size of the cruiser would have its bottom torn out if it dared venture within a hundred yards. Thus a mooring was relied on to hold the cruiser in place, and a dinghy was utilized to shuttle passengers back and forth from the dock.

The skipper left the dinghy tied to the cruiser instead of mooring it and hadn't even noticed his error until he was well out into St.

Andrew Sound. There was no sense in going back now. The effort would make him late, and his orders had stressed the importance of time.

As it was, the reinforcements were already standing on the dock at Crooked Bluff when he eased the cruiser toward them in the darkness. They stood side by side mechanically and might have been exact clones of each other if not for their different clothes. Some wore sports jackets and slacks, others jeans, and some even wore fatigues from their tours in the Special Forces. Their mixed bag of clothing indicated they'd been sent down on very short notice. The skipper wondered what made the woman back on the island so important that Torelli would go to such measures to ensure her safety. Christ, what did he think was coming?

The men looked impatient as he tied the cruiser down. He noted that the choice of weapons had been left to each one as well, a few hoisting gun bags or satchels with promised death inside.

"Your taxi is here, gentlemen," he said, immediately sorry for the humor when it produced no effect on the commandos. Speaking no further, he set off.

The night currents were slow, and the driver was glad for that much, for it made the journey quick and smooth. He reached the soft beacon over the cruiser's mooring in thirty minutes and tossed the line over to it. His passengers' eyes were on the rope as it looped over the mooring to anchor the cruiser, so none of them noticed the soft splash as a black figure slid over the side of the dinghy into the chill water.

CHAPTER 19

THE ISLAND'S COMMUNICATIONS CENTER WAS IN A SECOND-FLOOR den, a fairly elaborate setup that connected the man on duty with all patrolling guards as well as the cruiser.

"Come in, *Italia*," he tried again. "*Italia*, do you read me?"

Forty minutes earlier the cruiser had called to say it had picked up the reinforcements and was proceeding back. Since then there had been no word. The radio had been on the fritz not too long ago, so the man behind the console wasn't worried. The plan was for the *Italia* to call in for pickup by the Land Rovers after mooring up. If her radio was out again, maybe the passengers had just started walking.

"Patrol one," the man called to the jeep driver on duty by the fortress's front gate.

"I hear ya."

"Go down to the docks and check for the cruiser. She's overdue."

"Roger. Call you when I know something."

The man started his jeep down the island's single road, which wound its way through the brush straight to the waterfront. The best speed he could risk at night on the booby-trapped route was fifteen miles per hour. The road had been specially constructed to help ward off an attack from the beach. A vehicle trying for a faster speed would shred its tires on the jagged rocks deliberately placed on both edges of the narrow way. Even a vehicle driven slowly by someone unfamiliar with the terrain would be disabled.

The night was moonless and dull, and the man able to see little in front of him as he pulled onto the wooden planks that formed a pathway down the beach to the small pier overlooking the sea. As the planks gave way to the rickety wooden structure of the pier, he caught sight of the cruiser *Italia* tied out on its mooring.

"What the hell . . ."

Could have just arrived now, the man figured, shifting his jeep into neutral as he picked up the binoculars on the seat next to him, put them to his eyes, and turned the focus wheel.

There were dark shapes bobbing in the water.

There were more of them on the cruiser's gunwale and spread across the deck.

All dead, ten bodies at least.

Choking back his terror, the man went for his mike and had torn it from its stand when the hand latched on to his wrist. He tried to pull away, going for his pistol with his other hand, but the black figure that was suddenly over him pulled harder, and he felt the agony drive through his entire frame as the tendons and cartilage connecting his hand to his wrist snapped.

The pain slowed his reach for the gun. In the end he found its handle only when a second gloved hand jammed up under his chin, snapping his neck upward and back with enough force to tear it free of the vertebrae holding it. For one brief moment the man was aware of his head bobbing about like that of a top before the darkness closed over his eyes and the figure was forever lost from view.

"Patrol one, do you read?" asked the man on duty in the communications center.

"Cruiser's coming in now. Almost to the mooring," came the slightly garbled reply.

Damn radio again, thought the console operator. "I'll send the cars down."

"That's a roger," said Dreighton Quail.

Quail's battered Chevy had made Macon, Georgia, by dawn Friday, easily within range of the coastline by midnight or even an hour or so before. The journey east from Alabama had taken him down dozens of roads and freeways he had never used before, and the thrill was exciting, refreshing. Worried about time, he had actually driven an hour past the dawn, all the windows in the old Chevy sealed tight for fear some awful winged daylight creature would soar through and attack him.

The Dutchman wondered if the legendary Peet had taken most of his seventeen victims at night. Perhaps he had torn all the heads from their shoulders with the sun bearing witness. Either way, Quail was determined to go that one better.

He liked tearing his victims' hearts out. Using his hands. Always the hands, fingers being the key. Stretch out those hardened fingers and squeeze them together and they were as sharp as steel.

But not sharp enough yet. To better Peet, tearing a heart from a corpse's chest wasn't sufficient. Quail wanted to be able to drive his fingers straight into his victim, cracking ribs en route to the heart to be torn from the sinews restraining it while it was still beating and alive. Peet had waited until his victims were dead to twist off their heads. The Dutchman intended to go for the heart as the instrument of death itself, yank it out with the chambers still pulsing as if to move blood around.

Maybe tonight. Maybe the woman.

The Dutchman had reached Crooked Bluff not long after ten-thirty, already figuring that stealing a boat would be his only chance to reach the island. And that plan would have been carried out if Quail hadn't seen the large group of menacing-looking men standing impatiently on the dock when he arrived in the shadows. He blessed his fortune, not just because it was obvious that these men were here to be transported to the island, but also because it would provide an opportunity to kill such a large complement of the woman's guards in a short amount of time, a challenge that appealed to him.

He lowered himself into the water at the first sign of the cruiser's running lights, chose the moment when the soldiers were easing themselves from dock to deck to shift his frame over the dinghy, and covered himself with the tarp. The bumpy, uncomfortable trip bothered Quail very little, engaged as he was in considering his next moves. He had been told to expect upward of a dozen guards on the island, and this group doubled that number at the very least. If he could make use of the opportunity presented by having the passengers clustered so close together, though, the opposition's number would be halved again.

Quail would know what to do when the proper moment arrived. He had no use for guns. The only weapons he ever utilized other than his blessed hands were ones convenient enough to keep in his pocket, often fashioned by himself. He waited in the covered dinghy as the *Italia* slowed and her engines switched off, with the mooring coming up fast. Quail eased himself out of the dinghy and swam beneath the surface around to the cruiser's bow, where he poked his head over the gunwale.

The soldiers would travel to shore in the outboard dinghy in two shifts. The Dutchman was confident he could dispose of the first group of six and then the other before they even reached the island. In fact, he had to, because it was as a group clustered closely together that they were the most vulnerable.

The skipper was drawing the dinghy toward the cruiser by the attached rope when the Dutchman pulled himself onto the *Italia's* bow in a crouch. The toughest part would be to slither silently atop the precarious toeholds around the cabin to the deck where his victims lay.

Quail glided nearer the cabin in silence and pressed himself against its side. Six was going to be a tight squeeze in the dinghy, and three of the men had already lowered themselves into it. With six on board, space would be too cramped and the small boat too rocky to allow for any defense at all in the time he would give them. The key again was timing, to move between seconds, between the breaths and motions of others. Take the first six by surprise and then turn proximity against the six crowded into the dinghy.

As the sixth man started to step into the dinghy, Quail pounced. His leap carried him to a spot between the two soldiers at the rear of the deck, and before his feet had so much as gained purchase, he had a head grasped in either hand. Quail brought the two heads together hard enough to splinter both their skulls. There were no screams, but the deafening *crack* made some of the others left on board turn, and in the next instant Quail had already closed the gap, lashing out with a blow that shattered the windpipe of one. He spun next to snap the neck of the fourth man while still in motion.

The final pair still on the deck were smart enough to go for their guns instead of charging. Quail knew his quickest of lunges couldn't reach them in time, and there were still the forces in the dinghy to consider. As he rushed forward, his hands pulled from his pockets two small gray objects and hurled them at the two remaining soldiers. Like homemade arrowheads the objects were, his own unique variation. Miniature blades that were all edge.

One sank into a throat.

The other drove through a forehead.

The two men dropped in their tracks as Quail charged between them for the gunwale and the dinghy beyond.

The total assault had lasted barely seven seconds. Even fortune had proved his ally tonight, for the final man stepping down from the cruiser to the dinghy had lost his balance and fallen atop his fellows. The small boat's cramped confines allowed almost no space to maneuver, and the few soldiers who were able to draw their guns could aim only at a dark blur. The few shots that were fired struck nothing, and suddenly Quail was among them.

He had managed his landing in such a way as to ensure that the overloaded dinghy would collapse. As it started to turn, dumping the occupants into the water, the men's guns were spitting futile fire at nothing. The next moment all were thrashing about in the jet-black water, Quail's to take as a shark would.

The Dutchman had trained himself to hold his breath underwater for far more than a normal stretch of time. He dragged his first two victims down to finish them off the quick way, with a hand compressing each throat. When he resurfaced, he found himself attacked by another pair. He pushed one beneath the water and held him in a viselike grip between his legs. The other's skull he cracked with a single blow.

He saw the skipper's body floating near the cruiser and knew his head had been smacked by the overturning dinghy and he had drowned, which left two more soldiers alive. Both had chosen to flee, but neither was a strong enough swimmer to escape him. Quail caught the first easily and held him underwater until he stopped struggling and went limp, an easy kill. The second he caught only twenty yards from the dock and dispatched as quickly as possible because he knew the men from the fortress could be arriving at any time. He swam rapidly in and climbed atop the dock, saw there was no lookout, and turned to survey his triumph. A dozen killed in, how long? Two minutes maybe? Let Peet try to best that, just let him, Quail thought as the approach of the jeep forced him to shrink back into darkness to formulate the next stage of his plan.

Now he returned the microphone to its stand and propped the driver's body up in his seat so nothing would look strange to the drivers of the Land Rovers en route to pick up the arriving commandos. Two more men about to die, leaving ten perhaps.

A few more, a few less. It mattered not at all.

Lisa didn't know what it was that woke her, only that the digital clock on the night table read 12:06. For some reason she looked at the bedside phone as if expecting it to ring. Her mind slowly cleared, and memories were rekindled of the awful late-night call that had informed her of her father's death. The phone had rung, and she had known it was bad news on the other end, had resisted answering as if that might make it go away.

Now that same feeling returned to her in the coldness of this
strange room where she was a prisoner. She shivered and tried to
tell herself it was just the lingering effects of the nightmare Jared
Kimberlain had saved her from—saved her but not eleven employees she had watched die. Their ghosts lived in her memory, stole
her sleep, and threatened her sanity. So much violence, and so
senseless. They had died for nothing, and it was the feeling that
she was to blame that plagued her above all else.

But tonight there was more, though she couldn't have said precisely what. Outside her door Dom Torelli had stationed a gentle
brute named Chaney who could bend steel bars. Beyond him were
a dozen family soldiers, with at least that many more due in tonight
and maybe already on patrol. She should have felt safe.

But she didn't.

With the two Land Rover drivers dead back on the beach, Quail's
next step was to reach the grounds of the fortress. Clearly his best
bet was to make use of one of the Rovers to gain access.

Reaching the heavy steel gate fronting the wooden mansion would
be a simple chore, since the dark road led directly to it. His preliminary reports had included nothing about the jagged rocks lining
both sides, but his sharp eyes spotted these obstacles before he had
driven more than a few yards. After stopping to inspect them, he
slid along at ten miles per hour, allowing himself a bit more speed
only in the brief straightaways.

He was sweating horribly, and the layers of scar tissue he wore
for a face were sticking to the fibers of his chalky latex mask. The
mask could pose a real problem for him now. The guards at the
gate would know he didn't belong as he approached, would know
it even before they saw him, when they realized there were no
passengers in the Rover.

What then?

"Rovers One and Two, what the hell's taking you boys so long?"
the now familiar voice of the radio operator squawked through the
microphone.

Quail employed his seldom-used voice to grunt something about a mechanical problem in return.

A mechanical problem . . .

And with that he had his answer. The front gate came into view fifty yards ahead, and he flicked on the Rover's high beams to effectively blind the guards gazing outward. Next he probed under the dash and tore out the vehicle's ignition wires.

The Rover sputtered and ground to a halt, crunching hard gravel. Quail turned the key. The engine sputtered again, not even close to catching. But it made noise, and that was all he needed. He located the hood release and popped it, high beams left on to continue to blind anyone who approached.

He climbed down from the Rover and hurried to the hood, opening it all the way and crouching a bit so his vast size wouldn't be noticed until it was too late. He lowered his head way in toward the engine to further disguise himself and then waited.

He didn't have to wait long. The footsteps made crunching noises on the gravel. Quail didn't turn until the crunching had almost stopped, until the man was within easy reach. He had to wait for him to get right under the hood.

"So what's the tr—"

Quail's hand lodged in the soft flesh between the man's collarbone and throat, shutting his voice down and turning his face into a grimace. The pain made him scream; Quail wanted him to scream.

The man wailed again.

"Help!" the Dutchman blared now, sounding desperate.

The move achieved precisely its desired effect. The guard remaining at the gate rushed forward to provide assistance. Someone had been hurt, and hurt badly. Nothing else could account for that scream.

Meanwhile, Quail had slid his thumb over to the screaming man's windpipe and crushed it as soon as he was sure the second man was en route from his post. He timed his turn to coincide with the approach of the footsteps crunching gravel, timed it to perfection, smiling slightly as he grasped the horrified guard's head in one of his monstrous hands and smashed his face against the cooling engine. In the next instant, his free hand had brought the hood down on the back of the man's neck, and the crunch was almost as loud as that of the gravel compressing underfoot.

Two more dead, and Quail judged that there were perhaps six left.

He knew his time was limited. The screams would have drawn attention from those within the courtyard, who then might have relayed their suspicions to the communications center. But the night winds were his allies, camouflaging the direction of the sounds. Moving with those winds, the Flying Dutchman headed for the gate.

Lisa threw back the four bolts on the heavy wooden door. Pulling it open, she found the huge bearded figure of Chaney on his feet, his ear cocked.

"I thought I heard a scream," she told him, not caring if he saw her in the thin nightclothes she was wearing.

"Probably nothing. I'll check it out."

"You heard it too. That's why you're standing up."

"I heard something." And he started off.

"You won't go far," she called after him.

"I'll just go check things out. Won't be long. Bolt the door again. Don't open it for anyone but me."

Lisa wanted to tell him not to go anywhere at all, but instead she bolted herself back behind a ten-inch-thick solid wood door a grenade couldn't penetrate and tried to feel safe.

Quail wasn't going to enter the grounds through the gate. If the screams had drawn attention, that's where the remaining guards patrolling outside would gather, and he would be most comfortable entering through another route and then circling back to take them from the rear. The key was to keep them separate. A hundred men could be killed that way as easily as a single one if done so that one death did not warn of the next.

Ten yards from the gate, when he was just ready to veer off, the pair of flashlights grabbed his attention. One sprang from near the gate itself, and the other was halfway between it and the house and approaching. The snap of a lock being turned echoed in the night, and then the gate whined as it was drawn open.

"Yo, what's going on out there?"

The question was posed by the lead guard bearing the flashlight, a big man in dark clothing who was now starting cautiously down the road.

"Hey, you hear me or not?"

The man picked up his pace as if incensed by Quail's failure to answer him. The Dutchman slumped his shoulders, trying to look shorter. The guard stopped in terror when the flashlight caught his figure. He went for his gun, but the instant it took allowed Quail to rush straight up the beam. Needing to be quick, he killed the man in the same motion it took to toss him into the brush, then stooped over the body and retrieved the man's cap. He tucked it over his head as best as he could manage and kept his masked face angled down as he moved toward the gate, making himself stagger.

Again his timing proved perfect. The approaching guard reached the gate a second before Quail, shifting his flashlight to the turf as the wounded figure seemed to stumble just outside the gate. As the man reached for the latch, Quail flung his hands through the gate and brought the man's face viciously against the bars. He kept it there so the man couldn't scream while pulling one hand back and angling his fingers into a steel ramrod that bit deeply into the flesh of the guard's throat even as the second hand was already sliding down toward the latch.

"Everything's all right," Chaney told Lisa when he returned.

"How can you be sure?"

"The communications center hasn't had a single report of anything gone wrong. With a dozen guards out there, we'd know if something had."

"What about the other guards, the new ones?"

"Should be reaching the estate any second. Rest easy, miss. Nothing to fear out there except boredom."

Lisa noticed the walkie-talkie Chaney had clipped to his belt.

He followed her eyes. "Can stay in better contact this way," he explained.

"Which means you won't have to leave the door again."

"That's the idea, miss."

CHAPTER 20

QUAIL FOUND HIMSELF ALONE ON THE GROUNDS INSIDE THE fence and knew that all the remaining guards would be inside the house. One of them was sure to be mannning the communications center, and he was clearly a prime target. The Dutchman wanted time to deal with the woman as he wished, and an alarm sent to the mainland could bring help fast enough to make him rush.

Extensive and neatly manicured grounds enclosed the mansion. Clinging to the shadows, Quail eased himself toward the well-lit area of the main entrance, ears attuned to sounds of movement in case he had somehow missed any of the outside guards. Nearer the entrance, Quail crouched low. There were a pair of video cameras to concern himself with now, but with the proper timing he could reach the door by darting between their sweeps. Quail studied the cameras closely and, with their rotations spread widest, lunged.

The image on the video monitor looked like no more than a darkened shadow, a black splotch that went as quickly as it had come. The man in the communications room might have disregarded it altogether had not a red light and a warning buzzer alerted him to the fact that the front door had been penetrated.

"What the hell . . ."

His eyes swept across the other screens for hints of movement on the grounds among the floodlights. Nothing. No guards, no intruders. Why no guards, though? Could all of them be out of camera range at the same time?

Someone had entered the house, someone unfamiliar with the proper procedure for entry. It could have been one of the commandos just brought in and thus not briefed yet, but the console operator felt otherwise. No matter. The two interior guards were posted downstairs to handle any intrusion. The man flicked a pair of switches which brought the picture from the first floor onto two screens.

There were no guards visible on the monitors. *No one* appeared on the monitors. It was as if the intruder had moved between sweeps of the camera and used those motions to eliminate both interior guards in less time than . . .

Impossible! Or was it?

In the end it was a gnawing, all-encompassing fear that drew the man's finger to a small black button that would automatically send an emergency message to Dominick Torelli wherever he was. The boss would take things from there. There was help just minutes away once the signal got through.

The man had just pressed the button when the door to the communications room eased quietly open.

Lisa was seated in a chair facing the door when the knock came. She had only just given up her futile attempts at rest and dressed in jeans and a blouse.

"It's me, miss," came Chaney's now familiar voice.

She cracked the door open and gazed at his shadowy bulk in the dim light of the third-floor hallway.

"I'm having trouble with this box," he explained, pointing at his walkie-talkie. "Can't raise anyone."

"What should you do?"

"Check things out a bit. Thought I heard something a few seconds ago.'' The walkie-talkie was back in his belt in the next instant and a huge square pistol in its place. ''Lock the door, miss. I'll be right back.''

No, you won't, Lisa almost said, terrified by the certainty of her notion.

The black button brought no lights blazing or alarms shrilling, but Quail knew all the same that its signal meant trouble for him in the form of reinforcements of some kind. He killed the man behind the console by squeezing his headset well into his ears until the parted flesh swallowed the soft plastic ends, making them one with his skull.

His concern with the black alarm button had made him careless, though, and when he turned back toward the door, it was without proper consideration of his surroundings. He saw the gun come up before him and to the side, knew it was too late to prevent the shot and merely twisted to avoid the bullet as the large shape whirled before him.

Lisa heard the shot explode, echoing through the suddenly empty house. She waited as if certain there would be another, and when it didn't come she was unsure of what this meant in terms of her own fate.

The terror within her was more than a feeling. It was alive and moving through her stomach and chest, wrapping around her lungs as if to shut off her breath. She found herself standing with her back against the wall without remembering getting up from her chair.

She had to do something herself, and she had to do it now.

Quail's next conscious thought as the gun was pointed at him again was that its wielder was big, huge even, but still smaller than he was. He managed to lash his hand out in a blur and strike the gun on its hot barrel, surprising its holder with the power of the blow and tearing the weapon from his grip.

The man seemed fazed for only an instant, and he backpedaled agilely as the Dutchman lunged with his other hand. The man managed to deflect the blow with a lucky swipe, but the gun had been his only true hope, Quail knew, and he went for the kill.

Lisa sensed she was alone now and knew her best hope was that the killers didn't know which room was she in and would thus have to check each door before reaching this one on the third floor. She briefly considered taking her chances in the corridors in an escape attempt through the main entrance, but she dismissed the notion when she realized it was the surest way of delivering herself straight into their hands. Then she thought of the roof. Would that do as an escape route? No—the slightest slip and a three-story plunge would await her. The key was to make a stand, lay a defense here. Take advantage of what she had already and find more to add to it while she clung to the hope that help would be coming from the mainland.

First things first. Holding her breath, she unbolted the heavy wood door and grabbed hold of the chair Chaney had been sitting on outside the room so there would be nothing to make this one stand out from the others on the hall. This done, she refastened the bolts and went to her handbag. Fighting to stay calm, she rummaged through it as she went toward the bathroom. Since this was only a guest room, its medicine cabinet and the area under the sink were not terribly well stocked, but she would make do.

The best she could salvage for her planned use was a can of Lysol spray disinfectant and a jar of Crystal Drano drain opener. Working fast now, making every second count, she dropped a capful of the Drano in each of two heavy-duty plastic cups and then filled both three-quarters full of water.

The hissing started instantly, followed almost as quickly by the rise of an incredibly noxious vapor. The addition of water to the crystals created dangerous lye, and she placed the two hissing cups in different parts of the room equidistant between the door and the window. Still hurrying, she shook up the can of Lysol spray and left it on the bureau. She remembered that she had seen a cigarette lighter on the dressing table. She picked it up and put it on the bureau next to the Lysol. Then she again turned her attention to her handbag. Tossing the contents about, she came up with a nail file and a Cross ballpoint pen, the kind you twist at the top to make the hard steel writing ball emerge. Both able weapons but only in close, and if it came to that . . .

Footsteps in the corridor! Gliding more than stepping, and coming straight toward her door. Lisa held her breath and fought hard to still her shaking. At the last moment she jammed the file into her hair just above her ear and clipped the pen to her belt.

No longer hearing the footsteps in the corridor, she padded lightly toward the door with the Lysol can in one hand and the lighter in the other. She was testing the lighter, watching the flame flick high, when the door exploded inward.

True to his word to Kimberlain, Dominick Torelli had arranged for his private helicopter to take him to the island as soon as the evening's business was completed. The chopper was streaking toward St. Andrew Sound, with Crooked Bluff behind them, when the pilot handed him a headset.

"It's for you, boss!" the man shouted over the chopper's roar.

Torelli held the headpiece to his ear and mouth. He never spoke, just tossed the set aside, his face stiff with rage and determination.

"Step on it!" he ordered the pilot and turned to advise his bodyguards that he was leading them into a war.

Quail had known his time was severely limited, but he couldn't make himself rush. Such a huge house, so many rooms. Every door on both the second and third floors was locked, as he expected them to be, and looking behind every one would waste too much time.

But how to know which door?

The answer didn't come to him until he saw it. Halfway down the third-floor hall he found a pair of deep impressions on the carpet running down the center, as if a chair had been there until just minutes ago, occupied by a man of considerable weight. Quail smiled. The woman was clever to have removed the chair, but in that moment of cleverness had given away the fact that she was alone in the room.

Anticipation of the coming kill, of tearing the heart from her chest while it still beat, fueled Quail's strength, and he flung himself against the wooden door.

Lisa was conscious only of his shape when the figure crashed through the door. She had no true grasp of his size and features yet, other than the bare minimum required to aim the Lysol spray nozzle up and forward—at his eyes. She struck the lighter and sent the spray outward in the same instant his attention settled upon her.

Perfect.

She heard herself screaming as the stream of Lysol was turned into a blow torch speeding toward the figure's face. The flames illuminated it briefly before getting there and she noted, strangely, that it didn't look like a face at all. Worse, she had misjudged the figure's incredible size, so the flames reached him low and missed the eyes, striking lower around the nose and mouth.

Quail squealed in terror and agony as the flames struck him. His beginnings came back in the blue-orange flash, the night the flames had swallowed him in their fury and his new self had been born. But his new self couldn't be stopped by anything now, including flames, so he determined to race into the jet of fire, swiping at it boldly as if to knock the flames aside.

Lisa saw the arm flailing toward her and flinched, pressure on the lighter lost, reducing the Lysol to mere scent again. A pair of hands black with gloves were reaching for her as she abandoned the Lysol and reached toward the lamp stand holding the first of the plastic cups containing the liquified Drano. Her eyes were already burning from its hissing vapors as she drew it forward in line with the figure's face.

That face . . . There was something horribly wrong with the face.

The cup's contents sprayed out and forward. Some flew past the figure in black, but enough found his face to bring another scream and send his hands flailing up in the direction of his eyes.

I've done it! Lisa thought and started round him toward the door. She sensed that he was the only attacker, that he alone had somehow killed or disabled all the guards posted around her.

He reached out and grabbed hold of her just before she reached the corridor. Not a tight grasp, but firm enough to draw her back into the room and toss her against the wall near the window she had opened to allow some of the noxious Drano vapors to escape. Her eyes gazed up into a terrifying visage—what looked like white latex strips hanging from the monster's face. She knew now that it had been a mask the Drano had melted and not flesh, and what lay beneath the latex was . . . hideous.

In the darkness broken only by the spill of light through her window, Lisa could see that the monster had no face, just eyes pounded into something ghastly and unreal. She blessed the darkness for keeping that sight from her, but she couldn't prevent the bottomless scream that escaped from her throat. Despite the terror she managed to find and launch the second cup of her Drano mix straight at the monster's head.

Quail came straight at Lisa and saw too late that she had thrown another cup of liquid pain at him. Though he closed his eyes and turned his face, the agony burned this time into the side of his head, eating through his mask where it ran from his temple to the remnants of his left ear. He fought to ignore the pain searing his raw, nerve-exposed flesh, reaching again to grab as she darted toward the window.

To Lisa the grip that closed on her felt inhuman, for both its size and its strength. As the monster pulled her back into the room, she felt how useless it would be to resist and reached instead for the dagger-sharp nail file she had tucked behind her ear. In one swift motion she jabbed it as hard as she could into the monster's arm.

She missed her intended target as he yanked her mightily, but the nail file found the back of his huge gloved hand and dug deep.

He lurched sideways in pain, howling, past the window providing her best look at him yet.

Lisa gasped in horror.

No face, no face at all!

Before he could recover, she lunged again toward the window, and this time she got through it and out onto the sloping shingles of the roof. The mansion had roofs at different levels, which meant a leap would take her down one story instead of three. She couldn't afford to jump, though, for her momentum would certainly carry her over the side of the second-story roof as well. She had to maneuver in a manner she could control.

Lisa reached the bottom of the roof's slope and knelt down. Her intention was to grab hold of the rain gutter and then lower herself, greatly reducing the distance covered and thus the risk involved. She had started to ease herself into position when the monster's huge black hands grabbed her and flung her backward toward the window once more.

She landed hard and looked up to see the monster stalking her, angling himself so he could cut off her two possible escape routes. Whichever she chose—the ledge or back inside through the window—he could get there ahead of her. She found her feet again and then her balance.

Through the stillness of the night, a new sound reached her ears.

Wop-wop-wop . . .

A helicopter! It was a helicopter!

A beam sliced through the blackness, rapidly brightening as it neared the island, giving her a surge of hope. If she could avoid the monster for another minute or so, help would be here. But he saw it too and charged. Lisa tried to sidestep, but the slope of the roof betrayed her and she slipped, crashing hard onto the shingles. The dark shape loomed above her now, ready to pounce. The steady, vibrating *wop-wop-wop* of the helicopter was very loud, and the edges of its powerful beam were reaching the house. But none of that mattered, because the faceless monster was over her, his bulk blocking out even the night.

Quail hesitated, with his hand in the air. Tonight he was going to do it. Tonight he would call on the pain springing hot from his face and hand to tear this woman's heart still beating from her chest. He felt a hate for her like none he had felt before for any of his victims, because she had surprised him with her strength and determination to live.

His hesitation gave Lisa Eiseman the chance she needed to remember the Cross pen clipped to her belt. She grasped for it as a last resort as the monster uttered a throaty scream and started his hand down for her chest.

Lisa shoved the pen upward, steel ballpoint first.

The monster's blow pounded her ribs and knocked the breath from her body. But the blow had been slowed enough to save her at the last moment, when the pen lodged deep in the monster's throat. His eyes bulged as he swiped to tear it free. In the process he lost his precarious balance on the sloped roof and went tumbling.

Lisa watched him pitch over backward, heard the thud on the second-floor roof below, and found strength enough only to cry out. The helicopter had come directly over her, illuminating the whole back half of the house as it lowered, with Dominick Torelli already halfway out. Lisa slid to the ledge and gazed over into the light cast down onto the various roof levels and the ground below.

Nothing.

The monster was gone.

THE CHAMBER OF HORRORS

Saturday, November 21; 4:00 A.M.

CHAPTER 21

Iᴛ ᴡᴀs ꜰᴏᴜʀ ᴀ.ᴍ. ᴡʜᴇɴ ᴛʜᴇ ᴘʜᴏɴᴇ'ѕ ʀɪɴɢ ᴊᴀʀʀᴇᴅ Kɪᴍʙᴇʀʟᴀɪɴ from a restless sleep.

"I'm sorry for calling at this hour," Torelli said, and went on to provide an extremely brief summary of the night's events.

"I warned you."

"I've been punished enough already for not listening. Twenty-six of my men are dead."

"But Lisa's all right."

"Shaken and talking gibberish. Something about the man who attacked her having no face."

Kimberlain felt himself go cold. Quail! Peet had been right. Peet had known!

"We're trying to figure out how they got onto the island," Torelli was saying. "Helicopter must have spooked them, and they fled before we could—"

"Not 'them.' "

"What?"

"Not 'them,' not 'they.' Him, he."

"One man?"

"Just as Lisa said."

"Be serious. There isn't a man alive who could do what was done on the island tonight."

"His name is Dreighton Quail, also known as the Flying Dutchman."

Torelli hesitated. "You know him?"

"Of him, mostly."

"I'll move Lisa somewhere safer, triple the guard, bring in a fucking army, seal her in a vault if I have to."

"He'll get her. She needs something more than you're capable of providing, Dom."

"More than a friggin' army?"

"That's right."

"And I suppose you just happen to have it handy."

"As a matter of fact," said Kimberlain in spite of himself, "I do."

He had not been able to fall asleep again from the time Peet left the room. He could have rushed into the corridor seconds after him, had the hospital sealed and police on the premises within minutes. Or he could simply have waited and given the authorities the phone number Peet had given him. In the end he did neither. He tried to fall asleep again, only to dream different versions of the same dream every time he managed to doze off. In each he would awaken with Peet hovering over his bed with a vicious smile on his lips. In one the giant would be holding a gun, in another a knife; the weapon was different, but the intention was the same. Finally Kimberlain gave up and tried to keep his eyes open.

Why didn't I turn him in?

Because inside I know he's right.

Because I need him.

It was the second response he had dwelled on the most. If Peet was right and they *were* the same in more ways than they were different, that alone might have stopped him from calling the authorities. He hadn't killed the monster when he had his chance, and had chastised Kamanski and the system when they proved no more able to. Inwardly, though, he supposed he was glad when Peet had been spared, and perhaps just as glad when he had escaped. It was as if Peet provided scale, purpose, and definition to his being. Everything he had based his new life on concerned abstract differences between good and evil, extremes pulling and pushing, needing each other to justify themselves. But did good and evil exist independently, or were they simply differing interpretations of the same material, as Peet believed?

Kimberlain turned his thoughts to the practical now, still lingering on that second rationale for leaving Peet at large. He *did* need Peet, because Quail wasn't finished with Lisa yet, and Peet was her only hope of surviving his next assault. What was the phrase—set a thief to catch a thief? In this case it was set a monster to stop a monster.

But obviously there was something vital he was missing. The Hashi had tried to kill him at Mendelson's office and by extension were behind the murder of Lime and the others. Now, seemingly out of nowhere, the Flying Dutchman had entered the scene. Evidently he had been called in to finish a job the Hashi had bungled, and what Kimberlain needed to know was who had contacted him. Where was the link?

For the moment, Kimberlain gave up thinking and reached for the phone to dial Peet's number.

"You didn't tell me you'd called in Zeus, Jared," Kamanski shot out as soon as he came through Kimberlain's door later that morning. "You involved him in this, and you didn't tell me."

You don't know the whole of it, Kimberlain thought as he finished dressing. "You said it yourself last night, Hermes. We're both just private citizens now. Since we're facing far more than we bargained for here, I thought some outside help might come in handy."

"I won't work with him anymore. I can't believe you would."

"Don't compare my case to yours," Kimberlain said harshly. "My term was up; yours wasn't. You abandoned the old man at the first sign of the investigation. Didn't want to risk a blemish on your outstanding career. The FBI opened its doors to you, and you walked right on through. Zeus could have pulled the plug on you at any time, but he didn't, which probably means I had him a little wrong. *I* certainly would have." He started putting on his shoes, taking one of the chairs Peet had sat in the night before. "What have you got on Jason Benbasset?"

"What do you know?" returned Kamanski, glad to be off the subject of Zeus and the past.

"Assume I know nothing."

"Benbasset was a billionaire five times over, but one who was charitable and civic-minded on an international scale. Hell of a man. Three years ago on Thanksgiving Day he and his family fell victim to a terrorist bomb in the Marriott Marquis on Broadway, where they were spending the day. Benbasset was killed along with his wife, two sons, and a daughter. There was incredible damage—most of three floors totally wiped out. I'll leave you the file so you can go over the details for yourself."

"Now I know why it wasn't clear to me," the Ferryman realized. "It was just after Peet, and I was in the hospital. Were there any survivors in the family?"

"No. A bunch of Arab groups claimed credit for the bombing, and it's a safe bet one was responsible. Figured they had good reason since Benbasset was very big with the United Jewish Appeal and a public advocate for Israel. What the Arab bastards didn't know was that he had visited a half-dozen Palestinian refugee camps and was in the process of setting up a fund to care for them. He was a man who shot from the hip and didn't play favorites. He had a dream of world peace and was willing to fight for it. The fight died with him."

"Maybe not," said Kimberlain, not sure yet exactly what he meant.

Kamanski fumed in frustration when Kimberlain left the room soon after without offering an explanation of his plans. He told Kamanski simply to have the complete file on Benbasset ready for inspection by midnight, when they would meet with Zeus in an attempt to sort out what was going on. That gave the Ferryman nearly sixteen hours to accomplish what he regarded as an equally important task.

A rental car brought him to a private airfield in northern Massachusetts, where he arrived just in time to see Dom Torelli's private plane come in for a landing. He was out of the car and standing next to the runway by the time the jet squealed to a halt.

"I expected a larger reception committee," Torelli noted from the steps before allowing Lisa Eiseman to emerge. "If I was smart, I'd get back on that plane and take Lisa somewhere safe."

"The only place safe would be the sky, and sooner or later you'd run out of fuel. There's a different level," Kimberlain added, feeling the need to elaborate, "beyond all the commandos and Green Berets and hired killers. It's a level of existence where few men operate and even fewer are aware of."

"Yeah," said Torelli, his deep voice resonating. "I'm starting to figure that myself. See, I'm not crazy about handing Lisa over right now, and I wouldn't to any man but you. She's pretty scared, and as I see it you really are the only man who knows how to keep her alive, 'cause I gotta figure you're on that different level too." He hesitated, the next words clearly coming hard. "Last night, if it had been you after her on my island, things would be pretty much the same, wouldn't they?"

"Except she'd be dead."

"Yeah, I figured that too. Like I said on the phone before, I got the rundown on you. Pretty impressive, but I gotta figure it don't tell half the story."

"You wouldn't want it all, Dom."

"Maybe, but I still wanna help. Anything I can do, friend, you just name it.

Kimberlain named it.

Quintanna stood before the black curtain, waiting to be recognized. He had formed the lie over and over again in his head. No reason for the man to be told the truth, because the truth was inconsequential—as was the lie. He could not dare risk further disappointing the man who had brought him so close to achieving the goal he was born to achieve. The man needed Quintanna, but Quintanna needed the man more. There was still information to be passed on, information that was vital to the fulfillment of his goal. If the man denied it to him for any reason . . . Well, Quintanna had to avoid any distractions that might bring that about. The mystery of the man, the certainty of *his* goals, made him someone to be feared.

Beep . . . beep . . . beep . . .

"Good morning, Mr. Quintanna," the voice greeted finally.

"The woman is dead," Quintanna reported.

They reached the Maine Turnpike not long after noon. Lisa, who was sitting beside Kimberlain, was already calmer and more composed.

"Tell me more about where we're going," she requested.

"Fully furnished cabin nobody knows about in the wilds of Androscoggin County. I built it myself."

"But it won't be you who plays watchdog for me."

"No," Kimberlain told her. "Somebody just as good."

"That man from the island—you know who he is, don't you?"

Kimberlain didn't hesitate. "Yes."

"I want to know. I want to know everything you do about him."

"I'll tell you, but later. You have a right to know."

She smiled. "I was expecting an argument."

"Just being practical. It helps to understand what you're up against, who your enemy is."

"Spoken in the present tense. You think he'll be back, don't you?"

"If he can find you, he'll be back."

She almost chuckled at the flatness of his statement. "I'm not used to being around such honesty. Business world, remember?"

"I didn't pull any punches in Atlanta, and it wouldn't be fair for me to start pulling punches now, either."

She squeezed her eyes closed and held them that way briefly. "I didn't treat you very well at first. It's just that, well, I understood what you had come for, and I couldn't accept it."

"I came to help you."

"That's the point. See, the thing of it is, all my life I've never wanted to admit to anyone that I couldn't do everything for myself. That's why I don't have any maids or chauffeurs. Manage a five-hundred-million-dollar corporation during the day and go home to do the dishes. It was always me, just me, and that got magnified even more when my father died. Now all of a sudden the only reason I'm alive and hope to stay that way is because somebody else stepped into my life out of nowhere."

"There's nothing wrong with being dependent, so long as you pick and choose your spots."

"And who are you dependent on, Jared?"

"Lots of people," he responded immediately. "Most of them have plenty in common with you. They've been screwed around, and somehow they learn I'm out there and that I can help them. I'm dependent on them because they're my only shot at making up for the damage I did to the world during a period of my life I'd prefer to forget."

"So that's what I am to you," she said softly.

"That," he returned, "and more."

The cabin was located on a dirt road that ran off Route 121. The car bobbed and weaved, straining its shocks until they seemed useless. The cabin appeared as a dark splotch amidst the dwindling foliage, built to meld with the landscape in a way that made it hard to spot even when looking directly at it.

"Place comes complete with a forty-thousand-BTU generator, and the heat comes courtesy of a wood stove," Kimberlain said as he led Lisa toward the front door.

The air inside the cabin was musty, full of the smells of disuse.

They kept their coats on while the Ferryman tended to the wood stove, loading and lighting it.

"When was the last time you were here?" Lisa asked.

"Two years ago, maybe two and a half."

Kimberlain filled the generator with gasoline and got it started after only a brief struggle, while Lisa put away the groceries they had purchased on the way up. By 3 P.M. the fireplace and wood stove were both going and the temperature had risen enough for them to take off their coats. Peet would be arriving by five, and Kimberlain found himself eager to be out of this place he'd built to forget the pain of the Caretaker years and get back on the trail of the truth behind what was going on. At the same time, though, he was not so eager to take his leave of Lisa Eiseman. They settled down in front of the fire to warm themselves before going about the task of clearing the dust away.

She made him tell her about Quail and about how he had come to know him. The answers led to more questions about his years with The Caretakers and the scars left behind. Everything he told her had been told before, but never all to one person in a single sitting.

Their sharing should have remained merely verbal, of course; he hadn't expected or planned anything different, but he felt it start when their shoulders pressed together and he took her hand. He turned to find her staring up at him, and they kissed, wrapping their arms around each other. Lisa knew then that they would make love, knew she would enjoy it, but she wanted desperately to make it enjoyable for him as well. So in bed she teased and made him put off the final act of lovemaking in an attempt to be yet something else he would see himself having to overcome. She knew she had to appeal to this side of him if there was ever to be mutual desire, and the ploy worked beyond her wildest expectations. He returned her passion with even more of his own. Physically his capabilities were incredible. To give him the pleasure he needed, she had to reach deep inside herself for parts she didn't know existed. And at the same time she could feel him put all of himself into every motion, all of his vast being and power. His focus was singular. Anything he undertook he could only excel at. There was room for nothing else. Yet similarly she could feel deep down his discomfort with the motions, his virtual embarrassment that appeared in the pauses that came through their joining.

"It's been a long time, hasn't it?" she asked him at the end after they had moved back into the living area to be warmed by the fire.

"Since before I built this cabin." He thought for a moment. "Long before. I don't know, it just didn't seem important to me anymore. After The Caretakers, little did."

"Sex?"

"And love. Each person only has so much passion to go around, and it can be channeled to only so many different places. Maybe it's like a reservoir. When it's gone, it's gone. It can come back, but it doesn't always. After what happened to my parents, all of my passion went into The Caretakers and what they represented. And after The Caretakers, it went into the paybacks."

"You're using what you call passion as an excuse to avoid love. But it's not really love you're talking about, it's dependence, need. I know how it feels, because it's in me, too. There's always been a reason not to get involved, something else to do. Excuses, rationales. I always thought that by giving myself up to someone else I'd be weaker somehow, and I couldn't allow that, couldn't expose myself to that kind of vulnerability."

"In my business, vulnerability can get you killed."

"I wouldn't have thought the same could be said for my business, but . . . Just hold me, all right?"

Kimberlain did.

A car grinding down the dirt road announced Peet's arrival, and by then Kimberlain had dressed and was ready to meet him. It felt incredibly awkward to look at the giant as an ally, much less a sorely needed one. By force of habit he kept his distance, a fact Peet noted with the slightest of smiles.

He had told Lisa exactly who Peet was and what he had done,

and much to his surprise she nonetheless took to him from the start, utterly enthralled by his calm and charming demeanor. Peet still possessed the capacity for violence, but it seemed tempered by his ability to control it and this reaffirmed Kimberlain's decision to utilize his unique skills. Yes, he was leaving Lisa Eiseman in the hands of a man who had used them to kill seventeen people before he was caught. The hands might have been the same, but the man wasn't, just as the Ferryman wasn't the same person who had served with The Caretakers. If he could change, then why not Peet?

The sun was setting when Kimberlain zippered his jacket and walked outside to his car. Nearby, Peet was effortlessly chopping wood. Before moving on to the next log the giant swiped at it with his hand and tore off a section of bark.

"I would never do this to a still standing tree, Ferryman," he told him. "All that happens on the surface affects that which lies deep down."

"I assume there's a point to that."

"Be careful of what transpired between you and the woman before I arrived."

Kimberlain didn't bother trying to hide his shock. "Does it show that much?"

"To me it does. My concern is that its impression on your surface may have ramifications that run deeper."

"It wasn't something I planned," he said defensively.

"And therein lies the problem, Ferryman. Everything happens moment by moment, but each moment must be undertaken with an awareness of what will follow after. When all this is over, I must return to The Locks. You *must* return me. I know and accept that, yet here today we stand free as allies. Not that I will be any less free back in my cell, since freedom is a state of mind and not of being. The point is that moments create their own definition, and the woman you will see after this one will be a different person indeed. The Locks is my prison. But everyone has his own cell, which he must sooner or later return to or risk living in a state of limbo for eternity. I'm worried that you're starting to stray too far from yours."

"I'm keeping it in sight, Peet."

"Keep it in mind as well, Ferryman, for your own good."

CHAPTER 22

"EVENING, CAPTAIN," KIMBERLAIN SAID TO THE SHAPE HUD-dled in the doorway of Petrossian's, which occupied the ground floor of an ornate Beaux Arts building on Seventh Avenue and 58th Street. The exclusive restaurant had been officially closed for an hour, but since it was Zeus's favorite New York establishment, he had obviously arranged to borrow the premises for the meeting.

"Yo, Ferryman."

Kimberlain noticed that the captain was wearing just a denim vest over his shirt. "Bit nippy to be sitting outside."

"Wasn't about to go in there without you, boss."

"Then you're out of excuses."

They walked up a small flight of steps, which brought them to a large wood bar flanked by a deli cabinet filled with an assortment of chilled fresh and smoked fish. To the right of the bar lay the small dining area, fifteen tables at most. Seated at one, out of view from the street, were Zeus, his ever-present wordless hulks, and David Kamanski.

"Ah, Ferryman. On time as always," the blind man said. On the table before him sat a sterling silver tray that featured three different kinds of caviar. He packed another spoonful onto a triangle of toast lifted from a warmer that prevented sogginess and slowly raised it to his mouth, prolonging the motion. His lips were already smacking together in anticipated satisfaction. "Now look at me, forgetting my manners. Can I offer you some?"

"Maybe later."

Zeus finished chewing and then clapped his hands happily together. "Look at us, together again. Truly a joy! Old times rekindled. Truly!"

David Kamanski sloshed the ice about in his water glass.

"Nervous, Hermes?" the blind man taunted. "I elect to hold our meeting at one of the city's finest establishments so that we might enjoy a fine meal, and you arrive with the apparent conviction that the food on your plate has been poisoned and you will die from a single taste. As if you thought I was displeased with you for abandoning the network when you did. Not to worry. I was displeased with you well before that." Zeus went back to his caviar and toast points. "Where shall we start, Ferryman?" he said between mouthfuls.

"Where Mendelson's last words pointed us—Jason Benbasset."

"Then we start at a dead end," Kamanski said.

From his spot at the far end of the table, Captain Seven snickered.

"I don't think so," Kimberlain argued. "Three years ago Jason Benbasset appeared to be killed by terrorists. Their act turned all the good he had accomplished into a travesty. Now, in the last year, we've been faced with more than a dozen murders of leading industrialists all possessing a connection to the military community Benbasset blamed for the world's problems. You know how I feel about coincidence."

"Revenge killings?" Zeus said.

Kimberlain nodded. "Assume Jason Benbasset didn't die in that explosion. Assume he somehow survived, but his family was wiped out. What then?"

"He'd thirst for vengeance, in all likelihood," Zeus said.

"On whom?" Kimberlain asked Kamanski.

"The killers, of course."

The Ferryman shook his head. "Your field of focus is too narrow, Hermes. Benbasset would have looked at them as creatures of their environment, of civilization as it currently stands. So his vengeance would likely be much broader based. He blamed a militaristic form of thinking for much of the world's problems, so why not go after those he viewed as perpetuating that kind of thinking, people like Jordan Lime and Lisa Eiseman whose discoveries threatened to compound the problems."

"Yes," echoed Zeus. "Geometric thinking. I like it, Ferryman."

"Pure conjecture," said Kamanski, and Captain Seven snickered again.

"There's more," Kimberlain told him. "I had a conversation with Dominick Torelli earlier this evening. It seems that about a year after the attack on Benbasset, Torelli and several others in similar positions were approached about fielding an army of sorts. The links were tenuous, but they led back to Benbasset Industries."

"Which proves little at best," persisted Kamanski.

"You're not thinking ahead. You're not thinking at all. For a variety of reasons, Torelli and the others were unable or unwilling to meet the requirements specified. Benbasset was forced to go elsewhere: to a group willing to do anything if the price is right."

"The Hashi!" Zeus exclaimed.

Kimberlain nodded. "They were behind the bizarre killings you called me in on, David, but my guess is they were just filling out the specifications Benbasset gave them. Mendelson made the water cannon for them, and when he found out through us how it had been used, he became a potential liability. But the Hashi knew about the contact, just as they knew I'd be coming, so they didn't eliminate him until I arrived on the scene, because, of course, I was supposed to die too."

"Old hat," muttered Kamanski.

"Trouble is I *didn't* die," the Ferryman continued, "and their assassin let slip a clue to the next stage of the plan."

"A million will die in front of fifty million," Zeus intoned, "using the missing C-12 explosives. On what, though? Where will they die? And when? The only clue in our possession is Mendelson's penned-in-blood note your mystery woman made off with: '719, 720, 721 PS.' My people tell me it's mumbo-jumbo, something he didn't have time to complete before he died."

Captain Seven laughed, and all eyes except Zeus's turned toward him. "Your people got shit for brains, pal. Tell 'em to light up some lava bed smoke. Clear their minds real good."

"What is this man trying to say, Ferryman?" Zeus said.

"I'll tell ya what I'm saying," the captain replied before Kimberlain could break in. "The 'PS' stands for Penn Station. And '719, 720, 721' must be public storage lockers this doctor dude was trying to call your attention to. All you had to do was ask."

"I arranged for the bomb squad to raid the three lockers in question," Zeus told Kimberlain the next morning. They had met by the blind man's suggestion on the 86th-floor observation deck of the Empire State Building. Construction had closed it down temporarily but had ceased on Sunday. The outer promenade was torn up, with brand-new long-range viewfinders ready to be cemented tight.

The wind whipped through Zeus's surprisingly thick hair as he spoke. "Hermes will be delivering the findings to us up here. He's good at delivering things."

Kimberlain smiled at that. The old man loved manipulating, always had. Subtly, without notice or fanfare, Zeus was in control again. The old man returned his eyes, still encased in sunglasses, to the lenses of the viewfinder leaned up against the low wall in front of him. There was a click that Kimberlain knew signaled the end of the time a quarter had bought him, and one of Zeus's bodyguards came forward and inserted another.

"I was enjoying the view, Ferryman," Zeus said and swung toward him.

"I can see that."

"But I can't, can I? Blind since birth."

"So you tell me."

"But the mind has its own eyes, Ferryman. It can sketch any sight requested of it. Would you like to know what I do when I come up here?" He didn't wait for a reply. "I press my eyes against the lenses and have one of my men describe a sight or a building pictured beyond. I can see it in my mind, and I imagine I can see it through the lens as well. It's probably the same for you when you're inside the head of a madman you're pursuing. Your mind forms impressions based on available data, forms them so well that you know who or what you're facing before you even see, much less confront, him."

"It's important for you to understand that," Kimberlain said in what had started out as a question.

"You would have expected any different?"

"But it comes down to control again, doesn't it? If you can grasp how I work, then you're in a better position to exert your control."

Zeus turned away almost sadly. "I won't deny that that's so, but it's inadvertent. I didn't ask to meet up here for that reason. I have just shared something with you I have shared with no other man besides my guards. I wanted to make you a part of it because, goddamn it, I like you, and I want you to like me again." He paused. "During your final months with The Caretakers, I allowed the wrong people to provide my impressions. Yes, the form sketched was mine entirely and thus the responsibility mine to bear. But it is a picture I gravely regret now and realize how wrong I was in framing."

Kimberlain did find himself liking the old man and didn't bother resisting it. "There's more, Zeus."

The blind man nodded and tried not to look any more vulnerable than he had already. "The C-12 was my responsibility. A man can survive either by duty or by ideals, but disgrace strips away both." His dead eyes bored into Kimberlain's from behind the ever-present sunglasses. "If those explosives are employed as part of this master plan you believe is underway, then I will have nothing. You are the

only man who can help me, Jared. It's why I came to you to begin
with. It's why I wanted you to meet me up here this morning. So
you'd understand. You do understand, don't you?''

Kimberlain nodded very slowly and knew the blind man could
sense the gesture. He might have responded verbally if Kamanski
hadn't appeared through the doors leading out onto the west deck
of the promenade to join them.

"The lockers were empty," he reported, which drew a sigh from
Zeus. "But the C-12 had been inside them all right. The traces
were clear but fading. Report says they were emptied between forty-
eight and seventy-two hours ago."

"Any way of telling how long the explosives had been stored
prior to their removal?" Kimberlain asked.

"Best estimates say at least two weeks."

"The final missing batch of the C-12 was lost three weeks ago
almost to the day," Zeus noted gravely.

"They must have moved it when we started to catch on to their
plan," Kamanski said. "Your visit to Mendelson must have spooked
them because of what he might have said."

"Mendelson didn't know a damn thing about the explosives,"
Kimberlain said. "He must have used the same lockers as a drop
point when he delivered the unassembled components of the water
cannon. He was just trying to give us a lead. The C-12 being moved
had nothing to do with him at all. It was moved just as the schedule
had dictated all along."

"But that would mean it was going to be used here. In New
York."

"A million will die before fifty million," Zeus reiterated.

"That's right," the Ferryman acknowledged. "They'll die unless we stop it." He moved to the viewfinder and rotated it, with
Zeus's quarter still clicking away, until he found what he was looking for. "I couldn't figure out what Jason Benbasset was doing in
a rented suite at the Times Square Marriott on Thanksgiving Day.
It just didn't make sense until I read his file. The answer was in it
plain as day. Three years ago this Thanksgiving—next Thursday—

was the day he was allegedly killed. He and his family took the
suite so they could watch a parade go by down Broadway. Here,
see for yourself.''

All the breath seemed to leave Kamanski as he focused on the
view Kimberlain had left for him. "Jesus Christ, Jared. Jesus fuckin'
Christ.''

The sight the viewfinder was focused on was a bold marquee
with a banner running beneath it:

M
A
C
Y
'
S

THANKSGIVING DAY PARADE JUST 4 DAYS AWAY!!

CHAPTER 23

COMMANDER MCKENZIE BARLOW HAD DRIFTED OFF TO SLEEP IN his quarters on board the *Rhode Island* when he was jolted awake by the sound of the door bursting open.

"I'm disappointed in you," Jones said, closing it again so they were alone.

"Excuse me?"

"You underestimated me, Commander. I hate many things, but I hate being underestimated most of all. Others underestimated me once before, and soon they will be made to pay as well." His eyes had sharpened to match the edge in his voice. "Did you really expect me to allow you to send that follow-up message? Did you really expect me to believe that the 'repeat status grade' request from your COMSUBLANT had not been engineered by you somehow in a previous report so you could send a more accurate message to them?"

Mac felt himself go cold, the elation of what he had felt certain had been a successful ploy sliding down into his gut like a poorly chewed piece of meat.

"You told them your ship had been hijacked," Jones continued.

"Interesting code, the way it keyed off the numbers in the coordinates you supplied. Very simple to break, however."

"You switched off the sending relay," Mac said, suddenly realizing the truth.

"But I wanted you to go through with your show. I wanted you to feel the desperation you feel now in the wake of what you felt so sure was success. It hurts, doesn't it? I wanted you to feel that so you don't dare try it again." Jones paused. "Even if your message had gotten through, they wouldn't have known where to look for us."

"They would have known something was up. That would be enough for starters."

"Would it? I think not. They can't track us, and they have no conception of where we are because you don't."

"But since no reply was sent to their 'repeat status grade' request, they'll fear us lost. They'll comb the ocean. Sure, there's lots of water to cover, but at least they'll be trying."

"Trying to find a ship which by definition cannot be found. I'd say you've outsmarted yourself."

"Which places us in an interesting dilemma, Mr. Jones," Mac said, and he knew then that he was about to say more than he should. "If I don't give you the enabling codes for whatever reason you want them when we get where we're going, you'll kill my family. But in the meantime you can't contact the goons who are holding them while we're on deep lie passage, especially now that we're probably thought lost, which means I'm free to do anything I can to stop you before we reach our destination."

"You want me to tie you up, is that it, Commander?"

"You can't bind my mind, Jones, and even if you could, you wouldn't for fear of what the effects might be. I'm too valuable to you for you to take chances with my well-being. So you may have me by the balls, but my fingers aren't far from yours, either."

Mac had expected anger in response, even rage, but what he got looked to be sadness. "Keep reaching, Mac," Jones said placidly. "You won't find anything because mine had already been clipped off. Years ago. You think I don't know what it feels like? You think I took your ship simply because I was ordered to do so by some all-powerful force? I only wish it were that simple. But it can't be, because what I'm doing was set in motion so far in the past. Maybe this will help you understand,'' he said as he rolled up the sleeve of his charcoal-gray turtleneck. "Maybe this will make you see how similar we really are.''

Mac's eyes fell on what first looked like a blackened smudge just below the elbow but then sharpened into a swirl of letters that drove a numbing sensation through him inside and out.

It couldn't be!It just couldn't be!

He wouldn't have thought things could have got any worse, but they just had.

From the Empire State Building, Kimberlain went straight to Roosevelt Hospital, where Dr. Simon Kurtz, the assistant chief of emergency medicine, was waiting to see him. Kurtz had been the chief resident on duty the Thanksgiving morning Jason Benbasset and the others had been brought in.

"Do I remember that day?'' Kurtz asked, repeating Kimberlain's question as he shoveled the overly long hair from his forehead. "I still have nightmares about it. I never saw war, but thanks to that day I know what it must look like.''

"How many people died as a result?''

"I can only give you the figures from this hospital. A hefty number were taken to St. Vincent's as well. But there were thirty-seven DOA here, and another dozen within the next twenty-four hours. It was hell here. An ungodly mess.''

"Do you remember Jason Benbasset being brought in?''

"I heard talk. Never did examine him personally that I recall. No one was asking names. There wasn't time. And as for faces, well, several of the bodies brought in didn't have any to speak of. Benbasset was one of the DOAs, I believe.''

"He and the others, their bodies would have been claimed by the next of kin here, correct?''

"Or as close as we could find," Kurtz said. "Remember, a lot of the victims were from out of town. It wasn't pleasant making all those phone calls, and add to that the fact that identification in many of the cases was impossible."

"But all thirty-seven were claimed eventually."

"I can't say for sure but—"

"You can't."

"The numbers, I mean. I can check for you. It's all on the computer."

"Do it."

Kurtz turned to his computer terminal and started punching keys. It was two minutes before the information he requested came up on the screen. He looked at the white-on-green message quizzically, as if trying to change it with his eyes.

"That's odd," he said without turning back toward Kimberlain.

"What is?"

"It's probably just a foul-up in the paperwork, or maybe my memory's going on me, but I show only thirty-six bodies claimed from those labeled DOA. Hold on, let me cross-check the death certificates." A new set of letters and numbers appeared on the screen. "No, thirty-seven death certificates were issued for the DOAs, but only thrity-six bodies were claimed."

Kimberlain just looked at him.

"I don't know what you intend to make of this, but you weren't there. You can't know what it was like. There were hundreds of wounded that needed to be treated, on top of the dying and the dead. Mistakes could have been made, *were* made, I'm sure of it. People didn't have time to keep their clipboards up to date. It was inevitable that certain inconsistencies in the paperwork would show up, but they're meaningless, I assure you."

"Maybe," Kimberlain said matter-of-factly, pulling a photostat of Jason Benbasset's death certificate from his pocket and handing it across the desk to Kurtz. "I can't make out the signature on this."

Kurtz examined it quickly. "Howard Poe. He was one of the neurosurgeons on call that day."

"Where can I find him now?"

"Private practice on the East Side. Does quite well. One of the best in the business, most say."

Kimberlain stood up. "Thank you, Doctor. You've been very helpful."

"What was all this about, Mr. Kimberlain? What are you after?"

"Ghosts, Doctor."

Howard Poe had risen as usual on Sundays at ten A.M. He went into his study to switch on his stereo before doing anything else.

"Hello, Doctor," came a voice from a chair by the window as he reached for the switch.

"Who are you? How did you get in here?" he demanded, backing up toward the door. There was a revolver in the next room. But the stranger suddenly stood before him, and Poe's bravado vanished.

"What do you want?" he asked.

"To help you, Doctor," the Ferryman told him.

"What are—"

"Where did the money come from to start your office?" Kimberlain asked before Poe could finish. "I find the timing of your move to private practice interesting. Four months after a certain terrorist strike three years ago. You remember the strike, don't you?"

Poe's heavy swallow spoke for him.

"Your signature is on Jason Benbasset's death certificate. Only he didn't die. You or somebody else fabricated his death after somehow saving his life. Make a nice story for the newspapers. Maybe even television."

Poe stood very straight. "Are you here to blackmail me?"

"All I want is the truth."

"How'd you find out?"

"That's my business."

"Why is this important to you?"

"Stick to the issue at hand. You saved Jason Benbasset's life and then you signed a fake death certificate, correct?"

Poe winced. "I saved him, but then I . . . lost him."

"You mean he died?"

"I mean I lost him."

Poe told the story from a soft leather chair set next to a wall of cherry-wood bookshelves holding an extensive collection of leather-bound medical books. He still hadn't turned any lights on, and only a little sunlight penetrated the cracks in his half-drawn vertical blinds.

"I was working on another patient when a pair of men grabbed me. They seemed to know who I was—I don't know how. They said they were with Jason Benbasset at the hotel when the explosion happened. Or maybe they were waiting for him in the lobby—it's been so long I can't remember for certain. Anyway, Benbasset had just been brought in—or more accurately what was left of him had. His injuries were . . . extreme. He was behind one of the partitions, and as soon as I learned who he was I went to him immediately."

Poe stopped for a moment to take a deep breath.

"I looked at what was left of him and thought surely he was dead. He had to be, right to the glazed eyes. But then the eyes blinked. His lips moved. He was conscious, damn it. Don't ask me how. Medically I can't account for it, but there he was, trying to talk. I lowered my head so that my ear was next to his mouth, and I heard him speak. The words bubbled up inside him, but they emerged clear enough: 'Save me.' "

"And did you?"

"I tried. I'll spare you the technical details. There wasn't much left to work with, but with the help of machines I stabilized him. I tried to tell the two men how futile it was, how cruel it would be to prolong his pain when there was no chance of survival. But they were adamant. Obviously Benbasset had issued his orders to them as well. I've never seen such loyalty."

"It must have taken hours," Kimberlain said, "and required an entire surgical team."

"Right on both counts. We never could have spared it under the circumstances, but the men fixed things. I never asked how. I didn't want to know. In all the chaos, I suppose anything was possible. After I failed to persuade them against the surgery, one of them handed me a death certificate that had already been filled out for Benbasset. All I had to do was sign it, perform the operation, and I would be taken care of. I didn't really understand what that last phrase meant, so I stood my ground and refused to falsify a document."

The breaths were coming harder now.

"They pulled out a piece of paper with an address on it, the address of my current office. They said it and the practice of the man then occupying it would be mine if I signed. Beneath the note was a folded check. The amount was staggering. There it was, my dream placed within reach, and I grabbed for it because it didn't seem to make a difference. There was no way Benbasset could survive even the night. I wouldn't really be lying about anything except the time of death."

Now Poe's breathing slowed.

"After the surgery I went back downstairs and worked for hours more on the incomings. It was well after dark when I returned to Benbasset's room. He was gone without leaving a trace. It was as if he had never been there. No life-support machines. Fresh sheets on the bed. Nobody knew anything. I asked them. I confronted a few of the nurses who'd been on the surgical team. They looked at me like I was crazy, pretended they didn't know what I was talking about. That's what I meant when I said I'd lost Benbasset. Literally. I tried to tell myself he died after the surgery while I was downstairs. But then why would the nurses be covering up? Then I realized he *did* die. The death certificate with my signature was already filed."

Kimberlain assembled the facts in his mind. He looked for openings, holes in the story he had just been told. "Thirty-seven DOAs were recorded that day, but only thirty-six bodies were claimed," he noted.

"And I'm sure if you check the log at St. Vincent's, a similar anomaly will show up in the form of a body that vanished before the family could claim it."

"Then substituted for Benbasset's . . ."

"It wouldn't be hard," Poe said, "once they found a corpse with reasonably similar wounds. So long as the facial features were obliterated, no one would know the difference."

"You're telling me Benbasset survived. That's what all this comes down to."

"He survived that day, yes, but he couldn't have held out much longer. Physically it wasn't possible. There just wasn't enough of him functioning to support life. Both his legs were crushed. One of his arms was gone, and the other was close to it. The right side of his neck was . . . Well, you get the idea."

"Yes," said the Ferryman, "I think I do."

Kimberlain considered it all in the time it took the elevator to arrive and then descend back to the lobby of Poe's building. Jason Benbasset had survived the attack that claimed his family through sheer force of will, a will that would have formed a purpose for him in survival even then. Those who advanced the technology of the military would have to be punished for perpetuating the world that had destroyed him. On that level his desire for vengeance would be intensely personal, as if Lime, Lisa Eiseman, and the others had somehow rigged the bomb at the Marriott Marquis.

Benbasset's pattern of thinking was linear, predictable in the same ways as that of the killers he had stalked previously. Peet, Quail, and the others had created a purpose for their actions until the actions came to justify themselves. His strike on the Macy's Thanksgiving Day Parade would have evolved with the actualization of his own power. A symmetrical and logical progression culminating in a twisted but fitting end. The difference between the

madman and the sane one is that the madman can rationalize anything he wants to do and as a result can do far more.

The elevator doors slid open, and Kimberlain emerged into the
lobby. If all this was going to be stopped, the search for Benbasset
had to begin as soon as possible. The possibilities would be analyzed, reduced, investigated. A good start would lead ultimately to
a satisfactory finish.

The doorman was holding the door open for him, and Kimberlain
noticed that he was a different man from the one he had passed not
even an hour ago. He was already lunging for the man when several
others sprang forward from the lobby's recesses and alcoves. His gun
was drawn now, but the doorman managed to lock it against his body
as the figures converged upon him. The Ferryman felt the sting of
something in his shoulder and then the long fall into darkness.

In a month long past . . .

The Mind had stirred after fighting for rest. Long ago, in the first
life, its rest would have been called sleep, but the rest no longer
felt like sleep—it felt more like sliding into a daydream that runs
on and on. Often, too often, the daydream had presented surreal
visions of what had been, as if to taunt the Mind with memories of
what was now so far removed as to seem never to have been. In the
memories there was still the body, so incomplete, so utterly helpless against the shapeless wrath of man.

But the Mind wasn't helpless.

Of the moment when the first life gave way to the second, there
was virtually no recollection—just an instant of blinding heat and
somewhere deep the realization of a transition as intense in form
as it was in meaning. From the body's perishing, the Mind was
born. Since it could not feel, it feared nothing. It was immortal,
invincible, in search only of purpose. Often, though not often
enough at first, the Mind grasped its reason for being from the
dreamlike state it found itself drifting into.

There had to be retribution. What else could account for its very
existence? In the daydreams it could see those who had destroyed

the first life and brought the pain. But not its own pain. Something far beyond the body had been lost, something infinitely more precious. The Mind saw the faces and strove to touch them. It could not feel and yet it felt pain, and the only thoughts that eased the pain were of retribution. The makers of death would be vanquished, one at a time, in ways fitting the establishment of the madness they perpetuated. Not one would be spared. Not one.

For a brief time these thoughts served the Mind well. Yet the vastness of the retribution that was required soon mirrored that of the pain the Mind could not force from its being. It could not feel and yet it felt. A paradox. The memories conjured up the faces again and again, and perhaps it was the faces that at last showed the Mind how to alleviate the pain.

Where the pain had begun lay the means to vanquish it forever. *Yes!*

Another instant of blinding, terrible heat and the Mind would be soothed. Strange how everything had become so clear so quickly. With the craving for more had come more. Desire and attainment were merely different sides of the same coin.

The Mind's rage eased. It rested. For a time.

Because passion was fleeting. The coin had a third side in which satisfaction was again denied. More, always more. Each time one vision began to crystallize to soothe it, another began to take form, and the pain would flame anew, different yet the same. Pain from the first life that thrived on beyond the world the Mind had constructed for itself. Thus, the answer. It had escaped the first life, but the first life continued. Another paradox.

And with that the Mind had begun to ponder on the ways to resolve it.

CHAPTER 24

He wasn't sure what awakened him—not a sound so much as a motion, or a sudden change in it. He awoke to the awareness of figures around him, realizing it just too late to keep his alertness secret from his captors.

Those around him tensed and shifted uneasily.

All the men were seated, Kimberlain noticed, and some had twisted themselves around at strange angles in order to face him. This was a small jet, a twelve-passenger craft, with only four guards and himself presently seated. The motion that had stirred him had been that of the wheels locking down as they approached some airport in the night.

His head throbbed badly. He wasn't sure how long he had been out, but the effects indicated somewhere between six and eight hours, allowing ample time to fly to any number of places. But the darkness beyond the window was the late-night kind, which meant that perhaps he had been brought to Europe; the time change would account for the degree of darkness.

He didn't have to move much to find the tight wire binding him to the seat's arms. The slightest tug brought a grimace of pain to his face. Whoever these people were, they were experienced. All the rope in the world isn't as effective as well-placed wire across the wrists. If he pulled too strongly he'd run the risk of severing his own arteries. The guards would be needed for when the time came to remove these bonds—on the fast-approaching ground, perhaps.

The small jet's tires grazed the runway, and Kimberlain felt himself bounce slightly in his chair. He tensed, squeezing his hands tight to the arms to keep the wire from digging in, but his captors knew how to leave just the right amount of slack.

With the squeal of brakes in his ears, he looked around from one set of cold eyes to the next. The men's role had simply been to deliver him here from New York. Someone else would undoubtedly be waiting outside the plane. But not the Hashi, or he'd already be dead. Who then?

The small jet ground to a halt, and already his captors were positioning themselves strategically throughout the cabin to thwart any possible escape maneuver on his part. And if all else failed there would always be the wire laced to his wrists, with the other ends held by men who could disable him instantly if they needed to.

Wordlessly a pair of men beckoned him to rise after they disconnected the wire from the armrests; as Kimberlain had expected, each held one of the now free ends, almost as if they were leashes. Kimberlain rose, secure only in the notion that he would have been dead already if that was the ultimate plan for his capture. All he needed was time. If they were bent on keeping him alive, then the chances of escape were all the greater.

They were leading him toward the jet's exit door now. Another of his captors pushed it open to allow a flood of damp cold air to pierce the cabin's warmth. As he reached the door, one of the men holding the wire was starting down the steps while the other lagged a few paces behind Kimberlain. Arms thus forced into a spread, the Ferryman began to descend.

The throaty sounds of jets taxiing and taking off drowned out all others. A blanket of fog was draped over the scene, but a blanket not thick enough to obscure the lights in the back and foreground.

This was London's Heathrow Airport. They had taxied to a distant runway closed down by the fog. The damp mist chilled Kimberlain to the bone: any speed would be hard to summon, and he would need all he could muster when the time came. The procession moved onward, the pair of men attached to him by wires on either side and another pair keeping a steady distance to the rear. They knew who he was. They had been warned.

Twenty yards later, Kimberlain made out another series of figures through the mist on a runway standing near a similarly small jet. He counted five, but the mist was thickening and could have affected his vision. Drawing closer, he saw his original count to be correct, along with something else.

In the center of the group stood a woman dressed in slacks and a brown leather jacket. She was barely discernible through the thickening mist, which was starting to swallow the area, but Kimberlain could nonetheless see that her hair was blond and knew somehow that it was the woman from Boston, the woman who had taken Mendelson's dying message from him. Brutish-looking men flanked her at every angle—more deterrents against his trying anything.

Kimberlain's captors stopped when only a single macadam strip separated them from the group. The blond advanced a few steps. His eyes were drawn from her to the brutish-looking men. Something about the way they held themselves was wrong, the way they seemed to be trading glances with one another. The Ferryman realized the truth an instant before they broke into a spread, but the instant was long enough to take him into a dive beneath the first barrage of their gunfire, ignoring the pain from the wires tightening across his wrists. The roar of a jet hurtling into takeoff swallowed the blasts, so all that remained were orange flashes from the bores and the crumbling bodies of his two captors.

Kimberlain pulled free of their death grips and rolled toward the nearest of them with the wires dangling about him. The brutes were still firing, but their aim had turned on the pair of guards bringing up the rear, which gave the Ferryman the time he needed to tear one of his dead captor's guns free. Palming it, he realized the mist around him had turned thick as soup. He could hear the brutes shouting at each other in the confusion that had been created and wondered what had become of the blond woman who'd been at the forefront of the assault. It made no sense. She had let him live in Boston, only to have him transported across an ocean to be killed.

Behind Kimberlain another jet had just landed and had begun to taxi deliberately down the mist-shrouded runway. His first impulse was to fire back at the gunmen, but with his cover assured, escape was a far better option. He rushed in a crouch backward through the fog and cut a diagonal line to the passing jet. Bullets reached his ears as muffled spits, fired lamely, wildly, desperately, by men struggling to make themselves heard above the sounds on the tarmac.

The Ferryman reached the taxiing jet and sprinted alongside it for added cover. Holding his pace, he jammed the pistol into his mouth to free both hands for the chore of unwrapping the wire laced round his wrists—no easy task under the circumstances. He dropped the tangled wires and retrieved the gun from his teeth. The wet air invaded his lungs and nearly choked him. He fought for breath. The black cold chilled the sweat forming on his face.

The jet was swinging toward its gate now, and Kimberlain swung with it and then bolted away between another pair of jets with the red TWA emblem affixed to their sides. He made his target a door between the passenger jetways marked NO ADMITTANCE and charged toward it as fresh bullets found a bead on him. With the pursuit closing in, he took the final three steps in a single lunge, and as he yanked open the door a bullet tore off a huge chunk of wood just over his head. Before the next could find him, he had plunged inside.

The warmth of the terminal revived him, but the effect was short-lived. He leaped over the handrails of a moving footpath designed to help weary travelers more easily negotiate the lengthy walk to customs. Kimberlain was running now, weaving between just arriving passengers and hurdling over their carry-on luggage deposited on the moving walkway. An attempt to disguise himself by mixing with them would be futile, he reckoned, for his lack of an overcoat would betray him to his pursuers even before the lack of a passport to get him through customs and immigration did.

The Ferryman sped on. The warmth inside the terminal made his breathing easier. He had fallen into that state where desperation pushes out all fatigue. Behind him he could sense the pursuit accelerating, and he put on another burst of speed. To some he might have seemed an impatient traveler in fear of missing a connection. No one noticed the pistol he had wedged into his slacks back on the tarmac.

A swing to the left brought him down yet another endless corridor. His best chance lay in staying within the crowd for as long as possible and then dealing with customs when he got there. After that there would be taxis nearby, and once inside one he would be safe. This was London, after all—a friendly place for anyone who knew the territory.

He had reached the head of the procession of travelers by the time a quick descent and two more turns brought him to the customs station. The lines before the occupied booths were surprisingly long for this time of night. Kimberlain picked out an unoccupied one and sped through it, ignoring the shouts and screams at his rear from immigration officials. Baggage claim passed next in a blur, and several customs and immigration officials were still reaching for their walkie-talkies when he rushed by them. One stepped out in his path, and Kimberlain brushed effortlessly by him. To his rear the sounds of pursuit could mean either more authorities or gunmen following in his wake. No time to find out, and both were his enemies now anyway. The Ferryman sped out of Heathrow into the night.

A swift right up ten yards brought him to the taxi stand, where a number of the familiar square black English taxicabs sat lined up in a row. He plunged into the back of one and had pressed the pistol

bore up against the rear of the driver's head through the open plexiglass partition before the man could turn.

"Drive!" came his command.

"Just tell me where," the driver said fearfully, shifting into gear.

"London. The rest later. Fast now! Go!"

The driver obliged, streaking from his perch toward the lanes
that would take him from the airport complex and onto the M-4.
Kimberlain kept the plexiglass partition fully open so he was a grasp
away from the driver's head. The man had his window open a crack,
and cold, damp air flooded the cab's rear seat. The Ferryman settled back low, making sure only the cabby could know the gun was
still pointed at his head.

Questions raised on the runway returned. The whole incident
made no sense. The brutes obviously represented a different faction
from the men they had slain. And with that in mind, which faction
did the blond belong to?

No matter. He had other thoughts to concern himself with. London was a haven for power; its finer hotels catered to it. Several
maintained a code to be passed at the front desk in an emergency.
Do so and a room would be his without pain or record of registra-
tion. A room and, just as important, a phone.

The cabby was pushing his car fast down the M-4. It was almost
midnight, and the huge motorway was eerie in its near-emptiness.
Kimberlain's head was throbbing with pain and fatigue. His wrists
were scraped raw from the effort untangling the wire had caused
during his rush down the tarmac. Whatever they had given him to
knock him out was still in his system, and he had to battle the
lingering effects of that as well. Each car that passed them revived
his senses with the rising of his neck hairs.

Kimberlain stretched his legs out all the way in the spacious rear
of the cab. He was beginning to think he might have outrun his
pursuit by the time the driver turned off the M-4 onto Kensington
and the last leg of the journey in the damp London night. The cabby
gazed back as if to ask for further instructions.

"The Hilton on Park Lane," Kimberlain told him.

Minutes later, they caught up with Park Lane traffic and made their way toward Hyde Park Corner. The towering Hilton was just across the way. Kimberlain breathed easier as the driver swung into the hotel's private circle. The cabby had started to brake when the Ferryman spotted the two figures flanking the revolving doors.

"Keep going," he told the man as he hunched low.

"Sir?"

"Drive!" he said while sinking still lower as the doorman approached.

He could have been overreacting, yes, but something about the two figures seemed wrong to him. Instinct had gotten him this far, and he had learned always to trust it. The driver swung out of the Hilton onto a side street and then turned left onto Piccadilly. There were other hotels available to him, but if the Hilton was under watch, why not the others? And if all of them were under watch, that meant the opposition's resources were incredible and . . .

The Hashi! Here! After him now!

Kimberlain was starting to rethink his next move as the cab eased by an underpass and slid to a stop at a red light. It gathered motion again only long enough to reach the next traffic light at the corner of Half Moon Street.

A pair of headlights flashed in the rearview mirror, and Kimberlain noticed they had approached much too close. He was halfway to the cab's floor when the back window exploded. The cabby's head rocked forward, then back, blood splattering the cab's inside and spraying up against a closed section of the plexiglass partition. The light had changed to green. Automatic fire continued to pepper the interior.

Rather than stay a sitting duck for the gunmen, Kimberlain steeled himself for an offensive response. With bullets still thudding as the trailing car pulled alongside to complete the job, the Ferryman came up and pushed himself through the narrow partition separating him from the front seat. He reached for the cabby's leg with one hand and the steering wheel with the other, abandoning his pistol in the process. The killers' car had pulled up next to the taxicab by now, bullets continuing to stream inward, when Kimberlain jammed down on the cabby's knee to force the accelerator down. The cab screeched and shot forward through the intersection. The trailing car was momentarily left behind, but it gathered speed and caught up quickly. Upholstery exploded in bursts of fluff, and the rest of the windshield disappeared. But Kimberlain let the killers draw right up along his left side before swinging the wheel hard and fast that way.

The killers' car was midsize and dark, no match at all for the heavy bulk of a London cab. The cab sideswiped the lighter vehicle, and Kimberlain kept the wheel turning in, forcing the killers onto the sidewalk and straight toward an office building on the corner, just past a Mercedes-Benz dealership. The gunman in the rear fired until the very last moment but succeeded only in pricking Kimberlain's face with splintered glass. The front end of the lighter car crashed through the front wall, shattering glass everywhere, and ending up half inside, with its front end compressed like an accordion. The Ferryman managed to right his cab into a spin which took it across Piccadilly. It had barely come to a halt before he was out through the open rear window and moving again.

Horns honked from all directions; people were shouting and screaming. If more of the killers were about, he was too easy a target out in the open. The Green Park underground station had an entrance a block or so back that was camouflaged well enough in the darkness. Kimberlain weaved through the snarled traffic and rushed back toward it. He took the stairs leading down quickly and lunged through the entrance without bothering about a ticket. A swing left and then right at the bottom of the first set of steps brought him to a group of people heading for the Jubilee Line, which was as good as any for an escape route from the area.

He took the last staircase at a dead run, ignoring possible pursuit from the rear and focusing on the thundering train he had to catch. The doors had just started to close when Kimberlain surged through them and pressed his shoulders hard against the wall to steady himself. He had caught his breath by the Bond Street stop and his senses by Baker Street, where the exit of all the remaining passengers told him this was as far as the train went at this hour. He eased himself out among them, trying to feel if any of the Hashi had managed to follow him this far.

He slid past a man checking tickets and after a short climb emerged into the well-lit sanctuary of Marylebone Street. He started walking, eyeing the dome-shaped figure of the London Planetarium and its famed neighbor, Madame Tussaud's Wax Museum, just across the street from him. He crossed over with the intention to continue walking until he had enough time to consider his options.

The Ferryman had passed the Planetarium and was moving by the advertising windows of Madame Tussaud's when the figures came around the head of the building thirty yards in front of him: coming down the street, coming too fast, hands starting into their jackets. Behind him he caught the clickety-clack of heels gathering pace, heels that had just turned onto the street from his rear. They had him boxed in, and there was no reason for them to rush, since there was no place left for him to go and his gun was back in the abandoned taxi.

Suddenly the group-sales door of the Wax Museum opened and a nighttime janitor started to come out with a garbage can. Kimberlain spun to his left, and in the next instant the janitor had been shoved aside. He was still fighting to regain his balance when the Ferryman sprinted up a set of stairs past a wax couple eternally greeting patrons, even tonight well after closing time.

Another staircase lay down the hall past the right-hand ticket booth, and Kimberlain charged up it into the center of Madame Tussaud's.

CHAPTER 25

KIMBERLAIN STUMBLED IN THE DARKNESS BROKEN BY THE SPILL of light from exit signs. He tried one of the doors only to find it locked and its steel-reinforced construction against fire impossible to shoulder through. He spotted another door and emerged into the darkness of the Tableaux, the section of Madame Tussaud's reserved for historical figures. Suddenly the dim overhead lighting snapped on and he found himself face to face with a lance-bearing guard in a Civil War exhibit. The Hashi had turned the lights on to aid their pursuit, and he could hear a pair of them following his path up to the Tableaux, trying the same doors he had. There would be many others, with different routes of approach chosen to cut him off from all possible avenues of escape. As the nearest footsteps came closer, he knew his first stand would have to be made here. A weapon. He needed a weapon.

Giving the matter no further consideration, the Ferryman stripped the ten-foot lance from the wax guard figure and took up a position to the side of the door. He tested the lance's balance. It was a weapon meant to be wielded by the strongest of men. Its heft did not please him but its blade still held a rusted edge. Kimberlain held it with hands spread down the center of its shaft at waist level.

The first Hashi came through the door well ahead of the second, instantly finding the Ferryman's shape in the dim light. Kimberlain brought the flat edge of the lance blade up under his chin, stunning him, then rotated the weapon so that the lower portion of the wooden handle cracked against his skull. The man slumped directly into the path of the second Hashi following in his wake. The second man hurdled over him and lunged into the Tableaux firing a pistol. But Kimberlain had shrunk back into the flowing robes of Mary Queen of Scots, and by the time the killer might have noticed, the lance was coming at him. The man gasped as the ancient blade parted his midsection and wedged stubbornly in bone.

More footsteps thundered up the staircase, and Kimberlain started on again, stopping at the figure of Guy Fawkes leaning over one of the kegs of gunpowder he had sought to use to blow up Parliament more than three centuries before. The gunpowder was only a prop, of course, but the sword sheathed in his belt was as functional as the lance. Kimberlain tore it free and rushed toward a shaft of white light coming from a doorway at the other side of the Tableaux.

The light came from Madame Tussaud's Conservatory, which was devoted to a collection of figures from the entertainment world. With the footsteps pounding fast after him now, Kimberlain had time only to drop down behind the figure of a constantly smiling, saluting doorman on the right of the raised entrance just inside the doorway. When the first of another set of Hashi passed through the doorway, Kimberlain tipped the doorman over to distract him while he whipped Guy Fawkes's sword in a slash across the throat of the second Hashi, who staggered backward with blood jetting between the fingers he had futilely raised to stem the flow. By now the first Hashi had shoved the figure of the doorman aside and was swinging around with his pistol raised. Kimberlain held his ground and lashed out with the sword blade. The Hashi killer wailed horribly as the edge sliced across his brow, blinding and disabling him. The gun slid from his hand, and he stumbled forward directly into the path of a bullet fired by a third Hashi who had entered the Conservatory through a door on the other side of the hall.

The Ferryman dove over a white wooden railing rimming the entry pedestal as the killer's pistol continued to spit. The head of one of the Beatles, who'd been propped up on the railing in a display, was obliterated, and Kimberlain took cover behind a white piano between two more of the famed quartet.

More bullets cascaded against the piano as a second Hashi gunman joined the first from the Conservatory's other end. The impact rocked it slightly, and Kimberlain heard footsteps pounding between the shots as the Hashi charged forward to better their positions. Above him, one of the downed men's pistols lay teetering on a step. He managed to grasp it as fragments of the stairs exploded around his wrist. Kimberlain fired twice and knew he at least had the gunmen pinned. But time and position remained on their side, especially since the gunfire would attract more of them to provide the reinforcements needed to finish him.

Kimberlain could see only one possible means of escape, and he seized it. He lowered himself against the piano and stretched the pistol around its side to keep the pair of Hashi in place while he thrust with all his strength against the frame, right shoulder shoving to supply momentum. Instantly the piano's wheels began to turn, and it picked up speed quickly. Kimberlain kept firing, and by the time his clip clicked empty the piano had crashed into the white pedestals the gunmen were using for cover. The pedestals toppled, and the piano went after them, with Kimberlain heaving it upward at the last moment. The force of his lift carried the piano up enough so that its top-heavy weight smashed down on both Hashis' faces, and only their feet were left exposed.

The Ferryman grasped one of their still-smoking pistols as he found his balance and bounded through the remains of the Conservatory up a set of steps past a grinning Telly Savalas. Near-darkness welcomed him, and he found Sylvester Stallone staring down from one side and Grace Jones from the other. The leather-clad Jones exhibit featured a heavy chain draped in front of it, and Kimberlain tore the chain free before continuing on. He had a gun now, but using it was the surest way of alerting whatever Hashi remained to his precise location. A better strategy was to keep his kills and disablings as quiet as possible while he searched for a way out.

He had lost count of how many he had felled already and how many more might remain. This was the Hashi he was facing, after all. They had been prepared for him in London, an army marshaled in expectation of his arrival. He was facing at least a portion of that army now and had to remain patient if he expected to leave the museum alive.

With the chain in one hand and the pistol in the other, he passed into another darkened exhibit hall that mainly featured music superstars. Slinking on, he had just registered the fact that the dark, bearded figure holding a machete on the pedestal diagonally across from Michael Jackson was out of place when the figure leaped at him, blade glinting in the dim light. Kimberlain got his gun up, but a sharp clang sounded as the edge of the machete grazed it, separating it from his grasp. The big man whipped the blade around again, and the Ferryman ducked so that Michael Jackson caught the brunt of the blow. As the singer keeled over, the song "Thriller" began to play.

The man was quick to launch another strike, and this time Kimberlain deflected it to the side with his chain. The Hashi quickly swept it at him in roundhouse fashion, but Kimberlain was equal to that as well, backing off with his chain spread wide between his hands. The big man came in with an overhead strike, and Kimberlain caught the blade in the center of his chain and twisted his hands to lock it tight. Forcing the blade down, he tried for the big man's head with an elbow, but the Hashi twisted to avoid the blow and the result was a stalemate as they grappled across the floor toward a statue of David Bowie. With Michael Jackson silent, Bowie was now shrouded in theatrical smoke, as "Changes" played in the background.

The big man was fighting to work the blade free when Kimberlain noticed the duct beneath Bowie's platform through which the fake smoke emerged at regular intervals. The blade was almost free of the chain binding it when Kimberlain realized he had to change his strategy. With one eye on the duct, he released his hold on the machete. A slight *poof* signaled that more of the smoke was about to emerge in the instant the Hashi brought his blade overhead for another strike.

The Ferryman let him bring it down, whipping the chain up against the steel at the very last instant to knock it aside. The big man regrouped quickly, but the momentum of his blow had forced his upper body and head downward so that in a perfectly timed motion Kimberlain could force the head down still further toward the duct belching smoke.

The Hashi's huge eyes were bulging when the noxious smoke found them. He screamed horribly as his lenses seemed to catch fire. But his screams were cut short when Kimberlain worked the chain up and under his neck, jerking and pulling until the snap came and the dead Hashi sprawled on the floor.

Kimberlain headed on after retrieving his pistol. Finding an exit was still uppermost in his mind, and now he left the half-dark of this gallery in favor of a winding descent down a staircase layered in pink, the light brightening as he approached Madame Tussaud's historically elegant Grand Hall. The light would help him find an exit, but as he emerged into the hall he saw that once again his plans would have to be rethought.

Hashi with guns drawn were coming in his direction in a silent spread from the opposite end of the Grand Hall. They must have emerged from the cavernous underlayer housing the Chamber of Horrors, those at the head just now making their way around a display of Charles and Di's wedding. Kimberlain dropped to the floor and crawled on his elbows to an exhibit of Henry VIII and his six wives—the close proximity of the figures allowed for excellent camouflage. He crept between the figures of Jane Seymour and Catherine Parr and rose up just enough to steady his gun and eye between them.

Out of view from his position was the doorway across the Grand Hall which led down into the Chamber of Horrors. The chamber's darkness was what he needed now most of all in order to find an exit. For the time being, though, he had the light to contend with, and creating confusion among the approaching Hashi was his best chance of countering it.

The Ferryman could see eight of the Hashi mixing among the historical figures, only their movement betraying them. They had chosen a wide, defensive spread to keep him from a rapid assault but had limited their own options in the process and left him with a vital one. One of the Hashi slid cautiously behind a pedestal displaying current leaders of European nations and moved right into Kimberlain's line of fire. He sighted carefully and fired once, then immediately went into motion to take full advantage of the distraction and resulting confusion. The Hashi all turned first in the direction of the shot's origin and then toward the downed gunman, who had taken the wax figure of Helmut Kohl with him to the floor, but by then Kimberlain was frozen behind the draping robes of an Arabic national leader display. In all the chaos they could not possibly pick him out before his next shot. The key was to fire at targets as far away as possible to keep them off guard.

A Hashi padded toward him. The Ferryman didn't dare turn. He knew his strategy would have to employ a double, almost simultaneous kill now. He held the pistol at hip level, tilted up—a difficult shot. Across the hall a Hashi moved toward the kneeling figure of William the Conqueror. Kimberlain righted his pistol and fired.

The echo of the shot had barely sounded when the Ferryman turned quickly toward the Hashi who was standing with a clear view of him. The man had just realized the shot's origin and was bringing his own gun up even as the dead Hashi across the way collapsed across William. Spinning ever so slightly, Kimberlain turned his gun on the man and fired his last bullet, in motion before the reality that he was now weaponless again had a chance to sink in. As the man fell, shots began to ring out everywhere, Hashi screaming into the silence that had prevailed just seconds ago. Kimberlain used the chaos for the cover he needed and crept behind more of the wax figures, continuing on toward the doorway that would take him into the Chamber of Horrors.

* * *

The staircase wound dark and low. At the bottom a bell chimed, stunning his ears and making him swing wildly around. But it was just a sound prop. Gunshots thundered and again he spun, this time to find a Gary Gilmore figure acting out a firing-squad sequence. He swung away from that and came face to face with an electric chair sizzling to accompanying flashing lights. He started forward when a wax newsboy's call almost cost the figure its head.

"Extra! Extra! Read all about it."

The Ferryman realized happily that the sounds of the Chamber of Horrors made the best camouflage of all, for it negated anything that the ears of the Hashi could tell them once they reached this level. He moved slowly on through this waxwork testament to the macabre. Beneath him the tile flooring changed to cobblestone, and a fake mist rose through a brilliant reproduction of a Victorian London street where Jack the Ripper's next victim lay eternally in wait and a past one lay dead in an alley with a waxen hand clutching at a steel rail. The sound of a horse-drawn carriage was real enough to make him gaze over his shoulder as he passed by the front of a dimly lit pub called the Ten Bells, complete with laughter and the sound of mugs clanking together or on tables. The clippity-clop of the horse-drawn carriage sounded again but was intermixed this time with very real footsteps coming rapidly down the stairs he had just descended.

Kimberlain looked into a reproduction of a small bedroom containing a cowering child long enough to dismiss it as a hiding place, since it was too confining. Much better was a musty, dust-covered stairway featuring a pair of body snatchers sinking low to hoist up a crate containing their latest theft. He hurried up the steps and crouched down behind the display.

An instant later a flood of at least a dozen Hashi poured through the Chamber of Horrors and down the cobblestone walk, but they were distracted by the colorful sights and sounds. One yanked open the false door of the Ten Bells to find only partial figures and painted shadows within. Another ducked into the small room Kimberlain had dismissed for refuge and kicked the cowering wax child aside to search under the bed. The Hashi were obviously confused, thrown off the track of what should have been a logical and successful pursuit. They continued on, certain Kimberlain must have as well. On the chance he had not, though, guards were certain to have been left behind in case he backtracked. Stalemate again, and it would continue until ultimately their superior numbers wore him down or he made a mistake.

Kimberlain searched the walls and ceiling for a smoke detector. If he could set one off somehow, help would be here in minutes. But no smoke detector was in sight, which left him with . . .

Yes, he reckoned, just one bit of strategy left to him. They had him boxed in but would never expect him to turn the tables by following the ones who had preceded him through the rest of the Chamber of Horrors. Soundlessly the Ferryman glided back down the steps, leaving the body snatchers to themselves, and started on through the final stretch of corridor with his back pressed as close to the wall as he could manage.

The wall ended in a death's row prison display, and he went through it quickly, with Charles Manson the last on his route before he came to another set of stairs leading back up to the ground floor. Near the stairs was a set of double black exit doors, and next to them was a red fire ax in a rack. He was thinking of using the ax against the doors to burst free when footsteps closed on him from behind. Those who'd been laying in wait had grown impatient, or perhaps had stayed the specified period of time before joining the chase. Kimberlain had to move.

Cannon fire burned his ears as he sped into an exhibit immortalizing the Battle of Trafalgar. A gun deck complete with cannons shifted back and forth in rhythm with the blasts, and soot-blackened men manned them in the darkness splintered by eruptions of white smoke. Kimberlain leaped onto the platform and crouched in a dark corner near a pile of cannonballs.

The cannons continued to recoil and the taped cannon fire to sound as Kimberlain watched more of the Hashi pass by, unable to spot him in the lifelike scene. To survive, he had become part of a living exhibit to soldiers and causes long dead, and, though the irony struck him, for now there was only his own cause to concern himself with. His escape might be as close as the fire ax and the black exit door. He eased himself carefully along the rear of the exhibit, watching to avoid the recoiling cannons, and then cut quickly to the front railing, climbing down as close to the exit as he dared. He was reaching up for the ax when the double doors slammed open and the emergency signal began to wail nonstop.

And directly before him stood a blond woman in a brown leather jacket who had by now become very familiar.

CHAPTER 26

"**Y**OU!" WAS ALL HE COULD MANAGE AS HE RUSHED THE FIG-
ure who was standing as rigid as one of Madame Tussaud's figures.

"Hurry!" she said, beckoning to him. "We've no time!"

Kimberlain was already through the doorway, grasping her at the
neck before she could counter, death a twist away.

"We're not enemies!" she gasped. "Please, you must believe
me! We can get out of this, but we've got to move!"

As if to echo her point, bullets split the cold air around them as
the alarm bells of the museum continued to shriek. In the next
instant, lacking another choice, Kimberlain found himself running
with the blond woman by his side. There were more shots in their
wake, and he longed for a gun of his own, though he wasn't sure
if he needed it for the Hashi or this woman. They sped across the
street and down a narrow alley, both running mindlessly, trusting
their fate to a strong will and an even stronger head start. The
minutes were as difficult to measure as the distance, since their
route was erratic, crisscrossing over some streets they had passed
before. But gradually the sounds of pursuit lessened and then
ceased. They emerged at the outlying reaches of Hyde Park near
the Marble Arch and then made their way back to Bond Street,

where Kimberlain let the woman lead him down the steps into the underground.

She had reached the automatic ticketing machine when Kimberlain grasped her harshly by the arm. "I'll give you as long as the ride to explain who you are."

"We'll have the whole night for explanations, Ferryman, and we'll need it."

The car was virtually abandoned. They had a dozen seats all to themselves.

"My name is Danielle."

"That doesn't tell me who you are."

"I'm many things. I'm—"

His face showed disgust. "Please, no riddles." He grabbed her again at a pressure point in the shoulder, intense pain just a squeeze away.

Danielle didn't so much as flinch. "Hurt me if you want. It doesn't matter. I've been hurt before."

"Why did you save me at the museum after setting me up back at the airport?"

"I *didn't* set you up. My team was infiltrated, compromised. I was supposed to die too." She stopped, as if expecting him to interrupt. When he didn't, she continued. "I'll start where this began for me. I orchestrated a raid on a Hashi stronghold."

Now he did interrupt. "You *what*?"

"Let me start here, *please*! The rest can come later. For now just accept what I'm telling you."

"The Hashi don't get raided every day, miss."

"Just listen! During the raid certain information was recovered. That information led me to Boston, to Mendelson—"

"And to me."

"Coincidence, unless I miss my guess. We're pursuing the same thing along different lines. That's why we needed you."

"So you kidnapped me."

"It was the safest approach. To understand, you have to learn the truth at the source, not from me."

The train slid to a halt.

"We get off at the next stop," she told him. "Charing Cross."

"The source?" he asked.

"Hardly. That will take until morning. The fallback plan is already in place."

The train was moving again. An older couple and a pair of teenagers had entered the car, the teenagers complaining that the ticket clerk hadn't believed they were under sixteen.

Danielle lowered her voice. "We can help each other. We *must* help each other."

Kimberlain looked at her coldly and released his grip at last. "What I *must* do is get back to America to stop a madman from murdering a million people on Thanksgiving and then fig—"

"What . . . man?"

"How could it matter to you?"

"Because this million you refer to must be just the start," she said.

A train rumbled over the tracks perched on the underpass they were approaching in Charing Cross. Huge steam vents blew hot exhaust air into the otherwise cold night, making this a haven for the city's destitute and homeless. The authorities had managed to shoo them away successfully for months, but the problems raised by that policy were greater than those they solved, so London had relented and the home of the homeless had become just that again.

"We'll hide here until morning," Danielle said. "There's no choice. The Hashi will still be everywhere. If we're lucky, they won't look here."

Kimberlain agreed with her assessment and followed her toward the smoldering fires and the boxes many of the bums used for sleeping quarters. The stench as they approached was stifling, an amalgam of odors from cheap whiskey to urine to vomit. Even the smell of the greasy restaurants nearby seemed to settle here.

Another train pounded overhead.

"What happens when morning comes?" the Ferryman asked.

"A plane out of Gatwick. We could try for it now, but I'm not sure I could raise the pilot. Besides, morning will bring crowds, and it will be easier to hide. The Hashi may have given up the chase."

"The Hashi *never* give up the chase."

"You've dealt with them before."

"Not as much as you have, apparently."

They stopped at a large box set slightly apart from the rest. Kimberlain took his cue from Danielle and reached his hand into the box's dank innards. He grasped a leg and pulled at it.

"Hey," came the whining, drunken protest. "Get out now. My box. Mine!"

Kimberlain stuck his head into the stink and made sure the meager light showed the five-pound note handed him by Danielle. "I want to buy it from you," he offered softly.

"Huh? Who the bloody hell are . . ." Then the bum saw the note and made a move to snatch it.

Kimberlain pulled the bill back. "Out of the box first."

The bum dragged himself from it, no possessions in hand other than a soiled green department store bag—Harrod's of all places. Kimberlain gave him the five pounds. The bum noticed Danielle and started to speak.

Kimberlain grabbed him with a suddenness that tore his breath away. "Not a word."

The bum shuffled off without looking back. Danielle worked her way inside the box and made room for Kimberlain. The box was barely large enough for one person, never mind two, and the stench was revolting. She stiffened as the Ferryman brushed against her, and they settled on their sides facing each other a hair's distance apart.

Danielle pulled a pistol from a holster in her boot and handed it to Kimberlain. "We should both have one."

His surprise was evident. "Surprised you didn't show one of these before."

"We're on the same side, as I told you."

"But approaching from different perspectives."

"Yes. What led you to Mendelson?"

"A water cannon he developed that was used in a bizarre murder."

In the darkness he saw her nod. "A similar device was used to drill the pipeline for Spiderweb. It led me to him as well."

"Yes, he mentioned something about that. But what is this Spiderweb?"

"An installation of oil fields in Antarctica."

"Oil fields? You're telling me all this is about oil fields?"

"Only to a point. There are pieces here, fragments that by themselves add up to nothing. You have some, I have others. We must put them together."

"Fine by me. Just don't try and tell me a million deaths don't mean anything."

"Most of them will die anyway."

"No more riddles!"

"Give me time, please. What brought you to that doctor in New York? What were you after?"

"A dead man."

"Now who is posing the riddles?"

"Not me. Does the name Jason Benbasset mean anything to you?"

Danielle seemed to shudder. "Billionaire philanthropist killed by terrorists three years ago."

"Only thought to have been killed. He was blown up all right, but he didn't die. His 'death' was engineered. He wanted to disappear, and not for the happiest of reasons, I'd imagine."

"My God," she said, almost gasping. "It fits. It all fits. Stone mentioned his name. He was part of Spiderweb from the beginning. That's how the Hashi were privy to the details." Her eyes flashed in the darkness. "This million, when will they die?"

"At the Macy's Thanksgiving Day Parade, the site of Benbasset's apparent death three—"

"And the meaning of that note I took from Mendelson's office?" she broke in.

"Lockers in Penn Station that were used as a drop point for Mendelson to deliver the water cannon, used subsequently to store the plastic explosives to be utilized on the parade."

"Then we have barely four days. Quicker than we expected."

"Who exactly are 'we'?"

"An order whose sole reason for existence is the ultimate destruction of the Hashi. In that raid I told you about, pages were salvaged from a fire. Plans mostly. One set for Outpost 10, the main station of the Spiderweb oil network. The other was a set of blueprints for the prototype of the new class of super-Trident submarines."

"You're telling me the Hashi are planning to go after a *nuclear sub*?"

"I'm telling you they must already have it. The timetable you just detailed assures it."

"What timetable?"

"Thanksgiving Day. The end will come then."

"End of what?"

"The world, Ferryman, as it is presently known."

They were silent for a time.

"So we've got a bunch of Antarctic oil wells and a nuclear submarine. Mind telling me how that adds up to the end of the world?" Kimberlain said finally.

"That can be explained better tomorrow."

"Yes," he said, nodding. "Your plane at Heathrow tonight was meant to take me somewhere else."

"Malta."

"Why not just fly me there direct?"

"Our standard security dictated a change in personnel. Those involved must have their knowledge kept to an absolute minimum."

"Rather intensive operation."

"With good reason. We're vastly outmanned. The slightest leak under normal operating procedures could destroy us. You saw what happened tonight. In spite of all our precautions we were infiltrated, and now everything has changed as a result. The remainder of the order has gone underground. There are only the two of us . . . and one other."

"In Malta, of course."

"He'll explain what I've been unable to."

"But he won't know about Benbasset either, will he?"

"No," she said distantly. "I suppose he won't." Then, even more distantly, "The irony of Benbasset hiring the Hashi to do his work for him . . ."

"Why ironic?"

"Because it wasn't terrorists who were behind that bomb blast. It was the Hashi."

"How could you know that?"

"Because I was part of the team."

Danielle hadn't intended to tell him the story. It emerged in spite of herself, as if someone else were telling it. She had heard of how the Ferryman was spending his days now, settling the problems of others who sought him out with their lives and their trust. She had heard about what had led him to this and thought perhaps he had found a better way than she to give back some of what he had taken. For the same reason, she believed he would understand her better than anyone else. He was the first person to have heard her tale from start to finish. A confession was what it amounted to, but it did little to purge her. It was more important that someone—that *he*—understand.

"I never even conceived it could be like that," he said when she had finished. "The Hashi socializes *children* who know no better into killers."

"They choose their subjects carefully, ones they feel they can motivate, and of these only a tenth at most actually become soldiers. The rest, well, in times past they might have become slaves or servants, but these days they just disappear.''

''How civilized.''

''And as such for centuries—since the Crusades,'' she told him. ''Hired assassins, the first terrorists, trained almost from the cradle. Back then women were impregnated just to supply more potential soldiers to the Hashi cause. The cause,'' she added bitterly, ''was everything.'' She paused. ''The end for me came suddenly. I guess it started with the Benbasset bombing in New York, but I didn't realize it until after. My next mission came three months later. In Lebanon. Even that connection was meaningless in itself, a stray thought lost in a past that had ceased to exist . . . until we reached our target: a refugee camp.''

''My God.''

''Maybe it was the Israelis who hired us, or more likely someone who wanted the world to *think* it was the Israelis. Everything was ready. We were going in commando-style against hundreds of unarmed, hungry people. I watched them inside the camp and I started remembering. It was like recovering from amnesia. They had taken my mind, but they hadn't totally taken my memory. The machine in me seemed to die. Most of the people we were about to massacre were kids, damn it. Kids! I looked in there and saw myself fifteen years before. Then I remembered the incredible carnage that followed the bomb blast in New York. I didn't know so many would die; I swear I didn't. I didn't even know there was such a thing as a Thanksgiving Day parade. But in that last moment before our commander gave us the order to attack the refugee camp, I superimposed what I had been part of in New York over what I was about to be a part of in Lebanon. I couldn't allow it, not by me or anyone else. I shot the commander in the throat. Then I killed the rest of the team. It was over very fast. You might even call it a payback.''

Kimberlain strained to see her in the darkness.

''The camp was a panic. The shots scattered the occupants everywhere, and again I could see myself the night the Hashi came for me. I started running. I knew I had nowhere to go and had sentenced myself to a life on the run—and, worse, a life without purpose. I had disavowed everything I was, and before that I had been a nameless nothing.'' She hesitated long enough to take a deep breath. ''But there was someone else in the area of the camp that day, a man who'd been tracking our team with the intention of doing what I had done, a man who was part of an order bound to destroy the Hashi, just as the Hashi were bound to disrupt the orderly flow of civilization for profit. In his words lay a new purpose. He gave me what I needed. He made me one of them.''

''One of what?''

''The Knights of St. John.''

Kimberlain's eyes widened at that. He was familiar with the Knights of the Order of St. John, just as he was familiar with all great warrior creeds throughout history. Left in 1565 to defend Malta's Fort St. Elmo with 120 men against 10,000 marauding Turks, they held the invaders off—incredibly—for thirty-one days. Many referred to that as the birth of guerrilla warfare, because the knights employed strategies such as mining the harbor with chain mail and swimming out beyond the Turks' lines to toss makeshift bombs onto their decks. The drawn-out seige marked a major failure in the attempt of Sultan Suleiman I to destroy Christianity with a spearhead group of Ottoman Islamics he had joined forces with and who had gained legendary fame during the Crusades—the Assassins, often referred to as the Hashi, shortened from ''Hashishi'' for their purported use of the drug hashish prior to entering battle.

The Knights of Malta, as they were also called, had handed the Hashi their worst defeat ever but been wiped out themselves in the process, only to reappear in later years as a mundane religious order with all warrior ties lost. At least, that had been the tale.

''A pair of knights survived,'' Danielle continued by way of explanation, ''and vowed to secretly rebuild the order in its original form, with only one task in mind: to destroy the Hashi forever. Their fervor waned somewhat with the defeat of the Ottoman Empire, as the Hashi retreated into the shadows. But the vow lived on to be passed from generation to generation, though the knights were more watchdogs than warriors then, until the last twenty years have returned the Hashi to prominence.''

"Terrorism," Kimberlain said.

"Exactly. They were available for hire to anyone who wanted them and had the funds to pay. They broadened out and set up chapters of their perverse society in every major and several minor countries. They formed a subculture of sorts, thriving beneath the surface without the world knowing. They had no politics, but they provided an inexhaustible supply of manpower to groups such as the IRA, the PLO, Black September, the Red Brigades. They've become professional terrorists, not even worthy of being called assassins anymore.''

Kimberlain nodded, recalling similar words he had spoken to Zeus while he was still with The Caretakers. "I knew they were out there, but I never got close enough, never found hard proof. All I had was innuendo. No one believed I could have been right.''

"Which has served as their greatest ally for a thousand years. People won't believe in them, so for all intents and purposes they don't exist. But something changed. We uncovered their stronghold in Nice because suddenly they had begun to surface, leaving a trail where none had ever been left before.''

"Think about it," Kimberlain said. "Benbasset sought them out to be of service to him, but I'm betting they agreed to do so only for a unique fee. Imagine a group like the Hashi emerging *prepared* into the ruins of the world Benbasset's plot leaves behind. That's what the surfacing you referred to must be about. They have to surface in order to be ready when the time comes. It's like being at the point of Suleiman's charge again, except this time it's not just Christianity they're trying to overrun, it's the whole world.''

"You're giving them credit for principles they no longer possess.''

"Why wouldn't they, or at least enough of them? If enough of the Knights of Malta have managed to stay true to their cause for over four hundred years, why not a similar number of Hashi? The world in the wake of whatever Benbasset's got in store for it would be a world made for them.''

"I'll accept that, but it still doesn't explain Benbasset. If he plans on destroying the world anyway, why bother with a separate plot aimed at the Macy's Thanksgiving Day Parade?''

"For the same reason he bothered killing a number of industrialists with links to the military. I've had some experience with this type of thinking before. The ends were different, but the thought processes were much the same. Basically Benbasset isn't a paranoid or a psychotic; he's an obsessive, and an obsessive nature requires escalation. All this must have started with the notion of the murders. But even as he planned and began to initiate them, they were no longer enough. So he turned his attention to the event in which his family was killed, Macy's parade, not as replacement so much as extension. From there his field of focus widened to the whole of civilization he had lost faith in. Why not punish the whole of it? The extension was logical in terms of its progression, and Benbasset won't pull back, even if he knows we're on to all phases of his plan, which may give us our only chance to stop him.''

"And yet he's really not much different from you or me, is he?'' Danielle said. "Both of us are here now because we're trying to make up for the way we led our lives in the past. In the context of the time, they weren't mistakes, but the context is meaningless. We've all formed our own versions of paybacks, not trying to right the wrongs but at least pursuing a balance.''

"And that's where we all go wrong, because the scales keep shifting.'' He remembered something Peet had told him. "The mistake we too often make is to try to escape from our prisons instead of making do with them. Everybody is searching for something, and when they find it, they search for something else. I used to drive myself crazy trying to put a number on how many paybacks it would take before I had fulfilled my purpose. I'd gone from being the prisoner of one sort of morality to being the prisoner of another. My actions have been basically the same; only the justifications have changed. And even though I realize all that, I can't lie here and tell you I have any regrets, because at least I can sleep straight through the night now without waking up in a sweat like a kid out of a nightmare. But it was worse for me, because I could never remember the last thing that had been in my mind. It was buried so deep, I kept losing it.''

"Charon was never this philosophical when he ferried people across the River Styx.''

"He was seldom as busy as I've been lately.''

The Mind had been torn. The problem, it realized, lay indeed with the first life. But not just its own. The instant of blinding heat had birthed the second life and the truths of a new level of consciousness. Yet the pain had remained, so more than another instant of blinding heat must be required to accomplish what it had to in order to find the peace it sought.

So simple! So obvious!

Civilization's first life had failed and desperately required a second one for the whole of it. The Mind looked to fate, and fate looked back. Just as clear as the necessary ends were the means, drawn from the shadows of the Mind's memories from the first life. How fitting that such a marvel of the first life should hold the means for giving birth to civilization's second. Indeed, in the Mind's perspective this was a birth more than a death, or birth *out of* death.

At last the relentless, raging pain of its thoughts were soothed. The faces no longer haunted the dreamlike state it called sleep. They had shown it the way, and the Mind understood that fate was not only looking but smiling.

Finally the Mind rested.

THE KNIGHTS
OF ST. JOHN

Monday, November 23; 8:00 A.M.

CHAPTER 27

THE FLIGHT BY SMALL PRIVATE JET FROM LONDON TO LUQA AIR-port outside Malta's capital of Valletta took three hours, proving as uneventful as their post-dawn trek to Gatwick had been. Kimberlain had by then resigned himself to not learning the final details of Benbasset's plan—the connection between the hijacked sub and Spiderweb—until they reached their final destination.

The explanation came a half hour later, after a drive through the comfortably cool Maltese air. A car had been left for Danielle at a prearranged spot at the airport. She pulled it into a space just beyond the courtyard of St. John's Cathedral and led Kimberlain toward the steps fronting the building. The cathedral had been built in 1577 as a testament to the great siege of the Knights of St. John and to this day retained all of its simple yet majestic elegance. A pair of bell towers, one adorned with a huge clock, rose over the facade on either side. The entrance was between a pair of bronze cannons Kimberlain wouldn't mind restoring to add to his armaments collection. The bizarre mixture of the military and the religious, he supposed, was part and parcel of the Maltese culture.

Danielle led the way up the marble steps, beneath a portico supporting a balcony, and into the cathedral itself. Its depth and beauty

257

struck the Ferryman instantly. The cathedral's high, narrow vaults towered over the nave's floor, which was covered entirely with multicolored marble atop the tombs of the Knights of St. John, their individual, distinctive coats of arms creating the effect of a massive stone carpet. The ceiling was rounded and equally glorious, separate ribbed sections extending like a tunnel toward the choir. The nave was virtually deserted, but Kimberlain watched Danielle eye the few apparent tourists warily.

Running down both sides of the nave were carved archways leading into the cathedral's separate chapels. The third bay led to a flanking passage connecting with the building's south wing and the Oratory of St. John. The oratory wasn't as long as the nave, but it was just as wide, with pews on both sides and an aisle running down the middle toward the altar. Several people were seated, some in positions of prayer. Danielle walked straight down the aisle until she came to a monk in brown robes kneeling half out of the pew and half in it. She signaled the Ferryman into the row behind him, and seconds later the monk crossed himself and slid backward until he was occupying the aisle seat next to Kimberlain, with Danielle on the other side.

"Hello, Ferryman," he said softly. "Know me as Brother Valette."

The monk had taken the name of Jean de la Valette, who had led the original Knights of Malta in battle back in 1565, and Kimberlain wondered if he might be an actual descendant.

"We must be quick about this," the monk said. "There is little time, and as Danielle has no doubt explained, our order has been compromised. Trust no longer exists. It is, must be, just the three of us."

"You're the leader of the Knights," Kimberlain concluded.

"And you are a warrior of legend, Ferryman."

A group of choirboys, dressed in white robes, made their way down the center aisle. Brother Valette was silent as they passed on their way to the choir stalls near the altar, and Kimberlain used the opportunity to study him where his monk's cowl allowed inspection. His was an old face, but tanned and vital, the eyes a piercing green. It was a face that showed none of the desperation present in his words.

"I assume Danielle has informed you of the scope of what we are up against," Brother Valette resumed.

"Pieces. Fragments."

"All she was made privy to, I'm afraid. She passed on the information. The conclusions were left to us."

"Concerning the connection between a stolen nuclear submarine and a secret network of oil installations."

"Such fragments are joining to form a cataclysm such as no man has ever seen. Are you familiar with the Book of Revelation, Ferryman? The Apocalypse?"

"A little."

"Before each of the seven great woes, a trumpet blast was heard. The eighth is about to sound now." He shifted to face Kimberlain more directly. "Something called Outpost 10 forms the heart of Spiderweb eight hundred miles from McMurdo Base beyond the Transantarctic Mountains. Pipelines five to ten feet in diameter lead in and out of the complex, worming and weaving their way across much of Antarctica."

"Crisscrossing the continent like veins," Kimberlain elaborated.

In one of the choir stalls by the altar, beneath a huge red tapestry combining an ornate crucifix with the Knights of Malta coat of arms suspended from a chain, the boys' choir had begun warming up their voices.

"But the continent is fragile," Brother Valette was saying. "The many levels of ice, some as thick as three miles, account for its vast weight and mass. Only Dr. Mendelson's water jet system made it possible to lay the Spiderweb pipeline without disturbing the delicate environmental balance, but it also created a deadly vulnerability."

"To be exploited through the submarine. But how?"

"I'm not sure, but it must be the missiles."

"Procedure on board any Trident requires four men to use their codes before firing can take place. I can't envision how the hijackers' plan could assure that."

"You miss my point. If they simply wanted to fire the missiles they could have done so from the sea, perhaps already. The key must lie with Outpost 10 itself. Utilize its status as the central control station to somehow destroy the pipeline—and the continent along with it. Imagine Antarctica fracturing along the lines of Spiderweb the way porcelain breaks on ancient fracture lines when dropped. The Eighth Trumpet, Ferryman, at the very least."

On the choir platform, the boys were fishing through their robes for their music sheets.

"I know a man who can get the entire 82nd Airborne to Outpost 10 overnight," Kimberlain said, thinking of Zeus. "We've got three days, assuming Benbasset sticks to his progression."

The man dressed as a monk looked almost relieved. "You can see now why it was crucial for us to make contact with you. The more we uncovered, the more it became obvious that we lacked the resources to stop the enemy, because suddenly that enemy seemed to wield limitless power. Obviously there was something we were missing—the unholy alliance you describe between Benbasset and the faceless Hashi leader we know only as Quintanna. The direction may have come from Benbasset, but the men behind the killings and those on board the submarine are unquestionably Quintanna's. Each of them has goals which require the resources of the other to be achieved. Yes, an alliance forged in hell and one we—"

Brother Valette's words were cut short as the first burst of automatic fire sliced across their pew, followed by a half dozen more. His body jumped horribly, was caught by another series of bullets, then crumbled as the wood around him splintered into the air.

Kimberlain and Danielle had hit the floor by this time, struggling for their pistols and searching out each other's eyes as if to confirm the impossible sight each was trying to respond to.

The bullets were coming from the altar, fired by members of the boys' choir! A boys' choir with weapons tucked beneath their robes instead of music sheets.

"Hashi!" Danielle gasped in realization, covering her head as more wood splinters flew dangerously about, with the children's automatic fire homing in on them.

Kimberlain accepted her words incredulously. He could believe her story about children trained to be killers, but to see them actually *as* killers . . .

Danielle gazed over at the still corpse of Brother Valette, her eyes filled with rage. Her pistol was a fourteen-shot FN Highpower, and the one she'd given Kimberlain was similar. There were eighteen boys to use the bullets on at most, and time was on their side because the few tourists who'd managed to flee at the first sign of fire would certainly summon help. Young figures danced about the altar from the choir platform to better their positions and angles.

Danielle raised her pistol.

"No," Kimberlain told her firmly, hand latched onto her wrist.

"They'll kill us otherwise!"

"We'll find another way."

He looked forward and up beyond the altar. Danielle began firing shots very near the boys to ensure they would remain behind what cover there was on the altar and not venture down for a rush. Kimberlain was focusing his eyes on the brilliant Caravaggio painting, the *Beheading of St. John*, which hung behind the altar and overshadowed all else, except . . .

Stretching down from the ceiling across virtually the entire length and width of the altar and choir stalls was the ancient tapestry featuring the Knights' coat of arms with accompanying cross. It was held in place by beautifully braided rope strung to each of the four corners, the ropes joining together over the center and suspended from a chain which began at the ceiling thirty feet above the altar. If he could shoot out the chain, the tapestry would tumble and temporarily entomb all who lay beneath its weight. But he needed to get close enough to assure himself of the perfect aim and angle required to pull off such a feat.

Kimberlain's hand eased over to the bloodied robes of Brother Valette. Bullets flailed the air around him as he pulled the dead man's pistol free and handed it to Danielle.

"Keep firing up at them," he instructed her. "Not to kill. Just to keep them pinned down. Use both guns, different angles. Make them think it's still the two of us returning the fire."

Without waiting for a response, the Ferryman crawled to the far side of the pew, toward a narrow aisle that ran between it and the wall. Once there he pushed himself forward toward the head of the oratory, relying purely on his sense of direction to get him close enough to the altar to make the shots he needed. He would have to expose himself to fire, and it would in all probability take at least three hits on the chain to bring the tapestry down.

His ears rang with the echoing volleys of automatic fire, intermixed with the purposely errant shots fired by Danielle to keep the boy killers where they were. The approaching din of sirens joined the chaos, and Kimberlain knew help was coming fast, but would it really be "help"? The children would discard their guns with the arrival of the authorities, killers turned into apparent victims; as simple as that. He and Danielle would be cast as the offenders here, and even if they lived to tell their side of the story and witnesses corroborated it, valuable time would be lost in the process, while the Hashi would be able to reach them at their leisure. Under either scenario, the society of assassins would come out victorious.

The Ferryman reached the third row from the front and rose to a crouch. He could see the overhanging tapestry clearly now, as well as the chain supporting it. To obtain the firing angle required he would indeed have to chance standing up. His only hope for survival at that moment was Danielle: she had to intensify her fire at that very instant to provide him with the time he needed.

He had barely cleared the pews concealing him when Danielle's gunfire became more rapid and her bullets closer to the mark, both pistols firing away. He reached a full standing position with aim already locked on, pulling the trigger just as the first of the boy killers spotted him. He managed to get off five shots before the expected onslaught of their fire forced him back down, but not before three of his bullets had done the job. It must have been the fifth and final shot that did the trick, for the steel chain snapped and the tapestry slid into a floating fall. Descending, descending, it seemed to move in slow motion as the first of the children gazed up helplessly.

It landed upon them with a *plunk*, followed by the sounds of the altar's rostrums and pedestal ornaments toppling under its weight. The children were taken down as well, encased in the weighted darkness, struggling against the heavy material, in search of a way out.

Kimberlain charged back to Danielle, and together they rushed down the center aisle of the oratory past the trembling, prostrate forms of tourists who had dived for cover at the first sign of trouble instead of chancing flight. Passing into the small entryway, they caught the sound of footsteps pounding toward them from the cathedral nave beyond.

"This way!" signaled Danielle, directing him to a set of stairs that led up to the church museum and an alternative exit from the building. She had realized, as had Kimberlain, that with the wail of sirens still approaching, the footsteps could belong only to Hashi who'd been lying in wait to serve as backup, perhaps even dressed as Maltese police in cool-weather khaki uniforms.

Halfway up the staircase, Kimberlain grabbed her when his ears detected similar pounding coming from the museum above. More backup! They were surrounded, the enemy charging from both directions!

Kimberlain could see the results clearly in his mind. Maltese security police would shoot and slay the gunmen who had killed a monk and fired on innocent children in the sanctuary in an obvious act of terrorism. After the Egypt Air fiasco that had left a planeful of corpses, the Maltese people would embrace such a response. The police involved would be hailed as heroes—if they were ever found.

With no other choice, the two of them fled back down the steps.

Just past the bottom, Kimberlain threw open another door, only to find a narrow closet. No help at all until he saw what was hanging within.

The pounding steps were closing on them from both directions.

"Quick!" he said, tearing the first of the robes from its hanger and thrusting it at Danielle, then reaching back in for a second. He had it on, its hood covering his head, when the doors at the top of the staircase crashed open.

Danielle was pulling her robe tight when Kimberlain yanked her down. She caught his intention instantly, and in the next instant a sea of khaki-clothed figures converged upon them from the steps. Danielle rested her head on his lap, hair tucked beneath the robe's hood, feigning serious injury.

"They shot him!" the Ferryman screamed as if these were really the police. "Holy Lord Jesus, they shot him!"

The men in uniforms looked at the downed pair of clergy and then at each other. "Where did they go?" one demanded.

"Back into the oratory. A door behind the choir. An exit corridor. Stop them! *You must stop them!*"

The uniformed figures responded as if to do precisely that. They charged toward the door leading back into the narthex just as the second set from the cathedral nave crashed through it. The two groups joined up, numbering nine in all, and rushed off down the aisle in the direction of the altar with guns drawn.

Kimberlain and Danielle rose together with the awareness that they had to continue their ruse until safely out of the cathedral. He feigned sobbing as he passed back into the third bay off the nave and swung left toward the main cathedral doors, never even looking at the group of children just now emerging behind him, who had by now freed themselves from the fallen tapestry.

"A doctor! I must get the father to a doctor!"

By this time the real Maltese police were inside the cathedral and did not challenge or accost Kimberlain but simply moved aside. The children, meanwhile, were all crying, their weapons miraculously gone. The truth was so impossible to believe that no sense could be made from it, and a more rational explanation would be created in its place by the authorities. The murder of the nameless monk would be pinned on the pair of escaped strangers to fill at least part of the scenario.

They were nearly to the open cathedral doors now, the courtyard in view and their steps clacking against the stone. People were rushing past at each second, several stopping to offer assistance. One of these blocked their way in the process. "May I help, Father?"

"Yes," Kimberlain told him. "Make sure the call has been made for an ambulance and help clear a path for me down the steps."

"Yes, Father!"

Almost there now! Almost there!

The collection of pattering footsteps coming from the rear alerted him to the approach of the robed choirboys even before their sobs reached his ears. They had figured out the ruse and were coming for them, to finish now what they had been unable to finish before. Kimberlain gazed down at Danielle and could tell she realized it as well. He had only two bullets left in his gun, and even the idea of using it in this situation was ludicrous. The children might even hope for that, for it would accomplish their goal just as surely as killing the targets themselves.

Not children, Kimberlain reminded himself, Hashi. Escape would be on their minds as well as completion of the task. The strike would not come until they were outside. Quick and sure. Kimberlain felt chilled as another thought struck him. A number of the boys would have hidden their guns again where they would never be found: within their robes.

Kimberlain and Danielle passed under the cathedral's portico, with Danielle walking just enough under her own power to discourage the approach of bystanders. A huge crowd had gathered down the cathedral steps and within the courtyard. A quartet of Maltese police struggled to hold them back.

"Move aside," one of them ordered and began to clear a path as Kimberlain approached, still supporting Danielle.

The children were closing in, forcing more tears, victims of the panic rather than the makers of it.

More sirens wailed close by. Down the street just a few blocks, the Ferryman could see the first of the ambulances approaching. He had never really expected to make use of one, but with only a few slight moves they might be able to use it to make their escape. The ambulance was very near now.

But so were the boy killers, and they would never let their targets escape alive. They would kill them and take their chances that the chaos would shield the true origin of the shots. The crowd would scatter in panic, and they would scatter with it, joining the chaos they had created.

The boys were making their way down the steps now, moving quickly through the crowd.

The ambulance was screeching to a halt within a lane created for it within the mass of bodies. The boy killers were in range. The Ferryman could feel them tense, starting the process of moves that would surreptitiously allow them to bring out their guns once more, the bodies of some shielding the others.

In a motion as sudden as it was surprising, Kimberlain swung back toward the crowd gathered on the steps, his face solemn and proud.

"Lord Jesus be praised," he said, loud enough to be heard by all, with one arm still holding on to Danielle. "It was those children who saved us!" Pointing at them now for the crowd to see. "It was the children who pulled us out when those murderous heathen dared invade a holy place. Beaten back they were, beaten back by young lads who keep God close to their hearts. Lord Jesus be praised!"

The crowd took his final call as the sign to rush the boys with a hero's welcome, showering them with all due praise and adulation.

Almost to the ambulance's open rear doors now, Kimberlain looked back long enough to see the dust-streaked sea of white robes being swallowed by the throng. He met the eyes of one of the boy killers and expected to see hate, or at least disappointment.

But the face was empty, emotionless, as cold as the innocent blue eyes that framed it.

CHAPTER 28

THE MAN ACCOMPANYING KIMBERLAIN AND DANIELLE IN THE rear of the ambulance quickly realized the truth, but just as quickly Kimberlain showed his gun. After a few words of explanation, the man and the driver both pledged their cooperation. The Ferryman had them drive the vehicle into the countryside fifteen minutes outside of Valletta where he bound and gagged them, leaving them in the woods. He and Danielle continued on in the ambulance back to the outskirts of the city. They abandoned it in a parking lot, not wanting to risk being seen in a vehicle that might already be linked to them.

"They'll pin Brother Valette's murder on us," Danielle told him. "You know that."

"You're right," Kimberlain agreed.

"We must get out of the country. I have a route. It will be no problem to—"

"No," the Ferryman interrupted. "Utilizing any route would take too much time, and we can't afford to lose *any* if the proper authorities are going to be of any use. I've got to call the States—that man I mentioned. He's got to get help to Outpost 10. With the Hashi in possession of that submarine . . ."

267

"They'll be looking for us! Everywhere!"

"They'll be looking for a couple, not a single woman who checks into a hotel and says her bags were lost by the airline. She gets a room." He stopped. "I'll join you in it a bit later."

She looked at him, amazed at the pace at which his mind worked. It was as if he was constantly weighing every possible angle to arrive at the most logical and safest strategy to pursue. She sighed, feeling embarrassed by her failure to reach the same conclusion. She nodded her acknowledgment.

Danielle chose the Dragonara, both because it was nearby and because it was situated away from downtown, where the search for them would likely be concentrated.

Ten minutes after she checked in there was a knock on the door. She let the Ferryman in, and he moved immediately to the phone. A call to Zeus was first on his agenda, but the operator had difficulty finding an open overseas line and promised to ring him back when one became available.

"I ordered from room service," she told him.

"Not for two, I hope."

"I ordered fish, the largest portion available. A salad and soft drinks as well."

"That will do fine." He regarded her gently. "I'm sorry about Brother Valette."

She tried to hide her sorrow. "Besides you, he was the only other person alive who knew my entire story. But it was always something he anticipated and planned for. We of the Knights do not operate as traditional agencies do. Information is funneled on a shared basis. Our means of contact between various levels proceeds through very direct channels."

"Will you utilize them now to regroup?"

"There isn't time. My place is where Brother Valette would have wanted me: Outpost 10."

"That's insane!"

"Our entire quest is insane, Ferryman."

"But look at the reality of the situation. There's nothing you could accomplish at that station, even if you could reach it, that Zeus's people can't accomplish better."

She looked at him derisively. "The Knights exist purely to destroy the Hashi. Our mistake in the past has been to rely on others to do our work for us. They've seldom been up to the task."

"It's different this time."

"Maybe, but maybe not. The Knights gave me my life back, and in return I took an oath. Right now that oath dictates that I go to Outpost 10. Tell me you wouldn't do the same."

"I wouldn't. The difference between us is I know when to let go, when I've taken something as far as I can. Dedication is one thing, obsession something else entirely."

"Your definitions are only a matter of degree." And with that her stare grew sad. "And they articulate only one of the differences between us. In the church today I would have killed those children if you hadn't stopped me."

"It might have been the proper strategy, given the circumstances."

"Don't patronize me, Ferryman. You talk about drawing lines, and there are several you flatly won't step over."

"A lesson I learned long ago—and not the easy way, either. As a Caretaker I was forced to use others' values, pushing mine back in the face of what the orders made me do. But they couldn't stop me from looking at myself, and by the end of three years I couldn't stand the sight anymore. I vowed never to be faced with it again. I did plenty back then I could barely live with. Killing those children would have brought it all back."

"You would have preferred their killing you?"

"They didn't."

"They could have."

The phone rang.

"Ah, Ferryman," said Zeus, "I was starting to worry."

"Don't stop yet," Kimberlain told him. "I've got plenty to say. Might want to record this."

"The reels are already turning, old friend. You mentioned nothing about leaving the country."

"I wasn't given much of a choice. Suffice it to say that I was 'grabbed' by a network you've never heard of, with a purpose running parallel to our own."

"A network *I've* never heard of? Impossible!"

"This one's got a rather singular purpose. Details later. Let's start with what I learned before my removal. Jason Benbasset *is* alive."

"But I've searched for him everywhere, including all sixty-three floors of his crowning Manhattan achievement, the Benbasset Towers."

"Never mind. The key isn't where he is, but what he's about to do. The parade's just a part of it and a relatively insignificant part. The real plot's centered at the bottom of the world: Antarctica, specifically an installation called Outpost 10."

"You're speaking gibberish to me, Ferryman."

"Have your contacts at Defense yank the file out of Def-Net under ULTSEC seal. I doubt even the President knows."

"And what will the file tell me?"

"Lots about oil, but that's just for starters." And Kimberlain told him the rest as Danielle and Brother Valette had related it, a story even more chilling to tell than it had been to hear. When he elaborated on the potential theft of the submarine it was all Zeus could do to keep himself from shouting.

"Yes! There are rumors afoot that the prototype for the Jupiter class of super-Tridents has been lost at sea during its maiden voyage."

"Not lost, Zeus, taken—and for a very good reason. They're going to use the oil pipeline and the missiles to somehow fragment the continent. I'm no scientist, but it doesn't take one to figure out that we're facing the end of a good portion of the civilized world here."

Zeus sighed sadly. "To believe that such an installation could be set in place without my knowledge." His voice turned forceful now. "But my knowledge will be what assures the world's continued existence. I'll crack Def-Net personally, ULTSEC or not. I'll see to it that forces are marshaled and dispatched. Outpost 10 will be reached and protected."

"There's still the Macy's parade to concern ourselves with."

"The proper forces have been alerted. A simple phone call from me and an apparent strike will force the parade into a one-year hiatus."

Kimberlain felt a warm rush of triumph as he realized that at last they were winning. "There's something else," he said. "Something I need you to do while I'm on my way in."

"Of course. Anything."

"I took it upon myself to have Lisa Eiseman protected. But there's been too much penetration. I'm not sure her present placement is safe."

"Just tell me where she is and I'll have her delivered to a safe house."

"Tell whoever you send to be careful. The bodyguard I arranged for her doesn't have a lot of patience."

"I understand."

"I'll want him included as well."

"Certainly," Zeus said. "Know just the place. Cottage with a view of the Chesapeake." He proceeded to provide the address, after which Kimberlain furnished him with the details of where Lisa and Peet could be found.

"Hurry home," Zeus told him.

But getting home would be no easy task.

"The airport is out of the question," Danielle explained. "The Hashi will have it covered, and maybe the authorities as well. We're murderers now, remember?"

"We don't know that."

"I do. I know how they work. They're masters at short-circuiting legitimate processes or circumventing them to their best advantage."

"There must be alternative routes."

"Several, the best and safest of which open up after dark. We still have a number of hours."

"We," Kimberlain echoed. "I wasn't sure I was going to have company. Thought you were going south."

"I trust you," she said softly. "And right now I need that trust more than anything."

Danielle drew the blinds, shutting out as much of the daylight as she could manage. Neither of them had slept the night before, and they were exhausted; they could see it on each other's face.

Kimberlain started toward one of the room's chairs, but Danielle grasped his arm gently as he passed her. "Please," she muttered shyly, almost childlike. "Lie with me. Just . . . hold me."

She lay down on the bed atop the covers. Kimberlain joined her and wrapped his arms around her gently at first, then in a tight embrace. She clung to him, and the Ferryman thought of Lisa back at his cabin in Maine. He wanted Danielle more than he had wanted Lisa, but he knew he could never have her. Sex had happened only twice in her life, on both occasions violently. There could be no third until the bitter memories were put behind her for good. So they lay together with their arms entwined, Danielle for comfort and Kimberlain acting out of compassion, with thoughts of sexuality forced back. They hugged tight, and he felt her warmth before drifting off to sleep.

When he awoke it was to the awareness of darkness filling the room and his arms wrapped around cleverly arranged pillows instead of Danielle. He stumbled from the bed and located the light switch from memory. Her note was there in plain view, stuck against the mirror over the bureau. Kimberlain skimmed it the first time, eyes lingering on the detailed set of instructions she had left for getting out of Malta. He read the top last, because he already knew what message it would hold.

She had left, left him, to make a senseless journey to Antarctica and Outpost 10.

Kimberlain crumbled the note in his hand and felt anger flush through him. The similarities between the two of them were indeed striking. But equally striking were the differences. For her there were only two points connected by a straight line. For Kimberlain it was following the line that had become everything. She was caught up in beginnings and ends. The Ferryman had turned his life over to all that occurred in between, as if his existence had evolved into one continuous line, with no points to begin or end it.

He pushed his thoughts of her aside and retrieved the crumpled paper to better review her instructions for escape. They were complicated but shouldn't take too long to carry out. His mind calculated that, given the overseas time differential, he could be in Washington by the early-morning hours of Tuesday.

That would give him two full days before the start of the Macy's Thanksgiving Day Parade and not much more than that before the coming of what Brother Valette had called the Eighth Trumpet.

The strain was starting to tell on Zeus. He had followed Kimberlain's phone call with dozens of his own. Men had been rousted from meetings, meals, conferences. All had been reached over an emergency channel very few were even aware of.

"Who the hell is this?" demanded the first he'd managed to get hold of.

"Is that any way to greet an old friend, Colonel?"

"Zeus? You're calling on a dead channel, goddamn it. It's not cleared. I can't talk to—"

"You'll talk, Colonel, because far more than codes and clearances are hanging in the balance. I need information from you on one of your Def-Net installations. Outpost 10."

"Outpost *what*?"

"No games, please."

"This isn't a game. I don't know what the hell you're talking about."

It had been the same for hours now. Everyone he reached using outdated channels, long replaced since his reassignment, professed to know nothing of Outpost 10—and Zeus believed them. This puzzled as well as frightened him, because it meant that Outpost 10 was sealed so high up that it could conceivably resist all his attempts to penetrate it.

But it was a matter of pride as well as of necessity now. Hearing old voices—and new ones—rekindled in him the old fires of power, when he had held the reins and sent out orders without need to account to anyone else. It was a strange sort of retirement they had created for him—the illusion of power more than the reality of it. Yet the two were close enough for him to believe he could get the proper authority on the phone and ensure that the right precautions were taken at Outpost 10.

It was past midnight when one of his four lines rang.

"I shouldn't be calling back," a voice told him.

"We all do things we shouldn't."

"Outpost 10 doesn't exist."

"Really."

"Listen to me. We're talking levels here. Not the President, not the Secretary of State. Behind the scenes, yet above them."

"Good. I want the control for the project. I want him on this line within an hour. This isn't the kind of story one wishes to tell twice."

"Then use me as a conduit."

"Zeus doesn't use conduits, old friend."

The speaker still persisted. "Damn it, you don't know what you're dealing with here!"

"Unfortunately," Zeus countered, "I do."

The blind man sat by the odd-shaped phone on his desk in the near blackness of his study, the lights on only for the sake of his two bodyguards. He heard one of them approaching now.

"I brought you some coffee, sir."

Both the men were fiercely loyal to him, assigned originally by the government as much for its safety as his own. A man like Zeus couldn't be allowed to wander on too long a leash. No telling who he might talk to or what he might say. It was strange thinking back now to his reassignment following the dissolution of The Caretakers. Through it all, his greatest concern was whether they would let him keep his anonym. Stripping it away would be as bad as killing him. But they had left the blind man that much, a slice of identity large enough to build from.

Zeus raised the coffee mug to his lips. The steam rising off its top told him it was too hot, and he merely grabbed a taste before he heard a clatter of steps rushing down from upstairs followed by the second bodyguard's hurried entry into his study.

"There's someone outside," the man reported.

Zeus stilled his thoughts, tried to feel about the outer perimeter of his grounds with his senses. Yes, there was something out there, something big and evil, a disturbance not unlike a great storm announcing itself with soft lightning in the distance.

The second bodyguard was at the closet tearing out weapons. Zeus busied himself by identifying each by the clamor it made on contact with the floor or wall.

There was a loud click, followed by a drawn-out sizzling sound.

"Lights are out!" one bodyguard blared.

"They've cut the power!" followed the second.

"Not they," Zeus corrected. "He."

He wasn't sure how he knew that so certainly, any more than how he could tell that his bodyguards had stopped to stare at him briefly.

A smell reached his nose, a smell of the cold outdoors intruding with a wisp of wind into the warmth of his house. Another scent followed with it, that of something stale and worn and oddly terrifying.

"He's in the house," Zeus said very softly.

His huge bodyguards tensed like jungle cats, commandos again now, back to the life they had been brought here from. They readied for the invasion, and Zeus could sense the change in their auras as they made sure he was sitting low and safe behind the cover of the desk, then taking up positions on opposite sides of the room with a clear view of the doorway.

And Zeus felt the scent that was near death itself grow strong enough to touch.

CHAPTER 29

"**S**OMETHING'S WRONG," KIMBERLAIN SAID, FOOT SQUEEZING the brake and bringing the car to a halt at the edge of Zeus's driveway.

He had followed Danielle's instructions precisely, leaving the hotel just after six to begin the fourteen-hour journey that would return him to the States to face the end of a plot he now realized threatened the entire world. A ferry to the Maltese island of Gozo was the first order of business, followed by a private plane to Sicily, where he just managed to catch a flight to London's Heathrow that would connect with another bound for Dulles Airport. Danielle had left plenty of cash with her instructions, along with a perfectly forged passport bearing his likeness.

Upon arriving at Dulles, he had rented a car and driven straight up to the safe house where Zeus had stowed Peet and Lisa Eiseman, relieved to find them okay, with only the ebb and flow of the currents for company. They were also awake, which meant little delay was required before the three of them set out for Zeus's. Dawn was no more than an hour away on what, for the Ferryman, had become a night without end.

Zeus's home was tucked in the woods off the George Washington

Parkway, far enough from the road so the lights and sounds were barely perceptible. The house itself could be glimpsed only in late fall and winter when the natural camouflage formed by the leaves was lifted.

"Ferryman?" Peet said from the seat next to him.

Kimberlain's hands tightened across the wheel. "It's the lights. Only the outside ones are on."

"Zeus is blind, you said."

"But his bodyguards aren't, and there's something about those outside lights . . ."

"We'd better check," Peet said, a huge hand moving to the latch on the passenger side.

Kimberlain turned around to Lisa in the backseat. "You stay here."

"Wrong, Jared. After what you guys have just said, the last thing I want to be is alone. I'll take my chances between the two of you."

Kimberlain nodded and wondered why he had bothered with the suggestion. Seeing her alive and well at the safe house had made everything feel right again for a brief time. Then the truth of the situation flooded quickly back, along with a nagging uneasiness. He found himself comparing her to Danielle, the love she could give him versus the love of another he could never have. He felt distant from Lisa, separate. What they had shared together at the cabin was only a memory.

Together the three of them climbed out of the car after Kimberlain had unscrewed the dome light to mask their exit. He had cut his headlights off well back on the approach road as a precaution he prayed was unnecessary. There were enough trees and brush around to hide their moving shapes in the darkness, and they left the car doors open so no distinctive clicks would betray their presence. They clung to the darkness as they approached the big house, Zeus's last testament to the power he once wielded and remained determined to again. With Peet in the lead, they squeezed up against the house's frame, moving from the side to the front, then lunged quickly onto the porch, with the front door just a grasp away. Kimberlain eased Lisa behind him as Peet tested the knob.

"It's open," he reported, and the Ferryman knew then that it was going to be bad.

They passed inside, with Peet still in the lead and Lisa silently bringing up the rear. Their eyes adjusted quickly to the darkness broken only by the spill of the moon through the windows, and they found themselves in a spacious entry foyer. A set of double doors was open down the corridor and to the right—the living room or library perhaps, or even Zeus's study. They started toward it.

The sole working floodlights they had noticed outside must have spent most of their spill in this direction, because snakes of light racing the outlines of the windows were reflected on the hardwood floor as they drew closer. Kimberlain had moved to the front, and now he looked into the room while staying in the hallway. He gazed past Peet at Lisa. "Stay here."

"I want to—"

"I said stay here! Don't look in. Do you hear me? Don't look in!"

He entered just ahead of Peet, the two of them taking in the scene to the music of trees and bushes whistling in the wind just beyond the windows.

The room was a shambles, furniture spilled and shattered, papers strewn about and still blowing in the wind coming through a number of shattered panes. The bodies lay separate from each other, two large ones framing a much smaller one in the middle, about ten feet from the others. The bodyguards had done their best to defend Zeus all right, done it by the book as well. But it hadn't been enough.

The first bodyguard's corpse was lying facedown, and Peet turned it over. Its entire front was drenched in blood; it was impossible to tell what weapon had caused whatever wounds there were. The giant gazed closer, intrigued by something.

"He was here," Peet said softly.

"Who was?"

"Quail."

"A feeling, Peet?"

"More than a feeling this time, Ferryman," the giant said, angling the body so its chest was caught by the spill of light.

Kimberlain saw the chest, or rather what was left of it. The ribs and bones over the heart had been shattered and splintered out. He wondered if the heart itself still lay inside. With all the blood and the darkness, it was impossible to tell.

It was Quail all right, recognizable by the one trademark he had occasionally allowed himself. That the Dutchman would leave his trademark here could mean only one thing: He wanted whoever found the bodies to know it was him. He wanted Kimberlain to know.

They found Zeus's body next, half on its side, with its head twisted obscenely around. The sightless eyes bulged open, locked in their death stare. Kimberlain knelt alongside the old man's body and thought strangely how this was the first time he had ever seen Zeus up close without his ever-present sunglasses.

Peet inspected the body of the second bodyguard, then eased himself around the room, stopping regularly.

"The guards did their best," he explained, "but they didn't know what they were up against. Bullet marks dot the walls in a dozen places. Quail was taunting them. The second guard's arm was shattered and yanked out of its socket. Quail must have let that man get close to him."

"The lights," Kimberlain realized.

"What about them?"

"Floodlights shouldn't be pointing in. He moved them, damn it; he moved them before he left. He wanted to make sure we found his work."

Peet tensed. "I'd have felt him if he were still around."

"But he was here, and not very long ago either."

For the first time since the *Rhode Island* was taken, Mac wanted Jones to appear in his quarters. It had been a day since the madman had yanked up his sleeve to reveal the mark of a ship he had once captained for the navy: *Thresher.*

The U.S. nuclear sub *Thresher,* lost undersea twenty-five years ago, with all its crew members presumed dead. Its captain was a man whose name Mac couldn't recall but whose face he had somehow held in his memory. Jones's face.

"But we never were on board," Jones had told him, his own eyes never leaving the tattoo. "No, that's not quite true. We were placed on board just long enough for everyone to see us steam out to sea. We were picked up a day into our patrol, two hundred and fifty miles off the coast of New England, where the story was we went down."

"I . . . I don't understand."

"Neither did we. All except me, of course, because I was the captain. Orders, always orders. A strong element in the Navy believed robotics was the way to go with subs. Perfect control that way, with computers running everything. It was to be a brief mission." He took a deep breath. "But something went wrong on her robot patrol. Her missile systems snapped on close to Soviet waters. The story was a Russian jamming device had rescrambled our signals for the computers to interpret. The ship went to countdown."

"My God . . ."

"Of course we couldn't let it get that far, so the brass panicked and shut all systems down, every one. Parts of the story began to leak out, and to cover their asses the Navy devised the cover that a power failure had sunk the *Thresher* with all crew members on board. Except, of course, we weren't on board. We were still alive, but we couldn't be permitted to 'live,' could we?, because there'd be too much explaining to do. We became prisoners, Commander. Oh, we ate well and had a whole isolated base to ourselves, but we were prisoners, all right, and it didn't take us long to figure out it was going to become a permanent condition. The Navy people told us to just give them time. They promised resettlement, different identities, with our families intact. We tried to be patient. After six months it got hard. A few of us tried to escape. I made it.''

Mac looked at him from across the desk. Jones's forearm was throbbing, the letters of his tattoo lengthening with each pulse.

''They took my family, Commander,'' he continued. ''The message was plain. If I talked, they'd be killed. I didn't talk; I focused instead on finding them. I followed a trail. Lots of cities, lots of jobs. It was about six years ago when I finally got . . . lucky.'' Jones seemed near tears. ''My wife had remarried. My kids were teenagers and didn't even know I was still alive. Maybe I wasn't. And the worst of it all was that the government had set everything up. My family was moved to ease the pain of grief and reduce the onslaught of reporters. Everything was so neat and clean. What choice did I have? I kept wandering.''

''But you're here now.''

''Because somebody found me. I still don't know how, and I didn't understand why at first. I'd been working on the docks in San Francisco, waiting for a first mate's position to open up on a merchant vessel bound for the Orient. There was a bar we all spent our nights in, and maybe there were a few of them where I said more than I should have. The next time I was alone a man approached me. We got to talking. I drank. He didn't. The man said he had a job for me, said just enough to raise my interest. A few nights later I met another man in the backseat of a limousine, a dark man with a face that could freeze you. He knew my whole story, goddamn it. Somehow he knew everything. I could barely stand to hear him tell it. But in the end he told me it wasn't finished. He told me there was one more chapter to write.'' Jones's eyes held Mac's. ''He arranged for me to learn how to run your ship, Mac, and he gave me the means to get back at the bastards who had stolen my life away. I owe them this much. I owe them more.''

''What about your crew?''

''The dark man's people. But I supervised their training, all six months of it. I'm not really sure how much they know. I'm not sure if they know what we're going to do.''

Fear slid down Mac's spine. "What exactly *are* we going to do?"

"We're going to change the world, Commander, and you're going to help us."

It was clearer than ever to Mac that Jones was mad, but his madness was singular in purpose, making him doubly dangerous. Mac was the only one who could stop him, stop this bizarre plot of revenge. They had searched his quarters up and down for possible weapons but had missed the razor-sharp Sandvik knife he kept taped to the underside of one of his drawers. Jones was the key. The plot lived or died with him.

So there was no choice. Mac had to use the Sandvik blade on Jones the next time he stepped through the door alone. The guards left in the corridor would almost certainly kill him, yet this strategy seemed to hold the best chance for his family. If Jones really was going to use the *Rhode Island* to destroy the world, then bargaining for their lives would be useless anyway.

Jones was in charge, and Mac was the only one who could enable the missiles that were needed to complete the plan. With both dead, the intruder crew might as well abandon ship or head for home.

Mac's eyes locked again on the door latch, willing it to turn, with the Sandvik blade within easy reach.

Quintanna stood in his accustomed spot before the black curtain, listening to the raspy sleep of the man within. The news of the blind man's murder, and thus the Ferryman's isolation, could wait until later. Quintanna found himself glad to be able to finally relay some good news. The string of recent failures culminating in the events in London and Malta had proven both embarrassing and unsettling. Kimberlain was much better than he had imagined, but alone even the Ferryman would be unable to prevent the plan from proceeding.

And he was alone now.

Quintanna reflected on what it all meant, on how far he had brought the Hashi he had been chosen to lead more than a decade back. Financial compensation had taken the place of ideals as motivator long before that, so long that the original purposes of their

existence seemed lost and forgotten. But Quintanna had never forgotten. At night in his sleep or after taking deep drags from his
hashish pipe, the spirit of the Hashi founder, Hassan ibn al-Sabbah,
appeared before him to show him the way. And when he had first
been summoned by the man behind the curtain, Quintanna was
certain it was the work of al-Sabbah himself.

Tomorrow the man would provide Quintanna with locations
deemed to be the safest from the coming cataclysm. Stockpiled
equipment and men would be transported to these places, and when
the new world settled, the advantage of organization and supplies
would translate into power. Quintanna would take his destined place
at the forefront of a great marauding army, just as al-Sabbah had
led the Hashi forces at the spearhead of the Crusades. Those in
their path would join as subjects or face destruction. With each day
more land and territory would fall to the Hashi, until all of the new
world forged out of the corpse of the old belonged to them.

The man behind the curtain had labeled him a scavenger. But a
scavenger lives off the dead with no thought of life or the living,
moving from one corpse to the next. Quintanna and his Hashi
weren't fighting over the dead: they were preparing to overtake
those left *among* the living. For nearly a thousand years their destiny
had lingered unfulfilled. But a new series of Crusades was about to
begin. And this time they would emerge victorious.

Quintanna heard the man behind the curtain stir slowly awake.

"Jared," droned David Kamanski melodramatically, "how good
of you to call."

"Did I wake you, Hermes? Accept my apologies and get your
ass out of bed."

"You got me out of the shower."

"Get dressed. We're meeting for breakfast. Zeus is dead."

"*What?*"

"Just listen to me. I'm on my way up from Washington right
now. There's a Holiday Inn just over the George Washington Bridge

on the Jersey side. Meet me in the coffee shop in two hours—make
it ninety minutes."

"What's going on, Jared?"

"Plenty, David, and none of it's good."

Kamanski had been waiting for almost forty minutes when Kimberlain stepped through the door of the diner looking ragged and
unkempt and at least as tired as he felt.

"You look like hell, Jared. What gives? Where'd you disappear
to two days ago?"

The Ferryman slid into the booth across from him. They had the
diner mostly to themselves. A pair of business types shared a booth
two over. Three of the seats at the counter were taken by similar
men sipping coffee to wait out the traffic.

"In a nutshell, Hermes, the world's about to get fucked, and
you're the last one left who can scream rape loud enough for it to
matter."

"You lost me."

"Let me try another metaphor. Humpty Dumpty sat on a wall,
et cetera. That's us—Humpty Dumpty—the whole fucking world.
And instead of using all the king's men to put Humpty back together
again, we've got to use them to stop him from falling apart in the
first place by arranging an airlift of troops to a base called Outpost
10 in Antarctica."

"I don't know what you're talking about."

"That puts you in good company. Zeus didn't either. I'll make
it short. Outpost 10 serves as a major pumping conduit for a secret
oil pipeline we've had going in Antarctica for five years now. The
Hashi, retained by a very much alive Jason Benbasset, stole the
prototype for the Jupiter-class super-Trident and sailed it down there
complete with twenty-eight missiles to be used on Thanksgiving
Day probably about the same time the Macy's parade is winding
toward its explosive end. That's as specific as it gets. The specu-
lation starts with what happens when they blow up Outpost 10 and
the entire continent fractures along the lines of the oil facilities,

which make up something called Spiderweb. Unless you play messenger again, Hermes, and get the goddamn goverment to believe me."

Kamanski's expression tightened. "That's very good, Jared. You always were the best."

The Ferryman recognized an unfamiliar tone in Kamanski's voice. He tensed and started to move. In his belt was a pistol lifted off one of Zeus's dead bodyguards in Washington. Before he could free it, the three men from the counter and two from the booth had lunged for them with guns drawn, too well spaced for Kimberlain to possibly get them all.

"You son of a bitch," the Ferryman snarled, still half out of his seat.

"Drop the gun on the floor, Jared."

"I could kill you before—"

"Before they kill you," Kamanski completed. "Yes, I'm sure you could. But you won't, because it'll mean your death, and under the circumstances you'll insist on putting that off for as long as possible."

Kimberlain's stare bore into the eyes across from him. "You're one of them! You're a Hashi!"

"In the flesh, Jared. But don't bother looking for the skull-and-spear tattoo. That's been maintained only to throw persistent bastards like yourself off the track. No tattoo, no Hashi. We maintained that connection in order to exploit it in a different way. Our pursuers are never aware of our actual number or the positions some of us occupy."

"Pursuers like the Knights of Malta?"

"Yes. I understand their leader was killed. Pity you didn't die with him—or in London, as was the plan. Made things rather complicated. Exposing myself was a last resort. I knew you'd be calling after word reached me about Zeus."

It was all becoming clear. "Every time I got close to the Hashi with The Caretakers, something would go wrong. I could never pin it on a leak, but that's what it was, wasn't it?"

Kamanski grew defensive. "Those pursuits were unsanctioned. You had no right going after us. They wanted you killed, Jared. At least I was able to keep you alive."

"A different strategy than the one you employed at Mendelson's office in Boston."

The men with pistols drawn had advanced a little closer.

"The gun, Jared. Now."

Reluctantly, the Ferryman let it clang to the floor. He looked Kamanski in the eye. "You've had your chances at me, Hermes, and you've blown them all."

"I've got one left."

"Maybe."

With that, a pair of the armed men spun him all the way around, one frisking while the other locked handcuffs onto his wrists. The three remaining gunmen nearer the counter warily kept their distance, eyes ready for any sudden motion Kimberlain might make.

"Why'd you bring me into this in the first place, Hermes?"

"I was ordered to by my superiors at Pro-Tech. They knew my file and my link to you. I wasn't worried. I figured I could maintain control." Kamanski motioned to the two men holding the Ferryman to start for the door. "Of course, I never expected you to get this far. Figuring out Lime's murder, stopping the attempt on Eiseman, latching on to Benbasset and the Hashi—my, my, don't you have a right to be proud of yourself!"

"Oughta be an interesting world once you boys take over."

"That's the idea."

"Except it hasn't got a chance of working. Now order your goons off and let's you and me walk out of here together. Shit, Hermes, I'm giving you a chance to stay alive."

Kamanski gawked at him disbelievingly. "You've got things crossed up this time, Jared. I'm calling the shots now."

"No, you're not. You're more of an underling than you've ever been, and if I don't kill you here today, you'll be dead anyway because you've outlived your usefulness to them."

"Let's get him out of here!" Kamanski ordered, and instantly

the two men grasped Kimberlain by his elbows and started to lead
him toward the door out of the coffee shop and into the parking lot.

The Holiday Inn was perched on a rise overlooking the bridge,
with a decent view into New Jersey. Most of its parking lot, however, was obscured from the view of passing traffic. They emerged
on the building's side and moved quickly around to the rear, toward
a black van parked by itself near the back of the lot. Kimberlain
assessed the situation. Besides the men holding him by either arm,
another pair with guns exposed flanked him on both sides, moving
slightly ahead. A fifth was a good five yards in front of the rest and
walked almost sideways so he could keep his eyes on Kimberlain
as he led the way toward the van. Kamanski brought up the rear,
well back, standing as the final defense and occupying the safest
position if the Ferryman tried to seize the offensive.

"Last chance, Hermes," Kimberlain called behind him, testing
the limited range the handcuffs allowed him. He knew if he managed to strip a gun free he would have to fire it with hands squeezed
together by iron. "Send the goons away and we'll talk. Time's
running out."

"My thoughts exactly," Kamanski replied.

The gunman from the right flank had joined the one in front at
the van's rear doors. The gunman on the left side hung there, and
the Ferryman's captors continued to hold him at either elbow. Guns
still drawn, the pair at the van started to open the doors.

They had just depressed the latches when the double doors blasted
open with a force that cracked steel into both their faces. Kimberlain watched them go flying as Winston Peet lunged from the inside.
Using the shock of his assault as an ally, the Ferryman yanked free
of his captors' grasp and launched a side kick to the knee of one
and smashed his foot around into the groin of the second. The
second man had had time to go for his gun before crumbling and
Kimberlain's next order of business was to retrieve it from the black
macadam surface even as he angled himself to finish the now kneeling first man with a vicious kick to the face.

Kamanski, meanwhile, had missed with his first two shots and was struggling for a third when Peet hoisted the slumping body of one of the dazed gunmen effortlessly into the air and tossed him at another. The man was just aiming his gun at the giant when the impact sent him tumbling, and he launched his bullet straight into Kamanski's chest. Kamanski gasped, reeling backward.

Kimberlain had the pistol steadied by then and aimed back behind him. He had to twist around toward the pair of men struggling to their feet with guns in hand. Peet was rushing them, but their pistols were rising too fast, and the Ferryman started firing just as they were about to, fired and kept firing, squeezing the semiautomatic's trigger as fast as he could. He wasn't sure which of his bullets found the two men, but before they could get off any shots of their own at Peet, both had crumbled to the asphalt. Dropping the smoking gun, Kimberlain rushed to the fallen Kamanski while Peet dealt with the final conscious man who'd recovered enough from the Ferryman's groin kick to try to scramble away.

Kimberlain knelt over Kamanski and saw the blood pumping freely from his chest and pooling on the ground. He coughed, and more of it oozed frothily from his mouth. Kimberlain locked eyes with his dying stare.

"Where's Benbasset, David? Where can I find him?"

The eyes barely even regarded him. "Fuck . . . you." And then they locked open.

Kimberlain rose as Peet pulled up next to him.

"Never did trust the bastard," the Ferryman said as much to himself as to anyone.

"Hold still," the giant instructed, working his way behind Kimberlain, where he proceeded to pull apart the steel chain that joined the individual cuffs together.

Kimberlain drew his wrists in front of him and stretched the blood back into his arms as they began to run toward the spot on the other side of the building where Lisa was waiting with the car. When they had pulled into the parking lot earlier they had noticed the black van parked at the rear. That had aroused their suspicions and put Kimberlain and Peet on their guard, resulting in

Peet's own version of an insurance policy that placed him in the isolated van's rear after Kimberlain had made his way inside.

"Where to now?" Peet asked the Ferryman as they drew up to their car.

"To catch a train. Sort of."

CHAPTER 30

LISA EISEMAN AND WINSTON PEET SAT ON THE COUCH IN THE converted train car in Sunnyside Yard, while Captain Seven finished picking the locks on the cuffs still wrapped around Kimberlain's wrists.

"Fucked-up company you're keeping, boss," the captain noted, eyeing Peet as he reached for the remains of a marijuana joint smoldering in an ashtray.

"Everything's relative."

"Yeah, well, I'd offer your friend a toke, but it might stunt his growth."

Peet didn't look amused, but his expression remained unchanged.

"I seem to remember a time when the two of you weren't exactly on speaking terms."

"Times change."

"Hold on a sec," the captain said and disappeared into the kitchen contained in the second train car forming his abode.

They had driven straight to Sunnyside Yard from the Holiday Inn, Kimberlain keeping his fingers crossed the whole way that Kamanski hadn't managed to locate the captain's hideaway. The

Ferryman wanted to know exactly what they were facing at Outpost 10 if the Eighth Trumpet, as Brother Valette called it, came to pass.

Seven returned with a pair of sunglasses in place and his bong. He plopped down in the black leather chair across from Kimberlain and chambered the bong with pot.

"Okay, I'm ready."

"Assume there's an interconnected network of oil wells scattered across the Antarctic continent," Kimberlain started. "Assume a pipeline links them up with a central pumping station called Outpost 10. You've got twenty-eight Jupiter-class nuclear warheads and you want to do the most damage possible to the continent. What would you do?"

Seven spoke only after coughing out a hefty measure of the smoke he had bubbled into his lungs while the Ferryman had been speaking. His voice emerged sounding like a man with a bad cold.

"Simple. An installation like this Outpost 10 would have two sets of pipelines, one to bring the oil into it and one to pump the oil into storage depots. Odds are those depots started overflowing a long time ago, so parts of the outgoing pipeline were probably laid all the way to various locations on the Antarctic coastline to allow easy loading onto tankers. Now since oil under such extreme temperatures would tend to coagulate and back up the works, each of the pipes would be fitted with a plug to push the oil along and clear the line. What I'd do is I'd place the individual warheads in front of the plugs within the outgoing lines and send them out into the continent to be detonated at your leisure. Hey, you shittin' me with this or what?"

"Just go on."

"Okay. You'd rig the enabled warheads on timer detonation. It wouldn't be the most exact science in the world, but the fucks behind the warheads would be assured of a damn good spread once detonation came, which is to say: drop a piece of china on the floor and you'll have a pretty good notion of what Antarctica would look like."

"Splintered? Fractured apart?"

Captain Seven nodded as he drew in another drag off the bong. "Lots of ice melted or set adrift." His eyes swung briefly to Peet. "Plenty for you friend over there to have his next drink on the rocks." And when Kimberlain didn't respond to the humor, "Hey, you *are* shittin' me with this, aren't you?"

Kimberlain's stare answered for him. "Tell me the implications of the fracture."

Seven started to lower the bong to the table, then thought better of it and tucked it into his lap. "Let's talk about the continent in general first. You know what Antarctica is? One monster fuckin' ice cube on top of a landmass that covers, say, about six million square miles—twice the size of the beloved U.S. of A. You can call its weight somewhere around nineteen quadrillion tons—that's a 19 followed by fifteen zeros."

"The weight's important?"

Seven sucked in some more smoke before responding. "Not weight so much as displacement. You wanna talk nightmares? Fine. On the one hand you've got a great portion of our ice cube almost instantly melted by the heat generated by the ultra-megaton force of the blast, while on the other hand you've got the incredible concussion generated by the blast, which will fracture ice at incredible distances. And remember, long after the mushroom clouds are history, the oil fires stretching through the ice shield are going to be burning. The fire will raise the heat levels and even more ice will bite the dust.

"Now the ice closest to the blast radiuses would get vaporized and be gonezo. But plenty more would melt, thanks mostly to the burning oil and soot blackening the landscape and helping to absorb plenty of that twenty-four-hours-a-day sunlight. So you've got all these tons of water plunging into the ocean in a matter of seconds, minutes, hours, days—take you pick. Conservatively you're looking at a rise in sea levels worldwide of two hundred feet. In fact, four might be a more realistic figure."

"Four hundred feet?" Kimberlain repeated disbelievingly.

"Give you an idea of the effect of that—over ninety percent of the entire state of Florida isn't more than seventy feet above sea level." Captain Seven blew a smoky kiss. "Good-bye, Miami. Along with every coastal city in the world. Give you an idea what we're talking about over seventy-five percent of every U.S. of A. lives within one hundred miles of a coast."

"Jesus Christ."

"It's not his fault. And I'm just getting started. It don't matter much what is the coast and what ain't, because there's not gonna be many left to notice. Let's get back to weight." He reached down to the table for the thin pick he'd used to free Kimberlain of the handcuffs and laid it across his index finger. He looked at Lisa. "Could keep this here forever, right? Why?"

"Because it's balanced," she replied.

Seven eased the pick a bit forward and it slid off his finger to the floor. "And now it falls. Why?"

"Because the weight wasn't balanced anymore."

He smiled at her the way a teacher acknowledges good work by a student. " 'A' for the day, young lady, 'cause you just described what the fracturing of Antarctica will do to the balance of the Earth. The stability of the Earth's spin axis will get fucked royally and cause it to tumble over like an overloaded canoe. So, Ferryman, you don't have to worry 'bout the world being turned into a giant swimming pool 'cause there won't be many left to take a dip."

"Go on," Kimberlain said.

"You want it all?"

"I want it all."

"Hope you got a strong stomach," Captain Seven muttered and settled low and deep in his chair. "Like I said before, the problem's one of of weight displacement. Not much different than my pick, 'cause losin' all that ice mass will topple the planet in similar fashion. We're talkin' here about what is generally and accurately referred to as a 'poleshift,' in which *everything* ends up tossed out of balance. Forces of nature don't like that much, and they want their balance back. So they try to find it. Violently. Hurricanes with thousand-mile-an-hour winds will sweep the globe. Tidal waves will be as common as Jacuzzis. Any volcano with any life left in it will burp lava and hot ash like you never did see. Earthquakes will splinter plenty of land areas, and, as a bonus, they'll swallow up lots and lots of nuclear reactors thereby causing the effects of a thousand meltdowns. Lots of radioactivity, my friend, set blowin' in the wind.''

Captain Seven started to raise his bong up again, then saw he was out of pot. ''Thing is we're talkin' here about a planet that hangs in a surprisingly delicate balance between the poles. Our axis is maintained by huge weight masses concentrated at top and bottom. Once those nukes displace all that weight in the south, what you're effectively doing is removing one balance point. Dig?''

''All too well.''

''The planet would wobble around in search of a new balance with probably tropical South America taking over as the South Pole and somewhere around Japan taking over as the North.''

That made Kimberlain think of something. ''If you could predict the location of the new poles, could you also predict zones least affected by the pole shift?''

''You mean so anybody who knew what was coming could find refuge? Theoretically, yes. But all this is untested, so nothing's for certain.''

Not nothing, the Ferryman thought. *The Hashi are in this to inherit whatever's left, and somehow they've found a way to survive the initial effects of the cataclysm.*

''The only thing that's certain is that whoever does survive might end up wishing they didn't. All of the crops and plants indigenous to the old world will have a heap of trouble making it in the new. So whatever few survivors are left won't have much to eat, and with all the aquifers ruptured by those quakes, a lot of the drinking water will be gone too. Freshwater bodies aboveground will be polluted with debris and poisons beyond repair. Yup, I guess you could say the world'd be fucked up good.''

Captain Seven lapsed into silence and went about refilling one of the chambers of his bong with pot. Kimberlain found himself speechless as well. What the captain had just elaborated on was the vision of a madman, the vision of Jason Benbasset. He was going to punish the world for what it had done to him, to his family, and he had chosen a means that would destroy civilization as it was known and force it to remake itself from scratch.

The Ferryman's mind turned back to the Hashi. Their leaders would have embraced the plan as a means to create the kind of world they wanted and were suddenly in a position to inherit. If those safe zones could be pinned down, if they could emerge relatively unscathed from the Eighth Trumpet, then all other survivors would be at their mercy, the world *theirs* to remake.

The key remained with Outpost 10. Danielle was en route there now, but even if she reached the outpost, she would need help to accomplish what she had to, and that help could only come through him.

"There's a senator," Kimberlain told the three of them in the train after summarizing his thoughts, "I arranged a payback for. I've never called one in before, but there's always a first time." He thought further. "But that doesn't help us with Macy's. The parade's got to be called off, and I haven't got the slightest idea of where to go, considering the authorities will have no reason to believe me."

"I do," said Lisa.

"TLP is on the best of terms with the Macy's toy department," she explained. "And we've got strong connections to the parade coordinators."

"How so?"

"We've sponsored a float every year in the last four. Every year except this one, that is."

"Something changed?"

"Yes," Lisa replied with a smile that came quite easily. "Someone destroyed the life-size models of our Powerized Officers of War that were going to make up this year's display."

* * *

While Lisa went to the seventeenth floor of Macy's main store across from Penn Station in Manhattan, Kimberlain drove to the Hudson Valley and the white, Queen Anne–style mansion on the river's east bank belonging to Senator Thomas Brooks. He called ahead, and the senator, home for the holiday, agreed to see him immediately. Brooks was there to greet him as soon as he rang the bell.

"It's been a long time, Mr. Kimberlain."

"Not really, Senator. A year and a half, maybe two."

"A long time in politics, son. Forgive me."

"It's you who must forgive me. This isn't a social call. I need a favor. I know I said there would be no compensation for what I did for you, but—"

Senator Brooks cut him off. "Please, Mr. Kimberlain, you have no need to apologize. If it's in my power, I'll do it." His voice grew reflective. "God knows I owe you. You saved my sanity. They took my grandson because of me, and I felt useless until you brought me back to life with that . . . payback. Just name it. Anything I can do to help you."

"Not just me, Senator."

They moved into the study. Senator Brooks had a fire going, and the Ferryman wished he could have enjoyed the splendid autumn panorama through the freshly restored bay windows.

"How familiar are you, Senator, with oil exploration in Antarctica?"

Brooks thought briefly. "Proposals for drilling have come up before my energy committee several times. It always turns into a battle of lobbies between the environmentalists and the oil industry."

"Just screens."

"Pardon me?"

"Senator, have you ever heard of an installation called Outpost 10?"

"No, I'm quite certain I haven't. Why?"

"Because it's the central part of an operation called Spiderweb. Oil drilling in Antarctica has been going on for some years already.

That's what I meant by screens. The oil industry's just going through the motions because they've already got what they want, and when the time's right they'll make the announcement to the country. There aren't many who know about it, though, since the whole project comes under the auspices of the Defense Department.''

"That's incredible."

"But quite real. Hundreds of live wells linked together by pipelines stretching thousands of miles, and all joining up at the master control station called Outpost 10.''

Senator Brooks no longer looked relaxed. The warmth of the fire could not stop his face from paling. "If what you say is true, there'll be hell to pay.''

"It is true, Senator, and hell's an accurate way to describe the upshot, but not for the reasons you might think. Are you up to interrupting the President's holiday retreat?''

"With sufficient reason, absolutely.''

"Then make yourself comfortable, sir. This story may take a while to tell.''

Senator Brooks was still trembling when Kimberlain left him, secure in the notion that he would contact the President after checking the story himself as best he could. It was already Tuesday afternoon, and because of the Antarctic Treaty the Ferryman knew the U.S. maintained no active military presence on the continent. That meant troops and equipment would have to be airlifted, which would take time under the best of circumstances.

That much, then, was out of his hands.

Lisa Eiseman had left a message for him with Peet at the midtown hotel they had checked into. She wanted him to meet her at Macy's as soon as possible. He arrived there at four o'clock and rode the mezzanine elevator up to the Special Events offices located on the seventeenth floor. The corridor was narrow, and he made out Lisa sitting patiently in a chair outside an office at the very end.

She saw him and strode over. "He canceled a host of meetings to see you, Jared,'' she told him. "They're taking this seriously.''

"How much did you tell them?"

"Just the basics. That we had discovered there was a possible threat to the safety of the parade, and that you would provide the specifics."

"Well done."

A balding, portly man noticed Kimberlain's appearance and emerged from inside the office. He extended his hand to Kimberlain rather cautiously. "Bill Burns, director of special projects."

"Jared Kimberlain, longtime customer."

The Ferryman had tried for humor with the remark, but gained barely a polite smile from Burns. "We can talk in my office."

Lisa followed them inside, and Burns closed the door when she was seated next to Kimberlain.

"I'm curious, Mr. Kimberlain," Burns started, "to learn exactly who you are. Miss Eiseman was rather vague in that regard."

"I'm a lot of things, Mr. Burns, but mostly I provide a service: I help people. You won't see my services listed in the Yellow Pages, but enough seem to find me when they're in trouble."

"And that's what we are, in trouble?"

"More than you realize."

"But I don't remember seeking you out."

"It was different this time. There was another matter I was called in on. That led me to you, to Macy's."

"And the parade."

"And the parade."

Burns hesitated. "Have you gone to the police about this?"

"I was hoping that wouldn't be necessary."

"How wouldn't it be necessary, Mr. Kimbelain? Under the circumstances, I mean."

"I was hoping you would be willing to cancel the parade."

Burns started to laugh and then stopped. "You're joking."

"Not at all."

"Are we talking about terrorism here?"

"A form of it, I suppose, yes."

"But we haven't received any threats, any demands."

"As I said, only a form. Three years ago an explosion ended your parade prematurely, Mr. Burns, just as it prematurely ended the life of one powerful man. But it didn't kill him. Instead it gave birth to a whole new human being. And now there's a new disaster about to happen—the one Miss Eiseman has explained to you—and this man has chosen your parade to begin it. The ultimate symmetry, Mr. Burns. A mad brand of logic."

"And just who is this man?"

"Jason Benbasset."

"My God. You're serious, aren't you?"

"I wish I could say I wasn't."

The phone on Burns's desk buzzed. He excused himself and picked it up, listened, and then spoke briefly. He turned back to Lisa and Kimberlain.

"When Miss Eiseman advised me of the potential severity of the situation and of your . . . interest, I took the liberty of having our security department run a check on you."

"I know."

"You *know*?"

"It's what I would have done in your position. But, you see, my file's sealed. Your security department wouldn't have found anything unless I unsealed it."

As if on cue, a knock came on Burns's door and a younger man in shirtsleeves entered the office and put a manila folder into the portly man's hand. Burns started reading, eyes widening and occasionally coming up to meet Kimberlain's as he thumbed through the single-spaced pages. When finished, he did nothing for a time other than gaze across the desk at the Ferryman.

"It would seem you underestimate yourself, Mr. Kimberlain," he said finally.

"Modesty's always been one of my virtues."

"You have my apologies and my attention. Please, what exactly are we facing here?"

"Five hundred pounds of the most potent plastic explosives

known to man that if properly placed could take out a large chunk of the city.''

"Lord."

"I wasn't finished yet. This plastic explosive can be melted into a liquid, heated into an explosive gas, formed into virtually any shape—the possibilities are endless."

"And the perpetrators plan to use it during the parade?"

"Not just during your parade, Mr. Burns, *on* it. No one will be safe. Not the people watching or the ones participating. You understand my point about cancellation now."

"Yes, but it's impossible for us to cancel at so late a time. I haven't got the authority, and I'm not sure any other individual does either. The number of people involved in this event is tremendous. And there's television coverage to consider as well. If we cancel without showing just cause, meaning absolute proof, we could be sued."

"Five hundred pounds of C-12 *plastique* should be plenty of 'just cause' for you."

"Unfortunately, on your word alone, it can't. Please understand me, Mr. Kimberlain. I sympathize with everything you've said, and I don't doubt your word. But it remains *your* word—one man's word. If we were to call the parade off based on that, then we would be submitting ourselves to a different form of terrorism, wouldn't we? And in another perspective the terrorists would have won."

"These aren't terrorists!" Kimberlain caught his voice rising in time to lower it. "They're not out to score points for their hopeless Third World revolution. They're here to punish society, starting with your parade. I don't know how closely you read my file, but you might have gotten the idea I know a lot about vengeance, getting even, what I like to call paybacks. This whole incident is Jason Benbasset's version of a payback."

Burns shook his head, confused and anxious. "I'm a PR man, Mr. Kimberlain, not a decision-maker. But I know how they function, and I can promise you that the parade will not be canceled on such short notice without absolute proof."

"If I knew where the C-12 was, this conversation would never have had to take place."

Burns's tone turned conciliatory. "Please, we're both after the same thing here. Neither of us wants a disaster while the country is getting ready to sit down to Thanksgiving dinner, but we must face the fact that the parade is going to go on. With that in mind, what's our next best option?"

"Security. Lots of it."

"That much I *can* arrange. I'll talk to the New York police myself; the FBI, too. I'll put every one of our security people on duty and arrange twenty-four-hour guards on all sites where parade equipment is being assembled or stored."

"Where's your chief of security?"

"In Philadelphia until late this evening. I can set up a meeting for you first thing tomorrow morning."

"I'll want to know everything there is to know about your parade, Mr. Burns. The route, the props, the floats, those famous balloons, the works."

Burns jotted it all down. "Anything else?"

"Sure," said Kimberlain. "Pray for a blizzard."

"There'll be over twenty-five hundred Macy's employees walking the route, Mr. Kimberlain. No one will be praying any harder than I."

THE EIGHTH TRUMPET

OUTPOST 10

Wednesday, November 25; 7:00 A.M.

CHAPTER 31

FOR DANIELLE THE LAST FORTY-EIGHT HOURS HAD BEEN A LIVING hell. She had slipped reluctantly from Kimberlain's embrace Monday afternoon sadly aware that it was unlikely they would ever see each other again. He was the only person she would ever meet who knew her for what she was and thought no less of her as a result. Her life had been so filled with secrecy and deception that her very name had been forgotten, and reaching for the truth was a difficult task. The Ferryman accepted her because he too had lived such a life, and now he was gone. By her own choosing. By necessity.

So she could find the only truth left that mattered at Outpost 10.

She had fled Malta with the Hashi close on her heels and had begun a long journey laced with frustration and a feeling of utter helplessness. Her route took her to Sydney, Australia, by way of Paris and then on to Christchurch, New Zealand, through which most planes in and out of Antarctica were channeled. Her cover for at least reaching the continent, specifically the American research station at McMurdo, was in place. From there she had no idea of how she would make her way the additional eight hundred miles to Outpost 10—over the Transantarctic Mountains to boot. And even if she did manage to reach it, she held little hope the weaponry would be available to thwart the takeover attempt by a well-trained force of Hashi commandos from the captive submarine. All she could do was reach McMurdo and take things from there.

And here lay the basis for her initial frustrations: all traffic in and out of McMurdo from Christchurch was being restricted due to airfield problems. Her arrival in New Zealand Tuesday night was met with the news that the C-130 cargo plane scheduled to take her across would not be leaving until six-thirty A.M., which left her an additional seven hours to wallow in her anxiety. Two journalists were scheduled to make the trip along with a half-dozen researchers who'd been away on leave and were now returning.

The weather in Christchurch was chilly, and she knew Antarctica itself would be much worse. Even though November was the beginning of summer on the continent and the sun never set, killer storms could whip up quickly and last for days. The temperature was tolerable but still frigid to one not used to the climate.

It was sunny and bright in Christchurch Wednesday morning, and after breakfast the small group of passengers was escorted from the barracks straight onto the airfield. At the foot of the stairs leading up to the C-130, a panting German Shepherd sniffed each passenger before he or she was allowed to make his way up. At the rear of the party, Denielle felt the grasp of fear, thinking of the pistol concealed in the thick padding of her down parka. As she drew closer, though, she saw the dog was concerned solely with sniffing for drugs. She petted him when he was finished and smiled at his disapproving handler.

McMurdo was 2,200 miles away. At top speed, the C-130 would make it there by mid-afternoon. Danielle finally managed to steal some sleep during the flight, content at least with the fact that the last leg of her journey and of her mission was upon her. The Ferryman's assurances in Malta had meant nothing. Brother Valette had said all along it would be left to the Knights to stop the Hashi's ultimate try for chaos in the end, meaning it was left to her. There would be no help coming from Kimberlain in the States. She felt sure of that.

She awoke just as the C-130 was going into its descent. The aircraft was equipped with ski bottoms to maintain control during the landing. The airfields of McMurdo were paved, but workers were helpless to fight off the onslaught of the blowing winds, which sent snow squalling over the tarmac to freeze quickly into ice. Accordingly, the runways were built on a slight upward grade, so the C-130's brakes would bring it to a gradual stop.

Danielle tried to look out the window, but the brightness blinded her, a great white blur for as far as she could see. Her eyes ached. She longed for sunglasses as she watched the other passengers donning theirs. Nothing but white—rolling, sloping, hilly white. The C-130 grazed the runway with its skis. It was like flying while on the ground, and it seemed as though it would never stop. But the plane did stop, and rather precisely at that, not more than forty yards beyond a green mini-bus that would take them the five-mile stretch from the airfield to McMurdo Station.

Outside, the Antarctic cold was like none she had experienced before. It pierced the thickness of her jacket and clasped her flesh in its icy grip. It was raw, wet, and made breathing difficult. Her exhaled breath turned white, and she longed for her exposed face to grow numb to spare her the feeling of needles prickling with each gust of the wind.

The air inside the mini-bus was warmer but hardly comfortable. She could hear the heaters struggling against the dwindling temperatures and losing the fight. The door had been opened long enough for the passengers and their gear to be packed in—and also long enough for all the hot air to rush out so the heater had to start anew.

"All buckled in?" the driver called back to his seated passengers. And without waiting for an answer, he tucked his goggles over his eyes and the van set off.

Danielle knew enough about the Antarctic climate to fear such cold temperatures, for in the summer season they could only mean a treacherous storm was about to descend on the area. If that happened before she found her way to Outpost 10, she might well end up stuck at McMurdo while the hijacked submarine brought its deadly crew and cargo to a comfortable distance from the base. She fought the thoughts back; there was no sense in considering them.

The road the mini-bus took was formed of chunks of ice so worn that it had lost much of its slipperiness. Lines of red and green flags wedged into the ground on bamboo stakes rimmed the road on both sides in order to help drivers keep their vehicles on the path in far worse conditions. The road was winding, and the van did not take the curves especially well. The most it had going for it was the fact that it had the route all to itself, and at last it swung around a large high mound known as Observation Hill, beneath which lay McMurdo Station.

Danielle saw the development at first glance for just what it was: a speck of civilization where it plainly didn't belong. McMurdo had grown from a simple American research outpost into a small town, much of it built on a slope in a cluttered composite of streets and buildings that battled for her eye with enormous storage tanks. There were dormitories, workshops, a huge mess hall, a chapel, laboratories, garages, an administration building, a bar—all linked together by dirt roads that were either frozen or hopelessly muddy. Sewer and water pipes ran above-ground from building to building, encased in corrugated tin.

The first thing Danielle heard after climbing out of the van was the sound of a helicopter. She squinted her eyes to see a huge red Navy chopper lifting off from a pad next to a sprawling structure, the depth of which told her it must be the McMurdo gym. Helicopters were crucial here, since they were the only means of conveniently traveling beyond the immediate vicinity. She could see that the red monsters manned by the Navy were fitted with extra-capacity fuel tanks, and she wondered if that rendered them capable of taking her all the way to Outpost 10. Even if so, she had no idea how to fly one, which meant any plan to seize a chopper had to include coercing a pilot as well.

Moving toward the processing center, she noticed the conglomeration of antennae and dishes that watched over McMurdo from positions on the surrounding ridges. Perhaps she could find a way to make contact with the outpost, but what exactly could she tell them? She was considering precisely that question when the station commander greeted her and the other new arrivals curiously and abruptly.

"What's eating him?" one journalist asked another.

"There's a big storm coming up, and he's got a pair of research teams in the field. Chopper just lifted off to pick them up. But it's gonna be close if the storm's as big and as close as they say."

Danielle swallowed hard. Unknowingly, the journalist might have just spoken an epitaph for all of civilization. The coldness racing through her now was from far more than simply the temperature. A storm sweeping in from the area of the South Pole would render any possible route to Outpost 10 out of the question. In a word, she was grounded, as was all other traffic in and out of McMurdo, including the C-130 that had brought her here.

Unless . . .

She found the pilot of the C-130 in the McMurdo bar, starting to drink away the hours he knew he'd be stuck here. She sat down close enough to him to make him notice her, and in case he hadn't she prolonged the motion of tossing her hair free of her parka's hood. Like everyone else in the bar, she wouldn't take the parka off until her body temperature had a chance to regulate itself.

"You were on the plane this morning," the pilot said to her from his spot two stools over.

She nodded, waiting for the bartender. "Nice flight. Meal service could have been better, though."

"Let me make up for that now," he said, sliding over next to her.

Beyond the frost-encrusted window she could see the sky already clouding with the first signs of the coming storm.

"What are you drinking?" the pilot asked her. He relayed her answer to the bartender, adding, "If you don't mind, that is."

"Not at all."

The pilot smiled then and eased himself even closer. "Name's Bob Padrone."

"Marla King, Captain Padrone."

"Bob, *please*. Last name's easy to remember 'cause if you change the 'd' and the 'r' you've got the word pardon, except for the 'e' of course."

"Pardon me, Bob."

The pilot forced a laugh.

The rest was easy, barely an hour's investment of time. She maneuvered the man shamelessly, each smile or dart of her eyes bringing her further into control. The pilot kept drinking, not overdoing it but not watching himself either. Danielle lingered over a second beer, with the warm bitter taste of her first one stuck in her mouth. He touched her; she let him. He drew still closer; she let him. Not forcing it, never forcing it. Finally his arm slid around her and they kissed, exchanged whispers, Padrone unable to hide his surprise at her request.

"You wanna go *where*?"

Even at the bottom of the world, money plays an important role. A crumpled twenty-dollar bill pulled from his pocket gained the pilot use of a four-wheel-drive jeep, albeit with a lousy heater, to take them back to the airfield, specifically the cockpit of his C-130, and if that wasn't a fitting name for it on this day he didn't know what was. First time for everything, he figured.

They stepped out of the jeep and Padrone eyed the darkening horizon before moving to the ladder that would take them up.

"Better not stay out here too long with that coming on."

"Let's just see what else can come on, shall we?"

Padrone was trembling with excitement as he ascended the ladder with Danielle close behind. Inside he hit a few switches in the coldness and the drone of a tired fan whirled through the cockpit.

"Won't be but a few minutes 'fore it's nice and toasty," he told her. "Till then we might have to rely on body heat."

Her response was a roguish smile as he flipped another switch which activated a single light over the console. Doing it in a space surrounded by windows would have bothered Bob Padrone anywhere else. But not here at the bottom of the world with a killer storm coming on fast.

"Now, what do you say we—"

He stopped when he saw the pistol suddenly gripped in the woman's hand, the stare on her face icier than the frost gathering on the outside of the windshield.

"I hope you're not too drunk to fly, Captain, because you've got seven hundred and fifty miles of it ahead of you."

"This is crazy!" Padrone protested fearfully when they were airborne. "Case you didn't notice, there's a friggin' mother of a storm heading straight for us."

"Right now we're heading straight for it."

The pilot looked at her as if she had lost her mind. Danielle didn't blame him.

"They got radar back at McMurdo. They'll know we took off."

"What do you expect they'll do about it?"

Padrone had no answer for that and gazed at the radio, forgetting again that the woman had turned it off.

"You've got us headin' for the friggin' South Pole, which means we've got to climb over the Transantarctic Mountains. There's nothing there. Believe me."

"Used to be nothing, Captain. Something changed."

"Nobody ever goes that way. Nobody!"

"Just my point."

"Look, let me turn this tub around. Circle for a while. Let's talk about this."

The first of the storm appeared before them as nothing more than a few snowflakes sliding onto the windshield.

"Oh shit, it's gonna be a big one. I can feel it. Cake up our engines for sure and end your charter real fast, lady."

"Just get me to where I told you."

"There's nothing there!"

"Then you won't have any trouble finding it."

"You're gonna get us friggin' killed!" Padrone blared, clenching his teeth as more of the storm appeared before them in a great white blanket that seemed to be rising out of the equally white landscape beneath it. "Jesus Christ!"

Danielle looked on with similar awe, her resolve tempered no in the least. "Can you climb?"

"Been climbing, lady. These tubs ain't like jet fighters, and with this kind of air it's even worse. Least let me turn the radio back on keep McMurdo abreast of what's happening. That way if we crash they'll be able to—"

"They won't be able to do a thing. If we crash, we die. Jus sooner than everyone else, that's all."

Every mile was more nerve-racking than the one before it. The force and brutality of the storm were incredible, tossing the C-130 about at will. It was like being in a boat on rough seas. Danielle had fastened herself into the copilot's seat as tight as she could.

In the meantime, Padrone had sobered up fast and was performing admirably. He'd given up protesting and had turned his attention solely to flying. He was a good pilot, a damn good one, and he quickly figured out how to time the severest onslaughts of the storm and maneuver the C-130 to ride the winds as much as possible Watching him was like watching a race car driver manipulate the course, slowing through the especially difficult turns. Speed was no a prime consideration, but he didn't dare pull back on their thrust fo fear of losing the precarious footing the storm now allowed him.

"We're almost to your damn coordinates," he shot at her, "and there's nothing there, nothing on radar. You're dreaming. Just like I told you."

Danielle turned the radio back on and handed the microphone to him. "Signal a Mayday."

"Little late, lady. In this storm McMurdo will never get the message."

"We're not sending to McMurdo."

"Then who the hell are we . . ."

Padrone gave up and worked the mike as instructed. Then he adjusted the controls and tried again.

"Storm's swallowing the signals before they get anywhere," he reported grimly.

Danielle felt as though a blow had caught her in the stomach. Her plan had been to force Outpost 10 to provide them with landing coordinates thanks to the Mayday call. Without those coordinates in such a raging storm . . .

A vast white thermal blanket rose up before them. There was a thud of impact as something crashed into their nose. The windshield shattered, and small jets of icy air sped through, feeling like needles against Danielle's face.

Padrone struggled valiantly with the controls, but everything seemed to seize up. He realized that they were going down and blindly felt for the switch that would lock home the landing skis.

Not that it mattered, since they didn't have enough fuel to get back to McMurdo no matter what. If the crash didn't take them, the cold would.

Danielle had thrown her hands up instinctively when the C-130 struck the snowy ground spinning. She was aware of screaming, hers or Padrone's she wasn't sure, and thrashed for something to hold on to.

Her hands were still thrashing when something white and cruel came up in front of the C-130 as it whirled and delivered a jolting impact that fractured the transport's steel hull at the center. She was conscious of pain and cold for only an instant before they were replaced by nothing at all.

CHAPTER 32

KIMBERLAIN WAS WALKING BACK DOWN THE CORRIDOR OF MAcy's seventeenth floor at seven A.M. Wednesday. Inside Burns's office a female shape was moving about.

Kimberlain went to the door and peered inside. "I'm sorry. I was supposed to meet the head of security here at seven."

"You found her," returned a ravishing Oriental woman. "The name's Cathy Nu, Mr. Kimberlain."

Jared took her extended hand. "Whoops."

"Apology accepted," she said with a smile that made her look even more beautiful and radiant. Her dark hair tumbled past her shoulders, and her skin might have been wax, it looked so smooth and flawless. She was tall for an Oriental and lithe. Her handshake had been strong.

"I read the file on you that Mr. Burns left for me, Mr. Kimberlain. And where it left off I was able to fill in with some information obtained from friends in Chinatown."

The Ferryman smiled slightly at that. "Spent a little time there not too long ago."

"But made quite an impression. You've become a hero to the people of the shops. There are few men willing to stand up to the

Tong. In fact, some of the locals insist you were a spirit called from another time to do battle with the enemies of the masses."

"Only my tailor knows for sure, Miss Nu."

"Cathy."

"Jared."

There was a pause, broken by Cathy Nu. "I assume, now that we are formally acquainted, we can get down to facts. Mr. Burns briefed me extensively over the phone last night. For what it's worth, I'm going into this accepting everything you say at full face value."

"It's worth a lot."

"Maybe not enough." She shrugged. "If what you say is true . . . Well, just for the record, I told Burns we should find a way to cancel. His mind doesn't operate from a standpoint of security, so he had no real conception of what's involved here. A two-and-a-half-mile parade route, with maybe two million spectators lined up ten to fifteen deep. That's just too vast to guarantee anyone's safety no matter what steps we take, and believe me, plenty are taken even in a normal year."

"Did he go over my list of recommendations with you?"

"Yes, and I've already acted on several. I met with the police captain in charge of their security detail, and you can bet there are gonna be a lot of unhappy NYPD officers on this holiday: he agreed to pull an additional fifteen hundred from the off-duty roster. Some of them are already in place. This is going to cost the city a fortune in overtime."

"I'll cry later. What about the air traffic people?"

"Easily accomplished, and I didn't even have to get overly specific as to cause. All air traffic will be rerouted to avoid the grid over the entire city. Three police and two Coast Guard choppers will patrol the perimeter just to make sure no strays wander over. The Coast Guard choppers are outfitted with special radar they use to nab drug smugglers. They'll give us plenty of advance warning if any aircraft appear to be approaching." She stopped. "You don't think it's going to come from the air, do you?"

"Do you?"

"Given the scenario you've outlined, it's the most logical and simplest approach."

"Not when there's the C-12 *plastique* to consider. That changes the rules. The blast radius these explosives can cause from ground level means they don't need aircraft to accomplish their goal."

Cathy Nu recalled that section of the report. "A million dead, approximately half the people watching along the route. Okay, what do we do from here?"

"We walk the entire parade route. Take your notebook, Cathy. We've got a lot of lives to save."

"Were you born in Chinatown?" Kimberlain asked Cathy Nu as their taxi did its best to weave through the early-morning traffic.

She nodded. "The eldest of seven brothers and sisters and the only one born within Chinatown's limits. My parents waited until they were out to complete the family. What was the sense? They had left one China for another within the United States. My father referred to us as two different families representing the different stages of his American life." Her voice grew distant. "Often he told me he loved me best because I bridged the gap between them. I was eleven before my first sibling was born, and nineteen when my father died. A freshman at NYU with a full-time job at Macy's. The store saved me. I had to support my family, and they supported me every step of the way. I owe Macy's so much. If I can help stop this from happening, then . . . You get the idea."

"Sure. We all owe something to somebody."

"So it would seem."

"Where are we going?"

"The Lincoln Tunnel."

"I thought we were going to the parade's starting point."

"We are."

"Technically," she explained when they were inside the tunnel, "Macy's Thanksgiving Day Parade starts here tonight at one A.M.— Thanksgiving morning actually. The floats that compose much of the parade are worked on year-round in an old candy factory we own on the Hoboken waterfront. We call it the Float Palace. A crew of twenty will begin work on next year's parade come Monday.''

"We hope.''

"Yes, we hope.''

"Bring your notebook, Cath?''

She produced a memo pad from her purse.

"Good. Here's the first thing to make note of. Get your police contacts to dispatch a few of their trained dogs to that warehouse to sniff for C-12. Bring them out tonight after all construction is complete.''

"It's a bit more complicated than that.''

"How so?''

"Well, the floats are constructed in Hoboken, but nothing larger than twelve and a half feet high and eight feet wide can pass through the Lincoln Tunnel. So at one A.M., when they reach the Jersey side, they're disassembled for the trip through and then reassembled on the other side.''

"Must be time-consuming.''

"Not really. They're built to come apart and then go back together, and they're also incredibly solid. Remember, they carry singers, dancers, and actors who perform, or at least smile and wave, constantly throughout the parade.''

Kimberlain thought briefly. "Fine. We post guards within and on both sides of the tunnel starting at ten tonight. After reassembly, just to be on the safe side, we let the dogs have another go at the floats to be sure nothing new has been added that shouldn't have been, and we keep guards right on top of them until showtime.''

Cathy jotted down some more notes, adding a few suggestions of her own. They emerged from the tunnel, and she instructed the driver to head back into Manhattan.

"How many floats?'' the Ferryman wanted to know.

"Fifteen major this year.''

"Which brings us to the balloons. I remember them from when I was a kid."

"Don't we all. There are twelve this year, the most ever. They're constructed in another warehouse in Hoboken."

"Composition?"

"Urethane-coated nylon filled with helium and air. They're composed in sections so that a leak or tear in one section won't ruin the entire creature. The largest is Superman, at seventy-eight feet. Snoopy's about sixty including his roller skates. Kermit the Frog's about the same."

"Difficult to get them through this as well," Kimberlain noted as the cab headed back through the tunnel.

"Of course." Cathy smiled. "They're inflated a section at a time near the starting line on Central Park West tonight. It's quite a spectacle. People stay up the whole night with us watching. The balloons are delivered on trucks and laid out flat on sheets of cloth on the street. Nets are placed over them so they won't escape once inflated."

Kimberlain felt his neck hairs prickle. "You're aware that C-12 can be converted into an explosive gas."

"I am now."

"Let's say the enemy has a way of pumping that gas into the balloons mixed with your helium."

Cathy made some notes before responding. "We'll check each and every canister before it's used to inflate individual balloon sections." She paused and looked at Kimberlain. "Under that scenario, how could they be detonated?"

"Combustion, almost surely. A simple spark would be all it would take. Picture the New York skyline as it rises over Broadway. A dozen snipers, each perched on a rooftop or at a window, with instructions to fire into a particular balloon at a precise moment."

Cathy Nu sighed nervously and went back to writing. "We'll have to have men posted on almost every rooftop as well, then."

"Be difficult to handle all potential windows."

"Spotters from both ground level and above," Cathy proposed. "Each with a particular grid to sweep."

"Fine, but there's another possibility as well: detonation from a ground-level stimulus. Tell me about the people underneath the balloons."

"The handlers, you mean? Thirty-five to fifty people on each one, depending on its size and complexity. All volunteer Macy's employees."

"Make sure there are sufficient numbers of police and security people sprinkled in for good measure. All should be equipped with walkie-talkies tuned to your channel."

They passed out of the tunnel and sunlight flooded the cab, stinging their eyes.

"Forecast's the same for tomorrow," Cathy reported. "Only warmer."

"Let's check out the route."

"This is the real starting line," Cathy Nu told him as they stood at the corner of Central Park West and 77th Street. "The parade forms here and proceeds eighteen blocks to Columbus Circle. From there it veers onto Broadway and proceeds straight down it across Seventh Avenue to the finish line at 34th Street and Herald Square, the back of our store. Two and a half miles from start to finish."

"A million spectators per mile?"

"With tomorrow's forecast, it could be more."

"Give me an idea of the timing and organization," Kimberlain said, ready to visualize it.

"The floats, balloons, and bands are lined up separately, awaiting their signal to pull out into the parade as it proceeds down Central Park West. It's quite a show in itself, watching it all evolve through the early hours. Anyway, clowns mostly fill in the gaps between the major displays, also serving to keep route delays to a minimum."

"What do you mean delays?"

"Television dictates our schedule, for the most part. A number of bands and most of the floats stop at the finish line for a one- or two-minute performance. The rest of the parade is halted from around 36th Street back to protect against bunching."

"When is the lead of the procession scheduled to reach the finish line?"

"Ten A.M., give or take five minutes."

"What does television do for the first hour?"

"They cut back and forth between the starting line and Herald Square. Live entertainment, interviews with parade participants, lots of fluff basically to kill those minutes until the first of the parade reaches the cameras at Herald Square."

"Then no cameras follow the parade at the center."

"Not consistently. A few mobile cams, that's all."

Kimberlain gazed ahead down the sprawling length of Central Park West. "Then we'll be safe until ten o'clock at least. When are television ratings traditionally the highest?"

"Between eleven and twelve. Could be as many as fifty million tuning in during that period."

Kimberlain almost shuddered at that comment, recalling fifty million to be the same number a Hashi killer had claimed would serve as witnesses.

"That's the hour the explosion will be planned for," he said finally. "Optimum effect that way." He walked a bit down from the starting line with Cathy at his side. "What else will happen by way of preparation tonight?"

"To avoid possible snaring of the tethers, traffic lights will be removed and lampposts turned away from the streets."

"Blows one of my pet theories," Kimberlain told her. "Thermal explosive detonators rigged into the streetlights. Turn them on all at the same time while the parade is passing and *bang!*"

They continued walking, crossing over to the Central Park side of the street. Kimberlain's eyes moved between the park grounds and the apartment and office buildings that towered over the scene across Central Park West. His feet grazed a steel grating which vibrated as a subway train passed beneath.

"The subways run the whole route?"

"Yes."

"And they'll be active all day tomorrow?"

She nodded. "With extra trains added."

"What are the chances of shutting them down?"

"About the same as canceling the parade. With so many streets closed off and holiday parking rules in effect, it would be a disaster of a different kind to shut the system down on a day like tomorrow."

Kimberlain stopped and looked at her. "You want to talk about disasters, Cathy?" He hesitated long enough for another subway car to rumble past them. "Subway trains create a great deal of vibration. Assume the underside of Broadway along the route is packed with the C-12. When the vibrations reach their peak, perhaps increased by the weight of all those spectators, the explosives are detonated."

Cathy was writing again. "Police and transit personnel will be checking everywhere as soon as I get back to my desk."

"Have them check the subway ceilings too. Chunks and shards of asphalt being blown upward would be as deadly as shrapnel. C-12 could be packed in a way to imitate the effects of a localized earthquake."

More writing.

"The point," Kimberlain continued, "is that we've got to plan on two fronts: one, that they've somehow already got the *plastique* in place; and two, that their plan entails its not being present for us to find until the moments immediately prior to detonation. Which means advance security is all well and good, but the real cruncher is going to be those early hours of the parade."

"Is it possible they'll call off the attack, knowing we're onto it?" Cathy wondered.

"No," the Ferryman replied with total certainty, thinking of the mad obsession driving Jason Benbasset. "It's not possible at all."

They walked silently for a long stretch. Pedestrian traffic thickened as they neared Columbus Circle, the sidewalks cluttered by the time they veered left onto Broadway. In his mind Kimberlain was visualizing the floats, balloons, and bands making their way toward the heart of midtown, enclosed and thus trapped by the buildings lining both sides. Starting at ten o'clock and stretching for two hours beyond that, all of Broadway down to Herald Square would be filled by the parade and the lines of spectators. He gazed up at the buildings again and thought of all the glass forming their windows being ruptured by the percussion of the vast C-12 blast. The effect would be akin to a billion darts fired down from the sky upon spectators crammed too close together to move along the entire Broadway stretch of the route.

Cathy Nu had moved slightly ahead of him as they walked on, past the Marriott Marquis, the half-price ticket booth, the Newsday Building, and other landmarks Kimberlain stored in his head for future reference. At last the rear of Macy's vast building rose up before him in Herald Square.

"The parade ends here for each participant with a right turn and a brief stretch down 34th Street, where the process of dismantling for next year begins," Cathy explained.

"Let's hope so," said the Ferryman.

"What do you think, Captain?"

With night fully entrenched over the city, the Ferryman had briefed Captain Seven on all the security deployments and precautions that would be taken prior to and during the parade. As of now, two thousand security personnel were already on duty at the Macy's warehouse in Hoboken, as well as along the entire route, on rooftops, and watching from windows, the greatest concentration centered at the starting line, where crews had already begun work. Before meeting the captain, Kimberlain had spoken again with Senator Thomas Brooks. Brooks had been unable to get through to the President until early Wednesday morning. It had taken the chief executive only a short time to confirm the existence of Outpost 10 and then to learn that all reinforcement efforts would be forestalled by a killer blizzard raging over the entire region.

Meanwhile, the *Rhode Island* continued her deadly journey

southward, continuing to avoid what had become a massive detection effort, just as she was supposed to.

"Can you come up with any chinks in the armor?" Kimberlain asked Seven.

The captain had lowered himself to his knees and was sniffing at the sidewalk along Times Square.

"This macadam's new," he said, gazing up. "I'd say not more than a week. Have it analyzed." Back on his feet, he crossed dangerously close to the traffic streaking down Broadway. "And the white lane lines."

"What about them?"

"Say our boys melted the C-12 into a liquid and treated it to come out white. Then they hit Broadway a few days ago disguised as the Department of Public Works and repainted the lines. Detonation could be ultrasonic or timer. Results the same."

"What else?"

"Love the way you're having all the contents of the balloons checked, but you forgot about the float tires. They gotta be inflated too, right? I'd check them just as close."

"Good idea."

"Of course. It's mine."

"Fine, and if you're done stroking your ego . . ."

"I'd like to get something else stroked, and as I remember, Times Square is just the place."

"When all this is over, I'm buying," Kimberlain told him.

"Promises, promises."

"Anything more?"

"All those ropes used to control, hold, and steer the balloons. Say you covered them with a clear liquid version of C-12 and really let it soak in. Ropes wouldn't see sunlight again until the day of the parade. Could be rigged to be heat sensitive. Go *boom!* when the air hits a certain temperature and heats them up."

Kimberlain shook his head. "I don't like it. They couldn't depend on it being a warm or a sunny day."

"You're right. I don't like it either."

"You've got more, I assume."

Captain Seven shrugged. "What I'm out of is cannabis. Been so busy lately that I've neglected my bodily needs. How about working me up some from your police buddies?"

"I like seeing you without smoke coming out of your eyes."

"You want me with a clear head, better get me some grass is what I'm saying. I'm gonna need the extra perception, 'cause the thing we gotta do, we gotta think of every little thing no matter how trivial it seems. See, the trouble is what we're facing here is the fact that this fucked-up plan would have taken into consideration the possibility we would have found out about it. So every step we're taking, they'd have expected us to take. Maybe they stay that one step ahead of us—a mile under the circumstances. So we look for more. We see every potential phase of this route as a potential weapon, and we see it the way they do, and when it's over you use your new police friends to requisition some fresh lava bed stash for me out of the evidence lockers." Then, after a pause, "We can't stop the enemy from trying, Ferryman. We can only stop him from succeeding."

Lisa Eiseman caught up with Kimberlain just as he reached the parade starting point at Central Park West and 77th Street. As expected, a large crowd had gathered to view the inflating of the balloons and other work. The Ferryman knew hundreds of the security force were scattered among them and was glad he was having trouble picking most of them out.

"You don't look overjoyed to see me," she said, fighting to catch his eyes.

"Actually I am," Kimberlain told her. "It saves me the bother of tracking you down to say I want you to fly back to Atlanta tomorrow morning."

"I'm a part of this too, in case you've forgotten."

"I haven't. But I don't want you on the streets tomorrow during the parade. I don't need more to worry about."

She looked at him harshly, determinedly, mind already made up.

Something had changed him after the time they'd spent in the cabin. The warmth she had tapped into had retreated deep inside him, making her feel that a touch of his flesh would freeze her fingertips. She couldn't leave without trying to find out what had happened. Leaving now would mean losing him forever.

"Don't tell me to go back to Atlanta and suffer through it all on television, Jared, not knowing where you are or how close you are to dying, because if you succeed here there's still Outpost 10 to worry about, and Atlanta's only a hundred feet above sea level." She wanted to reach out to him but stopped herself. "This is where I belong tomorrow."

"Not tomorrow anymore. It's after midnight. Happy Thanksgiving."

"Mr. Quintanna has told me much about you, Quail," the voice said to the figure in black standing before the video camera. "Did he explain why I had him summon you here?"

Dreighton Quail shook his huge, masked head, making sure to do so in the direction of the lens.

"You like death, Quail. You worship it. You must help me. We must help each other. Mr. Quintanna, give it to him."

Quintanna came forward with a black device the size of a transistor radio in his hand. Keeping his distance, he placed it in the outstretched glove of the Flying Dutchman.

"My new life began three years ago tomorrow, Quail. And so shall the new world. Tomorrow. In the very place where my new life was forced upon me. The circle must be closed appropriately."

Beep . . . beep . . . beep . . .

"That black box holds death, Quail," the voice continued. "More death than you can possibly imagine, violent and awful. Imagine a million screams sounding at once. How far will that sound travel, Quail? How many ears will be scorched by it?" The voice let the questions linger with the expulsions of its thickening breath. "Mr. Quintanna will provide the details of your assignment. You will follow them to the letter. Is that clear?"

Quail nodded, barely able to contain his growing excitement.

A million screams sounding at once. And he was to be a part of it.

The expectation set him trembling as he held the black box tight in his hand.

CHAPTER 33

DANIELLE AWOKE TO THE SOUND OF DRIPPING AND THE FEELING of warmth where there shouldn't have been any. Around her all was white, time suspended in the moment frozen when the frigid air assaulted her after the C-130 piloted by Bob Padrone crashed.

"She's coming around, Doctor."

Suddenly there was a woman by her side. Her thoughts cleared along with her vision. She was no longer out in the ice and snow, the violent storm circling all around her. She was in some sort of hospital wing or sick bay, spacious and well furnished. She smelled alcohol and realized the dripping sound was a glucose IV draining into her arm.

A man in a white coat hovered over her and turned a penlight on before her eyes, blinding her once more.

"Hold still," he urged and maneuvered the penlight closer.

Her memory sharpened. She had crawled from the smoking wreckage of the C-130, dragging the unconscious Padrone behind her. She had stayed close enough to the heat generated by it to keep them alive. The rest came back to her in splotchy recollections. Figures had emerged out of the white, emerged from a huge beast belching diesel smoke. It was a Snowcat, a larger version of the kind of vehicle used at mountain ski resorts. Someone had seen the crash. Someone had come to save her.

Someone from Outpost 10.

They raised her and Padrone by stretcher into the Snowcat and laid them out flat. Danielle recalled propping herself up enough to see what they were approaching out the front windshield. There was a complex of buildings all but lost in the storm and the harsh whiteness of the landscape. Outpost 10 was smaller than she had expected, with a central structure of three stories flanked by two others of one and two stories respectively. From the outer edges, long narrow buildings reached out far ahead of the complex into the Antarctic snowscape, looking much like arms extended from a chest and head. They were housings for the incoming oil lines, she assumed. This must have been where the pipes rose from underground to join up and utilize the vast pumping power of this one facility.

As the Snowcat had drawn closer, Danielle saw the installation more clearly and heard the nonstop grinding of gears turning to keep the pumps active. There was no gate, just a single road plowed through the buildup from the storm, amidst the frozen, sloping tundra, leading toward the main complex of buildings. They drove up to a garage door that opened for them automatically. Before they pulled inside, Danielle managed to sit up higher and saw a number of Quonset huts containing a variety of heavy construction equipment. Work on Spiderweb, she guessed, was still going on. There would be a lot of people stationed here, and that would work to her advantage in the hours to come.

Hours . . . Did she have that long left now? At least Outpost 10 hadn't been overrun yet. Reason for hope, though not much.

"Can you hear me?" the doctor asked her.

Danielle tried to speak, but no words emerged. She could feel her lips moving, struggling to form sounds, and in the process more memories came flooding back to her, mostly of the complex itself. She remembered passing living quarters, dining halls, recreation rooms, and many arrows pointing to the base's technological centers. It reminded her somehow of a school, so ordered and symmetrical.

"Can you hear me?" the doctor repeated.

"Yes," Danielle managed finally and tried to form new words.

"Louder, please."

"How . . . am I?"

"You lost nothing to frostbite, but you came close."

"What about the pilot?"

"Unconscious but stable. Came out of it a bit worse than you so far as injuries go. He must have overshot McMurdo in the storm."

"No . . . I wanted to come here."

"What?"

She knew what she had to say next. "Outpost . . . 10."

The doctor pulled back at that and might have been about to move away when Danielle found the strength to latch on to his arm with her still numb fingers.

"What time is it? What day?"

"Thursday morning. Coming up on three A.M."

"Your leader. Bring him . . . to me."

"I was just on my way to get him," the doctor said, freeing himself from her grasp. "I'm sure he's got some questions of his own."

Danielle's senses sharpened by the minute as she awaited the arrival of Outpost 10's leader. The nurse maintained a constant vigil in the chair at the foot of her bed, and she assumed the doctor had made sure a guard was stationed outside the door as well.

Finally she heard voices in the corridor, and then the door to the small ward she alone occupied opened. Danielle saw the wheelchair before looking at the man occupying it. He had thick salt-and-pepper hair that showed only slight signs of thinning, and large brown eyes. The bulging bands of muscle in his arms and chest were offset by a pair of withered legs that dangled uselessly to the floor. Their eyes locked as he made his way over to the side of her bed, almost level with her head from his wheelchair.

"The name's Farraday, miss. You can call me 'Commander' for short."

"You're in charge here, I assume."

"Surprises you, doesn't it? Surprised me, too. Hire-the-Handicapped Week, right?"

"I didn't mean it that way. I just had to be sure before we talked."

"The only thing you've got to be sure of, miss, is that you're in one hell of a mess. This place isn't supposed to exist, in case you didn't realize."

"Its existence is known to more people than *you* realize." She paused. "What about the troops? Have you heard from them? Are they coming?"

Commander Farraday looked both puzzled and angry. "What troops?"

"You mean you haven't . . ." Danielle stopped. Clearly there was no reason for her to complete the thought. It was just as she had felt all along: something had gone wrong on the Ferryman's end, and it had become her lot alone to stop the Hashi from taking Outpost 10.

"I think you'd better tell me exactly who you are," Farraday said.

"I'm someone who wants to see your installation saved, Commander."

"What?"

"Can we talk alone?"

"Whatever suits you, miss. Neither of us is going anywhere for a while in this storm." Farraday raised one of his muscular forearms to indicate that the nurse and doctor should leave. When the door was closed behind them, he spoke again. "If you know what this place is, you know the kind of trouble you're in by coming here. We picked you up half dead after your plane crashed. Maybe we should have let you die."

"It might not matter," she said, almost too softly for him to hear. "Is your radio functional?"

"What? No. Wait a minute, what does that have to do with—"

"Then it's just us against them."

"Us against *who*? What in hell are you babbling about?"

Danielle lifted herself up to a sitting position. She was looking down at Farraday now. "This installation is about to come under attack," she said flatly.

Farraday almost laughed. "In the middle of an ice storm? Miss, nobody is going to have any more luck getting here than you did."

"Unless they come in a submarine."

"Submarine? I've had just about all I can—"

"How far are we from the Ross Ice Shelf?"

"Seventy miles. But that's over the Transantarctic Mountains. Hard for a sub to negotiate those babies."

"Yes, they'll have to come up through the shelf and find another way here."

"You're serious, aren't you?"

She looked at him harshly. "It's a new Jupiter-class super-Trident, the prototype for an entire fleet. The people coming here hijacked it, along with its twenty-eight atomic missiles. They're going to use them to destroy the Spiderweb pipeline, Commander. They're going to blow it and the continent to hell from this very spot."

Farraday wheeled himself closer. "Maybe I should get you a shrink. We've got real good ones down here. Lots of people need them. Might be the air, some say. I'm hoping your story can be attributed to that too."

"What would you like to know about your installation, Commander?" she challenged him. "Would you like to know how many barrels of oil a day your vacuum pumps suck up along the pipeline? Would you like to know the locations of your storage dumps? Would you like me to point out your major drilling sites on a map? They compose something called Spiderweb, but unless we do something they won't be there tomorrow."

Commander Farraday was staring up at her in shock. "And you've come all the way out here to warn me?"

"Not just warn. Help."

There was a long silence during which Farraday sat transfixed in his wheelchair, wondering what his next words should be.

"Accepting your help," he said finally, "presupposes that I believe this incredible story of yours."

"There's more. I left out the details. I was only trying to get you to listen."

"Tell me everything."

Danielle's tale was interrupted on several occasions by individuals needing Farraday for something or other. Not once was the commander short with his people, and Danielle could tell from their stares that their respect for this crippled leader was as intense as their love for him. She wondered how long a tour lasted for these people of the ultra-secret Outpost 10. A year? Maybe two? The longer it was, the more responsibility would fall on Farraday's shoulders to maintain a pleasant atmosphere. Here at the bottom of the world she supposed tempers could run hot enough to keep everyone warm.

"My God," was all Farraday could manage at the end. "I don't know what to make of it all. I don't know what to say." He paused. "Assuming I believe you, what exactly do you expect me to do?"

"Defend your outpost, Commander. With no help coming from the outside, it's our only chance."

"I'd love for you to tell me what to defend it with."

"This is a Defense Department installation, isn't it?"

"Only as far as funding is concerned, miss. If we're found out here, we've got another cover prepared entirely, and to make sure it holds, our weapons cache is well within limits set by the Antarctic Treaty. We've got approximately fifteen guns: six sidearms, six M-16s, and three shotguns—if they're all functioning, that is. The only soldiers here are six Marines who do a nice job of breaking up fights and maintaining a presence for the one hundred and twenty-five workers we have at anytime at the outpost."

"Seven soldiers, Commander. You mentioned you were in the Army as well."

"Sorry, miss. Corps of Engineers going back to Nam. Never did see real combat. I volunteered for this command because it was mostly administrative and far enough from the rest of the world to help me forget a little about all the things I can't do anymore." He gazed down at his useless legs. "Drunk driver crossed the center line six years ago."

Danielle kept her mind on the subject at hand. "What about calling McMurdo for reinforcements?"

"Even if we could get through to them in the storm, they would never be able to get help out in weather like this. I've seen storms last a week this time of year, and this one's barely a day old."

Danielle put it together in her head. "Fifteen weapons against a force I would estimate as at least four times that number."

Farraday wheeled himself closer. "With a nuclear sub you really figure they'll try and take us assault-style?"

"They haven't got a choice. They've got to take the installation intact, but they'll be expecting their attack to take us totally by surprise. We can make that work for us."

"With fifteen guns, miss?"

"There's more, Commander. It's just a question of finding it."

Farraday wheeled himself down the long corridor that connected the one-story wing housing the infirmary to the main three-story complex. Danielle walked by his side, still fighting to shake off the effects of her extended stay in the bitter cold.

"The complex seems too small for all that has to be done here," she commented.

"That's because most of the living quarters and recreation areas are underground, within the ice. Helps for insulation and makes it so we don't stick out too much."

Above them the corridor was lined with windows shaped like portholes which showed the signs of being battered by the ice blizzard raging beyond. Every time the wind gusted the whole building seemed to tremble as the cold made its best effort to penetrate the walls.

"I've got ideas for some things we can do," she told him. "But I don't know how to implement them."

"If they're good enough, I'll take care of the implementation. We're an engineering outpost, remember? We're pretty good at creating things out of nothing fast."

"I've got to see the outside. I need to have an overview of the layout to see if the things I've got in mind will work."

"You can see better from the inside looking out."

Danielle followed Farraday into an elevator which took them to the third floor of the main building. Once out of the elevator, the commander led the way down another hall and around a single corner, which brought them to the complex's observation deck, featuring a wall formed of insulated glass two feet thick. There was some distortion as a result, but with the storm Danielle wasn't able to see much anyway. The front of Outpost 10 was as white and thick as the rest of the landscape.

"What have you got for heavy equipment?"

"Besides the Snowcats, plenty of loaders and dozers, all made especially for our lovely climate. It means that about half of them are malfunctioning at any given time."

"Half will be enough."

"For what?"

But Danielle's mind was already moving on another track. "The oil does come through here from the wells en route to the storage dumps, doesn't it?"

"Of course. Why?"

She looked out at the dead white beyond the window: it was perfect camouflage. In her mind she was getting her bearings straight and trying to figure out the most logical route of approach for the Hashi after they cleared the mountains. They'd be best off moving with the wind instead of against it, which meant a frontal assault. All that stored away, she turned back to Farraday.

"We need to set up lines of defense utilizing the skills and resources available to us. For the first line of defense, we'll have the element of surprise on our side. For the others, the enemy will have regrouped and will be expecting a fight. That means we've got to get plenty of them fast while we save our best cards for last. It's our battle. We're the only ones who can win it. Commander, how fast can you assemble all installation personnel and have them ready for duty?"

"About the same time it should take you to explain to me what exactly they've got to do."

"Ah, Mac, how good of you to join us," Jones said when the trio of guards led McKenzie Barlow up to the bridge.

Mac had been sitting behind his desk when the door to his quarters opened minutes before. He had started to reach for the knife but pulled his hand back when he saw the guards enter instead of Jones. No sense in trying to smuggle it out. And sure enough the bastards searched him thoroughly before escorting him up to the bridge.

"We've arrived at our destination, Commander," Jones continued happily. "I thought you might be interested in witnessing the final stage of our journey."

"Where are we?"

"Steaming beneath the Ross Ice Shelf. Almost to its northern tip. Vertical sonar is looking for a light spot we can pierce through with our sail."

"And then what?"

"We surface." Jones came closer. "And then you and I will have a little trip ahead of us."

Not if I can stop you, you bastard, Mac almost said, but he focused instead on containing his own rage. He wondered if he could kill Jones with his bare hands here and now. He'd been trained to do so often and well, and even though his skills in this regard weren't battle tested, he felt certain he could do it. What stopped him from trying was the realization that a dozen men would be upon him before he could land a single blow.

"Thin ice above, sir," reported the sonar man.

"Ahead slow," Jones ordered.

"Ahead slow," a voice came back.

"Drifting speed. Hold us steady."

"Aye, Captain. Steady as she goes."

"Thin ice, sir," came the sonar's voice again.

"Thickness?"

"Seventy-five feet. Fifty . . . Thirty . . ."

"All stop!"

"All stop."

"Take us up."

"Coming up, sir. One thousand meters . . . Five hundred . . . Two-fifty . . . One hundred . . ."

Seconds later the *Rhode Island* rocked slightly as its sail impacted against the layer of ice above. She seemed to be stuck in her tracks for a brief moment before a slight grinding sound came and she began to surge quickly upward.

"We're through, sir."

Jones allowed himself a smile. "The door's open, people."

He gazed at Mac as if expecting praise for a job well done. What he got was a stare as cold as the sea above.

"That takes care of the shelf," the commander snapped. "But if that mass I notice on radar is a storm, there's no way you'll be going anywhere else."

"You'll see," was all Jones replied.

The beauty of Danielle's plan lay in its simplicity. There wasn't time to erect anything elaborate, and even if there had been, she had to keep in mind that these were engineers she was dealing with, not soldiers. She had explained her proposals for three separate lines of defense to Farraday and the former Corps of Engineers soldier in him rose to the challenge. Now, four hours later, they were outside supervising the work and surveying what had already been completed.

At the start, Farraday had hailed his people over the PA system. "Now hear this," he announced. "Don storm gear and assemble in the briefing room in twenty minutes. We've got ourselves more than just a blizzard to fight off today."

When they had assembled as ordered, he told them an enemy force was coming to overrun the installation. Murmurs passed through the crowd, but no one bothered interrupting for questions, though several noticed the stranger seated just behind him. It was up to them to save themselves, he continued, and it could be done so long as everyone pulled their share. The personnel were broken into teams and sent to various stations, where the work commenced almost instantly. Now, four hours later, they were still at it, though into the home stretch. The raging storm and fifteen-below-zero temperatures forced them to work in shifts which rotated with the sounding of a horn every twenty minutes. This had the added effect of keeping the workers fresh and constantly renewed in their resolve and enthusiasm. They couldn't see a foot in front of themselves in the storm, but everyone could see the fear on the face of the fellow closest to him, even through the woolen ski masks that were part of the storm gear.

Farraday was the only one to stay out for virtually the entire duration, permitting himself only ten minutes inside per hour and that only to warm and oil his wheelchair fittings so he could move it about as needed.

"Dead legs come in handy for something," he told Danielle. "Heart doesn't have to work as hard getting blood down there. It can focus its energies instead on keeping the rest of me warm."

For her part, Danielle could only stay out until the dizziness started to overcome her every twenty-five minutes or so. Each trip outside brought numbing pains to her chest and a light-headed feeling, and only her sense of urgency gave her the strength to avoid collapsing. Venturing back out into the storm with the four-hour mark just past, she had trouble finding Farraday. She pulled herself along the tow line that had been erected all over the complex at the start to make sure the workers had something to fall back on if their bearings deserted them. People had been known to freeze to death ten yards from a door in this kind of storm.

She found the commander at last beyond the camp line at the outer perimeter, where the finishing touches were being put on the first line of defense.

"We do have those six Marines," she had told him at the outset, "and it would be foolish not to utilize their skills. Question is how to get close enough to the enemy to make a difference with their guns in this storm."

"We could camouflage them."

"You mean dress them up in white?"

"So to speak."

What he had meant, Danielle saw now, was a series of layered mounds which were being finished off so smoothly as to seem a part of the natural landscape. The white-clad Marines would take cover behind them and poke their rifles through a slot carved in the snow-ice blocks for them. The only thing that might alert the near-ing enemy to their precise location would be the orange bursts that came with each shot fired. But if they were lucky the storm would hide enough of that.

As soon as the opposing forces scrambled for cover following the initial barrages, the Marines would pull back to the complex to serve as an additional line of defense if the next two failed to finish the job.

"What do you think?" Farraday asked her, having to yell to make his voice carry over the biting wind.

"Looks great. Can't be sure until I see the men in position, though."

She could tell that beneath his mask the commander was smiling. "They're already in position, miss."

Danielle smiled back at him through hers.

Together they moved back to the second line of defense. The snow had caked up on Farraday's wheels, and Danielle went about the task of pushing him, quickly out of breath but stubbornly shoving on.

"We've got to make use of those loaders," she had told him hours before, stunned by the size of them. Three were absolutely monstrous; perhaps a ton of snow and ice could be carried or pushed by their shovels. Chains were wrapped around their specially con-structed tires to provide traction.

Again Farraday's engineering background supplied the answer. The problem here, too, was one of camouflage, of making sure the enemy didn't know the loaders were there until it was too late, even though the fact that they were in for a fight had been made known to them by the Marines. Snow mounds big enough to conceal the loaders would stick out too much and might impede their rush. The solution he came up with was to drape snow-encrusted tarpaulins over the huge machines, with their shovel assemblies dangling straight overhead. That way, as soon as the shovels were lowered, the tarps would be swept away. From there the drivers could use the loaders to attack the invaders by overrunning them. Even at their relatively low speed, it was certain they could outpace men weighted down and slowed by huge, heavy boots in the storm.

Still, Farraday wasn't satisfied. The cabs were too open, the volunteer drivers too vulnerable to bullets. The answer was to weld steel plating over every part of the glassed-in cabin except for a six-inch slot that ran the entire length of the windshield to allow for adequate vision. That task had only just been completed, and now work had commenced on encasing the tarpaulin coverings with an even layer of snow and ice.

Satisfied, Farraday asked Danielle to wheel him on to the last and most complicated line of defense. Huge insulated pipes had been laid from the main pumping station into an area roughly a hundred fifty feet in front of the central building and the same distance from the resting place of the loaders. Fifty of the outpost's personnel had rotated the chores of digging a foot down into the snow and packing what lay beneath that layer into ice. Their progress was slowed by fresh showers of snow and crystal poured into their neatly cleared areas by the storm. Yet their perseverance paid off, and they were now finishing up the first stage of the job by leveling out the pit with acetylene torches.

With the trench finished to his satisfaction, Farraday supervised the placement of the insulated pipes linked up to the pumps inside the foot-deep trench and then ordered the spigots opened. Seconds later, thick black crude oil began rushing into the freshly dug ice pit. It coagulated like clotting blood and slowed for a time, but not many minutes later the entire pit was full to the brim and they were ready to implement the next phase. Men bearing hoses filled with heated water to prevent even the insulated rubber from freezing began casting a heavy, even spray over the oil the thickness of which held it on top long enough to freeze into a sheet of ice an inch thick. The storm helped them here by blanketing fresh snow atop the man-made fire trap. Outpost 10 personnel went to work next with shovels

and smaller dozers to deepen the snow so that the fire pit would
take on the same proportions and look just like the rest of the
grounds, even from up close.

"Incredible," was all Danielle could say for this ploy that made
up their final line of defense. "I saw the oil being poured and I still
can't pinpoint where it is."

Fortunately it was clear to the men laying the specially sealed
fusing from the fire pit back inside the complex. The fusing was
unique in that the flame it carried would burn on the inside rather
than the outside, where it could be too easily extinguished by storm,
wind, or cold. It was standard issue in cold weather regions where
construction was going on.

Danielle and Farraday gazed about them. The work was nearly
finished. They had barely allowed themselves a small smile of satisfaction when a call came for Farraday on his walkie-talkie from a
spotter placed atop a snow mound a quarter mile from the outpost.

"This is Farraday. I read you, son."

"I see them, sir. Fifty, maybe more, coming fast."

"Coming fast? How?"

"Snowmobiles, sir."

"Say again."

"Snowmobiles."

Farraday gazed at Danielle to make sure she had heard.

CHAPTER 34

"*T*HE SIXTY-THIRD ANNUAL MACY'S THANKSGIVING DAY PA-
rade is coming to you live and in stereo from New York City. . . ."

Kimberlain was close enough to a television monitor poised near
the starting line to hear a woman's opening narration as a trio of
red-jacketed Macy's personnel led by Bill Burns started down Central Park West before a banner that read HAPPY HOLIDAYS! carried
by a quartet of handlers also responsible for a balloon bearing the
store logo. The first of thirteen marching bands fell in immediately
behind, and the parade was officially underway to a chorus of whis-
tles and drumbeats.

"And now, let's go uptown to your host—"

Before the narrator could finish the name of the teenage heartthrob serving as uptown host, shrieks and ear-piercing screams rang
out and, barely out of camera range, the Ferryman instinctively
drew his gun. He reholstered it, embarrassed, when he realized the
noise was due to a host of teenage girls screaming their adulation
at a curly-haired teenage boy who had appeared among them. Kimberlain moved away from the throng when the boy started speaking
and gazed about him again.

The logistics were indeed incredible—a work of art in themselves.

He watched as the next band in line readied itself on West 77th Street, held in place so the first of the major floats could move in ahead of it. Not far down the other side of 77th, Woody Woodpecker grew impatient as he waited to become the lead balloon in this year's parade. It was minutes past nine A.M. on a bright, sunny Thanksgiving. Temperatures were already stretching into the fifties and by the finish at noon could be expected to have risen another ten degrees. Much of the crowd was clothed in simple spring-weight windbreakers, prepared to shed them at a moment's notice.

The lead band was playing a brassy rendition of "That's Entertainment" as it strode down Central Park West with military precision, flanked on all sides by drum majorettes.

"Come in, Jared," called Cathy Nu on the walkie-talkie clipped to Kimberlain's belt.

He backed up further from the crowd and raised it to his lips. "Read you."

"I'm at Columbus Circle. Sounds from here like things are underway."

"You got that right. Everyone in place?"

"Seems like we've got as many security personnel as spectators, but it's probably just wishful thinking on my part."

"For sure."

His mind drifted back to the six A.M. final briefing at a midtown Manhattan police precinct packed solid with leaders of the individual SWAT and surveillance teams. A captain named Donahue laid out the specifics: there was reason to believe the safety of the parade was in jeopardy, and the presence of explosives was feared. Since the entire area of the route had been swept and found clean, those behind the attack were believed to be planning their appearance for after the event's start. Donahue was vague because he had little to offer that was specific. Then he signaled for the lights to be turned off, and he switched on an overhead projector. The route of the parade had been mapped out in different colors to denote grids, ten in all, which grew progressively smaller in size to be more adequately covered as they drew closer to the Herald Square finish

ne. The result was that seventy-five percent of the security force
would cover the route from Columbus Circle on down, with fully
sixty percent of the total in the last ten blocks.

"Let's take it back now to my co-host at Herald Square," the
curly-haired teenage heartthrob was saying.

Kimberlain gazed up and saw a sleek pair of New York City
police helicopters buzzing the skies. Farther off in the distance the
Coast Guard choppers made a steady sweep of the larger perimeter,
working their radar diligently.

"I'm going to start walking the route," Kimberlain said into his
mouthpiece as dozens of clowns rushed past him to take their places
ahead of Woody Woodpecker on Central Park West.

"Stay in touch," said Cathy.

And the Ferryman turned to find himself face to face with the
ever-smiling heartthrob, whom he had never laid eyes on before.

"Wow!" the teenager exclaimed to him, wide-eyed. "This is
great! Never seen anything like it in my life!"

"I'll bet you haven't," said Kimberlain.

Kimberlain walked even with the first phalanx of clowns and
elves, who were costumed in droopy red suits with floppy hats and
shoes to serve as advance notice of Santa's imminent approach. By
the time he passed Tavern on the Green he had counted over a dozen
sidewalk food vendors and wondered if Cathy Nu's security precautions had included a check of all contents of such steel containers. It wouldn't take too many of them to be packed with *plastique*
and abandoned to . . .

His fears were put to rest when he saw one of the police's German
shepherds sniffing his way down the street. The dog passed a hot-
dog stand with nothing more than a wide eye at a potential meal.
There were a half-dozen such dogs walking up and down along the
entire route, and anything he or Cathy might have disregarded their
highly tuned noses would certainly pick up.

Above him one of the police choppers was streaking straight
overhead down Central Park West, keeping a discreet height to

respect the rising shapes of the huge balloons, which were starting to pass into their slots in the parade at regular intervals now. So far only Woody Woodpecker and Kermit the Frog had begun their walk, just to wet the whistle of the fans lining the route.

The Ferryman faded back a bit until he was even with the first of the major floats, a Masters of the Universe display featuring a green rubber dragon belching synthetic smoke as its head reared left and right. It seemed to be roaring as a muscular blond man stabbed at it with a fake sword.

He had spoken to Senator Tom Brooks just ninety minutes earlier to learn that much of the southern portion of Antarctica was still caught in a savage ice storm that prevented an airlift or help of any kind from the outside to Outpost 10. Soviet subs were steaming toward the area to lend assistance, and the carrier *John F. Kennedy* was en route as well, though three days away at top speed. It would be up to Danielle, then, to save the outpost, assuming she had been able to reach it before the storm hit. Kimberlain preferred not to consider the odds of that and turned his thoughts back to the problems at hand.

A whole troup of Macy's employees dressed as clowns glided by him, and he noticed a figure in cutoff blue-jean shorts moving between them from the other side of Central Park West.

"Jesus H. fuckin' Christ!" Captain Seven blared when he reached the Ferryman. "You didn't tell me about all these fucking bands! How was I supposed to know about them? You think I sit home and watch this shit every year? Christ, you coulda told me the Seven Dwarfs were the grand masters and I wouldn't have known any different."

"What about the bands?"

"You got any idea the kind of vibrations their instruments make? Great way to set off a bomb, let me tell ya. Could be anywhere—above, below, to the sides. And how about the inside of all those drums? You have anybody check them?"

Kimberlain realized he hadn't. "Hang in there, Captain. And

stay close. Come in, Cathy,'' he said into the walkie-talkie pressed near his lips. "Cathy, come in."

"I read you, Jared. I'm heading toward the finish line."

"We might have a problem."

"What's that? I didn't hear you."

Kimberlain stepped further away from the band passing him. "I said we might have a problem. Did anyone sweep the instruments these bands are using?"

"I supervised it personally."

"Thank God."

"I'm beginning to think we've got it all covered, Jared. I'm beginning to think we might have this whipped."

"You can rest assured we missed something, Cathy. The trick is to find it before it's too late."

Kimberlain was uneasy as he approached Columbus Circle. It was nearly ten o'clock, and the fact that the vast security detail had turned up nothing was reason for alarm rather than celebration.

They haven't found it because we're missing something.

He turned behind him and watched as the Spiderman balloon rode through the skies with muscular latex arms extended as if he were ready to topple one of the nearby skyscrapers. Before him at Columbus Circle an ancient-castle float passed, featuring a fairly famous actress confined to a tower room where throughout the parade it was a dashing young hero's lot to repeatedly strive to free her. All the major floats seemed populated with celebrities in costumed roles. Made for better viewing, he supposed.

"Come in, Jared," Cathy Nu called.

"Read you," said Kimberlain into his walkie-talkie.

"I'm at the finish line," she replied, and in the background he could hear the brassy beat of the lead marching band. "The head of the parade just got here, and Woody Woodpecker will be passing me before you know it."

The Ferryman watched as before him the parade slowed to a

crawl and then a stop to allow the band at the finish line a two-minute performance.

"It can happen anytime now, Cathy."

"It can't happen if we've stopped them from planting the explosives."

"We haven't stopped them yet. You can rest assured of that."

The key was timing, Kimberlain thought to himself. There had to be a specific moment the explosion was planned for and a reason behind it. Perhaps that was what they had missed. Perhaps . . .

A huge clown came up alongside of him, and the Ferryman turned in his direction.

"I think you've found your true calling, Peet."

Even the painted-on orange smile could not hide Winston Peet's displeasure with the remark, or maybe it was just his displeasure in general.

"He's here, Ferryman."

"Quail?"

"I can feel him."

"Why would he be here, Peet?"

"It will all be left to him in the end, Ferryman, and it will be left to me to stop him."

The white-painted face and orange wig made him look ridiculous, yet children seemed fascinated by his size and drawn to him. Even as he was standing next to Kimberlain, a trio of boys appeared and pulled at his green outfit, stretching their hands upward to see how high they could reach on him. Instantly Peet melted back into the disguise by producing three balls to juggle adroitly as he moved to take his leave.

"There is a balance to everything, Ferryman, and Quail is a part of this one. What was before will be again, but then never more."

Kimberlain felt a coldness creep over him. How could he have been so negligent? Of course, damn it, of course!

He was stripping his walkie-talkie from his belt and inspecting his watch in the next instant.

"Come in, Cathy!"

He would have to keep it simple, no time for long explanations.

Now he knew how to determine the "when," but still not the "how."

Lisa Eiseman was standing on West 50th Street when the sight grabbed her attention. She saw it just as Woody Woodpecker cleared the finish line and Kermit the Frog was passing in front of her, with Snoopy on roller skates not far behind.

An elf, one of the hundreds in the streets but the largest by far, and looking uncomfortable in his role, drew her eye.

Nearby a far smaller elf hugged a pair of twin girls and showered them with candy canes. At the same time a young boy had started tugging at the huge elf's belt on the other block.

The elf whipped an arm backward and tossed the boy to the sidewalk, sliding back into the crowd as the boy began crying.

Lisa started following him along the parade route. Something about this elf was wrong. Her first thought was it was simply his attitude, but there was more, though she couldn't say exactly what. She moved faster to close the gap, now making her way across to West 49th Street.

This elf had no interest in the children shouting up at him or trying for purchase on his floppy red costume. He beat a straight and narrow path down Broadway, looking as if he had taken a wrong turn somewhere and ended up among other human beings. Lisa closed the gap to half a block and kept on his tail. Her heart began to thud. She looked about for Kimberlain or even Peet dressed in his fanciful clown outfit.

But what to tell them?

Trying to answer that question for herself, she pressed on.

Quail was aware mostly of time. Time was everything today, and time distracted him from the uneasy feeling of being out in the sunshine. His eyes hurt. He couldn't stop squinting, and the unseasonable warmth made him feel hot and sticky within the confines of this ridiculous costume the circumstances demanded that he wear.

The black detonator the man behind the curtain had given him was pressed in his bulky outer pocket. It was necessary for him to be here now on the chance that the substance of the plan was uncovered prior to the magic moment he was to press it, thus forcing him to detonate the explosives early. Quail figured he would need five minutes to rush out of range of its effects.

The million deaths would make him the greatest murderer of all time, finally bring him out of the shadow cast by Peet. The world might not know, but Quail would, and that was all that mattered. All those nights cruising the freeways and back roads of the country looking for prey were nothing compared to this.

No, he couldn't achieve his goal of tearing a still-beating heart from a chest under these circumstances, but the cries of one million dying in horrible pain would be better than even that.

Much better.

Cathy had greeted Kimberlain's report with stunned silence.

"I can't be sure," he finished. "But it fits. It fits!"

"Give me two minutes."

The Ferryman started moving faster down the route, veering left with the parade onto Broadway. He kept the walkie-talkie pressed to his ear the whole time and had moved in front of the crowds viewing yet another high school band at 52nd Street when Cathy's call reached him.

"The explosion three years ago happened at precisely 11:03," she reported.

"Christ," Kimberlain snorted, checking his watch to find there were fifty-three minutes to go.

"You think it means—"

"I'm sure it does. But it doesn't solve our problem. Knowing the 'when' doesn't help us with the 'how.' "

"I'll alert the grid leaders. Now that we know the 'when,' maybe the 'how' won't matter."

The Ferryman didn't bother arguing.

* * *

Lisa had lost the huge elf in Times Square in the shadow of the Newsday Building on West 43rd Street, where the crowd was fifty deep in some places. She held her ground as another band with too many drums and cymbals marched past her followed by a float made up as a turkey carrying riders dressed as pilgrims. In the swollen mass of bodies it was impossible to pick out a single figure, even a huge one dressed all in red.

But wait. Was that him just across the center divider moving beyond the blue and white Traveler's Aid stand on 42nd Street? Yes! Yes! Still driven by her feelings, Lisa hurried in his tracks.

The subways charged with funneling the great masses of people to and from the parade area had been doing a yeoman's job. The lines that ran closest to the route had been jammed to capacity all morning, despite the extra trains added to prevent a massive human backlog underground. As it was, the lines were long but they moved, and on such a beautiful holiday, spirits could tolerate that much.

The Seventh Avenue Express number-two train had just pulled out of the 42nd Street station with twenty-eight cars in tow when the on-board lighting died and the train slid harmlessly to a halt along the tracks directly beneath the parade passing above. Emergency lighting snapped on immediately but made barely a dent in the darkness engulfing the crammed-together passengers as well as the transit cops assigned to every single car.

"Power failure," a father explained to his sons. "They'll get it cleared up in no time."

The father was only half right, for he could not have known that an explosion at a major subway transformer had shorted out the entire track system from the Harlem River to Brooklyn. The Seventh Avenue Express was dead on its tracks beneath 39th Street.

At 10:19 Kimberlain was walking along with a sixty-foot Garfield by his side when Cathy Nu's frantic voice grabbed his ear.

"Jared, come in. Come in!"

He spoke while still raising the walkie-talkie to his lips. "Here, Cathy."

"It's the subway. The whole system's out! There's a train stuck beneath the parade route, five blocks from the finish line."

A bitter chill flooded his body. Their precautions had left nothing out, had made sure everything was checked, *except* the subway cars themselves. The explosives must have been packed into them, the timing of the rigged power failure made to correspond to when the cars in question were beneath the route after ten o'clock.

"Where are you?" Cathy Nu was asking.

Kimberlain gazed up from beneath the green overhang of Tony Roma's Place for Ribs. "Forty-seventh, no Forty-eighth."

"I'm at Thirty-seventh. Meet me at the Forty-second Street entrance to the Times Square subway station."

Kimberlain was already running, charging past the confused line of spectators before him as he outpaced bands, floats, and balloon handlers alike.

Damn you, Benbasset! Damn you!

There were barely forty minutes left until 11:03.

Quail saw the police figures with walkie-talkies stuck to their ears sprint by him en route to the nearest subway entrance. The subway! They must have figured out where the explosives had been placed. His orders were explicit in this regard: he was to use the detonator as soon as he was a safe distance away. But that wasn't enough, he had realized.

He *had* to see it happen, had to see it all. And there was a way, even now with the substance of the plan so drastically altered.

He had just turned to head toward a fresh destination when a hand reached up for his shoulder and the Flying Dutchman swung to gaze into a pair of eyes he had seen before.

Lisa's pursuit of the huge elf was so intense that she hadn't even noticed the police charge by her. The elf seemed distracted, lost almost, when she reached him at last just beyond 42nd Street. But

he twisted like a cat at her touch, and Lisa felt the shudder rush
through her even before her eyes locked on a face trapped behind
rubber and plastic that wasn't a face at all. She had seen it before
in all its horror, seen it that night on Torelli's island when she had
barely escaped with her life.

The giant glared at her from behind his elf's mask. His hand
came up to strike her, but the crowd closed in and deflected the
blow into a glancing one. Lisa reeled, and the crowd absorbed her.
Quail raised his hand to strike at her again.

Lisa screamed.

Oblivious to everything but his search for the Dutchman, Winston Peet was sweeping the area beyond Times Square when he
heard the scream. It went through him like a knife, and his eyes
snapped to its origin.

He picked out Lisa Eiseman instantly. And someone else. An elf
about to strike her who suddenly changed his mind and, as Peet
watched, turned back into the crowd and headed for the finish line.

Quail!

Peet began to move, from a trot to an all-out sprint down Broadway with his orange clown's wig ripped off to reveal his bald dome
above his made-up white face. The Dutchman gazed back once,
and in that moment their eyes met and locked, and in the next
moment Quail was through the crowd, charging down the street
with Peet following barely a block behind.

The two of them were sprinting just beyond the edges of the
parade, seeming a part of it to onlookers, including the police,
many of whom were also disguised as participants.

The crowd appeared to think it was all part of the show, a clown
chasing an elf, and applauded as Quail and Peet charged by.

Kimberlain reached the subway entrance just ahead of Cathy Nu.
Together they bolted down the steps past the mass of people who
were emerging, frustrated by the power failure that had stranded
them here.

"We've got to clear the streets!" he bellowed between heavy breaths.

"No! The panic! People will be trampled, children! We know where the explosives are. We'll deactivate them. The bomb squad's already on its way!"

They had reached the turnstiles and hurdled over them with no tokens in hand. Kimberlain didn't waste the energy of telling Cathy the *plastique* would have been packed in a way to prevent it from being found quickly, much less deactivated. No sense in even looking. The streets had to be cleared, a panic risked . . . unless the cars could be cleared from the area instead.

The flight of stairs descending to the track level for the Seventh Avenue Express train was crammed with bodies moving toward the streets. Kimberlain and Cathy Nu pushed their way through and rushed to the quickly thinning platform where Captain Donahue was already in conference with a Transit Authority engineer whose nametag listed him as O'Brien.

"I tell ya the power's out on *all* the tracks, not just the express tracks," O'Brien was explaining.

"We've got to repair it, that's all," Donahue insisted.

"Mister, I don't even know where to start looking. I got maybe fifty thousand people trapped in the middle of hell, and if you ask me—"

"Is there another way to move the stalled cars of the number two?" Kimberlain interrupted.

"What is it about the number two that makes it so much more important than—"

"Just answer the question! Can we move it, shove it forward somehow?"

O'Brien thought briefly. "One of those new trash barges could do it. They're powered by diesel, not electric. They push instead of pull."

"Then get one here, damn it, and hurry!"

O'Brien started to raise his walkie-talkie to his lips as floods of police personnel, including members of the bomb squad, rushed onto the scene. He looked back at Kimberlain.

"Look, pal, you're going to need someone to drive this thing once it gets here, and I just happen to be one of—"

"Don't worry," the Ferryman broke in. "I've already got a driver lined up."

CHAPTER 35

JONES'S MEN ABANDONED THEIR SNOWMOBILES ON HIS SIGNAL TO proceed the final three hundred yards on foot toward Outpost 10 through the blizzard. Strange how such a common machine had emerged as the key to his operation, but without it there would have been no way to transverse the rugged gaps in the Transantarctic Mountains from the submarine. Just as the trek itself would have been impossible if not for the space-age "cold" suits provided for them, which utilized heating coils to recirculate the body's warmth. None of his men would have gotten a mile without them.

The skimobiles had been left for him months before in a specially designed Quonset hut built to blend in with the scenery. Even with the coordinates, Jones had barely been able to locate it. Inside, in addition to the small machines, were a pair of Snowcats outfitted to carry cargo—in this case the twenty-eight warheads that had been removed from the Jupiter missiles on board the *Rhode Island*. Only one Snowcat was needed, with the other serving as backup. The Snowcat traveled at roughly one-third the speed of the skimobiles, which meant it would probably pull into Outpost 10 not long after Jones and his men had the complex secured. He had placed Barlow in the Snowcat as well, under the watchful eye of four of his men,

so that the commander could provide the final element of his plan
without delay.

Outpost 10 was about to be overtaken. Jones tightened his goggles and gave the signal to move out.

The half-dozen Marines of Outpost 10 were garbed in white that
made them one with the landscape. They rushed from the warm
indoors of the station into the raging storm as the enemy forces
approached after abandoning their snowmobiles. The storm winds
had switched from north to south, an advantage for the Marines,
since their eyes would steer with the winds now, while the enemy
would be forced to look straight into it.

"I should have figured this," Danielle was saying to Farraday.
"I should have known snowmobiles were the only way they could
reach us fast enough."

"We should be pleased," Farraday told her. "After all, they'll
be hard-pressed to carry their warheads with them this way."

"You're missing the point. There's no way they could have loaded
the snowmobiles on board the sub in the wake of taking it over.
That means the machines were left somewhere near the Ross Ice
Shelf for them, along with whatever other equipment they required."

"Christ," Farraday realized, "a Snowcat—"

"To bring the warheads in. Probably making its way here now
at about a third the speed of the skimobiles."

"Shit."

It took several minutes for the Marines to use tow lines to find
their way to positions carved out of snow mounds for them and to
insert their M-16s into the tailored slots provided. By this time the
drivers of the three massive loaders were trembling from the cold
inside their cabs and perhaps the fear of being entombed in the
darkness forever. From the observation deck on the third floor of
the central building, Danielle and Farraday could see nothing; everything beyond was a white blur. Even knowing where the Marines
and the loaders had been placed didn't help them. They took this

as a good sign, for if they couldn't find the initial two lines of defense they had laid in the storm, then certainly the approaching enemy wouldn't be able to either.

"Front line leader, do you read me?" Farraday asked the head Marine.

"I read you, Commander."

"Can you see them yet?"

"No, sir. Storm's too powerful to make anything out at a comfortable distance. The best we're gonna get is motion through it to fire at, and even then we're gonna have to wait till they're up real close and personal."

"You know the plan. Once they begin to scatter, pull back to the outpost and leave the rest for the loaders."

"Will do, Commander."

"Fire at will, Sergeant."

"Roger."

Danielle could see that now, for the first time, Farraday was tense because it would be up to him to tell the loaders when to move. If he was an instant late in picking up the white-clad enemy forces who survived the gunfire barrage from the Marines, his men's lives could be in jeopardy. He needed visibility to properly command his engineers-turned-soldiers, but visibility was at a premium.

Farraday lifted the binoculars to his eyes and gazed off into the distance. Danielle watched him stiffen.

"Christ, here they come. Dozens, and well packed to boot." He lowered the binoculars deliberately. "Even after all we did, part of me wouldn't believe what you said until I could see it for myself."

"But you acted, Commander. Every man and woman who survives here today owes their life to you."

"Commander, this is front line leader."

"Go ahead, Sergeant."

"They're a hundred yards from the perimeter and closing. Their pattern's a little more spread out than I was hoping for. I'm gonna have to wait longer to give the fire order."

"It's your call, Sergeant."

"Thank you, sir. I'll wait until the fifty-yard mark."

Farraday gritted his teeth and went to the binoculars again, lifting them from his lap. In the distance beyond the snow mounds he registered the approaching enemy as motion amidst the white blur. That was all; no distinct forms or shapes, just objects that were noticeable only for their movement. Farraday did not envy the Marines for the shots they would have to take. If the approaching forces numbered sixty or more, how many would the initial defense line have to fell if they were to have any chance at all? And if the remaining lines of defense left too large a complement of the enemy alive, how could the complex defend itself from a direct charge?

Farraday shoved the questions aside and returned to his binoculars.

The brief walk had been treacherous, and Jones found himself exceedingly glad it was drawing to an end. Two hundred yards back, Outpost 10 had risen from the snow and storm. It seemed to beckon them onward.

Jones turned his attention to the detailed schema his mind held of the complex, specifically the pump room, where miles of insulated piping wound about, connected to the huge pumps that pushed oil through the vast pipeline and into the various storage dumps. Place his missiles in front of the plugs designed to clear the lines and they would be sent hurtling into the continent, to be detonated on a timer designed to give him and his crew enough time to return to the *Rhode Island* and dive deep beneath the blast's far-reaching effects.

Closer to Outpost 10 now, Jones had the sensation it was abandoned, deserted. The storm swallowed everything, left nothing with which to form impressions. The base looked like a toy castle piled amidst the whiteness. So quiet. So alone.

They were just over two hundred yards from the complex of buildings when a man three over from Jones slipped and fell. The next man joined him, and Jones's first impression was that they had wandered into an ice field with semicomical results. It was the puff of snow bursting upward into his face from ground level that made him realize the men weren't slipping, they were being shot!

He swung into a dive, already going for his walkie-talkie, when more snow bursts erupted around him. Everywhere, on both flanks, his men were going down, too many of those left standing locked as they were, unsure what to do next. And behind this first line others simply kept approaching, the storm disguising the reality of what was happening. Jones grabbed for his rifle and fired a series of shots into the air after the walkie-talkie had proven useless to get the signal out. His men swung immediately toward the sound of his echoing gunshots. Another pair were projected backward, one with his chest ruptured and another flailing for the remnants of his skull as death claimed him.

Jones continued to watch helplessly as everywhere around him his men continued to drop, how many to safety and how many to the bullets fired from the invisible guns ahead he didn't know.

"How many, Sergeant? How many?" Farraday demanded.

"Can't be sure, Commander. We let them get right up close." The sergeant reflected on the blessing the storm had become by totally obscuring the sounds of their rifle fire. "I'd say fifteen down. As many as twenty."

"Pull back, Sergeant."

"We've still got clear shots, Commander."

"Pull back!"

Jones had pinned the gunmen's positions to the last series of muzzle flashes that came before the remainder of his men dropped into the snow for cover. He locked his eyes on those spots and searched for motion. When it came in the form of five or six shapes darting back into the thick of the storm, he lunged to his feet screaming, "They're pulling back! We're going in!"

He heard his own words repeated in various tones and levels a dozen times as word was passed on. By design and training his men took on a wide perimeter sweep, spreading out as they rushed forward through the snow, firing as they ran. The idea was to create a line of fire that would make flight for anyone caught within it impossible.

As of yet he had confronted only the evident realities of the situation. The fact that they were being fired upon now led him to consider that their presence had been expected and that the element of surprise was gone. This changed the rules for the encounter substantially. Instead of simply taking over the outpost, they were now in for a bloody battle.

No matter. Jones's men were prepared either way.

The Marine sergeant watched two of his men go down and then a third. He caught up with the final two and body-tackled them to the ground.

"Stay low," he whispered, "and dig yourself into the snow."

The men did so as he groped desperately for his walkie-talkie.

"We're pinned down, Commander. Three dead."

"Damn," came Farraday's reply.

"Our position is thirty degrees west of the loaders. Say twenty-five yards in front of the second defense line."

Danielle found them in her lenses and steered Farraday's vision. What looked to be forty or more enemy troops were converging on the area in a semicircle three rows deep and well spread out.

"Steady," Farraday told the Marine leader. "They're almost to loader range now. Almost to the second line . . ."

Farraday resisted the temptation to order the loaders to move now. To do so too early would eliminate the element of surprise he still held, so crucial to the success of this stage of the plan as well.

Farraday was gnashing his teeth, walkie-talkie close to his lips, thoughts stuck on the three Marines who were dead meat if spotted and the three who were dead already.

Danielle's binoculars were glued to her eyes. "The enemy is fifty yards from the loaders," she informed him. . . . "Forty-five."

Farraday counted out the seconds he estimated it would take for them to reach forty. When the loaders started rolling, there had to be a minimum of space and time for the invaders to adjust.

"Go!" he called to the loader drivers through his walkie-talkie.

The climatized engines turned over on the first push of the starter button, and the huge loaders roared to life. The drivers swung the shovels downward, thereby stripping away the white camouflaged tarps and clearing their line of vision.

"Thirty yards," announced Danielle.

Shovels still descending, the loaders started into motion toward the stunned lines of invaders. The loaders' tires were ten feet high, and their shovels stretched fifteen by twenty. They rolled through the mounting snow effortlessly, seeming to glide, moving forward far faster than the now retreating troops could either backpedal or turn and flee in the heavy drifts.

The three surviving Marines grabbed the opportunity to scramble behind the new line of defense created by the loaders and rush through the whiteness behind them toward the safety of the building complex.

Danielle watched the rest unfold the way a film does on a big screen. The loaders' shovels were almost to ground level now, the invaders just starting to fire at them. The shovels took the brunt of the bullets, sparks flying at impact. As the shovels continued to descend, more sparks showered from the steel-encased cabs while the giant machines picked up more speed across the snow-swept tundra, closing the gap to the fleeing invaders. She found herself looking at Farraday, wanting to hug him to show her thanks and appreciation for his brilliance in plotting and carrying out this defense.

And for believing her.

The enemy was rushing away now, legs churning as the loaders gathered huge mounds of snow before them and plowed it on. The effect was that of a mountain of white in motion, an avalanche rushing across level land. The fleeing troops couldn't hope to negotiate the drifts and piles from the still-raging storm. Many tripped and fell, pulling themselves along on hands and knees. Others trudged as best they could.

It didn't matter. The loaders were gaining speed as bullets

bounced off their steel hulls or were swallowed by the mountains of snow they pushed before them. The spacing between their frames worked well against the spread of the retreating troops. Danielle watched the first wave of gunmen disappear under the mounds of white and thought strangely of a wave at sea swallowing a surfer. The loaders rolled on, oblivious to the bodies crushed beneath their massive tires. The snow caught up with the others, one of whom had the foresight in a final dying motion to slide a grenade from his tomb, which wedged in ice beneath the onrushing monster. Danielle saw the smoke, first white, then gray, and finally black sprouting up as the center loader ground uneasily to halt.

The other two were raising their shovels, now packed with snow, and gathered fresh momentum. Farraday and Danielle watched as the surviving troops stopped their retreat and launched an all-out attack on the remaining loaders.

"Pull back!" Farraday screamed into his walkie-talkie. "Pull back!"

It must have been that the roaring engine sounds stole the drivers' hearing, or maybe they heard the order and simply disregarded it, because the loaders rushed forward into a barrage of fire. A pair of men had readied rocket launchers, focusing on the same loader that had just caught up with another group of gunmen and dumped a ton of ice-snow on top of them. The shovel was descending again in the next instant, as if to act as shield against the coming rockets, but too late. The rockets blasted with red-hot light into the engine and cabin, and a burst of orange flame centered in black smoke sliced through the white death of the storm.

The final loader was charging the two men bearing rocket launchers, who struggled desperately to turn to get fresh loads chambered. They backed up as they struggled and managed to fire just as the shovel was upon them. The rockets blasted into the mechanism and shattered it, but momentum carried the heavy, snow-filled steel forward and crushed the shooters. The last loader wavered, damaged heavily. The invaders surrounded it like a group of ants around a spider trapped in its own web and fired relentlessly until a soundless *poof* erupted and everywhere again there was fire and smoke.

"God fuckin' damn you!" Farraday shouted at the invading gunmen with tears in the corners of his eyes. "I'll get you for that! I'll roast everyone of you goddamn fuckers!"

As he spoke, Danielle was already grasping the handgrips of his wheelchair and steering him toward the elevator that would take them to the ground floor. There the fuses could be lit that would set off the oil slick concealed beneath the snow and ice fifty yards from the front of the building.

"How many do you think are left?" he asked her.

"As few as twenty. As many as thirty."

"Say twenty-five, then," he said as the elevator doors started open on the first floor. "Nice round number to kill."

"How fast does the fuse burn?" she wanted to know.

"Ten yards per second."

"Then five seconds is what we have to work with."

"And I plan on enjoying each and every one of them."

Their view on the first floor was restricted to what they could see out a single round window. Outside, the enemy was still regrouping. They would approach closer on an even wider angle to play it safe. Danielle had expected as much and was glad the fire pit had been constructed to keep that possibility in mind. The enemy troops fired as they ran, shots impacting upon the structure of Outpost 10 and each shot bringing them closer to the third line of defense.

Danielle gazed more closely at them. "They're not all going to cross through the fire pit."

"Damn."

"Don't worry. We should have expected this. We've got to make them move closer together."

"How?"

And then she had it. "Tell the Marines to return their fire. Tell them to shoot in a way that forces the invaders to bunch closer together. Tell them that's the object."

Farraday spoke the appropriate instructions into his walkie-talkie and almost immediately the three surviving Marines began firing from positions they had fortified on the third floor. He knew Danielle's plan was to make the enemy think the forces of the outpost had grown desperate, so when the firing stopped, they would have the illusion of victory.

"I'll get ready on the fuses," Farraday said and wheeled himself over to the spot in the wall where the three spools had been snaked through together so that one match would do the trick for all three. Once outside, beneath the ice, they would break off and reach the fire pit simultaneously to create first a ring of fire and quickly a pool of it. "Just give me the word," he told Danielle, fuse tips, lighter, and walkie-talkie ready in his lap.

Danielle peered out the small window. As she had hoped, the opposition had bunched themselves together, with the snow and storm forming most of their cover as they returned the fire coming from within the complex.

"Walker's hit, sir," came a report from the sergeant over Farraday's walkie-talkie. "It looks bad."

Farraday gazed at Danielle and thought of the more than one hundred other personnel huddled throughout the outpost. How many more were going to die before this was finished? Danielle nodded at him.

"Cease fire, Sergeant, and pull away from the windows. Is that clear?"

"Affirmative, Commander."

Outside, the invaders kept firing for a time before realizing their fire was no longer being returned. Next the front lines rose tentatively, every motion slowed by their prolonged exposure to the below-zero conditions. Danielle realized then that those troops spared by the fire pit would still have to brave the elements to overcome the forces of the outpost. She recognized their suits as a space-age design only recently available. But even these couldn't protect them indefinitely. A stalemate meant victory for her and Farraday and Outpost 10.

The waves of white-clad invaders began to move, one line gliding ahead of the other until the advance line plunged into the snow covering the fire pit and the rest began easing themselves the last stretch to the complex. The second line began to follow soon after. Danielle held her breath against the chance that one of them might notice the difference in texture of this section of tundra compared to the others. None seemed to. She couldn't tell how many of the remaining Hashi invaders were over the pit, but it was plenty, well more than half.

The storm obscured her vision, the winds blasting ice and snow against her small window. For a moment she lost track of the enemy entirely and managed to pick them up again only thanks to their commando-style tactic of crawling over the ice. There seemed to be around fifteen to twenty of them. Of the positions of the other ten or so, she had no idea.

The lead line of belly-crawling Hashi was three-quarters across the fire pit. She could wait for the rest of their number to join their approach no longer.

"Light it," she told Farraday.

The commander didn't hesitate. Face bent in a scowl, he flicked his lighter and pressed the flame against the fusing. The edges caught instantly, flaring for a second before turning to a soft orange glow that sped first to the floor and then through the hole made in the wall and out into the ice.

"Five," Farraday started, "four, three, two, one—"

The flames erupted in perfect rhythm with his count, turning the fire pit briefly into an oblong shape of blinding orange. The Hashi had time only to lunge to their feet before the ring of fire closed upon them in an instant. The white-clad men found themselves jammed against each other in the pit's very center, visible among the scorching flames only for a moment before the smoke and fire consumed them. The savage whistling of the storm swallowed most of their screams, but what rose above it was bloodcurdling. Danielle turned away when the flames became blinding, hiding whatever stray motion remained.

Her mind, though, was fighting to tabulate numbers. How many of the Hashi were left? All three lines of the defense had performed up to or beyond expectations. And the fourth, that of the bitter cold the remaining opposition would have to contend with, would show no mercy.

"How many left?" Farraday asked.

The screams extinguished, Danielle pressed her eyes back against the small window. The still-raging flames sliced through the storm over the mostly circular shape of the fire pit but caught no man in the spill of their light.

"I can't see any," Danielle reported. But she could sense them. There were still some out—

An ear-wrenching blast shook her and toppled Farraday from his wheelchair as he swung. She was diving to his aid when a second blast followed and the door at the far end of the hallway leading in from the outside blew inward.

Danielle saw the white of the storm and of onrushing men an instant before their rifle bores began to spit orange.

CHAPTER 36

"OLLIE'S ON THE WAY," O'BRIEN TOLD KIMBERLAIN AS THE first of the number-two train's passengers appeared down the dead tracks, evacuated by on-board transit police on Kimberlain's orders.

"Ollie?"

"What we call the trash barge. You'll see."

Kimberlain's watch read 10:33, which gave him all of thirty minutes. "What about the track line?"

"From here she runs straight toward the World Trade Center, then veers toward Wall Street before crossing the East River by tunnel into Brooklyn."

With that, the Ferryman knew immediately what he had to do. "What's in my way between here and the river?"

"We got a train stalled outside of Sheridan Square and another at Fulton Street. Ollie'll be able to handle the extra load just fine, long as you don't mind being slowed down a little."

"How long for the whole trip, say to the middle of the East River tunnel?"

O'Brien eyed him suspiciously before answering. "Ollie does thirty MPH tops. Say fifteen on your trip with all the extra weight that accounts for slowdowns when you connect with the other stalled trains." He thought briefly. "You gotta go three miles, so I figure you're looking at twenty, maybe twenty-two minutes."

That was going to make things very close. Kimberlain swung toward Donahue, who was standing next to Cathy.

"You'd better get a city engineer on the horn fast. Tell him the East River subway tunnel is going to blow just after eleven o'clock and to get ready for whatever the backlash of the water into the tunnel is going to do."

"Hey," broke in O'Brien, "what the hell are you saying? Blow the tunnel? Might as well nuke the whole system!"

"Better than the whole city," Kimberlain shot back impatiently as a steady beeping sound started from the far end of the tunnel to announce the coming of the trash barge. He thought about all those subway cars packed with five hundred pounds of C-12, about the effects on the city above if they were allowed to go off anywhere but underwater, where most of the blast and its deadly percussion would be smothered.

O'Brien was still arguing—with Donahue now. Both of them were swearing up a storm as a roaring black beast neared the platform belching smoke and drowning out their words.

Ollie had arrived.

With Peet following him, Quail streaked down West 34th Street beyond the parade route where many of the participants were gathered. Defying the orders of the man behind the curtain, he could not simply depress the detonator after he had moved a safe distance away. That wouldn't suit his purpose, because he'd witness none of the carnage, none of the death. He had seen the last of their lives while mixing among them, but to truly absorb those lives, to etch the impression forever in his mind, he had to see the end unfold before him.

Up ahead the means to accomplish this rose like a beacon in the night. Smiling as best he could, Quail charged on.

* * *

Peet had gained some ground but not enough. The Flying Dutchman had all of the dark force inside him now, and it was a powerful force indeed. Peet had learned that himself through all the years he had accepted it lurking within him. Killing had not been enough. The dark force had made him twist the heads off his victims after their lives had been effortlessly snuffed out. The act shouldn't have been possible, even for him.

He had done it, though. Again and again.

And to slay this dark force that had once owned him, he also had to slay Quail.

He saw the Dutchman veer for a massive shape that stretched for the sky and cast lengthened shadows in the November sun. Barely thirty yards back now, he watched the Dutchman disappear through the revolving-door entrance of the Empire State Building.

Working on the holiday wasn't Bob Mackland's idea of a good time, but triple-time pay was hard to refuse. Besides, reconstruction of the observation deck on the 86th floor of the Empire State Building now threatened to lag well into the holiday season, and that couldn't be allowed to happen. The building had agreed to close the deck down for a week, and Mackland agreed to have his crew work the holiday, with a two-hour break between eleven and one. It seemed fair.

The last to leave, he had ridden the express elevator down from the 80th floor and was looking forward to meeting his family for Thanksgiving lunch at a restaurant with a view of the finish line of the Macy's parade. Couldn't ask for much more than that, and triple time to boot.

The elevator doors slid open in the lobby. Mackland had started out when a huge hand grabbed him by the throat and hurled him against the wall with a force that cracked his skull as darkness swallowed him.

Quail got his hand in the elevator doors just before they slid closed. He flung himself through them with only one thought: to reach the observation deck so he could witness the results of his pressing the detonator. He wanted to enjoy the moment, savor it. A million deaths, all at his hand.

Quail stripped off his ridiculous elf's mask to reveal the form-fitting latex one beneath it, chalky white in all areas except where sweat had started to soak through. He kept pounding the CLOSE DOOR button along with the "80," knowing Peet was close. The doors started their slide and were almost closed when a massive arm clothed in bright green snaked through. The doors bounced back open and Peet lunged inside the compartment. Quail came forward to meet him, and the first impact between them was dizzying, neither man giving an inch, arms intertwined as they grappled in the compartment's small confines.

The doors closed once more and the elevator began to ascend the eighty floors that would take them almost all the way to the Empire State Building's observation deck.

The monstrous figures whirled about, and Peet managed to maneuver a bulging forearm up under Quail's throat. Peet had the Dutchman by six inches in height—his only clear advantage, and one he intended to make use of. The leverage it provided allowed him to keep the arm tight beneath the Dutchman's throat as the faceless man thrashed wildly, many of the blows connecting to Peet's midsection with enough force to disable any normal man. Peet, though, grunted the pain down and shoved Quail back against the compartment wall, the whole shaft shaking at the impact.

He knew he had the Dutchman, knew if he could keep the pressure up, maybe increase it, Quail would pass out in a few more seconds from lack of oxygen. But Quail didn't panic. Instead of struggling to break free, he snaked both his arms beneath the wedge formed by Peet's forearm and went for the bald giant's throat. Peet deflected one of the hands with his free one and locked with it. The other, though, closed on his windpipe and began to squeeze. He felt the breath bottlenecking in his throat and knew in that instant that Quail could finish him before he could finish Quail.

Peet gazed to his left, toward something red, and lashed his hand from Quail's throat for it. The emergency button depressed beneath his palm and drove the elevator to a sudden halt that upset enough of Quail's balance to allow Peet to pull free. Peet cracked the Dutchman with a savage thrust to the head. Quail blocked his next strike and came up with a knee which Peet blocked with similar agility.

The arms of the two giants intertwined again, each grappling for the neck of the other, trying for a snap that would end the fight quickly. They spun, and Peet's back slamming against the control panel deactivated the emergency button, causing the compartment to sail upward again.

Quail was big and strong but not patient, as Peet had learned to be. Peet held his own against the strength that was equal to his own, waiting for the opening he knew would come. Finally Quail went for a quick move up and under his outstretched hands which would have snapped Peet's neck in an instant if he hadn't been ready for it. The end result was to place him in an infinitely superior position. Using one of the Dutchman's arms for leverage, he wrapped his other hand around Quail's chin and began to pull them in opposite directions.

Peet felt all of Quail's muscles tense against the force being applied to his chin, the twisting certain to snap the neck if the Dutchman let up in the slightest. He flailed and kicked, but Peet maneuvered him about so he couldn't strike. In that moment it all came back to the bald giant, the feeling of tearing his victims' heads from their shoulders back when the demons had run rampant through his being. That memory was enough to paint his mind with a vision, and the vision filled his thoughts as he continued to twist.

Quail tried for Peet's eyes, but the bald giant kept twisting, spinning, throwing off Quail's sense of timing. For the first time in the life that he could remember, the Dutchman saw his own death. The next spin cracked his side against the elevator wall, and he felt the detonator jockeying about in his baggy pocket.

The detonator! If he died here and now he would fail to achieve the ultimate climax of his life's work. That he could not allow.

Peet felt the surge of strength an instant after Quail felt it. The Dutchman was suddenly scalding to the touch, and Peet imagined that if he gazed at his fingers the flesh would boil off them. Still he held fast until Quail twisted his upper body at an angle that seemed humanly impossible. He realized his grip was sliding off in time to reverse his direction before Quail's deadly blow could find him. The Dutchman missed, and a portion of the elevator's wall bent inward. Peet tried for him again, but Quail ducked under his outstretched arms. Peet felt his skull being rammed hard against the wall once, twice; felt himself slumping to the compartment floor as the doors slid open on the eightieth floor and the Flying Dutchman bolted for the stairs that would take him the final six stories to the observation deck.

The trash barge's diesel engine roared like a dragon and continued to belch gray smoke. It ran the length of two subway cars and was coal-black from stem to stern. In fact, the beast had the look of a huge, elongated mouth that was all muscle, jaw, and teeth. Its front grille was composed of a steel alloy that could push anything in its path without giving, a feature that gave it the appearance of a gentle scowl not unlike the one made famous by comic Oliver Hardy during his infamous battles with his sidekick Stan Laurel. Add to this the grille's curvature, which looked very much like a mustache, and the name "Ollie" indeed looked fitting stenciled across the barge's side.

O'Brien led Kimberlain to the cab, where the driver was more than happy to relinquish his seat.

"Ever drive anything like this before?" he asked the Ferryman. And when Kimberlain said he hadn't, the driver proceeded to provide a two-minute course in how to manipulate the various levers and gears to shift Ollie at the proper time and stop him when the need arose. "You'll feel yourself slow down when you pick up the trains in front of you, but Ollie'll pick up speed again real quick so long as you . . ."

The Ferryman followed it all as best he could and climbed into the seat.

O'Brien leaned in after him. "Sure you don't want me to come along?"

"I work better alone."

O'Brien nodded reluctantly. "Well, after you pass through the Wall Street station, the East River tunnel comes up real fast. It's just over a half mile in length, so if you hit it at twenty miles per hour you're looking at less than a two-minute trip tops. Want to start easing off the gas real quick to make sure those cars don't push themselves across to Brooklyn. The transit engineer backed away. "Good luck, pal."

Kimberlain's watch read 10:39 as he eased Ollie forward.

The cold came with the men through the door. It seemed to Danielle that they had dragged the storm in with them as she dove downward and stripped her pistol free. A trio of white-clad, ice-encrusted gunmen were charging forward. Her dive carried her over Farraday to where she could shield him as she pounded out three shots from her pistol, the only three she would get before the mechanism jammed from its prolonged exposure to cold.

She saw one of the gunmen go down and the other two struggle to fasten fresh clips. Danielle rose to surprise them with a rush of her own, using the butt of her pistol like a hammer on the forehead of the first she reached while the second abandoned his rifle in the close confines in favor of a knife. His first slash made a neat slice across her stomach. Danielle screamed from rage and pain and counterattacked furiously, locking a hand on the wrist with the knife and using her booted feet against the man's knees.

She felt one of them buckle as he gasped, and twisted to better her position. She saw the man she had downed with the pistol butt struggle to his knees with blood gushing down the center of his face. Blindly he felt about on the floor for his freshly loaded rifle. Danielle tried to kick it away from him, but in so doing the man she was grappling with tore his knife free and sent it plunging toward her rib cage. She managed to deflect it, but by then the second man had recovered his gun and was bringing it up for a clear shot. She was powerless to do anything.

Suddenly the figure of Farraday, muscular above the waist but withered beneath it, threw himself atop the gunman from behind. The maneuver forced him to the floor, where they were reasonable equals, Farraday using his upper-body strength to gain the advantage. In the same instant Danielle deflected the knife blade a second time and managed to gain control of it. She jammed both hands onto its hilt and turned its force back into the man's gut. He stiffened and fell, frozen as the wind whipped through the open section of the station and gunfire continued above.

Danielle started to drop when another figure managed to rush through the door, gun blazing. Farraday grabbed the fallen man's rifle and pounded the new intruder with its fire as a second door at the opposite end of the corridor exploded and more Hashi entered.

The nearest staircase was just behind them. Danielle started for it and helped Farraday along, tossing his arm around her shoulder so she could drag him. The stairs came hard, the commander's legs thumping up one at a time. Above them they could hear the containing fire of the Marines, who were determined to halt the rush of more of the enemy into the complex. For his part, Farraday was struggling with his free hand to steady his walkie-talkie at his lips.

"Pull back!" he screamed to whoever was listening. "Pull back and barricade all doors."

They might succeed in denying access to the outpost through any entrance except the front, but that was all the Hashi needed. Danielle and Farraday reached the top of the second staircase and passed through a door onto the third floor. She eased him gently down and took his keys to lock it behind them. Knowing the invaders possessed explosives, she knew that neither this lock nor any other would hold the Hashi back once the Marines' fire from somewhere on this floor failed to keep them pinned outside.

"Christ," Farraday moaned. "They'll be everywhere."

"No," she countered. "There aren't enough left. One more assault is all they've got left in them, and it won't come until they're absolutely sure of success."

She helped Farraday toward the rec room that he had ordered many of the occupants of Outpost 10 to seek refuge in. She opened the door and looked inside. The room was empty.

"They must have pulled back farther when the shooting started," Farraday realized as more of the Marines' gunfire sounded.

A door crashed open at the other end of the corridor and the Marine sergeant, bleeding badly from a head wound, lunged forward with rifle ready.

"Sorry, sir. I thought you were—"

"Yes. How bad you hurt, Sergeant?"

"I'll get by."

"Where are the people?"

"Sent them as far back as they could go, sir. Sent them to the pump room."

"I've got one man left keeping the rest of the bastards pinned outside," the sergeant explained. "We've got position on them, but our ammo's down."

"Pinned outside," Danielle echoed. "How many?"

"I counted ten."

"What about inside the complex?"

He shook his head. "None other than the ones you must've taken care of. They've backed off. They know we're low."

Danielle knew the installation would be theirs to take once the two surviving Marines' bullets ran out. A thought suddenly struck her.

"Commander, the hoses we used to form ice over the oil pit, where do they run from?"

Farraday looked up at her, confused. "The pump room. We ran them through ventilation shafts."

Danielle's mind was working frantically. "Sergeant, can you and your men hold out for another fifteen minutes?"

"Give it a damn good try, ma'am."

"What about us?" Farraday wondered.

"We're going to the pump room," Danielle told him.

Kimberlain was coming fast toward Wall Street at 10:49. Fourteen minutes remained until detonation, and Ollie had behaved brilliantly through the entire trip. The toughest moments came when impact with the second stalled train at Christopher Street had slowed Ollie to a crawl he seemed powerless to lift himself from. The Ferryman fought against panic and shifted up and down until the trash barge gathered itself for the last leg of its journey and the final train, which stood in its way at Fulton Street beneath the famed fish market.

Kimberlain knew better than anyone the difficulty of his plight. He could shove the explosive-laden cars into the East River tunnel, only to be drowned in the backlash of water if he didn't give himself enough time to flee. With a full fourteen minutes to go before detonation and only two more stations before the tunnel, that didn't seem a problem. He was going to make it with time to spare as long as little time was lost when he reached the stalled train beneath Fulton Street.

Ollie was rolling fast by the time the convoy surged around a bend at Chambers Street and sped toward the Park Place station. Fulton Street was next, around yet another bend, and playing it safe, Kimberlain started to ease onto the brake to avoid the kind of collision that could cause derailment. Ollie's speed dropped, but not fast enough. The final stalled train was perched precariously partway into the curve and partway on the straightaway that led into the East River tunnel. The impact shook Ollie backward, and the grinding pressure on the barge's gears forced it to stall. Kimberlain kept himself calm and moved his hand to the starter button. Nothing happened.

His thoughts began to race crazily. An explosion here would level the entire financial district in a blast that would shatter every window within a five-square-mile radius, shards of glass turned into deadly projectiles all the way to Central Park. He pressed the starter button again.

The engine ground, and wouldn't kick over.

It was 10:51, and he was dead on the tracks.

After finishing his six-story climb to the observation deck on the Empire State Building's 86th floor, Quail charged straight toward the west side and through a door leading outside onto the promenade. The winds howled up at him, and he struggled to lean over to find a view of the festivities far below. Construction equipment was everywhere in his way. The promenade was undergoing extensive renovations, and he could smell wood and sawdust. Many of the J-shaped bars, normally curling inward to form a safety railing atop the retaining wall, had been removed to allow easy access to the promenade from the scaffolding that had been erected four stories down the building on all sides.

The huge balloons alerted him to the Broadway parade site, and he focused down on the squeezed-together swell of humanity that would soon perish by his hand. From such a distance, they had no identity other than the faceless mass that they were, and when the screams came they would seem as one. Quail started to reach into his pocket for the detonator.

The shuffling of footsteps to his rear made him turn just in time to see the two-by-eight plank coming forward. He ducked but didn't sink low enough to avoid all of Peet's blow. The right side of his head flamed, then numbed. He was dazed but saw the next blow coming in time to twist out of the way, and Peet's plank splintered on impact against the concrete retaining wall that stretched just past their waists.

The Dutchman reached over to his side and tore one of the J-shaped curls from a section of steel grating. He leaped back to his feet just as Peet grasped hold of a five-foot-long iron bar and faced off against him. Quail held his piece of grating like a giant scythe. It wasn't razor sharp, of course, but it was finished in a tip that could slice through bone as easily as flesh. The two giants stalked each other around the narrow walkway running between the glassed-in observation deck and the retaining wall. The first corner brought both added depth and width for them to maneuver, and Peet seized the opportunity to launch an attack with his more cumbersome weapon.

The steel bar sizzled through the wind straight overhead at Quail. But the Dutchman deflected it with his scythelike piece of safety rail. The bar continued its momentum, and the cement beneath it fractured at the crash. Quail immediately followed up the move with a sideways swipe aimed for Peet's throat. The strike was too low, though, and Peet was too fast. He backpedaled and twisted sideways, so the best Quail could manage was to slice through his clown costume. Blood oozed through the green fabric from the gash, but Peet felt no pain.

Quail came in overhead with his promised curl of death, and now it was Peet's turn to block and retaliate. He met the scythe at one end of the steel bar and rotated the other down onto the Dutchman's head. Quail bellowed and reeled, swiping at the air with his weapon to keep Peet from closing while he was stunned.

But Peet had *already* closed for the kill, and he might have had it if luck hadn't proved to be on the Dutchman's side. Quail banged hard against the concrete retaining wall, and the J-shaped curl dangled low by his side and nearly slipped from his grasp. With the blur of Peet nearly upon him, Quail was merely trying to regain his grip when his awkward motion drove the tip of the scythelike weapon into Peet's thigh.

The pain and shock forced the bald giant backwards with over an inch of the curl's steel tip still stuck down deep in his flesh. He stumbled into a workbench and lost his balance, finding himself gazing up at the sky as he felt for the handle of the curl to tear it from his leg. While still down and dazed, he was already considering the dart that would plunge it into Quail. But the Dutchman had the sense to realize that what he needed most was another weapon when something caught his eye halfway between him and Peet.

A circular saw, still plugged in.

With a scream that echoed through the upper stories of New York City, Peet had just torn the tip of the steel curl from his own flesh—blood, muscle, and sinew trailing behind—when the Dutchman lunged. His impact caught Peet by surprise, and his leg exploded in fresh agony as Quail toppled him back over the workbench. Peet felt for the scythelike thing, only to find he'd lost it at the same time the grinding noise split his eardrums.

His senses sharpened in time for him to thrust his arms up toward Quail as the Dutchman lowered the circular saw toward his neck. It spun in a rhythmic blur, smelling of wood and lubrication oil. Peet was able to lock both his arms on Quail's descending wrists, but the Dutchman's next violent push forced one of them onto his face instead. Peet felt the mask Quail wore for a face stick to his palm as he tried to force the head up and away. Quail's neck muscles resisted the action and kept the whirling blade lowering slowly toward Peet's head.

It was close enough to tease his lips when Peet managed to rejoin his second hand to his first on the Dutchman's wrists. Quail, mask half pulled off, glowered at him with eyes straight from hell. Peet looked into those eyes and saw the part of himself discarded three years before, and he knew it would continue to live on unless he was victorious here today.

The saw began rising, the muscles of both giants throbbing and trembling from the strain. Peet tried to position his legs to kick at the Dutchman, but his position remained too precarious and Quail's saw too close to chance it. But the saw was electric, which meant there must be a cord, and his eyes found part of it running between the Dutchman's legs. If he could swing one of his feet far enough to loop his toes around it, he might be able to tear the plug from its socket.

Peet arched his back to better position himself, giving ground in the process, which brought the blade back down to less than an inch from his chin. Hearing its whirl, he felt the toes of his clown shoe close around the cord. Damn things had been lousy for running but were flexible enough to curl around the rubber. He yanked with his leg as hard as he could and felt the cord come free.

The saw stopped instantly. Quail registered that just as he registered Peet springing up in the same instant. The Dutchman let the saw go and lunged at him. But Peet still held the saw cord, and now he quickly brought it up and around Quail's throat. The Dutchman fought sideways, but by then Peet had wrapped the tough rubber around his flesh, pulling with all his strength. He felt Quail's bulging neck muscles contract under the pressure and knew he'd cut off the Dutchman's air. Still the Dutchman managed to flail and stagger toward the concrete retaining wall, which stretched just above his waist. Peet yanked harder, until at last Quail began to sink to his knees, an awful gurgling sound coming from deep in his throat. Peet felt the end near now, felt his greatest rival growing limp, felt him dying, and leaned slightly over to better finish the job.

With that, Quail snapped back to life. The illusion abandoned, he reached behind him to the poorly balanced Peet, grabbed hold of his baggy clown shirt, and yanked it hard enough to bring the bald giant up and over him. Peet flew over the building's edge, and the force of the projection carried him beyond even the scaffolding into the open air to a fall eighty-six stories below. There was no scream, not a sound. He just vanished into the void of blowing air.

Quail stripped the cord from his throat and grasped the detonator from the pocket of his elf's suit as, far below, his unsuspecting victims applauded the parade passing by them.

It was 10:55 and Ollie's engine still hadn't caught. With only eight minutes left to go before detonation, Kimberlain knew the point was rapidly approaching where even if he managed to get the barge started, there wouldn't be enough time to drive it into the tunnel *and* get out safely. Barely a half mile remained to be covered but—

Ollie belched a huge plume of black smoke from his exhaust pipes and sputtered.

"Come on," Kimberlain urged. "Come on!"

And Ollie roared to life with all the enthusiasm of the first burst the Ferryman had gotten from him back at the start. He began to edge forward against the huge line of stalled train cars before him. His pace picked up slowly, and Kimberlain shifted gears to provide added thrust.

There were six minutes left to go by the time he cleared the last of the Fulton Street turn, and less than four when he passed into the Wall Street station gathering speed. The speedometer needle locked at twelve miles per hour, and all the coaxing and shifting in the world wasn't going to get Ollie to move any faster, given his huge load and the time remaining. In seconds, the stalled train at the head of the convoy would emerge into the East River tunnel, with the explosive-laden cars still a lifetime behind.

The Ferryman figured he could still just barely get the job done but no time would remain for him to escape. If that was the only solution, then so be it. He tapped Ollie's dashboard almost tenderly. It was throbbing from the incredible weight it was pushing, and even at this low speed the tach needle flirted increasingly with the red.

Kimberlain blocked it out and surged closer to the promised death of the tunnel.

Quail stood there frozen, for how long he couldn't tell. The sight had to be relished, frozen in memory. He would never get another chance to capture a moment like this, and he had to prolong it. These were going to be *his* victims. Their screams would make him more alive than he had ever been before. Quail drank in the scene one last time, with the semblance of a smile rising to his mangled lips.

He brought the detonator up lovingly before him, started for the button . . .

And the huge shadow hurled itself over the retaining wall, the Dutchman's breath leaving him when it impacted upon him.

* * *

In the end the scaffolding had saved Peet's life. Plunging down he managed to reach out for a grip on anything. The saw cord had tangled on a beam, which slowed his descent long enough for him to latch on to the scaffolding. Even then he still had the task of shimmying up steel from more than a story down to reach Quail once again. Just beneath the retaining wall, he found the strength to push off with his arms and fly skyward over the edge legs first.

At impact, the black box of promised death flew from Quail's hand over the retaining wall and onto the top layer of scaffolding. The collision carried Peet past Quail initially, and the Dutchman recovered his senses enough to lunge over the wall with the detonator in sight.

The Dutchman's dive onto the scaffolding splintered a portion of the planking which Peet's leap shattered. Dazed, both men struggled against the powerful winds to reach their feet. Quail made it up first, but Peet's sudden kick sent the detonator sliding toward the edge, where it teetered briefly and then settled.

Quail bellowed in rage and rushed Peet, who met him head-on, faking a throat strike and going for the Dutchman's eyes instead. His massive fingers dug deep into one of Quail's sockets and twisted.

Quail shrieked and Peet's ears curdled. The Dutchman spun away, and his mask came off in Peet's hands.

What he saw froze him stiff.

The Flying Dutchman's face was a mass of purplish veins and ever-drying pus from scalp to chin. Most of his lips were gone, and only a portion of his nose remained. The eye Peet had gorged was swollen and shut, rendered useless or even torn out. The veins lining Quail's burned face seemed to throb as he rushed forward, wailing even louder.

Peet ducked low at the last moment, and the Dutchman flew over him toward the edge of the scaffolding. Somehow he caught his balance, though, legs dangling in midair, and reached out in front of him for the black box.

Peet wedged one of his arms in a crack when he ducked. Instead of pulling it out, he jammed his free arm down through the crack too. Watching Quail's hand reeling the detonator toward him as he remained suspended over the edge, Peet then hoisted his arms up simultaneously, with as much of a purchase gained on the splintered edge of the plank as he could muster.

Instantly the board separated from its place on the scaffolding and toppled upward and out. But not before Quail managed to pound a massive hand onto the detonator, depressing the button. His last thought was that it was 11:03, just the time it should have been.

Peet saw the hate, violence, and fury on the face that wasn't a face at all one final time before the abyss swallowed the Flying Dutchman and he plunged into oblivion.

It had been another glance at the speedometer that gave Kimberlain an idea of how both he and New York City could survive. With Ollie traveling at such a slow speed, he could maybe, just maybe . . .

The front cars were well into the East River tunnel when the Ferryman thrust open the cab door, to the deafening roar of Ollie's diesel engine, with exactly two minutes to go before detonation at 11:03. His only hope was to try for a jump that would carry him onto the next set of tracks. A quick sprint along them and up into the Wall Street station would enable him to survive the gush of water charging in through the ruptured underwater tunnel leading to Brooklyn.

Kimberlain let the clutch out all the way and upshifted to ensure Ollie would keep rolling along, shoving the cars packed with C-12 with him to the center of the tunnel beneath the East River. Then he swung both legs toward the cab door, ready to jump.

He never contemplated the motion itself. He simply lunged, feeling the incredible heat generated by Ollie as he pitched onto the adjacent track. He rolled upon landing and rose immediately into a spring, ignoring the bursts of agony to his ravaged knees.

The Ferryman ran down the center of the track that carried the number three train. His headlong rush was slowed just outside the station by a row of stalled cars he had to snake around. He had slithered by them, almost to the platform, when the blast came.

It reached Kimberlain the way a hot gust of air might when a baking oven is opened. The entire tunnel shook as parts of the ceiling splintered and collapsed. He climbed atop the platform to find it trembling as well and numerous cracks starting to appear through the concrete. His rush for the stairs that would ultimately take him back to ground level was quickened by the roaring sound of millions of gallons of water pouring in through the now ruptured tunnel. He glimpsed only a wall of white foam as high as the tunnel ceiling before the first set of stairs took him beyond the sight and he swung onto the second, toward the safety of ground level.

The Snowcat pushed its way through the storm, treads forming an uneasy alliance with the piles of white chewed up in their path. Mac shivered, though not from the cold.

It was almost time.

The men had bound his arms behind him before setting out and then squeezed him between two of them in the Snowcat's rear seat. Another two in the front, including the driver. Four to overcome in all, while contained in the Snowcat's storage bay were the neatly cushioned and stacked warheads, each about the size of a filing cabinet drawer. Mac needed only gaze behind him to reinforce his resolve for the task he was already committed to in his mind.

He had to stop this Snowcat before it caught up with Jones.

They had been driving for over two hours now. The men's attention had waned. They were taking his status for granted, barely even regarding him any longer, especially now that the end of their journey seemed near. Mac did nothing to draw attention to himself, just kept working at the rope binding his arms behind him. As a SEAL in Vietnam, he had been captured once by the Cong and bound in much the same way for transport by jeep. But he had learned his lessons of escape well—how to first weaken the knots and then slowly ease the wrists from the bonds by working them up and down, up and down, up and down . . . The flesh paid with rawness and pain, yet after a while he could make himself used to it. Just as he had done in Vietnam.

He'd had no weapon then either, but the Charlie by his side did, and Mac grabbed for it as soon as he was free and blew that man's brains out and the two in the jeep's front as well before they knew what was happening. The jeep had spun off the road and rolled over. Mac had been thrown to safety.

There were more men to contend with today, four instead of three, and two were virtually on top of him. Mac felt his hands about to come free and saw in his mind the assault strategy he would have to pursue: distract one while disabling the other. The man in the front seat was his biggest worry, though; there was too much space for him to maneuver. Mac would take him second and leave the driver for last. The two men he was squeezed between both wore sidearms on their right hips. Have to go across the whole body to grab one, lots of time taken, and maybe a bullet in his head before he could use it. But pull the assault off right and he might only have to kill one of them.

He was a SEAL again, behind enemy lines, just the way he liked it. Mac felt his raw wrists a pull away from being free. None of the men in the Snowcat were paying him any regard, not until he whipped his arms up and to the sides, twisting to the right and going for that man's pistol, going for it even as it seemed hopelessly out of reach.

"I think you're crazy," Farraday told Danielle, with the door to the pump room closed and barricaded behind them.

"But in theory it should work," she persisted.

"It's twenty below out there. Even if their suits do have thermal warmers, it *should* work, but so should a rifle."

"I'd never be able to hit all of them with this poor visibility. One burst would be all I could reasonably expect before they got me, and that might not even hit more than a couple of them. It's got to be this way!"

Two Outpost 10 engineers were helping Farraday walk along

Danielle's side around the pump room. It was huge and cavernous, the very heart of Spiderweb. It looked to be a cross between the futuristic gadgets and technology of a nuclear power plant and the old-fashioned school boiler room with pipes running in every direction, crisscrossing in a labyrinth of layers. She supposed each of the hundred or so pipes represented a piece of the Antarctic pipeline, the pressure required to pump the crude in and out originating with the monstrous generators this cavern contained. Actually located under the ice, it was larger than the whole of the aboveground outpost itself. Machines whirled and spun. Unless he was in the quiet of the glassed-in control room elevated against the far wall, anyone who wanted to be heard virtually had to shout.

Farraday had directed a pair of men to grasp one of the water hoses used to cool off the pumps from its perch and bring it over. Connecting it with a pair of others would supply the additional length required in the next few minutes. Meanwhile, Danielle dressed quickly in white battle fatigues for camouflage, wincing from the pain of the knife slash across her abdomen, which there had been no time to bandage. She covered herself with white everywhere except her face, which a ski mask would take care of.

Farraday was sitting on the floor beneath a ventilator shaft and was working the screen free with a chisel.

"We use these, believe it or not, to pump cold air in here," he explained as loud as he could when Danielle had reached his side. "Otherwise temperatures would exceed a hundred and ten degrees. The equipment would seize, melt even. It's going to be freezing the whole way through, and it'll get worse the closer you get to the other side at the front of the main building." The screen popped off, and he handed the chisel to her. "Use this on the other side to pry the screen free." An uneasy pause. "I don't know how much longer the Marines can keep them at bay outside. Five minutes, maybe less."

"Yes!" she realized. "It's got to be less! Once they stop shooting, the rest of the invaders will start forward toward the complex. I'll be able to take them from behind!"

Farraday nodded, still grudgingly, and watched Danielle plung
herself into the shaft after clipping a walkie-talkie to her lapel.

The first stretch was virtually straight up, and she pulled hersel
along using her hands, with the hose end tied to the back of he
belt. After the climb, things leveled off except for the temperature
which slid quickly toward zero and then below. Suddenly her breat
was misting before her and she had to stop to pull on her ski mask
By the time she reached the midpoint the shaft was in total dark
ness, but it didn't matter. The going was straight, with no intersec
tions to confuse her. Even in the blackness, all she had to do wa
keep going as fast as she could.

The shaft's layout, however, became purposely uneven, resem
bling a miniature roller-coaster, in order to better control the col
air flow. The down slides came easy, but the up climbs swiftl
became maddening, each seeming harder than the one before it
and made harder by her awareness that too many seconds wer
ticking by.

The sound of gunfire reached her just before the light at the othe
end of the shaft. The light came first as a flicker and then a splotc
that grew into a blinding white square shattering all hint of dark
ness.

Danielle grasped the walkie-talkie from her jacket. "I'm almos
at the end," she reported. "Have the Marines cease fire."

She reached the ventilator screen and unwrapped the hose fron
the rear of her belt, tucking it beneath her foot so it would be withi
easy reach. The Marines' gunfire had cut off as she went to worl
with the chisel. She saved the edges for the end, but her glove
made her clumsy and she yanked them off, exposing her fingers t
the numbing cold to finish the job more quickly. Her fingers stiff
ened, giving her only seconds to work the screen free—but second
were all she needed.

The screen came free in her hands and she peered out into th
storm as best she could. As expected, there were shapes moving
rising in a spread that narrowed as they closed on the blasted-ou

front of the complex, with the containing fire from the Marines having ceased.

"Turn on the water!" she ordered into the walkie-talkie, gloves back on and grasping the insulated hose.

She waited until the remaining Hashi were all within ten yards of the complex, gathered closer together, before she plunged out into the soft snow and raging storm beyond. Pressure from the powerful water rushing through the hard rubber turned it into a snake, wild and strong, demanding to be set free. Danielle grasped it firmly, hand on the nozzle, and circled around for a charge that would take the attackers from their rear flank as they prepared to rush the front of the complex. They remained orderly and precise in spite of everything—the trademark of the Hashi.

She had hoped to circle all the way around behind them and center herself to assure optimum effectiveness for her deadly spray, but there was no chance for that now. Time only to take the angle she was already approaching and hope for the best. She rushed at them hunched low, one with the storm. She turned the nozzle on to free the pent-up water within when she felt the hose lose its slack ten yards from the first of the Hashi.

It was then that the ones on the other side noticed her and dropped to the snow, leveling their weapons as the first stream of jet-fast water rushed out in a spray frosted white by the sub-freezing temperatures. The fierce pressure of the water carried it as far as the first wave of Hashi, encasing them in instantly frozen ice which brought on rapid unconsciousness and then death by freezing.

These first ones dropped their weapons and clawed frantically as if being attacked by millions of flying insects. In the next instant, they had fallen and were kicking and writhing in the snow. But those Hashi farther from her spray who'd dropped to the snow were now able to steady themselves and open fire as Danielle tried to shift the hose toward them, struggling with all her strength to contain the powerful snake trying to pull free of her grip.

A bullet pounded her thigh and blood gushed over the white of her uniform, congealing quickly in the cold into a thick ooze. Staggering, she started to go down but bit her lip against the pain and righted herself long enough to fire her water spray straight toward the exposed Hashi supplying the fire. Three of them managed to get off further shots, and at least two more bullets found her, one in the shoulder and another grazing her ribs. But Danielle swayed only slightly and brought her jet of icing water on the last of them she could see. Pressure built up behind her lips, and she coughed frothy blood which froze as soon as it hit the snow.

The red splotches dotted the white beneath her now, but the shooting had stopped, because the last surviving Hashi was fleeing toward one of the outpost's Snowcats to escape. She would cut off his angle. She would . . .

More blood dropped to the snow around her, Danielle finally sank to her knees, the powerful hose sliding from her grasp to dig deep chasms from the fresh powder before her. She slid into the soft cushion as the Snowcat tore away into the white of the storm.

Jones drove the Snowcat furiously, relying on instinct for direction. In his wildest nightmares he had never conceived of anything as terrible as this happening. Imagine, to be beaten back by the meager defenses of Outpost 10! But somehow they had known he was coming. Somehow they had known!

Jones could let himself dwell on that no longer. He had agreed to be part of the operation and to help the dark man because the end result suited him. To be able to accomplish that end using the same sort of naval vessel that had torn his life away made the operation even more satisfying and provided him with a sense of purpose. Now losing that purpose was worse than losing his life.

There was only one way to salvage at least a measure of this operation—and thus his purpose. He had to rendezvous with his Snowcat containing the twenty-eight warheads and utilize them as best he could. Plunge them into the ice shield rigged for timer detonation with enough time left to get back to the *Rhode Island* and dive to safety. The resulting nuclear explosions would have less far-reaching effects than the original plan, but significant damage would be done, enough to make him feel he had accomplished a measure of his goal. He would twist the enabling codes out of Barlow and achieve some portion of his vengeance.

Up ahead he could see the orange shape of his Snowcat through the storm, and he relaxed a bit as he straightened his course for it. Drawing closer, he saw that it wasn't moving. A mechanical failure must have stalled it here, which made his foresight to flee Outpost 10 in this Snowcat even more crucial. He had jumped down from his cab and started to approach before realizing that something was dreadfully wrong. Not far from his feet, looking like a small snow-covered mound, was the bound and gagged body of one of the men assigned to the Snowcat. He drew in his breath sharply and inspected the surrounding area. Two more snow mounds were visible not far way in the storm. He lumbered over the ice to the one nearest, then the next. Three of the men he had assigned to the Snowcat were out here, but where was Barlow?

Jones lunged back to his Snowcat's cab and drew out his rifle. Thinking of the warheads, he rushed past his men in a panic, his grasp on reason gone, and didn't notice a figure in heavy white garb angling toward him from the rear.

"Drop it, Jones," Mac said just loud enough to be heard through the storm. "I don't want to kill you."

But Jones twisted, and Mac saw the steel of his rifle barrel coming around. Mac fired a burst from the M-16 he had lifted from inside the commandeered Snowcat, knowing that Jones would never allow himself to be taken prisoner. The body of his captor was tossed backward and twitched toward death as the snow gathered in what would become his tomb.

EPILOGUE

"JUST TELL ME WHAT I'M SUPPOSED TO DO," LISA EISEMAN said to Kimberlain outside the Benbasset Towers in midtown Manhattan Friday morning.

"Wait in the car right here," he told her. "If I haven't come out within ninety minutes, call Senator Brooks at the number I gave you and give him the message."

"About Jason Benbasset being . . . inside."

"He'll understand," Kimberlain said and started to step out of the car.

Lisa's hand gently restrained him. "You could call Brooks now. You don't have to go up there alone."

"Yes, I do."

And with that the Ferryman was heading for the entrance to the huge office building. He had realized the truth the night before, an anomaly that made itself known out of the darkness. *We searched all sixty-three floors of the Benbasset Towers and didn't find a thing,* Zeus had assured him. But his eyes showed him something else as he thought he remembered it: the Benbasset Towers had sixty-*four* floors. The obscure fact had turned up somewhere in his research into Benbasset himself. Somewhere along the line a floor had been lost . . . or redirected.

New York City had survived Thanksgiving virtually intact. Miraculously, the Macy's parade had finished without incident, the only disruptions occurring at the various subway stations bordering the route as authorities scrambled to bar entry at all points of access. Earlier, the stalled cars had all been evacuated in time to avoid the flood of water which spared no station running the IRT line through Manhattan and Brooklyn. But only fortune was to blame for avoiding what would still have been a disaster of awful proportions. The blast beneath the East River created such shock waves that the last two subway tunnels on the Manhattan side collapsed, in effect creating a massive dam which greatly reduced the flow of water under the city. Otherwise streets would have collapsed, perhaps even the skyscrapers resting atop them. The tunnels had been further sealed overnight, and the system was being flushed of water even now. It would be weeks, months probably, before the subways were running at relative normalcy again. The disruption of service was a crisis in its own right, but nothing when compared to what might have been.

As for Outpost 10, an airlift was risked at the first break in the storm, the troops arriving to find cleanup operations already underway at the station.

"Hell of a battle went on down there," Senator Brooks had told Kimberlain. "The facts are still sketchy, but it's obvious a skeleton force at the outpost was able to fight off the assault by forces from the hijacked submarine, which, by the way, has been recovered unharmed."

"Anything about a woman?" Kimberlain posed hesitantly.

"Plenty. Apparently a woman was the spearhead behind the whole defense setup, but she got herself wounded in the final shootout."

"Wounded?"

"This is where it gets strange. As soon as the storm broke, they whisked her to McMurdo and from there to Christchurch, where they pulled a few bullets out of her. They kept her in intensive care overnight and put her in a private room when she seemed to be recovering. Then when they returned a bit later to check on her, they found her gone. She had completely disappeared.'' The senator paused. ''You don't seem surprised.''

Kimberlain thought back to Danielle's fierce resolve in fighting the Hashi. This failure wouldn't destroy them, but it would severely weaken them, perhaps enough for the Knights of St. John to destroy their murderous society at last. With Brother Valette's murder, Danielle would take it upon herself to reorganize the Knights with that goal in mind.

''She had unfinished business,'' he told Brooks at last.

And so did Kimberlain. He gazed one more time at Lisa and entered the building. He didn't have to bring her; he didn't have to bring anyone. In truth he wanted an excuse to see Lisa, to work out in his own mind what was coming for him next and whether or not she would be a part of it. Every time he closed his eyes to think of her, though, a picture of Danielle flashed through his mind. The Ferryman was wise enough to understand why. Danielle was gone from his life, so there was no harm in thinking of her. His feelings for Lisa, on the other hand, had to be faced directly, making them infinitely less appealing.

The river now flowing beneath the city had subsequently caused a massive power failure by shorting out thousands of underground cables. The governor had declared a state of emergency, and Manhattan was basically shut down this Friday, traditionally the busiest shopping day of the year. Benbasset Towers was eerie in its desolation, but Kimberlain knew the front door would be open, just as he knew the elevators would be functioning.

The upper elevator bank deposited him in the dead quiet of the sixty-third floor, and twenty minutes later Kimberlain found the private elevator that rose up a single last flight. It was operated by key, and he used one of Captain Seven's picks to activate it. The elevator shot upward and stopped, opening into a long corridor that led directly forward.

The Ferryman simply followed it along, aware of an antiseptic hospital-like smell permeating the air. He could sense life somewhere on this floor but not life as he had ever felt it before. At last he reached a pair of sliding white doors which opened automatically when he approached them. The alcohol smell within stung his nose. The room was spacious but stark, its only ornament a shiny black curtain forming a separate room of sorts against the far wall.

Beep . . . beep . . . beep . . .

That sound reached him along with a breathing that emerged in rasps and wisps, each one a struggle.

"I've been waiting for you, Mr. Kimberlain," a voice said through a speaker, and Kimberlain froze, pistol in hand an instant later. "You have no need for that here, Ferryman," the voice continued. "I've dismissed my keepers. Left myself alone to wait for you, as I'm sure you suspected I would."

Kimberlain reached the curtain and saw the video camera that had allowed the man residing behind it to view his approach.

"I've looked forward to this, Ferryman," the voice resumed. "I really have. You have no idea how much. We have much to discuss. Please, come in."

And hesitating only slightly, Kimberlain found the break in the curtain and stepped into the private world of Jason Benbasset.

The large number of machines grabbed his attention first, then the shape of a figure lying in the bed enclosed by them. Lights blinked, and squiggly electronic lines danced across a quartet of screens.

"This has been my home since my death, Ferryman," Jason Benbasset said and followed the words with the twisted semblance of a laugh. "Not a bad resting place, I suppose."

Kimberlain started to approach the bed but stopped in his tracks. He was close enough to see the figure partially covered by a dark blue sheet, and the sight was enough to assure him he didn't want to move closer. What remained of Benbasset was little more than a lump. Even with the sheet Kimberlain could tell both his legs were gone, one severed at the hip, the other just beyond the thigh. His left arm was a memory, and his right descended only as far as the elbow. One side of his neck and throat was covered in thick bandages, the edges of which revealed thick, raw scar tissue. Benbasset's exposed face, though, was almost normal-looking in spite of its paleness. He looked like a freshly made-up corpse, his features blank to the point of seeming part of a snapshot, right to the dark wisps of hair combed neatly in place. The only trace of motion came from the blinking of his eyes.

"There's no pain, Ferryman," the rasp from within the shell said. "In fact, I feel nothing at all, except in my thoughts. I should have died three years ago, but something kept me alive and kept me going, and I did not bother to question what. Last night, when my failure was made known to me, I gave up the will that had kept me breathing through all these months. But, alas, out of habit I couldn't let myself perish. I knew you would come here, and perhaps that is why I was not yet ready to accept my passing. Please, come closer."

The raspy voice spoke gently, calmly. Kimberlain approached to where Benbasset could see him.

"You of all people cannot tell me I was wrong in my aims. It was an evil and coarse world I sought to punish for its acts. War has raged over religion, land, politics, money for twenty centuries and more. The names change, the causes too, but always people die for reasons they either can't or won't understand. Tell me you can't see that."

Kimberlain said nothing.

"Fanatics drive truckloads of explosives into buildings, taking their own lives along with a thousand others. What does it prove? What does it show us? Life is too often defined in terms of death. The fanatics of the world can justify anything in life, because true life begins in their minds only when death starts. Such an empty justification . . . Yet it typifies all of them, even those of this very country. Are we any better than the rest of them? We think ourselves to be and thus we are not."

Benbasset's lung machine was working more quickly with each word, struggling to give him the breath he needed to keep speaking. Ultimately it fell behind, and he gasped for air, wheezing uncontrollably. Kimberlain came right up to the bed, as if there was something he could do. The medicinal smells flooded his nostrils, almost dazing him.

Beep . . . beep . . . beep . . .

"I was right to do what I did, was I not?" Benbasset managed. "I was right because the world took my family from me along with my life. I tried to help that world, and this was my payment. Surely you understand that I had to have my vengeance!"

"No," Kimberlain said suddenly, a chord in him struck, "because to achieve it you had to employ the very type of group you claim to loath. You hired the Hashi, Mr. Benbasset, cold-blooded assassins like none the world has ever known. And in doing so you became what you hated most." He paused. "The Hashi and others like them define the world in terms of its ugliness. The Caretakers were formed to rid the world of this, or at least keep it from America, but in the process we had to become what we were resolved to terminate. It's the same for you. You blame the world, yet people are basically helpless against the ugliness. Become part of it or hope it steers clear of you—there's no convenient third alternative."

"There was for you, Ferryman. The paybacks. You bridged the gap."

Kimberlain shook his head. "I *was* the gap, Mr. Benbasset. I was, am, merely a crevice that some people who've been wronged by the ugliness slide into. I give them a boost back up. I try to keep them from becoming a part of what nearly destroyed them."

"All the more reason for what *I* tried to do," the shape on the bed persisted between lips that barely moved, air drawn deep from within to force the syllables out as best he could.

"You can't destroy the ugliness if doing so means you have to join it first."

"It's not like that. I didn't employ the Hashi, I *used* them. It was all undertaken in return for my providing them with coordinates of safe zones from the coming cataclysm. What I didn't tell them was that those coordinates would have assured their destruction after the cataclysm. You see, I agree with you, Ferryman. Quintanna and his people would have begun the ugliness all over again. I could never have allowed that."

"It doesn't change anything," Kimberlain told him, "because it wasn't just the ugliness you tried to eliminate, it was everything. You blamed the world because you couldn't change it, and you blamed yourself for what happened to your family. But you couldn't hurt yourself any more than you'd been hurt already, so you turned your anger on the world."

"Tell me you wouldn't have done the same thing. You *have* done the same thing."

"I would have gone about it in a far different, more personal way. I would have gone after those who planted the bomb and maybe the ones who ordered it. I don't expect to be able to destroy all of the ugliness. Getting rid of some of it is enough."

Benbasset grew silent, and the sounds of his breathing machine emerged like a series of disappointed sighs.

"I had hoped you would understand," he said with as much sadness as he could manage.

"No, you hoped I would approve. That's up to God."

Beep . . . beep . . . beep . . .

"I knew you would be coming," Benbasset said again. "I needed you to come because I require a . . . payback. Life punished me first with the attack that left me as I am and now has stripped me of purpose. Life is the greatest enemy all of us must face, Ferryman, and I have faced it twice only to lose both times. My payback is to deny it a third victory. I have lingered and labored against my own mortality, and when at last I am ready to relent I cannot—life's final little joke." Benbasset's eyes sought Kimberlain's out and held them. "The plugs, Ferryman, pull them all. Strange, isn't it, that despite all I've accomplished I haven't even the power to end my own life.''

Kimberlain stood quietly and gazed at Benbasset. Then he nodded and reached for the first switch.

Beep . . . beep . . . be—

"I was getting ready to call Brooks," Lisa told Kimberlain as a blast of windy air entered the car with him. A cold front was swooping in, and temperatures were already plummeting.

"Not necessary now," he told her.

"Was he up there, as you thought?" she asked.

Kimberlain's stare turned upward to the tower's top. "He was up there. Not as I thought."

"Oh?"

"He was dead."

"Really?"

"For three years now."

"We've got to talk, Jared," Lisa said before Kimberlain started the engine. She continued speaking quickly so that he couldn't interrupt. "I know you've been thinking that I don't fit in your world. I could feel you trying to make up your mind about me every time you looked at me. You don't want to be dependent on anyone, and you're going to tell me it's all for my own good."

Kimberlain's stare told her she was right.

"Well, it's okay, Jared. You don't have to tell me anything, because I've been doing some thinking too. It can't work, not now anyway. You see, you don't fit into my world any more than I fit into yours. I've got a life and a business back in Atlanta, and that's where I belong. Now. Today. And it *is* for my own good—and yours, too. I think maybe I love you and maybe even you love me. But there are things both of us love more, and we'd be fooling ourselves if we think that's going to change anytime soon."

Kimberlain was still looking at her. Her words seemed formed of his very thoughts, but hearing her speak them brought sadness as much as relief.

"There's a long time that follows 'anytime soon,' " he said softly.

"There might be," came her reply.

Lisa had pressed him about the battle between Peet and Quail that had raged atop the Empire State Building, and Kimberlain reiterated that the body that had plunged more than eighty stories was identifiable only from the elf's costume that clothed it. He professed to know nothing else and in reality he didn't, though he could have added that Peet must by now have achieved the peace he was after. He didn't actually know where the giant had gone, but he had an idea.

And when he heard the voice of John Wayne coming from inside his Vermont cabin as he approached, he smiled and stepped inside to find Winston Peet firmly entrenched between the holographic figures of the Duke ready to shoot it out with the film's villain. Seeing Kimberlain enter, he flipped the machine off and the cabin's interior returned to normal. Peet rose, dressed in a tank top and work pants. Blood had soaked through one thigh of the pants, and when the giant advanced toward him, Kimberlain noticed the limp.

"Man's need for heroes fascinates me," Peet said.

"Makes our shortcomings easier to stomach," Kimberlain said. "We transpose their values over our own for scale. It gives us something to strive for."

"And yet so many times these heroes live their lives alone, in solitude, prisoners of their own standards. But to judge is the same thing as being unjust. We run from such truths for fear of the consequences of accepting them." Peet stopped. "You knew I'd come here."

"I knew."

"And you came hoping to see me, preferring my company to that of the woman you had me guard from the Dutchman."

"How did you know . . ." Kimberlain stopped the question in mid-sentence. Clearly there was no reason to pose it.

"You prefer to face me, Ferryman, because I remind you of everything you are. The woman reminds you of that which you can never have."

"Nietzsche again?"

"Merely Peet, Ferryman." And he smiled. "My work is done. I am at peace. I told you if I succeeded you could return me to The Locks. I'm here to book passage."

"The Ferryman only ferries the dead, Peet." He sighed. "I won't take you back there. I can't because I know you're not the same man who got sentenced three years ago. You've earned your freedom. Besides, you're right about the size of the jails we make for ourselves. It really doesn't matter where the cell is, because we're all our own jailers and each of us is the only one with the key."

"You're granting me my freedom?"

"No, because you're already free. You finished Quail and saved my life in the process. I'd say that did the trick."

Peet looked confused.

"I've got this cabin in Maine," Kimberlain continued. "I think you know it. Built it myself and haven't used it in years. Thought you might be interested in taking out a lease. Only neighbors you'll have are squirrels."

Peet nodded. "And fine neighbors they'll be. And what of you, Ferryman? What of your prison?"

"I've got the key all right. I just can't always find the door, and as you said, I'm not really sure I want to. I haven't been nearly as good at slaying my demons as you have. With each payback I get one, but another's always waiting to rise. I thought after all this I might be able to finally walk away. Now I doubt it."

"And what if they ask you to take up the search for me?"

"There is no search. You've been declared officially dead. You don't exist."

The prospect of that brought a gleam to Peet's face. "How fortunate. How very fortunate indeed."

"Let's go," Kimberlain told him, car keys in hand. "It's a long trip."

"Yes, Ferryman. I suppose it is."

About the Author

Jon Land is the author of THE DOOMSDAY SPIRAL, THE LUCIFER DIRECTIVE, VORTEX, LABYRINTH, THE OMEGA COMMAND, THE COUNCIL OF TEN, THE ALPHA DECEPTION, and THE EIGHTH TRUMPET. He is thirty-one years old and lives in Providence, Rhode Island, where he is currently at work on a new novel.

THE OMEGA COMMAND

A BLAINE MCCRACKEN NOVEL

Murder . . . Conspiracy . . . Revolution . . . Annihilation . . .
A top secret agent is brutally slain in a New York City pleasure parlor after completing the most dangerous assignment of his career. A desperate man thrusts bizarre information into the hands of a TV reporter moments before he dies. Power-crazed madman Mohammed Sahhan plans the first strike in his perverse campaign against the heart of America. The wicked union of power, money, and raw ambition lie smoldering, ready to explode. Rogue agent Blaine McCracken is brought out of exile to unravel the vicious mystery of Omega. Trapped in a web of ever-escalating danger, McCracken is all that stands between the world and its total destruction.

THE ALPHA DECEPTION

A BLAINE MCCRACKEN NOVEL

A town in Oregon dies instantly, wiped out by a laserlike beam, leaving nothing behind but a whirling cloud of black dust. A remote town in Colorado is taken over by a mysterious army that imprisons its citizens and begins strange activities on the far side of the mountain. The war is on for an ancient gemstone—the most precious mineral on earth and the greatest power source ever known to man—both key to the ultimate weapon and the foolproof shield against it. Renegade agent Blaine McCracken unites with beautiful Natalya Tomachenko, the KGB's number-one assassin, to gain control of this life-giving, death-dealing superforce, whose origin is shrouded in legend and buried on the floor of the sea.

LABYRINTH

"The Committee" has masterminded a fiendish plot, a malignant conspiracy rooted in the highest corridors of power. Code name: Tantalus. Tantalus strikes at the very lifeline of humanity. Its aim is enormous, horrible, and unknown even to the superpowers. Only one man, Christopher Locke, an unsuccessful college professor, can expose the trail that begins with the brutal execution of every person in an obscure South American town. From Washington, D.C., to an ancient castle near Vienna... from the mountains of Columbia to the north Texas prairie, Christopher Locke fights his way through a maze of deception and blackmail, torture and assassination, in a shattering race to stop Tantalus.

THE COUNCIL OF TEN

In Miami, four seemingly harmless grandmothers are professionally terminated. Then the shocking news is revealed: the victims are key links in a global cocaine operation. Journalist Drew Jordan discovers how dangerously deceptive appearances can be. The reporter turns killer... and target. Elliana Hirsch is the top operative of the Mossad. Her assignment is the penetration of a monstrous threat to world peace, one that has robbed her of the person she loved the most. The shadowy, all-powerful conspiracy—the Council of Ten—has but one aim: total domination. It is fortified by an awesome superweapon that can render America helpless. And only a desperate army of three can stop it.

There's an epidemic with 27 million victims. And no visible symptoms.

It's an epidemic of people who can't read.

Believe it or not, 27 million Americans are functionally illiterate, about one adult in five.

The solution to this problem is you... when you join the fight against illiteracy. So call the Coalition for Literacy at toll-free **1-800-228-8813** and volunteer.

Volunteer Against Illiteracy. The only degree you need is a degree of caring.

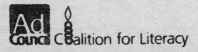

Ad Council Coalition for Literacy

LV-1